# UNDER THE DOGWOOD TREE

## KARI WIRTH

Black Rose Writing | Texas

©2023 by Kari Wirth
All rights reserved. No part of this book may be reproduced, stored in a retrieval system or transmitted in any form or by any means without the prior written permission of the publishers, except by a reviewer who may quote brief passages in a review to be printed in a newspaper, magazine or journal.

The author grants the final approval for this literary material.

First printing

This is a work of fiction. Names, characters, businesses, places, events, and incidents are either the products of the author's imagination or used in a fictitious manner. Any resemblance to actual persons, living or dead, or actual events is purely coincidental.

ISBN: 978-1-68513-263-7
PUBLISHED BY BLACK ROSE WRITING
www.blackrosewriting.com

Printed in the United States of America
Suggested Retail Price (SRP) $23.95

*Under the Dogwood Tree* is printed in Garamond Premier Pro

\*As a planet-friendly publisher, Black Rose Writing does its best to eliminate unnecessary waste to reduce paper usage and energy costs, while never compromising the reading experience. As a result, the final word count vs. page count may not meet common expectations.

*To the man who demonstrates daily what it means to be a husband.
I love you, Chad.*

# ACKNOWLEDGEMENTS

*Under the Dogwood Tree* would've remained just an idea without the help and support of some very important people. Interviewing sources is one aspect I thoroughly enjoy as a writer. Whether it's learning about a career or hearing personal stories and experiences from interesting situations, the information gathered is invaluable in bringing the characters and the scenes to life.

If it weren't for Ron Jentz, I couldn't have portrayed the main characters appropriately. Thank you for answering all my questions on police policies, verbiage, and scenarios from paperwork to patrol. Also, a special thanks to Dr. Cayleigh Blumrick for a detailed medical breakdown of surgery and recovery for a patient with a traumatic injury.

To my fellow author Lauren Hasbrouck who went line-by-line offering constructive feedback and pushed me to go deeper into the story. Thank you for letting me bounce more ideas off you than I realized I had.

Emily Tenter, my dear friend and forever writing buddy. I'll never get bored talking to you about this delightfully crazy industry!

A great big thank you to the Black Rose Writing family, beginning with Reagan Rothe for taking on *Under the Dogwood Tree*. Your guidance, insight, and belief in a novice author like me are appreciated beyond measure. When it comes to art and graphics, it's best that I stick with words. That's why I'm eternally grateful to David King for designing a spectacular book cover. It's a beautiful thing when authors support each other. To Kim Conrey, Michelle Caffrey, P.L. Jonas, and Karen K. Brees, thank you for reading *Under the Dogwood Tree* and giving reviews and feedback.

To my family and friends whose continued support drives me to write another book, I thank you

Last, but never least, Chad. For all the times I've said, "Just five more minutes," and "I'll be working on my book all day," your patience and understanding have allowed me to do what I love. Your perpetual encouragement to pursue my passion, dream big, and never settle is the reason this book made it to publication.

# UNDER THE
DOGWOOD TREE

# CHAPTER 1

Tony Lombardo arrived at the police station twenty minutes before his shift—a habit turned routine for the past twenty years. In the locker room, he changed into his black uniform, mentally preparing for another day on the job as a cop in the Pittsburgh suburb of Hilton. Anything from a traffic ticket to a shootout.

Unbeknownst to Tony, nothing prepared him for what he was about to encounter.

Max Brody stood next to Tony and hung his jacket in his locker. "Today's the big day."

Tony balanced his foot on the bench. "Yep," he said, tying his shoe.

For weeks, the Hilton Police Department had speculated who would replace Chief Elliott Kahn after he retired. A morning press conference was about to put an end to the well-guarded secret.

Max took off his sweatshirt. "Did you hear the latest?"

Tony brushed off the rumor as idle gossip. "What's it today?"

"Chief brought in an outsider. Wanted to give the department some fresh blood."

"No wonder Rosario's been so miserable. He was next in line." Tony clicked the duty belt that held his weapons. "Guess there won't be another star on his collar brass."

Max buttoned his uniform shirt. "Not surprised if the town board influenced the Chief. His sister-in-law is an elected official. Bet she's been chirping in his wife's ear."

Chet Dalton entered the locker room and dropped his bug bag on the bench.

"Speaking of wife, enjoy your last moments of freedom," Tony quipped to the officer.

"I got 'til December to live it up," Chet said. "Full-blown bachelorhood all the way, boys. No holds barred."

Max slid on his pants. "What are the big bachelor plans this weekend? A quick trip to Vegas?"

Chet hesitated. Busted. "Taste-testing cakes, finalizing flower arrangements, and choosing the song list."

Tony oohed at his colleague's so-called wild plans. "You're whipped, Dalton."

"Hey, it's my wedding, too."

"No, it's not. It's her day. Every guy knows that." Tony flicked Chet's arm. "Where've you been?"

Chet's voice elevated with concern. "I should have some say."

Tony poked the officer's pudgy midsection. "Only when it comes to the cake."

Chet smirked and replied, "We can't all be Italian gods like you, Lombardo."

"This is true."

Tony and the guys shared a rousing laugh. Bantering lived embedded into their blue brotherhood. Tony's fellow officers were like brothers to him, a bond that saved him from the dangers of being a cop.

Max tucked his shirt into his pants and zipped his fly. "Chet, all that talk about marriage being a trap, the whole 'Yes, dear' scenario is BS."

Tony wished his best friend hadn't opened that can of worms.

"I wouldn't trade life with Audrey for anything. Not for fame, or money, or all the women out there. I knew she was the one in tenth-grade biology." Max stroked his brown goatee, smiling. "She was all squeamish about dissecting a frog, almost puked in the classroom until I jumped in and sliced the sucker open. We failed the assignment for not doing our own work. I gladly took the F. She couldn't say no to a date with me after that."

"Aww, how sweet." Sarcasm seeped through Tony's words. "Frog guts brought you two crazy kids together."

Men weren't supposed to share their feelings about women. It was chapter one of *The Guy's Manual*, which Max apparently hadn't bothered to read. Part of Tony applauded Max's bravery for not adhering to the male ego. The other part was tired of his best friend fawning over his wife. *Audrey's the best mom... Audrey texted me to say she loves me.* Audrey this, Audrey that.

Max looked at Chet. "Why are you marrying Mia?"

The newbie cop hesitated. Like most men, he didn't want to appear as a mushy sap. "Well, you know. I love her and stuff."

"Right. Now imagine life with no Mia."

Chet mulled it over. "Kind of sucks, I guess."

"Marriage isn't a cakewalk. Mia and you will disagree. You'll have the dumbest arguments. Now and then, you'll feel like you're in a rut. But the longer you're together, the closer you'll be as a couple."

If Max had a side business doling out relationship advice, he'd make a killing.

Tony shut his locker. "Listen to the man, Chet. He's got the perfect marriage."

"No, I don't," Max said. "Audrey and I have butted heads over typical marriage stuff, but we're committed to each other to get through the battles. Never go to bed angry. It's one of our rules. Marriage is hard work. Period."

*Easy for you to say, pal. Too bad it doesn't work that way for everyone.*

Tony had believed in Max's motto before his divorce. He had made a mistake—the big one—and his ex-wife dumped him without thinking twice. Apparently, she'd forgotten the whole "until death do us part" agreement. After their daughter died, his wife left him, too. In less than a year, the two most important people in his life were gone. Tony had suffered the kind of loss he wouldn't have wished on his worst enemy.

Chet untucked his T-shirt. "Who needs bachelorhood? The best woman in the world wants to marry me."

Max slapped Chet on the back. "She's a lucky woman."

Tony had all he could take of the "How to Have a Happy Marriage Seminar" for one day and left the locker room. He went into the kitchen for a cup of coffee, then followed the rumble of voices into the lobby, where a media mob of reporters, cameramen, and photographers had formed.

Tony approached a man from the *Hilton Herald* and slung his arm around the guy's shoulder. "How did you get to cover the news story of the day, little brother?"

"I can write about more than feature stories on old ladies turning a hundred and the town's annual dog show." The reporter adjusted his blue tie and centered the press pass attached to the black lanyard hanging from his neck. "It's time my editor sees me as a hard-news journalist."

Tony cocked a suspicious eyebrow, sipping coffee from a Styrofoam cup.

The man wiggled out a confession. "We're down two reporters. I got called up from the bullpen."

"It doesn't matter how you get there, Joey," Tony said, grinning, "as long as you get there."

Joey held a pen to a notepad, ready for any scrap of information. "Any word about Kahn's replacement?"

"Nice try."

"What?" Joey lifted his shoulders with an exaggerated shrug. "I get the facts. That's my job."

"Even if I knew, I still wouldn't tell you."

Joey blew a mouthful of air. "Unbelievable. I have an inside source reporters would die for, but my brother—my flesh and blood—won't budge."

"Save the creativity for the article."

"Yeah, yeah," Joey mumbled, walking away.

"See ya Sunday," Tony called above the media chatter.

His brother turned around. "Not this week, you won't."

Tony drank a swig of coffee. "Ma's gonna kill you. The woman lives to feed us, and the Steelers are on prime time!"

"It's dinner. Not the Super Bowl."

Few exceptions qualified as worthy to bypass tradition in Italian families where food and family reigned supreme. If you lived in Pittsburgh, you were a Steelers fan until the day you died. A woman was the only acceptable excuse a Lombardo man had to blow off Ma's Sunday dinner and the Steelers.

"Who is she?" Tony asked.

"Rachel." Joey glowed as the name rolled off his tongue and more so the second time. "Sunday is her day off."

Tony downed the remaining coffee in one gulp. "You're off the hook."

Joey melted into the media circle as Lieutenant Mills announced five minutes until the press conference, sending reporters on a foot race to the conference room.

Tony tossed the empty cup into the trash can inside the kitchen. Rounding the hallway corner, he saw Chief Kahn talking to a woman. White uniform shirt and black pants, her backside facing Tony.

Mystery solved. The big secret—Kahn had hired a woman.

Tony had worked with a handful of female cops during his two decades on the force. Only one outshined the rest. Most of the men, too. Unfortunately, she'd been long gone from the department and his life.

The new chief emanated an eerie familiarity. She stood like a statue. A subtle nod of her head as it balanced her hat. Her stealthy movement as she tucked a loose strand of hair behind her ear.

Chief Kahn raised his chin. "Lombardo."

Tony nodded. "Morning, Chief."

Not an ounce of curiosity caused the woman to turn around and scope out one of her officers. Odd. Cold, too. Tony had a bad feeling about the new chief as he went inside the conference room. Reporters sat at the oval table while officers and detectives lined up along the wall.

Tony moved past his colleagues and stood next to Max. Leaning over, he said to him, "It's a woman."

"Who's a woman?"

"The new chief. Just saw her with Kahn."

"Which explains the hush-hush. Did you recognize her?"

"I didn't see her face. She wouldn't turn around. Some first impression." Tony grunted. "Kind of pointless to keep it a secret. Kahn picked a woman, so what?"

Max glided his arm through the air. "Look around, buddy. Not one female officer."

"If she can't handle the testosterone, she shouldn't have taken the job."

Chief Kahn strutted into the conference room alone. Muffled conversations ceased as he approached the lectern with microphones huddled in a bunch. He thanked the media for coming, then kicked off the presser with a preamble of his years as a cop, followed by passing the torch to a new leader. He paused, letting the interrupted applause ride out.

"She's no stranger to Hilton," Chief Kahn said. "In 2001, she started her rookie year here at the department."

Tony's ears took notice when he heard the year.

*No, it can't be.*

"For nine years she served the Hilton community, then transitioned to the Scottsdale Department, where she earned the ranking of captain. The department and community have honored her for her involvement with youth programs, among other achievements."

*This is not happening.*

Max elbowed Tony and whispered, "Are you okay? You look sick."

Chief Kahn ended with, "Her dedication to the force is admirable. It's an honor to have her back. Ladies and gentlemen, join me in welcoming Hilton's new police chief, Veronica Callahan."

Tony swore his heart stopped beating. Veronica strode inside, moving in what appeared to be slow motion only to him. His jaw dropped. His eyelids were paralyzed. It was as if someone had whacked him in the back of the head with a two-by-four as the roaring applause faded to a low-level vibration in his eardrums.

Veronica stood next to Chief Kahn, posing with a Mona Lisa smile during a rapid-fire of camera clicks.

There she was. The new chief. Tony's boss.

His ex-wife, Ronnie.

# CHAPTER 2

While not one for the spotlight, Ronnie soaked in the approbation like a sponge. The crowd of faces formed a blur. Except for one officer.

Tony Lombardo.

Her ex-husband looked as if he'd seen a ghost, yet for Ronnie, she had known Tony was still a Hilton officer before she accepted the position as chief.

A calculated move, one might say devious. It was spring the news on him the way she did or meet him in the parking lot after his shift to warn him there's a new chief in town.

*"Hey, Tony. How's life been since our split? Oh, by the way, head's up. I'm going to be your new boss."*

Ronnie made the right choice. Shock does not last forever. It wears off.

Ronnie hadn't seen Tony since the day they signed the divorce papers. He wore ten years better than most guys his age, making him one of the most attractive men she ever laid eyes on. Thick, jet-black hair. Dark brown eyes deep enough to drown in—she knew from experience. At five-feet-ten inches, he boasted a skin tone resembling a year-round summer tan. No beer belly or spare tire, which meant he still lifted weights at the gym. A solid build, strong like granite. At forty-two years old, time found favor with Tony Lombardo and skipped past him.

His stare bore into her. Time rolled back nearly two decades to her rookie year. The attraction between them had been instant, but Ronnie maintained a professional relationship. Guys with illegal looks spelled trouble. It was just how life worked. The better looking, the bigger the jerk.

Ronnie, however, eventually caved to Tony's charm and pursued a relationship with him outside the force. A relationship she counted on lasting forever, but forever didn't happen.

One month after their seventh wedding anniversary, she left him. What other choice did she have after what he had done? She had ended their marriage, leaving behind the Lombardo name she loved, even though there was not a speck of Italian blood in her.

Haunting memories followed her. Images she prayed would disappear because the hurt Ronnie had suffered was impossible to forget. She had to choose: succumb to loss and hopelessness or turn it into fuel to move forward.

Ronnie chose the latter, which resulted in her reward of being honored with the Hilton Police Department's most prestigious title.

Tony's slack-jawed expression had Ronnie relishing in his bewilderment. Only for a moment. Being the police chief, Ronnie had a responsibility to the citizens of Hilton and to the department. Her title wasn't a weapon to use against her ex-husband. Ronnie's father, Nick, taught her wearing a badge made him humble, not powerful.

The applause faded like the tail end of a song as Ronnie began her speech.

"Thank you for the warm welcome," she said. "It's good to be back. I've always considered Hilton my home. It's an honor to protect and serve this community. As police chief, my promise to you is Hilton will be a place you will be proud to call home. A place where you'll feel safe. A place where families grow and live for generations. At this time, I will take a few questions."

Voices tripped over one another in a hail of incoherent noise. Ronnie pointed to a reporter with brown hair from Eyewitness News 5.

He stood, deepening his voice. "Congratulations on your position. How does it feel to be Hilton's first female police chief?"

Of course, the first question out of the gate was gender-related instead of what she planned to do for the town. Important issues such as lowering the crime rate, keeping drugs off the streets, and officer training. Ronnie had prepared for this question with the help of YouTube tutorials on the dos and don'ts of media interviews.

"The real honor is being named police chief. The unit, like all police departments, is a brotherhood. A family. In a family, there are many unique members. As we do our jobs effectively, we create a strong team dedicated to upholding the law."

*That's how you answer a question without answering it. Thanks, YouTube.*

A second burst of questions erupted from the gaggle of reporters. Ronnie nodded at a woman with glasses from Channel 2 Action News who asked, "What goals do you hope to achieve by the end of the year?"

*At least someone cares about this town.*

"Great question. I plan to bring back initiatives aimed at helping our youth. They're the next generation of leaders, and I'll do whatever I can to help them succeed. Drug awareness and mentoring need attention. If we do our part as law enforcement officers, we can play a key role in these areas."

Ronnie watched her ex-brother-in-law look across the room at Tony. They resembled stunned twins.

She answered four more questions, thanked the media, and stepped aside as Chief Kahn ended the press conference. The reporters gathered their gear and left to work on the day's lead news story unless something more earth-shattering occurred before five o'clock.

Max approached Ronnie, congratulating her. "Welcome back, Chief Callahan. Looking forward to working with you again."

"Me, too, Officer Brody."

Max was a class act both as a cop and a human being, a doting husband and father from what Ronnie remembered. Having him on the force was an enormous asset.

He turned and looked at Tony planted by the wall as if he were saying, "What are you waiting for? Get up here."

Ronnie shook hands with her brothers in blue. After the room emptied, silence levitated like a thick storm.

It was just the two of them.

• • •

The ground shifted beneath Tony's feet. His slanted body fought for balance, as if he had stepped off one of those spinning rides at an amusement park.

Ronnie removed her hat and tucked it under her arm. Authority sliced through her razor-sharp tone. "Hello, Tony."

He stammered like a fool. "I—I had no idea."

Her lips formed a smug grin. "The look on your face was priceless."

"Glad to know I still amuse you."

Although he wasn't, not one bit.

Ronnie's hair made her unrecognizable from behind. It used to be long, past her shoulders. Brown, the color of milk chocolate. On duty, she had worn it in a low bun. The locks Tony's hands had wandered through were now the color of honey and cut at an angle dangling from her neckline.

Questions ran through his mind in chaos. "Not surprised you climbed the ladder, and so quick. Must've broken a record."

"I simply set a goal and achieved it." Her rigid tone sounded robotic, as if she weren't human.

"Scottsdale, huh? That's where you disappeared to."

"I relocated, not disappeared."

One hour. Ronnie had been only an hour away for ten years. Tony had assumed she moved cross-country after the divorce. Any woman would've after his egregious mistake. Regret of his infidelity had been a heavy chain around his neck.

Although Ronnie wasn't exactly innocent in all of this, either. She had thrown in the towel long before he screwed up royally. She had refused to save their marriage, leaving him no choice but to sign the divorce papers.

Thankfully, his satisfying career as a cop and supportive family close by had helped him weather the personal storm. Dating had changed after being married. The bar and club scenes attracted young, giddy girls looking to party and divorced women hunting for hubby number two to play daddy to their kids. Being a cop, Tony had to be careful. Hitting on a chick with a few drinks in her could turn into a sexual harassment allegation by morning. The Internet matching sites—forget it. He wasn't that desperate.

Tony's relationships after the divorce were few. His phone had exploded with texts from his first girlfriend, Trisha, begging him to quit the force. He already had an overprotective mother; he didn't need another. After breaking it off with her, he changed his number.

Bailey, girlfriend number two, had pressured him to have a baby with her. "I want to be a mother before I'm old enough to be a grandmother," she had chanted.

Parting ways went better than Tony had expected, which meant she only wanted a sperm donor.

Candace, girlfriend number three, was as jealous and insecure as they came. Ironically, she had dumped him for another guy.

No woman had compared to Ronnie. There was something special about Tony's ex-wife; he knew it the moment they met. Being cops connected them in a way only they understood. However, the job wasn't enough. Tony had never worked harder to get a woman's attention and feared he had lost his irresistible sex appeal.

Ronnie finally had agreed to a date. One. Tony's only shot to impress her. He had done something right because during the ride home to her apartment, she said, "Next time, I pick."

She had dragged him to an outdoor ice-skating rink by the river in January. Circling the block of ice, freezing their butts off, Tony knew he had found his future wife.

That life was a long time ago. Better moments from their relationship he had sent to the recesses of his memory.

Tony lowered his head enough to still see Ronnie. "I tried finding you, but you were gone. Natalie was tight-lipped, but not before screaming a few words I can't repeat."

"It was the one request I had for my mother she made good on." Again, Ronnie's reply mimicked a stranger's, not the woman he'd been married to for seven years.

Is this what time had done to her? Made her hard and distant. Priorities of duty and responsibility embedded so deep they overshadowed the Ronnie who had been his loving wife. Even her eyes had changed. Once warm and inviting, a delicate shade of brown with amber flecks, were now stoic.

Ronnie relaxed her posture. Tony, I'm here strictly for the job. This is about my career, not what happened between us. The first female police chief in Hilton is an extraordinary accomplishment. I assured Chief Kahn our divorce won't cause dissention within the department." She extended her arm, breaking through the trapped tension. "I'm willing to work together. I hope you can, too."

They cemented the agreement with a handshake.

Her dry skin seemed rougher than before. Then again, ten years had passed. She was creeping up on forty.

Tony headed toward the door. "I got to get to briefing, Ronnie."

"Tony?"

He expected her to say that it was good seeing him again. That she had missed him. Or maybe had forgiven him. Wouldn't that be nice?

Ronnie put her hat on and jutted her chin. "At the station, you are to address me as Chief Callahan."

Callahan—her maiden name. It sounded wrong. She had been a Lombardo. His Ronnie Lombardo.

Contempt cut through Tony's words. "Yes, Chief."

• • •

Tony recognized the tall man from the wavy ends of his grown-out silver hair. He stood to get his father's attention, and the older Lombardo headed toward Tony's booth.

The men greeted each other with a hug and a loud slap-pat on the back, garnering a few stares. The Lombardos' affection came with their Italian heritage.

"Thanks for coming, Dad," Tony said. "What time do you have to get back to the factory?"

"Vince practically runs the place. Your brother doesn't need me there. What can I say?" John waved a hand through the air as if he were swatting a fly. He cracked a smile. Lines formed around his mouth like parentheses. "Maybe it's time I do that retirement thing everyone my age talks about."

John Lombardo's thriving custom cabinetry business paved the way for Tony's older brother, Vince, who followed in their father's footsteps as a talented carpenter, to manage the business's day-to-day operations.

The waitress approached John and Tony's booth and handed them each a menu. John ordered a ginger ale. Tony, a Pepsi. They perused the limited lunch options: sandwiches, burgers, and wraps.

John's soft brown eyes adjusted through the glasses he had worn more in the last year. "The Swiss cheese mushroom burger looks good."

"Mm-hmm," Tony muttered in agreement.

John pointed at the menu. "Look at that. They've got sweet potato fries. Haven't had those in a while."

Tony yielded a half-smile. "Me, either."

"Okay, Tony. Out with it," John said, closing the menu. "What's buggin' you?"

The waitress returned with their drinks. She removed an order pad from her apron pouch when John stopped her. "We're going to need a few more minutes, ma'am."

"Take your time," she said.

After she left, John opened the menu. His eyes moved in Tony's direction. "I see Ronnie being named police chief threw you for a loop. Your brother called me after the press conference."

"Leave it to Joey to blab. He's got the right job for it." Tony made a noise between clearing his throat and grunting. "It's humiliating taking orders from my ex-wife."

"Because she's a woman, or because of how your marriage ended?"

"Both," Tony admitted.

"Kahn hired her because she's qualified. You've said it yourself a thousand times that she's a good cop. Now she's your boss. Be the better man. Respect her and her position. If you were in Ronnie's shoes and you were chief, you'd want the same from her, right?"

Tony didn't invite his father to lunch for a lesson in the Italian motto of respect. Respect your elders, respect your boss, even if she was your bitter ex-wife.

"The history between you two, well, what can I say?" John shrugged. "It's a harder pill to swallow."

"I don't want to quit the force."

"Who says you had to? Did Ronnie?"

"No, but I'm sure she wants me to." Tony sipped his Pepsi. "Being a cop is the only thing I've ever been good at. I'm not talented like Vince or educated like Joey. I'm no winner in the marriage department, that's for sure." He collapsed against the cushioned booth.

John was a straight shooter and not one to baby his boys. "Tony, stop with the pity party."

"You should've seen her, Dad. She acted all high and mighty, as if being the new chief meant she was better than me." Tony leaned across the table. "She waited for me to say what I did, but I didn't. Eventually, she'll bring it up. It's only a matter of time before she does."

"It seems to me your guilt is working overtime."

"I feel like it's happening all over again. Once was bad enough. I don't need a repeat."

"Son, you made a mistake. It cost you your marriage, but it's over. Let it go."

"I did until she came back to town. Why couldn't she stay in Scottsdale, where she belonged?"

"Look, Tony. I know Ronnie being chief is no picnic for you. There isn't one good thing you could possibly think of about her coming back to Hilton. But I can. And it's Vivian. Take this as an opportunity to talk to Ronnie about what happened. And maybe, finally, you'll both get the closure you need."

Tony shut the menu; he lost his appetite. "Ronnie doesn't talk, remember? And I doubt she wants to pry open old wounds."

# CHAPTER 3

Tony wished he was anywhere but at the station while Sergeant Dan Ortiz briefed the morning officers. He'd respond to a 10-31 (crime in progress) or 10-32 (man with a gun). He'd answer a 10-54 (livestock in the highway) if it meant not breathing the same air as his ex-wife.

"We've got a busy day, gentlemen." The sergeant's commanding voice boomed as Tony's mind wandered to Ronnie's office, where she had spent the week barricaded behind a closed door.

"We have surveillance video from the break-in at Stella's Antique Shop on Pine Street. Be on the lookout for two men, early twenties, Caucasian." Sergeant Ortiz passed out blown-up photos from the recording. "One suspect has red hair and a spiderweb tattoo on his neck. The other, a shaved head and a scar across his nose."

Tony felt trapped in a weird dream—the kind that tricked you into believing it's real because all your senses work. For Tony, however, there was no waking up. Ronnie was his boss. Which was more of a nightmare.

"Two vehicles were involved in an accident on Route 32 at six o'clock this morning. Property damage only. Scene cleared."

Ronnie. Police Chief Callahan. Her return had settled in like a nasty case of the flu.

Sergeant Ortiz continued. "The Autumn Harvest Festival begins tonight at the fairgrounds. It's a three-day event, and we need to beef up patrols around a five-mile radius."

Tony and Ronnie had gone to Hilton's five-decade-old fall outing every year, not as cops, but as a couple. They'd spend the day eating doughnuts and drinking warm cider as well as browsing the vendors' booths, where they bought goofy trinkets. They'd end the day with a ride on the Ferris Wheel and leave with a five-pound bag of fresh-picked apples.

"Firearms training is this week. Check the schedule for your appointed times." Sergeant Ortiz announced the patrol assignments without breaking stride. "Sector One—Lombardo, Brody, and Fields."

Officers Max Brody and Lenny Fields unanimously replied, "Yes, Sergeant."

Everyone heard Tony's gap in response, except Tony.

"Am I boring you, Lombardo?" Sergeant Ortiz asked.

Tony snapped out of his trance. "Huh?"

The sergeant tromped over to Tony and slapped his meaty hands on the table, rattling it. "Daydreaming about something more interesting than what I have to say?"

An officer behind Tony snickered. "Yeah, she's down the hall." He snorted, laughing, as the other officers joined in on the playful teasing.

"Knock it off!" Sergeant Ortiz barked.

News that Ronnie was Tony's ex-wife had spread through the station like a contagious disease. He had taken jab after jab all week, as if he were wearing a bullseye. He could take a joke. He had a sense of humor, but his brothers in blue had crossed the line, making him feel less of a man and less of an officer with her around.

Tony looked up at his superior. "It won't happen again, Sergeant."

"It better not. We're a police department. There's no time to be lazy. Not with the new chief riding our butts."

Ronnie wasn't winning any popularity contests. Not with Sergeant Ortiz, and certainly not with Tony.

• • •

Ronnie had spent the first week as police chief reviewing crime stats and trends, reviewing investigations, and keeping those below her accountable for every move they made.

Her office, with a private bathroom and a mini-fridge, had turned into a second home. The only thing missing was a bed.

Reminders of Ronnie's achievements encapsulated her. Two framed articles with photos hung on the wall: one of her with Elliott Kahn at the press conference, the other of her with a group of kids at a community event in Scottsdale. A plaque with her name engraved on it for the Drug Enforcement Officer of the Year, while her rookie photograph rounded out her personalized décor.

On her desk, memories of her father protected her like a shield. A photo of him in uniform. She and Nick at the Baseball Hall of Fame.

He had surprised her with the trip on her tenth birthday. Nothing made Ronnie happier than being with her father. She had him all to herself for an entire weekend. The seven-hour drive to Cooperstown. Sleeping in a hotel. Eating at greasy dives.

Nick's obsession with the All-American pastime had turned Ronnie into a baseball junkie by the time she was five. She and her father had played catch in the yard, even when the snow was up to their ankles. He had taken her to the batting cages to practice her swing. Nick was a season ticket holder, and had taken Ronnie to as many Cleveland Indians games as possible when he wasn't on duty.

Ronnie held the frame with the photo that meant the most to her. The one of her and Nick posing by his patrol car. It had been his last day as an officer before transitioning to the narcotics unit as a detective—and the last picture of Ronnie and her father together.

To the outside world, the duo had resembled father and son more than father and daughter. Known as "Ronnie" to Nick and her friends at school, only her mother, Natalie, addressed her daughter by her birth name, Veronica.

Ronnie hoped Nick was proud of her, wishing he'd been alive to see her graduate from the police academy. To have called him, letting him know she had made sergeant, then lieutenant, then captain, and finally chief.

Touching the photo, she fought feelings of abandonment he didn't mean to inflict on her. Comfort came from knowing he was in a better place where she imagined him smiling down on his "slugger."

*I'll see you again one day, Dad.*

She placed the frame back on the desk, allowing the peace of that knowledge to ease her heartache.

Time to get back to work.

"Who authorized you to switch sectors? Because it sure wasn't me. Your sergeant."

The unmistakable brash voice of Dan Ortiz led Ronnie out into the hallway, where he had cornered an officer. The sergeant was still the same brute. Just because he was as tall as a skyscraper, he thought he could intimidate the officers ranked below him.

The rookie cop, fresh out of the academy and old enough to be Ronnie's son, stood at military attention, taking the chastisement like a man. "Sorry, Sergeant. It won't happen again."

Ronnie approached the officers. "Gentlemen, what's going on?"

Sergeant Ortiz stopped her with a raised hand, his beady eyes piercing her as if she were an annoying little sister pestering her older brother. "I got this."

"Says who?"

Sergeant Ortiz towered over Ronnie, measuring six-foot-three. "Look, *Chief,* these men are my responsibility. I don't need your interference."

Ronnie ignored the wannabe Hulk and addressed the errant officer. "Officer Chambers, I need a moment with Sergeant Ortiz. Please excuse us."

"Yes, Chief."

The rookie cop left and disappeared around the corner.

With a cordial, outstretched arm, Ronnie ushered Ortiz into her office. The sergeant huffed, and she closed the door.

Good leaders didn't scream. Composure signified strength. They dealt with issues in a firm, constructive manner.

"These are my men." Ronnie tugged her collar. "See these stars? They're there for a reason. If the day comes when you're wearing them, you can call the shots any way you want. Until then, you answer to me."

Ten years ago, Ronnie and Sergeant Ortiz's roles were reversed. As Officer Ronnie Lombardo, she had taken orders from her bully superior. Little did she know her last run-in with him would cause her world to crumble.

Ronnie released the pointed end of the white shirt. "What happened?"

"It's your ex."

"Do not refer to Lombardo in that way, Sergeant. It is disrespectful and rude. He's a Hilton officer."

Ortiz complied. He got the message. "Lombardo switched sectors with Chambers in the middle of his shift, and he's been late to briefing twice."

Careful not to show her shock at Tony's rebellion, Ronnie remained calm. "Three infractions. All within a week, I presume?"

"I'll have a talk with him."

"No." Ronnie strode behind her desk. "The second Lombardo gets back, tell him I want to see him. No coffee. No going to the john."

Sergeant Ortiz turned his head with a heavy sigh.

Her voice tightened. "Are we clear, Sergeant?"

He looked directly at her. She felt his hostility saturating her. "Yes, Chief. Crystal."

"Good. Get back to work."

Despite Ronnie's ranking, the sergeant's blatant disrespect tested her anger and leadership. She had won one battle, but not yet the war.

Ortiz slammed the door behind him as he left.

An hour later, a knock on Ronnie's door alerted her gut that it was Tony. Nervous energy twisted inside her like a tornado. "Come in."

The door opened, creaking. Tony stood behind it. "You wanted to see me?"

Kudos to her gut. "Close the door, Lombardo."

The tension in the air rose twenty degrees, suffocating Ronnie like a shirt two sizes too small. Tony's bored countenance implied he had better things to do. If his eyes could talk, they would've said, "Get on with it."

Ronnie knew her officers would challenge her, testing to see how much they could get away with by crossing the boundary line. She didn't, however, expect the first one to be Tony.

Standing to her feet, her fingertips formed tepees on the edge of the desk. "Why did you switch sectors with Chambers?"

"I wanted a change of scenery." Tony folded his arms across his chest. "I've been patrolling sector one for two weeks. It's boring me."

"I'm sorry your job bores you, but you don't choose your sector, Lombardo. Nor do you have the authority to switch it on a whim halfway through a shift."

His mouth arched into an exaggerated frown. "No big deal."

*No big deal!* Tony knew better than to make that kind of a cavalier remark. He wasn't a rookie cop.

"I disagree. It's a very big deal," Ronnie said. "While you're at it, care to enlighten me on your reason for two tardies to briefing?"

Tony cackled like a teenage punk. The kind of reckless street thugs Ronnie had arrested for disorderly conduct and vandalism. "Don't get your panties all in a twist. You've got more important things to piss you off than me."

Ronnie's jaw dropped wide enough to fit her whole fist inside her mouth. "You ever speak that way to me again, I'll have your badge so fast, the only job you'll get is flipping burgers at McDonalds!"

Tony exhibited not one iota of fear as he shifted his stance with boldness. "Don't you threaten me."

"I don't have to. Consider it a promise."

"You don't have it in you."

Ronnie leaned across the desk. "If this is your juvenile way of acting out because I'm chief, then you're more of a coward than I pegged you for."

Tony glared at her, the crow's feet around his eyes deepening. "Cowards run away."

"And they have SEX with girls who pour coffee for a living!"

"Didn't take long for you to throw that in my face!"

Tony had baited Ronnie like a mindless fish. She had no intention of digging up the past she had buried ten years ago, especially to her ex-husband.

"*You,*" Tony said, pointing at Ronnie, then at himself, "left *me*. Not the other way around."

"If memory serves me correctly, my reason was more than justified."

"You gave up and walked out."

"You have the audacity to call me a quitter after what you did?"

"Bingo! You bolted before the ink dried on the divorce papers." Tony measured an inch with his fingers. "You didn't even try one bit to put our marriage back together."

Ronnie's brain pleaded for her to stop, but the argument had turned personal fast. She was in deep, like sinking quicksand.

"I'm not the one who broke it!" she said. "You want to lay blame, fine. Step in front of a mirror and take a good, long look!"

"Just admit it. What I did was the perfect out for you."

She rolled her eyes at the absurd notion. "I wasn't looking for one."

"Yeah! Right!" Tony arched his back with ridicule. "You got a lawyer, the divorce papers, and sold the house in a month. Very efficient of you!"

"Not that you gave me a choice!"

"Oh yes, I did! What about the one about giving our marriage a second chance? Does that ring a bell?"

"Don't you mean *you*, Tony? I didn't give you a second chance. This all boils down to your precious ego." Ronnie's arms shot out wide. "I mean, come on! How could any woman be stupid enough to leave Tony Lombardo?"

"You think I wanted to save our marriage to save *face*?" He choked on his laughter, and his mouth twisted with disdain. "A marriage is two people who don't bail at the first sign of trouble. They stick together. They're partners. They work it out no matter how bad it gets."

Ronnie tilted her head sideways. "How touching. Award-winning, even. But since I'm a nice gal, here's a free reality check. There was no way to rectify what you did. I had every right to end our marriage. Not a day goes by I regret my decision. So don't you stand there and make me out to be the bad guy."

Tony rubbed the side of his face as if a dull ache had settled in his jaw. "You're some piece of work."

"Think whatever you want about me. I don't care."

He sighed. "You're not the only one who lost her. We both did."

"I don't want to talk about it," Ronnie snapped. She didn't want to think about it either. She had done enough of that already.

"Nothing new there. Keep it all bottled in the same way you did after the accident."

Ronnie could do without therapy advice from her ex. No amount of talking would change how she felt. No one understood what she had endured—not even Tony.

"I'm not like your nosey family, Lombardo. I don't go around spilling my guts to every Tom, Dick, and Harry about my personal life."

Tony plopped his hands onto the desk in a wide stance with a *thud*. His dark eyes intensified, begging her to listen. "This is about our daughter, Ronnie. Our Vivian. Eleven years and you still won't talk to me about our little girl?"

"Didn't I make myself clear? You are to address me as 'Chief.'"

He pounded a fist on the desk, clenching his pearly white teeth. "That's all you care about? A title!"

"One I worked my butt off for, and don't you dare forget it!"

"How could I?" Tony stepped back, his hands in surrender mode. "All you did was work! Officer Ronnie Lombardo saving the world while her marriage fell apart, leaving me alone with the broken pieces."

The cold, hard truth hung in the air like a noxious odor. Ten years later, Tony was still playing the victim.

"Poor baby, you were lonely." Ronnie's mouth formed a condescending pout. "Good thing you had the slut to keep you company!"

Tony's chest heaved as air poured from his nose. "Two cheap shots in two minutes. Wanna go for three and call it a day, Ronnie?"

"Chief! It's Chief Callahan! Show some respect!"

"As soon as you show me some!"

A knock rapped on the door, and she screamed, "Go away!"

Ronnie and Tony had served each other insults like a ping-pong ball bouncing back and forth. Before ending the match, Ronnie took one last shot. "You're still not man enough to say it."

Tony's face contorted as if she had lost her marbles. "Say what?"

"The fact you have to ask means you haven't changed." Ronnie sat down in her chair and sorted through a stack of papers. What she was looking for, she didn't know. She saw Tony as a cop, not as her ex-husband. "Get back on patrol. Stick to your assigned sector. Don't make me remind you again."

• • •

"She is our boss."

"And my ex-wife." Tony's head lolled against the passenger seat headrest as Max drove the patrol car. His blowout with Ronnie left him seething.

*Chief or not, she was out of line. Who was that woman, anyway? It sure wasn't the Ronnie I knew all those years ago. Is it always going to be this way?*

"It still doesn't give you a pass," Max said to Tony. "It wasn't the smartest move you made talking to her like that."

"What would you have done if it were you? Stand there and take it like a spineless yes-man?" Tony shook his head. "Not me."

Max stopped at a red light. "Chief Callahan is trying to do her job. She always played by the rules."

Every mention of Ronnie's maiden name grated against Tony's skin like sandpaper.

"Yeah, well, all that power shot straight to her head." Tony sneered. "She'll see. She thinks everyone will bow to The Royal Highness because she's the Chief. Not these guys. Ronnie's no leader. I give her three months until she turns in her resignation."

The light turned green, and Max floored the gas pedal. "I'll take that bet."

"Siding with the enemy? Some friend you are."

"Tony, you're my boy. I got your back." Max grinned, taking his eyes off the road. "But you could try to get along with the Chief."

"We're divorced, Max. We're not supposed to be bosom buddies." Tony pursed his lips, bobbing his head. "She said it. Yep, I knew she would."

"About Kaitlyn?"

Tony's fleeting affair embarrassed him, especially around his best friend, the one with the perfect marriage. Max adored Audrey. He'd hack off his manly equipment with a machete before doing what Tony had done.

After the divorce, nights had been like a prison sentence. Tony had dreaded the mornings, knowing when he woke, Ronnie's side of the bed would be vacant. He missed seeing her next to him, curled in a ball with her mouth ajar and a tiny puddle of drool on her pillow.

Even after Tony's monumental blunder, Max stood by his side. He had kept Tony preoccupied with the typical guy stuff. A beer at The Tavern after their shift. Pirates games, a few Steelers games, too. Seats on the fifty-yard line were no easy feat. Tony had a standing dinner invitation at Max's house on the first Tuesday of the month. Max had been right about Audrey being a superb cook, unlike Ronnie, who couldn't boil water without burning the pot.

Max had played matchmaker, fixing up Tony with his cousin Renee—a real Southern Belle from Georgia. Sweet girl. Pretty. They had little in common, though. Halfway through their second date, they had ended the evening early and went to Max's house and played Monopoly with Max, Audrey, and their daughters.

"Ronnie had to bring it up, not once, but twice," Tony said. "Good thing she booted me out of her office before I said something I really regretted."

"I'm sure it wasn't her intention."

"Are you kidding? Ronnie's been a sniper ever since the press conference. Waiting for the chance to pounce on the cheating, loser ex-husband. All that crap about us working together was her way of blowing smoke."

Max turned left onto Middleton Avenue. "The Chief isn't the vindictive type."

"There's truth behind the saying about a woman scorned."

"Enough about the Chief. I need a coffee."

Max drove past The Grind Café; he knew better than to go there. At the intersection, he turned right onto Harper Street.

"I think it's time for me to leave," Tony said, his tone solemn.

A line burrowed across Max's forehead. "You mean the force?"

"If today was a preview of how it's going to be working with Ronnie, then I don't want to stay for the movie. I have my twenty years. I can retire."

"Then what? You don't exactly fit in with the over sixty-five crowd at the senior center."

"I'll work with Dad and Vince."

"And you'll be stuck all day in a factory on an assembly line."

The nine-to-five monotony wasn't Tony's cup of tea. Being a cop was unpredictable. Some days were lighter than others, filled with handing out speeding tickets or patrolling the sector repeatedly. Then there were times his training had him make an arrest, save a life, or be involved in a high-speed chase.

"Maybe I'll check out a trade school. Start a new career," Tony said with little enthusiasm. "I have other interests."

"Like what? Being a plumber or an electrician." Max jiggled his head. "You're a cop, Tony. You'd be miserable doing anything else."

"Not as much as I am right now. Max, she threatened to fire me."

Tony's best friend blew a heavy breath. "That must've been some argument."

"Fight," Tony quickly corrected Max. He and Ronnie had been like two boxers, only instead of throwing punches, they used words to knock the other down. "I won't give her the satisfaction of taking my badge."

"Then play it smart. Don't give her a reason to find fault with you. Do your job. Be the best cop you can be."

"I already am."

Max cocked his head, implying Tony could do more. "Be the better man."

John had offered the same advice. Did his father and best friend conduct conclaves to come up with this stuff?

"Look, Max, I know you're trying to help. But I won't walk on eggshells around her, waiting for the next Cage Match."

Max pulled into Starbucks and parked the patrol car. "Give it a few weeks before you do anything hasty."

They went inside and each ordered a coffee. Max opened his wallet. "I got it. You've been through the wringer enough today."

Tony tapped on the glass display of pastries. "Throw in a chocolate muffin since you're buying."

At a table with their drinks and food, Tony watched the youthful employees buzz around behind the counter. Kids with their whole lives ahead of them, reminding him of the day he had met Kaitlyn.

The day that had marked the beginning of the end of his marriage.

# CHAPTER 4

*May 2010*

Tony watched the blonde barista sashay from the register to the coffee machines, admiring the view. And what a pleasant view it was.

Her ponytail through the opening of a GAP baseball hat dangled over her shoulder. She added the final touches to one of those Frappuccino concoctions and handed a customer the medium-sized cup topped with whipped cream and drizzled chocolate syrup, then greeted Tony as he approached the counter.

"Afternoon, Officer. Welcome to The Grind. What can I get you?"

That was a loaded question. Tony's eyes shifted to the green apron covering her plump cleavage. "Coffee, black. In a mug."

"Sure thing." She turned with a bouncy step. Pouring his coffee, she looked at him with a coy smile. "That'll be two-fifteen."

He paid for the drink, and she gave him his change. He thumbed through a stack of bills in his wallet and dropped ten dollars inside the tip jar filled with ones and coins. Excessive, yes. But why not?

The generous gratuity made her smile as she slid the mug toward Tony. "Careful, Officer. It's *very* hot."

The underlining message was steamier than the coffee. Tony grinned. "Thanks for the warning."

"Anytime," she said, tilting her head sideways.

She leaned across the counter. Again, his eyes wandered to her chest. All she needed to do was lose the apron and he'd have a bird's-eye view down her shirt.

The innocent flirtation boosted Tony's ego. A pretty stranger had shown him more affection than his wife had in months, and it felt good. To have fun and not be treated like a leper.

Sitting at a circular bistro table, Tony sipped his coffee. A teenaged couple joined at the hip, their bodies fused into one, walked past the window. The girl stumbled while kissing the boy as he pinched her butt. Then an elderly couple passed by. The man pointed to the Irish pub and restaurant across the street. His wife nodded, agreeing with his suggestion. They waited at the corner for the signal light to turn red before crossing.

A man went by carrying a little girl on his shoulders while she held a cone, licking a stream of runny ice cream.

Tony used to carry Vivian like that. She had said she was a giant "way up here." Her brown hair parted down the middle in two braids, her scrawny legs thumping against his chest. Her tiny fingers ruffling his hair. The rollercoaster flow of her giggles as he jumped. *Again, Daddy! Do it again!* Her squeaky voice echoed in Tony's mind, and he wanted more than anything to hear it for real.

Tony lived isolated from a world of happiness besieging him. The normal life he once had died with Vivian, while his wife had turned into an aloof workaholic. He had tried talking to Ronnie about the accident, but she always clammed up. She hadn't cried since the funeral. The emotion of losing a child went into her own grave. She was dead inside and under the delusion she had grieved. Coping with a loss by working any and every shift was not healthy. Doubles, holidays, weekends, nights. Ronnie had spent more time in a patrol car than at home.

After the funeral, Ronnie had incrementally erased Vivian's memory. First, she had donated the child's toys to the Salvation Army. Next, her clothes. Another trip to the Salvation Army. Then, Vivian's bedroom.

Tony had come home from the grocery store to find Ronnie disassembling the bed with his electric screwdriver. Dresser drawers strewn on the floor; the mattress propped against the closet. She took one piece of furniture at a time to the curb and taped a sign on the mound that read FREE. However, the final gut-wrenching purge implied Tony's wife was worse than he had realized. Ronnie had packed Vivian's photos and the family albums into a box and stored it in the attic.

Tony had tried comforting his wife with hugs that were pushed away. Notes left on her dresser went unread. After the mushy stuff flopped, he had tried winning Ronnie over with the laundry—the chore she griped about the most. Wash, dry, fold, iron, and put away. Tony had done it all without a single thank you.

Then Tony had an idea guaranteed to pull Ronnie out of her funk. He had arranged a two-day getaway at a bed-and-breakfast on the lake. A weekend filled with hiking, canoeing, romantic dinners, flowers, the works. He had packed their suitcases and waited for her to come home from work. Ronnie had told him she didn't want to go and went upstairs to bed.

Tony had exuded great patience for months, but it was time to be a married couple again. He had convinced himself of their need to have sex, not only to satisfy his urges, though he felt divided in his feelings. Guilt had poked him for trying to reconnect with his wife in bed. Justifiable truth had reminded him he had an active sex life most married guys would kill for. It had been like a busted fire hydrant that was abruptly fixed.

One evening after dinner, Tony had made a move with a lingering kiss on Ronnie's neck. Her body stiffened, and she pulled away. He had broached having a baby, making the situation worse, and Ronnie accused him of replacing the child they lost with another. Their ensuing argument exacerbated the ever-widening distance between them.

Tony stared at the coffee mug, grieving his wife once full of life. The one who made him laugh with her poorly executed jokes. The one who woke him in the middle of the night while cuddling with him in her sleep. Until nine months ago, the one who couldn't keep her hands off him.

The Ronnie before the accident vanished. A shell of a woman took her place, existing but not living. From the look of things, Ronnie wasn't coming back.

"On the house."

Tony looked down at the blueberry scone on a plate, then at the blonde barista next to him.

She jammed her hands into the back pockets of her jeans. "You okay?"

"Why do you ask?"

Her shoulders lifted. "Just a hunch. I've seen you in here before, but today you seem... lost."

Tony picked at the scone, grateful for the young woman's intuition and to be noticed for a change. "It's been one of those days."

*More like one of those years.*

She nodded, implying she knew what he meant. "I'm Kaitlyn, by the way."

"Officer Lombardo." He reeled in the formality. "Tony."

"Nice to meet you." Kaitlyn stuck her thumb out like a hitchhiker. "I have to get back to work. My manager is in a cranky mood. Hope your day turns around."

He lifted the scone. "Thanks."

Tony watched Kaitlyn's tight butt swing side-to-side as she went behind the counter and wondered how it would feel in his hands. Thoughts like that occurred every time he saw an attractive woman. In line at the bank. Pumping gas. In the patrol car at a red light. Fantasies entertained him regularly, making them the closest thing to sex he could get.

He bit into the scone; sweetness filled him.

The pastry was good, too.

• • •

Tony checked his hair in the rearview mirror and went inside The Grind Café. Kaitlyn had mentioned she had to work the afternoon shift after he stopped by yesterday, but he didn't see her behind the counter.

No denying Kaitlyn was hot. She was the type of woman he had dated as a bachelor.

Tony was about to leave when she came out of the kitchen. She smiled and waved. She had wanted to see him as much as he had wanted to see her.

He ordered a coffee. With a tilt of his head, he motioned for her to join him at a table near the register. She spoke briefly to a coworker and tossed her green apron under the counter.

Kaitlyn sat down across from Tony with a to-go cup. It looked like tea from the string hanging over the edge. Her tight blue shirt ended above her pierced belly button. The shiny stud attached to her navel enhanced her tanned, flat tummy. She was gorgeous.

"Are you on break?" Tony asked.

Kaitlyn sipped her drink. "Yeah. I waited 'til you got here."

"Glad you did," he said and winked.

Their breezy chitchat mixed with flirty comments as her mellifluous voice aroused Tony.

Kaitlyn talked about her roommate's annoying habits but dismissed them because the girl was her best friend. She mentioned her parents and her two brothers, who treated her like one of the guys instead of their sister. She laughed it off, saying she "wouldn't trade those idiots for anything." Having two brothers, Tony related to the sibling dynamic.

She was a college junior majoring in education, thanks to her eighth-grade English teacher. He had assumed a cosmetology career was in her wheelhouse.

When she asked why he became a cop, Tony didn't have an "ah-ha" moment because he always wanted to help people.

Fifteen minutes flew by, and her break ended. Kaitlyn stood with reluctance. "I'm working Friday. Same time?"

Two days felt like an eternity to Tony. "If you're free, how about getting a bite to eat after your shift?"

"Tonight?" Her eyes widened. "Yeah. Great!"

Tony and Kaitlyn met at seven o'clock at The Texas Barbecue. He should've felt sleazy for being with a woman six months shy of legally ordering a beer, but Tony swept those feelings aside. Kaitlyn's company was like depending on oxygen to survive, making it worth hiding out in the back booth of a dingy diner to escape another lonely night.

Ronnie went on a last-minute trip to Akron to visit her mother for the week. Tony had offered to go with her, but she said it was unnecessary. Unnecessary? She was his wife, not a buddy from the gym. They both needed a break from the station, even if it meant staying with his mother-in-law. Maybe then Ronnie would talk about the accident. However, she had insisted on going to Akron alone. Suddenly, Natalie was the only person Ronnie needed. Didn't make sense. Then again, neither had the last nine months.

Tony stared at Kaitlyn's full lips shimmering in pink lip gloss. She wore more makeup around her gorgeous blue eyes that were fixated on every word he said, as if no one else existed but him.

While eating barbecued chicken sandwiches and coleslaw, the winding road of conversation ended at the front door of his marriage. Neither one had mentioned it until then. It was like knowing the house was on fire but saying nothing as flames burned around you.

Tony lamented Vivian's death. How he would never get to watch his daughter grow into a young woman. Part of him had died the day she ran into the street and got hit by a car driven by a seventeen-year-old. The other half was on life support because Ronnie had made him believe she had fallen out of love with him.

Sympathy drenched Kaitlyn's eyes as she reached across the table for Tony's hand. "I'd invite you to my apartment, but my roommate is studying for a big test."

"We'll go to my place," he offered without hesitation.

"What about—"

"She's not there. She never is."

• • •

A fruity fragrance jabbed Tony's nose. The same cloying scent that had his mouth buried in Kaitlyn's body, causing him to ignore the snagged thread resembling his life. Last night, he pulled the frayed piece from woven unity with the rest of the fabric until the last tug damaged it beyond repair.

Kaitlyn's body draped across Tony's bare chest, which was reserved for only one woman. It was as if the coffeehouse girl were trespassing, being in the bed he had shared with his wife for the past seven years.

Tony slid out from under Kaitlyn. At the end of the bed, he searched through the pile of clothes for his boxers and put them on. Watching Kaitlyn stir in her sleep, he twisted his platinum wedding band until his finger ached.

The reality of what Tony had done, purposeful and intentional, was now glaringly clear. Sunlight streamed through the window, offering hope for a new day, but loathing contempt was all he felt. He had lowered himself to having sex with a stranger. A kid.

Inside the master bathroom, Tony splashed cold water on his face. Nausea rolled through his stomach. He closed his eyes, unable to look at his pathetic reflection in the mirror. Darkness failed to blot out the images of leading Kaitlyn through the living room, past his wedding photo on the wall. Kissing her as they went upstairs and into the bedroom, where they had fallen onto the bed.

"Hey there," Kaitlyn said.

She stood in the doorway wrapped in the black and white Afghan Tony's grandmother had knitted for him and Ronnie as an engagement gift. Her flawless flesh peeked through gaps of stretched yarn as she held the fold between her cleavage.

Tony dried his face with a towel. "Hi."

Kaitlyn flipped back her tousled hair. Standing beside him, she kissed his bicep. "Last night was so *hot*."

He sensed her hope for a repeat encounter of their scorching night together and dried his face again, although there wasn't any water to wipe away.

Not taking no for an answer, Kaitlyn pulled Tony's head toward her and kissed him. She released the Afghan; it swooshed to the floor, curling around her feet. Tony pushed her away and moved past her as he went into the bedroom.

He took a T-shirt and athletic pants from his dresser drawer as Kaitlyn appeared wearing the Afghan. "Did I do something wrong?" she asked.

He pulled the shirt over his head.

"Oh, I get it. I'm just the one-night stand to get your mind off of your wife."

Again, he didn't answer and put on his pants.

"Tony," she whined, "talk to me!"

"What do you want me to say?"

Kaitlyn slinked toward him. Her delicate hands framed his jaw. "It was bound to happen between us. We're so good together. Don't feel guilty."

Tony's eyes clouded with tears. He had cheated on his wife. One night for sex. No matter how many times Ronnie's silence had filled a room or all the times she had rejected him, Tony never hated her. Frustrated, yes. Concerned, extremely. Worried, all the time.

He removed Kaitlyn's hands. "I can't give you what you want."

Her sweet countenance soured as she huffed. "But it's okay I gave you what you wanted. A few times."

"I was wrong. I made a mistake."

"You mean I was a mistake."

"I'm in love with my wife. It's that simple."

Kaitlyn's rounded eyes narrowed. "If that's how you love someone, how do you treat someone you hate?"

Tony gathered her clothes off the floor. Last night, he couldn't wait to get her out of them. Her skinny jeans that were practically painted on her legs. The low-cut shirt. Her matching red bra and panties.

He handed her the garments and her shoes. "You need to leave."

Tony turned, listening to Kaitlyn's movements as she dressed. She flung the Afghan onto the bed as if it were a cheap rag from one of those dollar stores and left the bedroom. Her footsteps thumped down the stairs, and she slammed the front door.

Tony pulled back the curtain, looking through the window at Kaitlyn's Ford Fusion in the driveway as she came into view. She must've sensed him watching her because she turned around and flipped him the one-finger salute.

. . .

"Ma? Dad? Anybody home?" Tony went into his parents' kitchen and saw John through the window in the garden. He went out the sliding glass door onto the deck in the backyard and jogged down the steps.

"Hey, Dad."

John spun around. "Tony! This is a surprise. What brings you by?"

"Thought I'd stop by for a visit. Where's Ma and Nonna?"

"Having a girls' day. Getting their hair done and lunch." John hugged Tony. "They'll be back soon."

Tony had little time alone with his dad. "What are you planting?"

"The usual. Cherry tomatoes, hot peppers, broccoli, and green beans." John lowered himself to the ground, dirt at the knees of his old jeans. He picked up a glass jar with seeds in it, examining it like a scientist in a lab. "These are from last year's harvest. They'll multiply twice as much."

Tony didn't care about bean growth. He had bigger problems to contend with, but appeased his father. "How so?"

"I'm not sure. It's a trick Nonna taught me."

"Is there anything she doesn't know?"

"Eighty-two years old and still sharp as a tack. She's full of wisdom, that's for sure. No one can ever accuse her of being senile."

*That wisdom must've skipped my generation.*

"How's work?" John interrupted his train of thought and pointed. "Pass me the broccoli."

Tony handed his father a tray with four sprouts. "Work's work. The same."

"No big arrests, robberies, or shootings?"

Tony squatted. "It's been a slow week."

John loosened a sprout from the container. "Good. The slower, the better. You know how your mother worries about you being a cop. The midnight shift you worked your rookie year, she was a wreck. Didn't watch the news. She practically wore away her rosary beads. Father Louis saw her more than me. She'd pace the floor all night, listening for sirens. The woman was sleep-deprived for a year."

Tony could recite the story; he had heard it a hundred times but acted as if it were the first.

"Ah, but she only did it because she loves you. No matter how neurotic she gets, she's proud of you. I am too." John tapped Tony's cheek like an Italian mob boss. "My son, the heroic cop."

*Some hero. If he only knew.*

"How's Ronnie?" John asked, digging holes with a gardening shovel.

"No change." Tony swallowed past the lump in his throat the size of Vermont. "She's in Akron visiting Natalie."

John secured the first sprout in the ground and dumped a scoop of soil around it. The news left him mystified. "Hmm. Didn't see that one coming."

"All of a sudden, she has to see Natalie. I don't get it."

John added a scoop of soil to the second sprout. "Maybe she needs someone to talk to who understands motherhood."

"She chose the wrong person." Tony snickered. "Natalie's too busy playing genie, granting Graham's every wish. Why doesn't she talk to Ma? She treats Ronnie more like a daughter than Natalie."

John finished the last two sprouts with soil. "Yes, your mother loves Ronnie like she was her own, but if Ronnie thinks Natalie can help, all you can do is let her try."

Tony stared at the grass. His clammy hands had enough sweat to water the broccoli sprouts. "Dad, there's something I have to tell you."

Gravity thickened Tony's tone, causing his father to take notice.

Tony dug his fingertips so deep into his forehead, he almost drew blood. He couldn't believe what he was about to say. "The other night... I was with a woman I met at The Grind. We had dinner... and..."

"Tony, you didn't. Did you?"

He looked up at his father. "I slept with her."

At Tony's confession, a gush of relief momentarily eased his guilt-ridden conscience—until John ripped into him. "What were you thinking? How could you be so stupid?"

Tony's knees hit the soft ground. "I feel awful."

"Awful?" John echoed, then drove the shovel into the ground like a stake. "I'd feel a lot worse if I were you!"

Tony hadn't seen his father that mad at him since his senior year in high school, when he had driven home drunk from a party celebrating the football team's city championship. After a twenty-minute tongue lashing that had his mother begging John to stop, Tony's father revoked his driving privileges for three months.

"Tony, life changed for all of us when Vivian died. I don't pretend to understand what it's been like for you and Ronnie. But was this woman worth breaking your marriage vows?"

John's disappointment hurt Tony almost as much as being a low-life adulterer.

"Dad, Ronnie works all the time. She's never home. And when she is, I don't exist." Tony glanced over his shoulder, as if someone were in proximity to him and John, and quietly disclosed his embarrassing admission. "We haven't had sex since Vivian was alive. Ronnie is so far away from me in bed, she almost falls off the edge. My wife won't kiss me; she won't come near me. Do you have any idea how that feels?"

John freed the shovel from the ground. "So, you get even? Is that it? Punish her by cheating on her."

"No! It just happened." The excuse rolled off Tony's tongue just as John cocked an eyebrow at his son's sophomoric excuse. "I didn't plan it. It's just been so hard."

"What about counseling? Someone you and Ronnie can talk to about Vivian."

"I had mentioned it, but she said she didn't want a stranger telling her what to feel."

"How about one of those, you know, groups? The ones for parents who lost children."

"If she won't see a counselor, she won't join a support group, either."

"Then make her go."

"How? Kicking and screaming. That won't help. The last thing I want to do is make her angry."

John aimed the pointed end of the shovel at Tony. "She needs to get mad. Carrying around pain is no good. She needs to let out those feelings, and she's been begging you to help her do that."

"Well, Dad, I guess I failed the class. Comforting My Wife 101 isn't an easy A." Tony slapped his hands against his thighs. "I wish we'd had this talk sooner."

"First things first. Come clean with her."

Tony laughed at his father's suicidal advice. "Are you crazy? I can't do that!"

He would save his secret for confession. Father Louis would absolve him from his mortal sin, and Tony would be on his way.

"Can't or won't?"

"Honesty isn't always the best policy, Dad. Sometimes to protect someone, it's better not—"

"To tell the truth?" John looked at Tony as if he knew better. "Your mother and I didn't raise you to be a liar."

*Or a cheater.*

"Dad, it was one time. One mistake isn't worth throwing my marriage away." Tony should have known better than to confide in his father. "Forget I told you, pretend it didn't happen. And, please, don't say anything to Ma."

John wiped his forearm above his sweaty brow. "Son, marriage is like a garden. There are healthy parts to it, but life's weeds take root. What you did was a weed. Rip it out. If you don't, the weed will grow bigger."

• • •

Ronnie flung a suitcase onto the bed. "Pack!"

Tony shut the lid.

"Fine, I'll do it for you!" She opened the case and took his clothes from the closet with the hangers still attached and smashed them inside the case.

The second Tony had said, "Ronnie, I need to talk to you," when she came home from Akron, he knew there was no turning back. Throwing him out prevented them from fixing the mess that had become their life. Tony did not expect Ronnie's forgiveness, not right away. But leaving? That was no way to mend their brokenness.

*Why did I listen to you, Dad?* Tony thought. He removed the clothes from the suitcase as if he were dismantling an active bomb. Gentle. Slow. Cautious. "Let me explain."

Ronnie threw the clothes back inside the case. "Spare me the pornographic details! You slept with a slutty barista because you haven't gotten any in a few lousy months!"

"More like nine."

"That doesn't justify what you did! There isn't a statute of limitations on cheating!"

Ronnie whipped opened Tony's top drawer, and it nearly fell off the track. She grabbed his boxers and socks, then froze.

Tony seized the opportunity. He'd tell her what a jackass he was, what a complete idiot he'd been, and that it wouldn't happen again.

Staring at the bed, Ronnie discovered the missing piece of the puzzle. One Tony conveniently had hidden.

She faced him with rage-filled eyes. "You brought her here. Into *our* bed!" The rawness of her words burned like acid. "That's how much you respect our marriage. Respect me? Why not take the slut to a trashy motel where she'd fit in? No vacancies?"

Ronnie dumped the underclothes into the suitcase and returned to his dresser as Tony approached her from behind. "You haven't been the same since Vivian died."

She whirled around and hissed, aiming her finger at him. "Don't you dare speak her name. Blaming this on a little girl."

"I lost a child, too!" Now Tony was yelling. "This has been hell for me! I'd do anything to have her back in her bedroom talking to that stuffed bunny she called her best friend. I want to hear her laugh and see her skip around the house. I even miss hearing her cry!"

"I was her mother!"

"Because you're the mom, you're the more important parent? Vivian was my daughter, too, Ronnie. I was her father! I loved her as much as you did!"

Just then, Tony saw Ronnie's internal crack spread.

"Do you know how many times I've been on patrol, driving around, bawling my eyes out?" Tony said. "You have no idea what it's been like for me because all you've thought about was yourself. What you lost!"

"So you let someone other than your wife console you. Is that it?"

"What other choice did I have? You've avoided me for nine months!"

"I suppose hopping into the sack with another woman made you feel all better." Disgust shot through Ronnie's sneer as if she were about to lose her lunch. "You make me sick. I can't even look at you."

Tony had given Ronnie space for months and look where it got him. Not anymore. They were going to have it out. If it meant screaming at each other, so be it.

"Stop shutting me out!" he said. "You've done it for too long. I'm not putting up with it another second!"

Ronnie slapped Tony's face so hard he saw double. He was moving his jaw to make sure it still worked when she went to hit him again, but he grabbed her wrists, harder than he should've, and held her against the wall.

Her arms waved ferociously. She was a scrappy officer trained to tackle a man before he knew what hit him. "Let go of me!"

"Not until we talk like two civilized people!"

Ronnie raised a leg to stomp on Tony's foot, but missed as he backed away.

"Stop it! Calm down!"

At Tony's command, Ronnie ceased her thrashing. She wheezed until she caught her breath.

He slowly released his grip. "We need help. A counselor or a support group. Something. Anything."

"Which group are you interested in, Tony? The one for couples without children, or the one for cheating husbands." Her sarcastic tone chilled his body. "There's no point in getting help. The damage is done."

"It was one night, I swear."

Ronnie took Tony's T-shirts and athletic pants from his drawer and tossed them into the suitcase. "You were with another woman. If you did it once, you'll do it again." Her voice rode a disturbed singsong wave.

"I don't blame you for being angry."

Ronnie laughed like a deranged mental patient. "Tony, darling. I'm more than angry. I'm done. It's over."

"One strike and I'm out? That's how you're gonna play?" Tony spun Ronnie around, forcing her to look at him. "Vivian's gone. Nothing can bring her back, but stop pretending she didn't exist."

"Don't do that, Tony! Don't change the subject! This isn't about her!"

"You can't even say her name. You haven't since she died. Ronnie, you can't keep doing this. Not remembering her. Not talking about what happened. It's eating you alive. I don't even know you anymore. I want my wife back. I want my Ronnie back. We need to grieve together."

Her chin trembled. "Grieve? All I've been doing is grieving, which is more than I can say for you. You're nothing but a typical, selfish guy who only cares about getting action below the belt!"

Ronnie took another suitcase from the closet and tossed his shoes inside. "What a fool I was. I knew how guys like you operated, but I let you work me because I liked the attention. Playing hard-to-get with the hot cop." She zipped both cases. "I was dumb enough to believe you were different. But, hey, it only took a decade for me to learn a brutal lesson."

Tony grabbed her face. "I made a huge mistake that I have to live with for the rest of my life. I know things are bad right now, but we can get our marriage back to how it used to be. We need to be together. I can't do it alone."

Ronnie clawed Tony's skin with her jagged nails, making him yelp. She shoved him once. "You took our life…" She shoved him again, harder. "Our marriage…" The last shove sent him stumbling backward into her dresser, rattling the mirror. "And you killed it in one night!"

She launched a framed photo of their engagement picture straight at Tony's head. He ducked, and it hit the wall, busting the frame as broken shards of glass fell.

Ronnie sank to the floor, where she fell onto her knees, wailing. "Every time I look at our bed, all I'll ever see is you in it with her."

Tony dropped next to Ronnie, holding her as she choked on her sobs.

She scrambled to her feet. "Don't touch me! Your filthy hands were on another woman! I hate you! I hate you!"

Ronnie screamed so hard the vein in her neck bulged. She hurled the suitcases at Tony like a shot-putter.

"Get out and don't ever come back!"

• • •

Tony had called Ronnie three times a day, each day, for weeks. Every call went to voicemail. He had left message after message; the mailbox was full, and no longer accepted new ones. His only hope was she had listened to one and heard his remorse and would call him.

She hadn't.

Ronnie had taken an emergency leave from work. Tony had gone to the house once. She wasted no time changing the locks. He had banged on the door, yelling for her to let him in while the neighbors gawked on their porches.

Tony had been staying at his parents' house for three weeks when one morning on his way to the station he was served divorce papers in the driveway. A week later, he and Ronnie were in a conference room. Her attorney by her side; his attorney next to him.

The man representing Ronnie handed her a pen and the document. "Mrs. Lombardo, sign there." She scribbled her name across the last page as if she were signing a credit card receipt. Void of resistance, no hesitation in movement.

Her lawyer slid the papers to Tony. "Mr. Lombardo, right there, please." The line where his name made it official symbolized the grave representing the death of his marriage.

Tony dropped the pen.

"Is there a problem with the agreement?" the lawyer asked.

It had been fair. Cut and dry. Tony and Ronnie would split the assets fifty-fifty—the sale of the house, their savings, and retirement fund. No alimony.

Tony stood. He went to the other side of the table and yanked Ronnie out of her chair.

"What are you doing?" she squeaked.

"Excuse me, gentlemen. I need a minute alone with my wife."

Tony dragged her into the hallway as both lawyers watched through the window. "Ronnie, I know you don't forgive me. I'm not asking you to, but we need more time to work this out."

She snorted. "You told her about the accident."

He squinted, confused. "Told who what?"

"Kaitlyn. I went to The Grind. That slut had the nerve to blame *me* for *your* cheating. She justified what you did."

"It doesn't matter what I told Kaitlyn or what she believes. I don't want her, and I don't want a divorce."

"Our marriage is in shambles. Our daughter is gone. There's nothing left, Tony. It's pointless to hold on to something that isn't there."

"Love's there. It hasn't left. I love you, Ronnie, and I know deep down you still love me."

Tony had hit a nerve; a layer of anger melted off Ronnie. For the first time in weeks, he had hope. "We'll tear up the papers and start over."

Ronnie didn't refute.

*She's listening. Thank God she's listening.*

"Baby, I'll do whatever you want. If you need time alone, I'll stay at my parents' house. I'll work the third shift. Whatever you want me to do, I'll do it. Even if it means separating for a few months. But please, don't make me sign those papers."

Ronnie straightened her posture. "We're through. I'm moving on. I suggest you do the same."

Tony reached for her, and her body flinched as if he had zapped her with a taser.

Her chin trembled. "Do you honestly believe I could let you touch me again after what you did?"

Day after day, Tony lived with the perpetual agony churning inside of him. Every day he had looked at his hands, remembering how another woman's body brought him pleasure. Ronnie was right. How could he make love to her again without her thinking about his infidelity?

Ronnie's desperation to move past the worst year of her life came through with one last request. "Tony, if you love me, you'll sign the papers."

Fighting for her, delaying the divorce proceedings, badgering her to mend their relationship, it all prolonged the inevitable. Tony knew he would lose in the end. He followed Ronnie into the conference room and signed the document. His marriage was over.

Ronnie's lawyer filed the document in his briefcase. "I'm sorry folks, I truly am. You seem like a nice couple, but sometimes people are better off apart than together." He smiled a disingenuous attorney smile and left the room.

Tony's lawyer clamped a hand on his shoulder, telling him he was sorry while thanking him for the business and left.

Tony waited for Ronnie to say something, anything, as she stared at her engagement ring soldered to the diamond wedding band. The circular promise that had once been a symbol of their union, now reduced to a piece of jewelry. With each tug of the banded rings, Tony's ache grew, taking permanent residence. Ronnie placed the rings on the table. The metal clinked against the glass top; it was the worst sound Tony had ever heard.

She was almost out the door when Tony said, "I love you." His voice cracked, desperate and broken.

Ronnie stopped, took a breath, then left.

# CHAPTER 5

Ronnie clicked "Send" as she emailed a town board member regarding the budget hearing. A knock rattled her office door. "Come in."

The door opened; it was Tony.

She had seen him twice since their argument last week. Once in the kitchen getting coffee, the other time in the parking lot after their shift. Neither one of them had said a word.

"What can I do for you, Lombardo?" Poised with authority, Ronnie showed a professional demeanor. She inhaled a familiar aroma tantalizing her senses. "Athens Deli?"

Tony placed a white paper bag with blue Greek lettering on her desk. "Chicken gyro. Feta, olives, no onion. Salad dressing on the side."

Ronnie uncurled the folded rim and peeked inside. A big, fat pita rolled in aluminum foil sat at the bottom, still warm. "You remembered."

"Hard to forget. You ate one every week for years."

The food symbolized a peace offering. Her ex-husband's way of apologizing, not a sentimental memory of years past. Two simple words of "I'm sorry" had always been hard for Tony to say. Pride or his ego on the line, perhaps both.

Ronnie refolded the bag and planned to eat the gyro later. "Thanks."

Tony held a second bag and looked out the window. "Let's eat outside. It's a nice day. Not too many of them left."

Her head jerked back in astonishment. "You and me? Together?"

"It's only lunch," he said, making the meal sound as nonthreatening as possible.

Ronnie thumbed through a stack of papers in a poor attempt at appearing busy, hoping Tony would take the hint and leave. "I'm buried here. The budget proposal for the town board is more work than I expected. I'll be chained to my desk the rest of the day."

Tony's expression softened, and with it came a dash of begging. "Please, Chief."

And then it happened. Her ex-husband's blasted dark-brown eyes had done it again. If Tony Lombardo had only one card to play, that was it. All he had to do was stare long enough at her and he could coax her into robbing a bank.

"All right," she said. "I could use some fresh air."

Tony held the door open for Ronnie, and they left the station in his patrol car. "Where are we going?" she asked as he drove down Phillips Avenue.

"Not far," Tony answered vaguely while focusing on the road. He turned onto Stovemeyer Road and entered Birchwood Park, riding the brake as the tires rolled with caution over the speed bump.

"Lombardo?" Ronnie pointed at the lush green space in question. "The park?"

"What about it?" he asked, as if it was an empty lot for a speed trap.

What did he mean "What about it?" If Tony remembered her favorite sandwich, then he knew Birchwood Park had been a special place to Ronnie before the divorce.

*Did he forget all the times we spent our lunch breaks here, getting away from a demanding job so we could be alone where we were just Tony and Ronnie? Did it slip his mind Birchwood Park was where he told me he loved me for the first time, under the dogwood tree by the rose garden?*

Tony parked the patrol car. Reaching for the bags of food on the floor, his arm brushed her calf. Takeout from Athens Deli, now Birchwood Park.

Why the need for a trip down memory lane? To reminisce about the good ol' days when they were wild for each other or have her admit she was wrong to divorce him? He would surely gloat about that.

This was a mistake. The food, the drive, the park. All of it. What made Ronnie believe being alone with Tony outside the station was harmless? She was the police chief, not the same rookie cop with the hots for a colleague.

Ronnie sulked as Tony exited the patrol car. He cocked his head to the side the same way he would if he were ordering a suspect to move. "Come on, I'm starving."

She followed him to a picnic table near a shady patch beneath an oak tree. The warm breeze, unseasonable for late October, whistled past them as they ate.

"How's the gyro?" Tony mumbled while chewing.

"As good as the last time I had one. What about yours?"

He displayed a confident thumbs-up.

Ronnie glimpsed at the dogwood tree in the distance. The memory of the crisp, chilly April day bloomed inside her like new flowers in springtime. Every detail as vibrant as a maple tree's crimson leaves flooded her mind.

Standing against the tree with Tony's hands on her hips, her heart had pounded with anticipation as she picked at a loose piece of bark.

"I love you, Ronnie. You're the only woman I've ever told that to, and I don't plan on telling it to anyone else ever again."

A hush broke through as he kissed her, reassuring her he had meant every word.

Unlike some men, Tony had been a proponent of showing affection, in public and in private. Ronnie attributed it to his Italian genes of hugs and kisses that were as natural as breathing.

He used to burrow his mouth into the curve of her neck when she washed dishes. Fondled her leg under the dining room table during Sunday dinner at his folks' house. After a stressful day at work, his killer massage proved he'd been a masseur in another life.

Ronnie shook off the memories, burying them with the rest of Tony Lombardo's touches that had turned her insides into mush.

Tony had the same roaring appetite as he devoured his gyro. His mother, Tess, had fed him well as a kid. An abundance of food and flavor filled the Lombardo home. Ronnie couldn't hold a candle to her ex-mother-in-law's five-star dinners and counted it a victory by making a grilled cheese sandwich without burning the bread, which happened about as often as a solar eclipse.

"How's the job going?" Tony asked.

"Good." Ronnie pulled a dangling shred of lettuce from the gyro and ate it.

"That's it?" He waited for her to say more. "Just good."

She turned up her palm. "What else did you expect to hear?"

Tony bit into his sandwich, chewing. "I'm not privy to life as a police chief. I thought you'd have some behind-the-scenes footage to share."

"I'm still a cop, just with a lot more responsibility. Everything lands on me." Ronnie dipped her gyro into the plastic cup of salad dressing. "How come you haven't moved up the ranks?"

"Don't want to. I'm fine where I'm at."

*Ten years later and still in the patrol car?*

Ronnie's telepathic powers sent Tony a message that he was too content.

"Officer ranking isn't good enough for you?" Offense pinged his tone.

"That's not what I meant. You misunderstood."

Ronnie bit into her gyro, thinking back to Tony's quirky behaviors. After brushing his teeth, he'd rinse out the toothpaste by sticking his face under the running faucet, swish the water around, and spit. He used to leave the toilet paper roll empty, expecting her to change it. He wouldn't eat the same brand of cereal three days in a row. He used the pointed end of a knife to loosen chunks of meat lodged between his teeth. They were minor irritations she had learned to live with.

Again, Ronnie looked at the dogwood tree.

Tony interrupted her wandering thoughts. "How'd you hear about the chief's position all the way over there in Scottsdale?"

"Maggie Richmond, the former receptionist at the station. She works for the town now."

"You kept in touch with her?" Tony's thick eyebrows drew together. "I didn't know you two were that close."

Ronnie shifted uneasily in her seat. "We'd get together for lunch or coffee."

"You came to Hilton?"

"Mm-hmm," Ronnie muttered, making light of her trips. "Passing through on the way to Akron."

Tony looked crushed, as if his best friend no longer wanted to play with him. Ronnie had been a mere hour away. All the times she'd been in Hilton and he never knew it. "It didn't cross your mind to stop by the station to say, 'Hi.'"

"It wouldn't have been appropriate."

Ronnie pictured seeing her former colleagues.

*Hey, boys! I'm back! Say, where's that cheating ex-husband of mine?*

A lull of silence stretched between them. Ronnie's surreptitious visits had Tony switch topics. "Did you like living in Scottsdale?"

*Good. A mundane, safe conversation piece.*

"It was okay, but it wasn't Hilton. My apartment was nice and the neighborhood was decent. But it always felt temporary." Ronnie stared past Tony. "Now I know why."

"Make any friends?"

"A few," she said and took another bite of the gyro.

Tony probed further. "Any… guy friends?"

"Are you asking me if I dated?" Without waiting for him to respond, she said, "If so, the answer is yes."

He wadded the aluminum foil and tossed it into the bag. "Anything serious?"

Tony's subtle dirt-digging needed fine-tuning. "This interrogation is awfully familiar. It reminds me of the one you gave me twenty years ago."

He leaned across the table in a flirty way. "How so?"

"You know the answer."

"I want to hear you say it."

Ronnie knew she was blushing because her cheeks felt warm, as if her face had been under a small heat lamp. Looking down at her half-eaten gyro, she answered, "You wanted to know if I had a boyfriend."

Tony tilted back his head and glanced upward as if he were pondering the purpose of life. "Ah, yes. It's all coming back to me. What can I say? Old habits die hard."

It was Tony's turn to sit in the hot seat. "What about you?" Ronnie asked. "I'm sure the ladies flocked to Tony Lombardo when word got out you were a free agent."

"I had a few relationships."

*Still cocky, eh, Tony?* Not that she expected any less.

Ronnie's phone buzzed with a text. She read the message while typing a response, then wrapped the remaining gyro in the foil and dropped it into the bag. "Captain Rosario needs to see me. Thanks again for lunch."

"You're welcome. We should do it again." Hope and desperation mixed in his words.

Ronnie didn't want to mislead Tony. Lunch was a nice gesture, but it wasn't going to be an everyday occurrence. She stood. "Captain Rosario is waiting."

• • •

The stalker took a final drag from his cigarette and flicked the smoldering butt out the window of his rattletrap truck while watching Tony and Ronnie eat lunch in Birchwood Park.

He scoffed, talking to himself. "You don't deserve to wear that uniform after what you did."

The stalker gulped the rest of his beer and threw the empty can onto the dirty floor. "You'll get what's coming to you, Ronnie."

# CHAPTER 6

At the helm of the conference room table, Ronnie's presence silenced the officers' chatter. "Good morning. I'll make this quick because we all have a lot of work to do. I'm bringing back the drug task force that was cut several years ago because of funding."

Grumbles rippled across the room.

"I see how excited you all are. Let me tell you more about it."

*Like it or not, we're doing this.*

She rattled off startling statistics. "There has been a steady increase in drug use among Hilton's teens in the past five years. Arrests, rehab admissions, and overdoses have all doubled. This epidemic is more than smoking a joint after school. Kids as young as thirteen are doing coke and heroin and getting their hands on opioids."

Ronnie noted two areas of the task force: to partner with the New Beginnings Youth Center and to have a presence in the schools.

"Chief, schools have resource officers for that," Officer Fields said.

"Correction. They had resource officers. Budget cuts have forced many districts to eliminate them."

"With all due respect, Chief, the task force is pointless," Officer Nelson added. "Kids are going to do what they want. They won't listen to us."

Ronnie's rigid stance unwound at her officer's honesty. "Look guys, I get it. It's impossible to have a 100 percent drug-free town, but if we help one kid say no to drugs—and it saves their life—then we've done our job. If it means keeping one kid off the streets so that one day he doesn't point a gun at one of my men..." Her throat tightened at the memory of her father's murder. "Well, then you'll get to go home to your families."

Her impromptu speech either hit home or was background noise.

"Who's my first volunteer?" she asked. "I need five."

The officers were as quiet as church mice, waiting for the guy next to them to be the first sucker.

With her hands behind her back, Ronnie took what she hoped were intimidating strides around the corner of the table. "Do I need to reinstate the draft?"

Still no response.

On the Scottsdale force, she had formed a similar team with more volunteers than she needed. The successful program had won her an award.

The longer Ronnie waited, the harder it got. There had to be at least one officer who had an ounce of faith in her. All she needed was one volunteer, and the rest would follow like sheep.

*Please, someone. Anyone.*

Tony cleared his throat. "I'll do it, Chief."

Ronnie acknowledged her gratitude with a firm nod. "Thank you, Officer Lombardo. Who else?"

Max called out, "Me, too, Chief."

Knots unraveled in Ronnie's body, putting her in a lighthearted mood. "I knew I could count on you, Officer Brody."

Max and Tony looked down the table at Chet. Their buddy's shoulders drooped along with his head. "Why not?"

Ronnie pumped her fist in the air. "Way to step up to the plate, Officer Dalton."

Three additional officers volunteered. She thanked her new task force for their participation, staring only at Tony.

• • •

November in Hilton was Ronnie's favorite time of the year. The sharp bite in the air required a coat but not yet gloves. The last smatter of leaves had fallen onto the ground. Orange, brown, and red decorations in their full glory brightened the business district. The aroma of pumpkin spice from coffee shops and bakeries lingered in the streets.

With the holiday rush circling her, Ronnie was due for an extended weekend off. Since becoming police chief, she had worked an average forty-hour workweek only three times.

Arriving at the station at seven a.m., Ronnie had planned to leave at noon, allowing her time to pack and be on the road to Akron just in time to avoid the day before Thanksgiving traffic rush.

She had finished changing into her uniform when her phone rang. She rolled her eyes when she saw the Caller ID. "Hi, Mom."

"Are you busy, Veronica?"

*I'm the police chief; I'm always busy.*

Ronnie turned off the bathroom light on her way out. "Is something wrong?"

"No, no. Not exactly." Apprehension softened Natalie's words.

Ronnie took the police academy mug she had bought after graduation off her desk. She was a bear before her morning coffee and avoided everything and everyone until that first sip of the hot brew. "Can it wait until I see you tonight?"

"Unfortunately, it can't." Her mother made a funny noise, the same one accompanying her passive pout.

"Mom, hang on a second."

Ronnie went into the kitchen. She filled the mug with coffee and grabbed a handful of individual creamers, sugar packets, and a spoon. With the phone balanced on her shoulder, pressed against her ear, she hurried to her office and closed the door. At the desk, she poured the creamers into the mug. "Okay. What is it?"

Natalie hesitated. "Veronica, I'm not sure how to tell you this."

If anyone other than her mother had said that, Ronnie would've been on the edge of her seat. She stirred in the sugar and took a sip. "Just say it, Mom."

"It's about Thanksgiving. I'm so sorry, but we have to cancel."

Ronnie threw the empty coffee paraphernalia into the wastebasket next to the desk. "What's it this time?"

"Graham and I are going to the Bahamas! He got a great deal he couldn't pass up. You know how much he hates this time of year, being so cold and snowy. I swear, once he retires, we're heading south with the birds."

Ronnie's stepfather had been a pain in her butt for the last twenty-five years. Of course, this was Graham's doing. The mastermind behind Natalie's submissive role as a wife. He had turned her mother into a yes-woman the moment she declared, "I do."

Natalie jumped at her second husband's every whim. Whatever Graham Taylor wanted, Graham Taylor got. If he wanted Mexican food instead of the dinner Natalie had cooked, she'd freeze the meal in Tupperware containers. If Graham wanted to go camping, even though his wife was allergic to anything green, Natalie took Claritin as if it were candy. If Graham wanted to keep his stepdaughter from interfering in his marriage, Natalie made sure Ronnie didn't get in the way. In return, Natalie got a husband who was a successful accountant, home every night at five—except during tax season—and she didn't have to worry about him getting killed on the job.

"Get a move on it, Natty. Keep packing. Our flight leaves in a few hours." There it was, Graham's condemning tone.

"Okay, darling!" Natalie shouted into the phone. "Veronica, I am sorry. I was looking forward to seeing you. Now that you're the police chief and behind a desk, I finally sleep like a baby."

"Natty," Graham whined. He sounded closer to Ronnie's mother.

Natalie giggled like a silly schoolgirl. "Graham, we'll have plenty of time for that once we get to the island."

Ronnie gagged at the image of her stepfather pawing her mother. "I have to go. Don't worry about Thanksgiving. I'll catch you at Christmas. If not then, Easter."

"I'm so glad you understand!" Natalie gushed. "Yes, Christmas! It's the better holiday. Goodbye, Veronica."

Ronnie murmured a "mm-hmm" and hung up.

Alone for the holiday. Again.

Ronnie looked at the photo of her father in his police uniform, remembering the last time she had seen him alive.

She had hurried home from school, peddling her bike faster than a Tour de France cyclist. Nick had promised to take her to the batting cages to practice her swing and out for a burger at her favorite restaurant, The Dugout—a baseball-themed diner. Nick had postponed the outing twice because of work, but that Thursday, he had the day off.

Ronnie dropped her backpack in the hallway entrance. Homework could wait.

She took her new bat and Cleveland Indians hat from the coat closet and wandered through the house searching for Nick. Ronnie found him in his bedroom in front of the mirror, inspecting his outfit: worn-out jeans splattered in stains, a faded navy-blue hoodie, and a ratty brown jacket.

He looked like a bum.

But that's how undercover narcotic detectives dressed for assignments on the streets.

Nick spotted Ronnie in the mirror. His arms shot out at his sides. "How do I look?"

"Like someone going to work."

"I was called in, slugger." An apologetic smile spread across his handsome unshaven face as he put on a green knit cap with holes. "We'll work on that swing tomorrow."

Junior high softball tryouts were next week, and Ronnie still had one heck of an upper cut. "Keep your swing level," Nick had reminded her, but she still managed to hit the ball straight up rather than across the field. A few hours at the batting cages with the world's best baseball coach, and she would correct the erroneous swing. Sure, Ronnie was disappointed that she had to wait until tomorrow. What twelve-year-old wouldn't be? But when it came to Nick's job, his zealous commitment to the force made Ronnie proud to be the daughter of the best cop in the department. She'd have the same fervor one day.

They went downstairs, and she kissed him goodbye. He was halfway out the door when she reminded him about the batting cages. "Tomorrow? For sure this time?"

His fist gently punched her chin. "Promise, slugger."

Nick didn't come home that night. The last conversation between Ronnie and her father had ended with a promise he hadn't known he couldn't keep.

• • •

Nixed holiday plans meant there was no reason for Ronnie to leave the station early. Keeping busy at work took her mind off being dumped for a beachy vacation. It wasn't the first time she had turned to her job to fill a void, and it most likely wouldn't be the last.

A knock rattled the door. "Come in."

Tony came in with an update on the drug task force. He had arranged an afternoon assembly at the middle school following Thanksgiving break. His sister-in-law taught science there and put in a good word, expediting the process.

The progress pleased Ronnie, but Tony noticed her mind was elsewhere. "What's wrong?"

She focused on the computer screen. "Nothing."

"Chief?"

Ronnie looked at Tony; he had done it again. *Those eyes.* She sighed. "It's my mom."

Tony stepped closer, concerned. "Is Natalie okay? She's not sick, is she?"

"Ha! Far from it." Ronnie's tone oozed sarcasm. She pounded the computer keys harder. "She's in a bathing suit, oversized hat, and sunglasses, sipping a fruity cocktail on the beach with Graham. Truth be told, I didn't want to drive to Akron for Thanksgiving."

Tony shook his head as if he had seen it coming. "Same old Natalie. Something better came along." He quickly removed the foot he had inserted into his mouth. "That came out wrong."

"No, you're right. A trip to the Bahamas or spending the holiday with her daughter." Ronnie used her hands to imitate weighted scales, alternating each one until the Bahamas one plummeted. "No contest."

"What are you going to do?" Tony asked.

"Maybe I'll fly down there and surprise them. Can you see it? One big, happy family reunion!" She frowned. "No, that won't work. I'd be like sand in Graham's swim trunks."

Tony stared at Ronnie with pity. "Seriously, what are your plans?"

"I suppose I'll get a few things done around here," she mumbled.

"On Thanksgiving?"

"Cops work holidays. It comes with the job. At least I'm always welcomed at the station."

Tony tapped his belt with his index finger. His famous trademark stance meant his wheels were turning. He snapped his fingers. "I got a better idea."

"It's too late to rustle up a new family. The deadline was last week."

He grinned. "Not necessarily."

"Lombardo, I was joking."

Tony came around to the side of the desk. "You can spend Thanksgiving with me." Quickly adding, "Along with the rest of the lively Lombardos."

The kind invitation lowered Ronnie's defense, but not enough for her to accept. "Thank you. But no."

"Come on, Ron—Chief. You don't want to be alone on Thanksgiving."

No, she didn't, but Ronnie didn't have a choice. Her family had blown her off. Natalie and Graham had been making plans and breaking plans since she was a teenager. She'd gotten used to the pattern and girded herself with numbness to the broken promises.

"I appreciate the offer, Tony. But I'll pass."

Disappointment shadowed him, and he went to leave the office. "If you change your mind, let me know."

"Okay," Ronnie said and continued working.

# CHAPTER 7

A hot-air balloon in the shape of Snoopy floated through New York City. Ronnie was tired of cartoon balloons, B-list celebrities promoting their new movies, and dance teams prancing around in scanty outfits in thirty-degree weather. It was just another Macy's Thanksgiving Day Parade. Ronnie didn't even like parades and turned off the television.

She went into the kitchen and surveyed the skimpy food selection in the refrigerator. The leftover takeout containers were as appealing as dog food. She tried the freezer. One microwavable dinner. Even less promising. She flung the dinky box back inside the cooler.

Her phone lay on the coffee table, calling her name. She tapped the device against her palm, mulling over Tony's invitation. It felt like his good deed for the day, as if he brought home a stray cat, fed it, then kicked it out into the cold.

Ronnie and Tony had maintained a professional work relationship. Cordial, too. But spend a holiday with her ex-husband and his family?

*No, it's ludicrous!*

She looked around her apartment. Loneliness had been her companion over the years, but today she wanted some different company.

Ronnie found Tony's phone number under her contact list and called him before changing her mind. Queasy waves in her stomach gained strength with each ring.

*I must be nuts.*

"Hi!" Tony's cheery voice bounced. "Happy Thanksgiving!"

"You, too." She paused before identifying herself. "It's Ronnie."

He chuckled. "I know. Your name blew your cover."

"Right. Caller ID." Ronnie bit down on her lower lip. "I was wondering... Never mind. You're probably on your way out. It's fine, no need to turn—"

"I'll be there in an hour."

"A-are you sure? I don't want to inconvenience you." For a split-second, Ronnie wanted Tony to renege his offer.

"You're not an inconvenience. I wouldn't have asked you to come if I didn't mean it. So, an hour?"

Ronnie's mouth lifted into a smile. "Works for me. Bye." She heard Tony say her name before ending the call and brought the phone back to her ear. He must've changed his mind. Bringing his ex-wife to Thanksgiving was a bad idea. She knew it was true, and now, so did he.

"I can't pick you up unless you tell me where you live."

"Addresses come in handy." She let out a breath she didn't realize she was holding in. "Three forty-one Cameron Avenue. It's a brick building. There's parking along the street."

"Got it. See you soon."

Ronnie hadn't been to the Lombardos' house in a decade. Arriving empty-handed on a holiday reeked of bad manners. She rummaged through the barren cupboards and the emaciated fridge in a panic, searching for a dish to whip up. Unless she counted a block of cheese, a box of Wheat Thins, a half-filled carton of OJ, and stale potato chips delicacies to work with, Ronnie had zilch. Even with the proper ingredients, her culinary skills were an embarrassment. Although, knowing the Lombardos, they'd graciously receive whatever she presented.

Still, an appropriate gift was in order. Ronnie looked at the time on her phone. Fifty minutes to scrounge up a gift and freshen up before Tony arrived. She went to the liquor store two blocks from her apartment, surprised at the myriad of customers.

*I wonder how many of them are buying last-minute gifts to bring to their ex-in-laws for Thanksgiving?*

The turkey. *White goes with poultry or was it red?* Ronnie's palate and alcohol didn't mix. Her drinking escapades had included nursing a Michelob Light beer for two hours with her police academy class after graduation and a glass of champagne at her wedding reception.

In the wine aisle, the plethora of varieties overwhelmed her. So many bottles, big and small. Sleek, sophisticated bottles to hillbilly jugs. Erring on the side of caution, she chose White Zinfandel and Merlot—John Lombardo's favorite. At the register, she added a festive holiday gift bag and a spool of brown and gold-colored ribbon onto the conveyer belt.

Back at the apartment, Ronnie changed into a pair of jeans and a gray cable-knit sweater. Much more appropriate than green yoga pants and a T-shirt with *What are You Lookin' At?* written across the front. She brushed her hair and applied a small amount of blush, lipstick, and eye shadow. Waiting for Tony, she paced long enough to erode a patch of carpet.

Looking out the window for his truck, Ronnie fussed with the ribbon on the gift bag.

*Did I tell him my apartment number?*

No, she hadn't. Nor did he ask. Walking three flights of stairs implied a date. This wasn't a date. It was dinner at her ex-in-laws on Thanksgiving Day.

*Uh-oh. Sounds like a date.*

Ronnie put on her coat, grabbed her purse and gift bag, and waited in the vestibule downstairs for Tony. A few minutes later, a red GMC truck came to a rolling stop next to the curb.

*Here we go.*

She climbed inside Tony's truck, greeted by the scent of Ralph Lauren Polo cologne. He still wore it. Ronnie had bought him a bottle for Valentine's Day when they were dating. Apparently, it was still his favorite. Hers, too.

While driving, Tony peeked inside the bag on Ronnie's lap. "When did you acquire a taste for wine?"

"It's for your parents. You told them I'm coming, right?"

His head turned with a single swish. "Nope."

"Tony!"

"Ma hasn't changed, Ronnie. If an Army battalion showed up, she'd say, 'What about your spouses? They have to eat, too, you know.'"

Ronnie fiddled with the bow. "All right. I hope she has enough food."

"That's hilarious." Tony laughed. It was a deep rumble Ronnie remembered so well. "I'll have to tell that joke at dinner."

"It's been a long time since I've seen your family."

John and Tess had treated Ronnie as if she were blood-related, while her own mother and stepfather made her feel like an in-law. After Ronnie had learned of Tony's infidelity, she had ignored John and Tess's calls, too. They would've tried talking her out of the divorce. As close as Ronnie was to them, she had left town without saying goodbye because it hurt her too much to see them one last time.

"Trust me, Ronnie," Tony said. "They'll be thrilled to see you."

He turned onto Crescent Drive, and the road curved into a semi-circle. The Lombardo house on the left at the dead-end came into view. A two-story colonial with ivory siding and black shutters. Tony parked in the double-wide concrete driveway. He and Ronnie were the first guests to arrive.

The house's exterior reflected the holiday season. Cornstalks covered two pillars, anchoring the enclosed balcony on the second story. Pumpkins sat atop haystacks on the open porch. An orange and brown wreath with a burlap bow hung on the front door, and a strand of leafy garland outlined its perimeter. Tess Lombardo's decorating talent could give Martha Stewart a run for her money.

Tony and Ronnie went inside the house, where the aroma of Thanksgiving staples and Italian favorites awakened Ronnie's appetite. She placed the gift bag on the floor of the entranceway and removed her coat, just as Tony came from behind, assisting her, and hung it next to his jacket in the closet.

Ten years had passed since Ronnie saw Tony out of uniform. The years had been good to her ex, who wore dark-washed jeans and a blue V-neck sweater. The fitted fabric defined his physique, outlining his biceps and broad shoulders she used to cling to. Around his neck hung a medallion of St. Christopher, the saint known for protection. Tony's mother had given him the sacred emblem the night before his first day as a cop and made him promise to wear it every time he was on duty.

"Ronnie?"

She snapped out of her trance and took the gift bag from Tony. "Thanks."

Following Tony into the family room, the volume from the television grew louder. She heard John clap and shout, "Nice play!"

Ronnie stayed behind Tony as he entered the family room, where John sat on the couch. "Happy Thanksgiving, Dad."

John stood and went momentarily mute when he saw Ronnie.

"Happy Thanksgiving, Da—John." Calling him "Dad" was an Italian tradition that had made Ronnie uncomfortable until he had introduced her as his daughter.

John hugged Ronnie as if she were his long-lost child. He'd been the only man to come close to filling the fatherly gap left by Nick. She handed him the gift bag. "This is for you."

"Thank you, hon." John examined the bottle of Merlot. His smile ran deep as his eyes twinkled with hope. "Are you two back together?"

"No," Ronnie and Tony answered unanimously.

John brushed off his presumption. "You're here. That's what matters." He stuck his head out into the hallway. "Tess! Come here!"

A faint voice came from the kitchen. "I'm a little busy, John! Dinner won't cook itself."

"It'll only take a second!" he shouted back, then winked at Tony and Ronnie.

Footsteps moved across the house. "What is it?" Tess asked, entering the family room. She was wiping her hands on a dish towel and dropped it when she saw Ronnie.

"Hello, Tess," Ronnie said. "Happy Thanksgiving."

The woman's pale blue eyes were stuck open. "You're here. I can't believe you're here!" Her big-boned arms went around Ronnie and squeezed her like a python. Tess was short, thick in the middle, but strong as an ox. Her blond hair and fair skin tone favored the Northern portion of Italy.

"John, Ronnie's here!" Tess came to the same mistaken conclusion as her husband, and her voice rose with joyful expectation. "You're back together!"

John, Tony, and Ronnie all answered with a soft, "No."

Tess flicked her wrists. "It doesn't matter. You're here now. That's what counts." She hugged Ronnie a second time, followed by an Italian slap-pat. "Sweetheart, you're so thin. Have you been eating enough?" Tess groped Ronnie's arms. "Just bones."

Ronnie maintained an average weight for a woman of her height, but to an Italian mother, average meant too thin.

"Ma, she eats." Tony said, countering his mother's paranoia.

"How do you know? Have you seen her?" Tess turned to Ronnie. "You didn't turn into one of those vegetarians, did you?" she asked, as if it were sinful.

"Heavens, no! I can't give up meat."

Tess breathed a sigh of relief. "Good. We have plenty of food, so don't be shy."

"Where's Nonna?" Tony asked in a clever move to veer Tess away from her obsessive need to feed the world.

"In the basement." Tess bared all her teeth, staring at Ronnie like a starstruck teenager. "She's making sauce for the ravioli. Your favorite, Ronnie!"

Italy's best chef couldn't come close to Nonna's delicious homemade cheese and spinach ravioli in her famous sauce.

"I'll set another plate at the table." Tess practically floated into the dining room.

Ronnie followed Tony down the steep staircase to the basement used as a second kitchen—a necessity in older Italian families.

Nonna stood at the stove stirring the sauce in a giant kettle fit for a restaurant. Perfectly round ravioli on baking sheets sat on the same table she used to bake and cook on.

Tony approached his grandmother. "Happy Thanksgiving, Nonna."

The old woman whacked the wooden utensil against the edge of the pot and placed it on a spoon rest shaped like Italy. *"Mio nipote!"* she blurted—Italian for "My grandson."

They simultaneously kissed the other's cheek. He towered over the petite woman with short white hair and wrinkled olive skin, speaking directly into her ear with the hearing aid. "I invited a guest to dinner."

"Who? Someone you police with?" she asked, her accent slightly noticeable.

Tony stepped aside. Ronnie came into view. "Happy Thanksgiving, Nonna."

Behind coke-bottle glasses, tears filled the rims of the old woman's eyes. She muttered something in Italian—Ronnie wasn't sure what—followed by a cheeky kiss. "Thanksgiving indeed."

Her hopeful eyes darted between the two of them, but Tony extinguished his grandmother's burning question before she could ask. "No, Nonna, we're not back together."

She took one of their hands in hers and kissed them. "You will be." Smiling, she shuffled to the stove and stirred the sauce.

Ronnie found the Lombardos' false impression of wedding bells ringing sweet. Not that it had surprised her. Tony had brought his ex-wife with him for Thanksgiving. The logical conclusion was an imminent reunion. What were the Lombardos supposed to think?

Tony tore off a chunk from a loaf of bread, dunked it into the kettle, and ate the sauce-soaked carbs.

"Well?" Nonna looked at him, on pins and needles as if it were her first crack at making sauce.

"Fantastic, as usual. It's not too late to sell it. You'd make a pretty penny."

"Never. It's a family recipe. That's where it stays. With family."

The smell of dough, cheese, and sauce made Ronnie salivate as she stood on the cold tile floor surrounded by the same gaudy Italian decorations hanging on the avocado-colored walls.

Tony approached her from behind, close enough for her to feel his breath on her neck. "Brings back memories, huh?"

Ronnie turned around to the sound of his sexy voice and equally sexy smile. More than food had sizzled in that basement.

The pantry had been their go-to location to make out. Shelves stocked with canned goods, baking ingredients, and beverages lined the narrow storage unit. Not the most romantic spot, but there was something so exciting about the overwhelming need to be with each other so badly that their secret hiding place was a grocery store of nonperishable foods.

One time, Nonna had walked in on them panting like animals. Ronnie nearly died of embarrassment and hid behind Tony. The old woman thought nothing of her grandson and his girlfriend going at it as she took two jars of canned eggplant off the shelf.

"I was young once, too. Continue."

• • •

Ronnie and Tony went upstairs to the main floor as Vince and his family arrived. Tony resembled his older brother, who had more gray hair. Vince's wife, Cora, was a pretty redhead and Ronnie had gotten along with her. Ronnie's unannounced visit floored them, too, but their hugs welcomed her back into the family.

She hadn't seen Vince and Cora's daughters, Tasha and Emma, since Vivian's funeral. For identical twins, her former nieces were as different as the sun and the moon. The tips of Tasha's chin-length black hair were reddish-crimson. Her fashion style fell into the layered, mismatched category. Anything goes these days, she thought. Dark-purple polish that looked almost black coated her nails. Emma, however, resembled a squeaky-clean model on the cover of a teen magazine from 1990. Her long, wavy brown hair was her natural color, and she opted for the less is more makeup theory, complimenting her gray plaid skirt, black tights, and a black sweater.

"Girls, you remember Ronnie," Tony said to his nieces. The twins stared at Ronnie as if she looked familiar. Tony clarified further for them. "My ex-wife."

Emma waved at Ronnie. "Good seeing you again."

"It's been a long time," Tasha added.

"Yes, it has." Ronnie had to think. "You're both what… seventeen now?"

"Seniors in high school," Cora said. "Can you believe it? Yesterday they were fighting over Barbie dolls. Now, they're practically women."

The giggling teens held their phones, fingers flying across the screens. Ronnie imagined they were posting on social media about their former aunt's surprise visit on Thanksgiving.

Joey arrived moments later. "Happy Thanksgiving, everyone!"

Ronnie had always had a soft spot for the youngest Lombardo boy, who had been a whoops baby when Tony was fourteen.

Joey hugged Ronnie, then cut a punch to Tony's arm. "Nice going, bro."

"It's not what you think," Ronnie said to Joey. "I didn't have any plans. Tony was kind enough to let me tag along."

Joey snorted. "Right. My brother, the holiday saint." He slapped Tony's back, grinning, and looked at the woman by the door. "What are you doing standing over there?"

He yanked the tiny blonde forward, causing her to stumble into the family circle. "This is my girlfriend, Rachel."

*If Tess thinks I'm anorexic, wait until she sees Rachel. She's small enough to get blown away by a windstorm.*

Joey rattled off everyone's name, and the poor girl appeared to have forgotten all of them by the time he was done. Ronnie used her weird scenario to ease Rachel's trepidation.

"Hi, Rachel, I'm Ronnie. Tony's ex-wife."

Rachel stared at Joey as if she were saying, "Are you serious?"

"She's his new boss," Joey said to Rachel. "Remember the one I told you about?"

The young woman stretched her green eyes like a doe caught in the headlights. "Nice to meet you."

The Lombardo men filed into the family room to watch the football game while Cora and the twins went into the kitchen. Rachel and Ronnie exchanged awkward smiles, and the new girl followed Ronnie into the family room.

Joey pulled Rachel onto the love seat and curled an arm around her neck as if she were a prize he had won at a college fraternity party.

The only seat available was the one next to Tony on the couch. He had a home-field advantage with Ronnie being on his turf—and he knew it.

She felt him summoning her. Standing drew attention and she sat down between Tony and Vince. *Don't move a muscle.* Holding a perfectly straight posture worked muscles Ronnie didn't know she had. Tony stared at her. Sexy smile number two.

The guys watched the football game, rooting for their team. The offense lined up; the center snapped the ball to the quarterback who scrambled in the pocket. Unable to get rid of the ball, he ran to the sideline and out of bounds to stop the clock. He signaled to go for it on fourth and twenty instead of punting.

"Geez! Come on!" John shouted. "What's he doing?"

"That's going to cost them the game!" Vince yelled.

The next play, the quarterback's Hail Mary pass for the touchdown had everyone on their feet shouting, except Rachel.

Vince sat back down. "I didn't know he had it in him!"

Ronnie chimed in, "He's been in a slump the last four games. The odds weren't in his favor playing against the league's fourth-rated defense. Plus, two offensive linemen are out with injuries, and Borden hasn't brought his A-game in a while."

John, Vince, Joey, and Tony turned their heads simultaneously in Ronnie's direction as her analysis left them flabbergasted.

"Since when do you follow football?" Tony said.

Ronnie didn't dare mention Harris, the sports fanatic she had dated for three months. His obsession with the gridiron had rubbed off on her. Harris, unfortunately, hadn't.

"Ten years is a long time, Tony. A lot has changed."

Silence descended on the room. John and his boys looked away, uncomfortable.

"I need to use the bathroom," Ronnie announced as she stood.

She cut through the living room to get to the downstairs bathroom, and it felt as if someone had punctured her lung. She struggled to breathe, staring at the pictures of Vivian displayed on an end table like a shrine.

An eight-by-ten framed portrait. Her daughter's toothy grin bursting with life. Red ribbons tied in bows dangled from her high pigtails. A black-and-white photo of Tony and Vivian making angels in a pile of leaves. There was also a picture collage of the girl's brief life from an infant to her last Thanksgiving. She wore a paper pilgrim hat and held a mini pumpkin.

Ronnie had packed away her daughter's photos. Seeing them every day was too painful. It still was.

Her head dropped into her hands.

A pair of arms wrapped around her from behind. Tess's perfume gave her away. "You're going to see her again, sweetheart," she said. "We all will. Knowing that doesn't make it hurt less. I know that, but Vivian is not alone. The angels are watching over her. She's so happy in Heaven."

Ronnie dried her eyes on her sleeve and threw herself into Tess. Her ex-mother-in-law's tone, soft and heartbreaking, while true and real, was just what Ronnie needed to hear.

Rubbing Ronnie's back in circles and kissing the side of her head, as only a mother would do, Tess said, "There, there. You let it all out, sweetheart."

. . .

After a good cry, Tess and Ronnie went into the kitchen.

Cora lifted the crock-pot lid and poked cubes of butternut squash with a fork to test the softness. "Girls, put those phones away and help your grandmother."

The twins continued watching a video.

"Hey, I said, 'help your grandmother.'"

One look from their stern mother, and Tony's nieces dropped their devices and went to work.

Tasha took a pitcher of water into the dining room. Emma lined two bread baskets with linen napkins and placed warm rolls straight from the oven inside.

Ronnie stood in the middle of the kitchen. "What can I do?"

Tess lowered a ladle into a pot of homemade minestrone soup with a wary glance. "Honey, you're a guest."

Ronnie's ex-mother-in-law looked at Cora as if she had dodged a bullet. The Lombardos were aware of Ronnie's inept culinary skills.

"There has to be something for me to do that I can't burn," Ronnie said.

Tess snapped her fingers. "The salad. How are your knife skills?"

"If I can operate a gun, I can maneuver a kitchen knife."

Tess's hands flapped in rhythm as she spoke. "A gun. You're too nice of a girl to be carrying around a gun." She made the sign of the cross, sending up a prayer.

Emma scoped out Ronnie's backside for a bulge. "Are you wearing it now?"

"Not today."

"Have you ever killed anyone?"

"Emma!" Cora snapped. "What's the matter with you? You don't ask those kinds of questions to cops. Or to military personnel. Taking a life isn't something to brag about."

Emma's cheeks turned pink. "Sorry, Ronnie."

"It's okay, Emma. To answer your question, no, I haven't. In almost twenty years, I haven't had to fire my weapon, which is a good thing."

"Maybe I'll be a cop like you and Uncle Tony." Emma spread her legs and pretended to hold a gun. "Freeze, dirtbag!" She looked at Ronnie for approval. "Pretty good, huh?"

Ronnie teetered her hand in a so-so manner. "Don't believe everything you see on TV."

"You'll be a cop over my dead body!" Tess shouted.

Emma giggled. "I'm just kidding, Grandma."

"A heart attack. Is that what you're trying to give me on Thanksgiving?" Tess tossed her hands in the air. "Enough cop talk. Emma, get the vegetables for Ronnie."

At the counter island, Ronnie sliced tomatoes, cucumbers, and a red onion while Tess and Cora put the final touches on the feast.

Tess strained the kettle of boiled potatoes and dumped them into a serving bowl. "Ronnie, honey, how's your mom?"

"Good. I haven't seen her since spring, but we keep in touch."

Cora removed a pan of stuffing from the oven. "What's she doing today?"

Ronnie looked at the time on the clock wall. "I'd say coming in from the beach right about now."

Cora and Tess stared at Ronnie as if they had misheard her.

Ronnie sliced through a tomato. The force of the knife struck against the cutting board. "She and Graham went to the Bahamas. It was a last-minute trip."

Tess's voice strained. *"The Bahamas?* Who wants to go there for Thanksgiving? It's too hot. They don't know how to do a real Thanksgiving dinner." She plopped a stick of butter into the bowl and poured in a generous splash of milk, then whipped the potatoes with a mixer.

Ronnie slid the diced vegetables from the cutting board into a leaf-decorated bowl with the dull side of the knife. "You know my mother. Graham comes first," she said in a singsong tone.

Cora and Tess flashed each other a pitiful stare.

Ronnie chopped the head of lettuce with the same force she had used on that poor tomato. "It's okay. I'm used to it."

"Natalie's loss is our gain." Tess turned off the mixer and tossed the beaters into the sink. "John! Time to carve the turkey!"

Nonna came into the kitchen carrying a serving bowl filled with enough ravioli to feed a small country. Cheese shavings fell like snow onto the pasta as she grated a block of parmesan over the bowl.

Once John had finished carving the turkey, Tess corralled the family into the dining room. The table decorated with china plates, crystal wine glasses, and a cornucopia centerpiece, flanked with lit pumpkin-scented candles, earned the right to grace the cover of *Better Homes and Gardens*.

Tess assigned Ronnie's seat next to Tony and winked at her son. Ronnie's ex-mother-in-law, the matchmaker. He pulled out her chair, and she craned her neck to thank him. Ronnie released the fanned linen napkin from the metal leaf ring and placed it over her lap.

John sat at the head of the table. "In the name of the Father, Son, and Holy Spirit," he said, making the sign of the cross, and the rest followed suit. "Lord, thank you for all your blessings. Let us not only be thankful today, but all year. Thank you for this delicious food, and all those who took part in preparing it." He paused. "Everyone say it with me."

"Amen," they all replied and closed the prayer with the sign of the cross.

Ronnie's wine bottles, along with two more, went around the table. Tess poured John a glass of Merlot. "Ronnie, honey, white or red?"

"Water's fine."

"I forgot, you don't drink." Tess hit her forehead with her palm. "They say the memory is the first to go."

"Does everyone have a full glass?" John stood, as if it were his cue. Everyone raised their glass, waiting for the Lombardo patriarch to continue. "A toast to my family. To everyone here tonight at this table. Past, present, and future. Salute."

The group echoed "Salute" and clinked their glasses with the person next to and across from them. Tony's stare warmed Ronnie, filling an emptiness that had lived with her for far too long. She clinked her glass with his and took a long sip to cool her flushed cheeks.

Dinner started with a bowl of soup, followed by Nonna's ravioli.

After the two courses were done, everyone passed platters of turkey and bowls of side dishes around the table amid multiple conversations. The twins chatted about their college plans. Emma had applied to Penn State; Tasha had planned on staying home and commuting to the University of Pittsburgh. Cora shared funny anecdotes of her middle school students. Vince mentioned the big order that had come in yesterday at three o'clock. Then John broached Ronnie's promotion to police chief.

"It's different, a ton of paperwork. I miss being on patrol." She sliced a turkey strip into bite-sized pieces, sighing with feigned irritation. "Then there's dealing with the media."

"Hey, I report the facts. I'm a journalist," Joey said. "Some nepotism would be nice, Ronnie. Me being your ex-brother-in-law."

Ronnie chewed a piece of meat, smiling. "No way, Joey. You get the scoop with the rest of the bloodhounds."

Tess huffed. "At least you're behind a desk, Ronnie. You don't have to worry about getting *shot*."

Ronnie immediately thought of Nick.

Vince rolled his eyes. "Here we go. Can't we make it through one dinner without Ma bringing up Tony getting shot?"

"Never mind, you," Tess snapped at her firstborn. "I don't want my son out there in the thick of crime, risking his life. For what? To chase criminals and break up brawls. Go on drug busts and talk crazy people out of letting hostages go."

Tony looked down the table at Tess. "Ma, I've been a cop for twenty years. When are you going to relax?"

"The day of your press conference to announce your retirement, that's when." She shoved a forkful of stuffing into her mouth.

"Tess, you're a broken record," John said while chewing. "We've been over this. Tony's a good cop. He wanted to be a public servant, to put others before himself. There's no talking him out of it."

Tony's mother huffed. "Did he have to pick one of the most *dangerous* jobs to do something commendable? There are lots of careers that are commendable and safe!"

"All we can do is pray the good Lord and the saints watch over him. So far, so good," John said.

Ronnie glanced at the St. Christopher medallion around Tony's neck.

*I wish Dad had had that necklace with him that night.*

"John, I've spent so much time praying I've worn away the cartilage in my knees," Tess said. "I'm his mother. It's different for mothers. We always worry about our kids. No matter what they do or how old they are."

John and Tess's voices were clear and audible, but the only words Ronnie heard were the ones in her head.

*Dad got shot. Dad died.*

Over and over again.

*Dad got shot. Dad died.*

Tony noticed Ronnie pushing her food with her fork and jerked his head toward Ronnie for his mother to shut up. "Ma."

Tess sucked in a breath at her insensitivity. "Ronnie, sweetheart. I'm so sorry. I wasn't thinking."

Ronnie smiled softly at her ex-mother-in-law. "It's okay. It's not a secret."

Rachel looked like a lost kid in a store. Joey filled her in as quietly as he could, but his voice carried over the silence. "Her dad was a cop. He died in the line of duty."

Rachel gave Ronnie an empathetic look. "I'm sorry."

"It was a long time ago," Ronnie replied, "but thank you."

"Me and my big mouth," Tess said.

John pinched his wife's chubby cheek as if he were telling her to forget about it.

"Tess, you have every right to express your concern," Ronnie said. "I'd feel the same if I were you."

She let the thought of Tony being shot roam around her head for a minute until Joey diminished the somber mood.

"Hey Ma, ask Ronnie to make a few exceptions for Tony. You know, now that she's his *boss.*"

"What I wouldn't give to be a fly on the wall at the station," Vince added, smirking.

Cora backhanded her husband's arm.

"Ow. What'd I say?"

Ronnie laughed at Vince's feisty wife, and instantly, a jovial mood returned.

Vince and Joey exchanged a few more digs at Tony. He clinked a butter knife against his glass. "All right, yes. Ronnie's my boss. What took you so long to harass me about it?"

Joey took a bite of mashed potatoes and waved his fork as he spoke. "It's cool. You got it made. She goes easy on you because you two were married."

"Wrong, little brother. She treats me the same as every other cop."

Joey clucked his tongue. "Too bad."

"Tony's one of my best officers, Joey," Ronnie said. "We're lucky to have him."

Tony went to sip his wine and stopped. "What do you mean, one of the best? Not *the* best?"

Ronnie tipped her head sideways and sipped her water. "Hmm, let's give it until spring. Then I'll re-evaluate."

Everyone laughed, except Rachel. Other than her apology to Ronnie, Joey's girl hadn't spoken since the first slurp of soup. She looked as if she were a puzzle piece that needed to be manipulated to snap into place.

"Rachel, where do you work?" Ronnie asked.

The young woman looked up nervously from her plate. Ten pairs of eyes waited for the cute blonde to answer. "I'm the manager at LeeAnn's Boutique."

Nonna strained to hear the quiet girl and looked at her son with confusion. John spoke loud into his mother's right ear. "SHE SAID SHE WORKS AT LEEANN'S BOUTIQUE."

Nonna bobbed her head. "*Si, si.*"

"I haven't shopped there, but I hear the clothes are fabulous," Ronnie said. "I'm in a uniform all week, so I don't have an extensive wardrobe."

Rachel shifted in her seat. "If you decide to stop in, I'll give you my employee discount. I get forty percent off."

Ronnie lifted her water glass. "Deal."

Rachel took a chance as she looked around the table. "That goes for all of you."

Joey, being Joey, cut in with, "Me, too, babe?"

Rachel elbowed him in the ribs. "I meant all the ladies."

Vince chimed in, "Rachel, my little brother would look lovely in a blue ruffled gown."

She must've felt part of the family because she came back with, "Vince, ruffles have been out of style for years."

Everyone laughed, and the bantering continued.

After dinner, the men huddled like cattle into the family room for the second football game of the afternoon while the women cleared the table and cleaned the dishes.

Tess brewed a pot of coffee and brought three pies into the dining room—apple, chocolate, and pumpkin—courtesy of Nonna, who had made homemade whipped cream to go with dessert. The Lombardos never used the artificial spray stuff from a can.

Ronnie volunteered to slice and serve dessert. She knew what Tony wanted without asking; it was always the same. A piece of apple pie and a sliver of pumpkin, both topped with a mound of whipped cream.

Handing Tony his plate, he thanked Ronnie with a third sexy smile.

・ ・ ・

Holiday meals at the Lombardos guaranteed there would be leftovers.

"What am I going to do with all this food?" Tess would say, handing each son a bag with Tupperware containers. "Now you don't have to cook for two days."

Tess had enough leftovers to give to the boys, Ronnie, and Rachel during a lengthy goodbye of hugs and kisses.

Tony kissed Nonna, then she slapped him.

"Ow," he said, rubbing his stinging cheek. "What was that for?"

"Not keeping your pants zipped." The old woman waved her bony index finger. If she were a foot taller, it would've been wagging in his face. "This time, don't mess up. *Capisci?*"

"Nonna, I told you, we're not back together."

His grandmother waved a dismissive hand. "I hear what you say; I'm not deaf." She shuffled to Ronnie and hugged her goodbye as his ex-wife suppressed a laugh at the comical chastisement.

Tony and Ronnie made small talk during the ride to her apartment. The food, the football games, and how his nieces had changed.

Ronnie held her sack of leftovers on her lap, content and peaceful. Without taking his focus off the road, Tony said, "Looks like you and Rachel hit it off."

"I've been in her shoes. Being the new girl in the family, hoping to fit in."

*You did, Ronnie. They fell in love with you the minute they met you. They weren't the only ones.*

"Not everyone can handle the culture shock of a verbose Italian family."

"Come on, we're not so bad."

"Your family's great, Tony. They're genuine and unpretentious. They always make everyone feel like part of the family." Ronnie quickly stopped and looked out the passenger window.

They arrived at her apartment building, and Tony parked the truck. They sat quietly for a few moments as if they were on a first date.

"Thanks for inviting me," Ronnie said. "I had a great time."

"Me, too." Tony drummed the steering wheel with his thumb. "Who knows? Might be a new tradition."

Her jaw dropped. "Bringing the ex-wife isn't a ritual your family wants to adopt."

"Ronnie, Ma hugged you so tight, I heard your bones crack. I bet she left bruises."

"She treats all her dinner guests like that."

"Cops are supposed to be observant. Get you out of uniform and you become an average civilian."

"Excuse me?" she said. "Was that a jab?"

"A friendly one." Tony took out another sexy smile from his arsenal. He had been doing it all day. Why not one more before calling it a night?

With it came an unnerving Ronnie, ending the playful bantering. She opened the door and stepped onto the sidewalk. "I'll see you Monday."

"Ronnie?"

Tony didn't feel the cold air rush inside. He had so much to tell her. Things he didn't expect to say until today. Being with Ronnie was like old times; Tony almost forgot they were divorced. She still fit in with the Lombardos. It was as if Tony's family kept Ronnie's place open, waiting for her return. Most of all, today reminded Tony of how much he and Ronnie had loved each other, a love he hadn't experienced since her.

"It was a nice Thanksgiving," he finally said.

"One of the best."

Tony watched Ronnie walk to the door. The porch light shining on her cast an angelic nimbus as snowflakes fell, sticking to her coat and hair. She went inside, and a warped image appeared behind the bubbled glass before disappearing.

. . .

Parked across the street from Ronnie's apartment building, the stalker watched Tony drive away.

Ronnie and her ex had been awfully chummy lately. They'd have to be to spend Thanksgiving with Lombardo's family.

The stalker had nothing to be thankful for in eight years. He'd been alone—thanks to Ronnie. All he had was a crappy job at a convenience store in the poorest, most crime-ridden section of town.

While Ronnie had been stuffing her big mouth with turkey at the in-laws, his Thanksgiving dinner was a lousy ham sub set to expire from the store.

He took a deep drag from his cigarette and blew the smoke, clouding the windshield.

"Enjoy it while it lasts, Ronnie."

# CHAPTER 8

"Hi, Chief. You remember my wife, Audrey?" Max said.

Ronnie shook the woman's hand. "Yes, I do. Nice seeing you again."

"Congratulations on your position," Audrey said. "It's about time that station put a woman in charge."

"I've got a great team, thanks to people like Max. I'm sure you're very proud of him."

"Thanks, Chief," Max said as Audrey swelled with pride.

Guests dressed in their finest attire trickled inside the church for Chet and Mia's wedding. The wedding coordinator power-walked through the lobby, scrolling the screen on an iPad while talking into a walkie-talkie. "The bride will make her arrival in eight minutes. Is the flower girl over her stage fright?"

On each side of the sanctuary's double doors stood a groomsman. They had escorted an elderly woman and a girl no older than twelve to their seats.

Ronnie waved at Officers Chambers and Nelson, each with a date, while on the lookout for Tony. The entrance door swooshed shut, and Ronnie rotated her head so fast she pinched a nerve in her neck. Rubbing the kink, she fished for information.

"Uh, Max, is Tony coming to the ceremony or just the reception?"

He glanced at his watch. "He'll be here soon. We'll wait for him inside."

Ronnie followed Max and Audrey as a groomsman's protruding elbow nearly hit her in the face. "Bride or groom?"

*How embarrassing, but the kid has a job to do.*

She took his arm. "Groom."

The young man with an acne breakout along his chin led her to the row where Max and Audrey sat. Judging by the floor-length arrangements with red and gold roses at each pew, Chet and Mia had cleaned out every flower shop in town.

Ronnie searched for Tony, even though she hadn't seen his truck in the parking lot. It was hard to miss. The beast looked like a fire engine.

Two weeks had passed since Thanksgiving. The following Monday, it had been business as usual for them both. Ronnie had reminisced often about that day with her ex-husband and his family. She could not recall the last holiday when she had such a good time. It had been worth her parents ditching her for the Bahamas.

Ronnie dug through her cluttered purse that resembled the inside of a junk drawer, searching for her phone, but stopped short of calling Tony.

Music playing from a three-piece orchestra drowned out murmuring guests. Candles flickered on the altar, adding warmth to the cold December nuptials.

The elegant setting reminded Ronnie of her own wedding. The white strapless dress with a short train had fit her slender frame like a glove. She had worn her hair in a simple half-chignon decorated with fresh baby daisies. The bridesmaids had worn indigo-colored dresses and carried bouquets of white roses. Vince had been the proud best man, while an eleven-year-old Joey had escorted a weepy Tess down the aisle. Tony had put every man to shame wearing a traditional tux—black bowtie and cummerbund.

Other than becoming Mrs. Tony Lombardo, the only other day Ronnie had been that happy was when Vivian was born.

"Hey guys."

Ronnie looked in the aisle at Tony. The suit he had on made him look even more handsome. Then again, he was a fine specimen, no matter what he wore. The man could wear a burlap sack and still look hot.

She pointed to the empty chair next to her. "We saved you a seat."

"Great," he said. "How about one more?"

Ronnie's smile plummeted. A woman emerged alongside Tony, snaking her arm around his elbow. Not any woman. His date.

She was gorgeous—supermodel gorgeous. The kind who strutted down the Victoria's Secret runway in heels, scanty lingerie, and big, fluffy angel wings. She was almost as tall as Tony with brown hair past her boobs that looked as if all she had to do was brush it one time through.

Tony introduced the woman to the gang. "This is Brianna."

The woman blinded Ronnie with the record for the whitest set of perfectly straight teeth that were, without a doubt, cosmetically enhanced, because no one naturally had flawless teeth like that.

Brianna and Tony sidled through the row. He sat between his ex-wife and his date, who ran her manicured nails through her hair, but the siren-red strapless dress with a slit to her thigh nabbed her the win for "The Hottest Date at the Wedding."

Then there was Ronnie, in a modest elf-green dress ending right above her knees. The sleeve length stopped at her elbow and a conservative scoop neckline revealed a bit more skin than a nun wearing a habit. Ronnie's gnawed nails lacked femininity, and she tucked the grotesque display between her knees.

Ronnie had never been a girly-girl. She would wear a dress when the occasion called for it, but she preferred athletic pants or jeans and a T-shirt.

*What had a guy like Tony seen in a plain Jane like me?*

Looking at Brianna, Ronnie deduced not much.

Having a daughter like Brianna would be a dream come true for Natalie. If Ronnie's mother had the power, she'd clone a younger version of herself, a giddy shopping companion with a standing monthly appointment at the spa for manicures and pedicures.

Maybe that was why Natalie called Ronnie "Veronica." The name was more ladylike than "Ronnie." Perhaps through repetition, Ronnie would see herself as a girl and not the tomboy she'd been for Nick.

The two groomsmen at the door pulled a red runner down the aisle. Then one by one, Mia's bridesmaids appeared, followed by the cute flower girl tossing pink petals from her basket, and the adorable ring bearer carrying a pillow he dropped only once.

The pianist played *The Wedding March* as guests watched Mia's father escort her down the aisle.

Ronnie imagined what it would've been like if Nick had lived to see her get married. The tough detective, teary-eyed, walking his only daughter toward the altar to his new son-in-law in the bittersweet moment of letting go.

Ronnie heard the groom's vows echo, as if she were in a tunnel. "I, Chet, take you, Mia, to be my wedded wife, to have and to hold from this day forward."

Then she heard Mia. "For better, for worse, for richer, for poorer, in sickness and in health."

Chet and Mia each took the other's wedding ring from where they lay in the minister's opened book. Chet slid the band onto Mia's ring finger. "With this ring, I thee wed. I give it as a symbol of my faithfulness to you alone."

Tony pinched the bridge of his nose, appearing as uncomfortable as Ronnie at the mention of fidelity.

Mia slid the ring on Chet's finger and repeated the vow.

After the minister pronounced them husband and wife, Chet dipped Mia and planted a sloppy, wet kiss on his bride. The guests applauded, hooting and whistling.

• • •

Holding her name card, Ronnie walked through the maze of tables in the reception hall until she spotted a number ten sign poking through a flowered centerpiece. At her table were Max and Audrey, along with Tony and Brianna.

*Solo at a tableful of couples. Here comes Ronnie—the fifth wheel.*

Two reasons had prevented Ronnie from bringing a date: a blank list of potential suitors, and more importantly, she had hoped Tony would have asked her to be his date. Since he hadn't, she assumed he was going alone. If they were both without dates, they'd be together like they were at Thanksgiving. Her expectations had tanked the moment she saw Brianna.

*Look at that, an empty seat next to Tony. Isn't that just dandy?*

Ronnie played spectator as superficial chatter circled the table until the newlyweds approached them. Tony and Max congratulated Chet with hearty handshakes while the women prattled over Mia's gown, hair, and wedding ring.

Despite the succulent steak dinner, Ronnie had lost her appetite and was full after eating only three bites of her filet mignon and half a roll.

Brianna's finger sliced through the air in a half-circle motion, pointing to Tony, Max, and Ronnie. "You're all police officers?"

"Yep." Tony acknowledged Ronnie for the first time since the ceremony. "Veronica is our new police chief."

Veronica? Tony had never identified Ronnie by her real name, except during their wedding vows—the ones he had broken.

"I go by Ronnie," she said in an icy tone, then took a long sip of champagne from the glass next to her plate.

"Brianna, where do you work?" Max asked.

"Unified Health Insurance. I'm a public relations manager."

He bobbed his head, appearing interested. "How long have you been there?"

"Four years in January," Brianna said, smiling.

Audrey pierced the last piece of her steak with her fork. "Do you like it?"

"Love it. I work with great people and have an excellent benefits package. I'm in the running for Director of Communications. I had my third interview yesterday. I should find out this week." Brianna crossed her fingers for luck. Her gleaming smile belonged in a Colgate commercial.

Ronnie sipped her champagne. *Great. Beauty and brains.*

Max thumbed at Tony. "How did you meet this troublemaker?"

Brianna stared at her date as if the story were humorous. "Believe it or not, a mutual acquaintance."

Someone at the table blurted in repulsion, "A blind date?"

Both couples glanced at Ronnie as she scoffed. A blind date was beneath Tony Lombardo's caliber. He didn't need help finding a date. One smile from him released a stampede of women.

Brianna giggled. "I know, I know. I was apprehensive myself."

*Apprehensive. A four-syllable word. She must be a scholar.*

Ronnie was all for a woman being smart and sexy, unless that woman was after her ex-husband.

Brianna moved closer to Tony, and her hand disappeared somewhere on his lap. "Joey promised me I wouldn't be disappointed."

"As in, *your* brother, Joey?" Ronnie's jaw tightened while waiting for Tony to correct her, to tell her he had a buddy with the same name.

He sipped his champagne. "Uh-huh."

*Mental note: Ban Joey Lombardo from all further interviews.*

Brianna stared at Tony like an animal in heat. "Remind me to thank him for bringing us together."

*Together? This girl moves fast.* More champagne. Ronnie needed more champagne.

With discretion, Tony gestured to Ronnie's near-empty glass and leaned toward her. "Go easy on that."

*Don't tell me what to do, Lombardo. I'm your boss!*

Ronnie gulped the remaining champagne. A waiter carrying a tray of drinks rounded the table, and she swapped her empty glass for a full one.

• • •

Guests formed a circle around Chet and Mia on the dance floor, cheering on the bride and groom as they showed off their moves to "Uptown Funk."

Ronnie found her place, but it wasn't on the square parquet. Sagged against the bar, she shouted over the music for a glass of champagne. Her fifth—no, sixth. She had lost track after three.

Max appeared next to her. She forced a smile that implied she was having the time of her life. "Nice wedding. Chet looks happy."

"He sure does." Max hesitated. "Chief, let me get you a cup of coffee."

Ronnie snubbed the offer and slurred, "Chet and Mia. Mia and Chet. Mr. and Mrzz Dalton. Today's the happiest day of their lives. Let's see how long they'll last."

"Did you have a piece of cake yet? It's delicious. I'll get you a slice."

Max reached for the champagne, but Ronnie held the glass close to her chest and took a sip.

She hiccupped. "They call it the honeymoon phase, Max. Before you know it, the newlyweds will bicker about his habits. She'll hate me for working him to death. Then, the kid comes. They won't have a minute alone together, ever again, for the rest of their lives."

Max touched Ronnie's elbow. "Why don't you sit down?"

She shooed away the suggestion and his chivalry.

"Then again, take me and Lombardo, for instance. He had teeny-weeny habits. Hey, that rhymes. I'm a poet and don't know it." Ronnie giggled. "Where was I? Oh, yeah. Me and Lombardo. We're both cops. Score for us! And the physical stuff in the boudoir..." With a hand against her mouth, her whisper came out loud. "A—mazing. The man's got a *fantastic* body and knows how to use it." She raised her glass, toasting his physique. "H-O-T hot. Know what I mean?"

"I'm not the person you want to talk to about this."

"Sure you are." Ronnie hiccupped. "You're Tony's best bud. His primo amigo. Which makes you my..." Ronnie's fingertips danced on her forehead. Her Spanish was rusty. "Um... my friend, too. You know what, Max? Tony and I had a good marriage. Pity it didn't last. We were together..." She counted off on her fingers. "Seven, um, yeah, seven years. Not a long time."

The mood of the music shifted as the energetic tempo slowed down. In a cruel dose of fate, the first two notes of "Stand by Me" hit Ronnie like a runaway train. Brianna pulled Tony onto the dance floor, and while they danced, she whispered in his ear and laughed.

Ronnie imagined marching onto the dance floor and prying Brianna and Tony apart, then giving Cindy Crawford's lookalike an earful that the song playing was her and Tony's song. The one they had danced to on their wedding day in front of three hundred people and had made love to for the first time in their honeymoon suite later that night.

Ronnie went to do just that, but her feet felt as if they were molded in cement shoes. As much as Ronnie wanted to claw Brianna's eyes out, she knew Tony's date was an innocent bystander. She didn't know Ronnie was Tony's ex-wife or have a clue what that song meant to the former Mrs. Lombardo.

With one dance, Ronnie felt as if Tony had betrayed her. Again.

In a hard gulp, she finished the champagne and twirled the empty glass at the bartender. "I'll have 'nother one of these."

She hiccupped.

• • •

"Excuse me, Brianna." Max's smile held an apology as he said to Tony, "I need to talk to you."

Tony touched his date's bare shoulder. "I'll be right back."

Brianna subtly licked her top lip. "Don't be gone long."

Max led Tony out of earshot of Brianna and pointed to Ronnie at the bar. "Do something about the Chief. She's been hitting the alcohol hard."

Tony put his hands in his pockets, perplexed. "Ronnie doesn't drink. What's gotten into her?"

"You're a cop, Tony. You can't be that oblivious."

No, Tony wasn't. The hurt in Ronnie's eyes when she saw Brianna made Tony regret not asking her to be his date instead. Too late now.

"What was I supposed to do, Max? Come alone?"

"Of course not. Don't want to taint your ladies' man reputation. Here's a thought, you could've asked the Chief. If she spent Thanksgiving with you, why wouldn't she go to the wedding with you, too?"

"We were with my family. It was different. Ronnie and I were in a good place until a few hours ago. You saw how rude she acted during dinner." Tony bowed his head and sighed. "She still hates me."

Max cuffed Tony's shoulder. "She doesn't hate you, buddy. But she does hate seeing you with another woman. How would you feel if the Chief came with a guy who belonged on the cover of *GQ* clinging to her like spandex?"

Women like Brianna intimidated Ronnie. Tony had rubbed salt on his ex-wife's wounded self-esteem by bringing the brunette bombshell easily named, "Most Gorgeous Woman of the Year."

"Look," Max said, "I don't do the whole sticking-my-nose in my best friend's relationship business thing."

"Good. Glad to hear it."

"But of all the police departments, all the positions out there, the Chief happens to come back to Hilton?"

Tony shrugged. "Freaky coincidence."

"Can't you see she used it as an excuse to get back together with you?"

Tony shot down Max's cheesy theory. "Ronnie doesn't mix business with pleasure. She was adamant the job had nothing to do with me."

"And you believe her?"

"Why would she lie?"

Max bent his head, scratching the back of his neck. "Man, you are blowing it. All you did was complain about not getting a second chance. Now, it falls from the sky and lands in your lap, and you're wasting your time with 'teeth' over there."

Tony wasn't in the mood for relationship advice from Doctor Know-it-All. Max was right about one thing, though. Ronnie was blasted. Tony watched her guzzle her drink and lose her balance.

"She can't drive home." Tony turned around and saw Brianna drumming her nails against the white linen tablecloth. "I need a favor, Max."

"Name it."

"Have Audrey drive Brianna home." Tony reached into his pocket and handed Max his keys. "Take my truck. I'll call you later for a ride. I'm taking Ronnie home."

Max tossed the keys and caught them in midair. "You got it."

"Thanks." Tony slapped his buddy's back, gratitude minus the sentimental speech.

"I'm your best friend. Who else is going to look out for you?"

Through the dimly lit reception hall, Brianna's smile beamed as Tony returned. She tickled his palm with a pointy fingernail, as if they were a couple and not two strangers who had met six hours ago. "Looks like you and Max were having an intense conversation."

The faster Tony ditched "teeth," the quicker he could get Ronnie home. "I'm sorry, Brianna, but we have to cut the evening short."

"Why?" she frowned. "What's wrong?"

"It's Ronnie. She's had too much to drink and needs a ride."

Brianna looked confused. "Then call her a cab."

"I don't want to embarrass her. She's the police chief. Word travels fast. It's best I take care of this."

Disappointment mixed into Brianna's pouty huff as she stood. "Okay. Let me use the restroom before we go."

*That's what she thinks.*

"Brianna, I'm taking Ronnie home by myself."

Her jaw dropped. "Why can't I go with you?"

Tony glanced at Ronnie at the bar. Her elbow had tipped back so many times, a sore arm was the least of her worries in the morning. "It's better if I go alone."

Brianna slammed her purse onto the table. "What about me? What are you going to do? Throw me in a dirty, smelly cab. It's too good for what's-her-name, but not for me."

Tony held his temper. "Her name is *Ronnie*, and she's my boss." *And my ex-wife.*

"How am I going to get home? Walk ten miles in the freezing cold; probably get attacked by some grungy creep lurking in the alley."

*What a drama queen. Time to appease, teeth.*

"Let a lovely lady like you go home alone? Not a chance. If you can't have me, you'll have the next best thing. Audrey will give you a lift."

Brianna plopped into the chair and turned her back on Tony, but he didn't give a rip. She was a date to a wedding and nothing serious worth pursuing. Ronnie needed Tony. Brianna didn't. But he had to smooth things over so he didn't look like a total jerk.

Tony moved his chair closer to Brianna. "I had a great time with you."

*Nada.*

Tony pulled out the cop card. "See, I'm never off duty. I'm always a police officer. The people I work with are important to me. I'd hate for someone to get hurt, knowing I could've stepped in and helped."

He touched Brianna's shoulder, and she unraveled her crossed arms from their tight fold. She turned around, taking him at his word.

*She bought it.*

Tony's irresistible grin worked like a magical charm. Brianna went from seething to sweet in seconds. "Maybe we can take another crack at this dating thing?"

"I'll call you," he said. A cliché line from back in the day after he had lost interest in a woman. Funny how he had used it again.

"Good night, Officer Lombardo."

Brianna pressed against Tony with a seductive kiss. Her mouth worked to separate his as her tongue tried just as hard to get inside. He watched Ronnie at the bar. Thankfully, she had her back toward him. Tony didn't have a snowball's chance in hell of driving Ronnie home if she saw Brianna sucking on his face.

He pulled back, hard and fast, and the release made a noise like a suction cup. Brianna's perfectly waxed eyebrows drooped.

*Keep the act going for a few more seconds. Throw in a wink. Yeah, women like that.*

So he did and topped the sundae with a cherry with a quick, barely touching, kiss on her cheek. "Bye."

Tony strode to the bar. He grabbed the champagne glass from Ronnie.

She twirled around, groping the wooden ledge for support. "Hey, what are you doing?"

Tony set the glass on the bar. "Cutting you off."

"You can't do that. I'm your boss."

"Not the shape you're in." Tony stayed calm. Ronnie wasn't in the right frame of mind. Anything she said, he wouldn't take personally.

"Go back to your *date*, Lombardo, and leave me alone." At each word, she poked his chest. Ten pokes in all.

"Spoken like a true drunk."

Ronnie snarled and turned her back on him.

Tony grabbed her by the elbow and spun her around. "What are you so pissed off about? Is it Brianna?" He knew he had his answer when Ronnie refused to give hers. "Because your skin color matches your dress."

She grunted at the absurdity of the accusation.

How could Tony have been so blind? His small window of opportunity was quickly closing. Ronnie's unprecedented drinking binge meant she still had feelings for him.

Tony held his stare, and in it, hoped Ronnie believed him. "Brianna isn't my girlfriend. I'm not dating her, and I don't want to. I only agreed to bring her to the wedding. That was before Thanksgiving."

"You don't owe me an explanation, Lombardo. I'm not your *wife*. Not anymore." Ronnie lost her balance, and Tony steadied her. "Hey!" she yelled, snapping her fingers at the bartender. "Another drink down here!"

Tony sliced a finger across his neck with the nonverbal cue that Ronnie had reached her limit. The guy spun around and moseyed down to the opposite end of the bar.

"Give me your keys," Tony demanded. "I'm taking you home."

"I don't need *you* to swoop in and *rescue* me."

"Use your head, Ronnie. Do you want tomorrow's headlines to read 'New Police Chief Busted for DWI'?"

"I'll get a ride, but not from *you*."

Ronnie took the champagne glass off the bar. As she went to take a sip, Tony lost his cool. "All right, I've had it. You're coming with me."

He bent down, grabbing her behind the knees, and threw her over his shoulder. She dropped the champagne flute, and it shattered into sand-like crystals.

"Put me down, Lombardo!" The back of Ronnie's dress rode up, and Tony pulled it over her butt. "You're a dead man! I'll have your badge for this!"

Ronnie threw a kicking tantrum as Tony strutted out of the reception hall like a cave dweller.

• • •

Tony drove Ronnie home as the seat belt harness cradled her head. He intermittently blew on his hands as the frigid air rushed in from the opened passenger window of the Toyota 4Runner. Ronnie had better odds of clearing the vehicle if she got sick.

Tony followed Ronnie to her apartment, prepared to catch her if she wiped out. She had insisted she was fine, but he knew better than to believe her after encountering countless drunks while on duty.

Her legs wobbled up the last two steps before she came to a brusque stop on the landing, balancing herself, then continued toward apartment 310.

Searching her purse, she mumbled, "Where are they?"

Tony jangled a set of keys.

Ronnie snatched them from him. To his surprise, maybe hers, too, she inserted the key into the lock on the first try, and they went inside.

Tony surveyed the tidy apartment with a few hanging pictures and a bookshelf in the living room. Minimal. Simple. Not much to bog her down. Same style since they were married.

Ronnie dropped her purse onto the glass coffee table. She wrestled with her coat, trying to take it off. Tony went to help her, but stopped.

*Who knows? She might deck me.*

Tony had done his job. Ronnie was safe at home, but he couldn't leave.

She tossed the coat onto the gray recliner and plunked onto the couch, her legs spread slightly unladylike, staring blankly at the window. "That was our song, Tony. You danced to *our song* with someone else. How could you do that to me?" Heartbreak riddled her voice as if she had been dumped by her first boyfriend.

Tony sat down next to Ronnie, wanting to apologize, but he had trouble owning up to his faults. "I didn't want to." His weak excuse was all he offered.

Ronnie slumped onto the back cushion. "I think about us a lot lately. You and me. Vivian. When we were a family. Before she left us."

"Me, too." The words came out harder than he had expected.

"We were happy, the three of us. Were you happy, Tony?"

Heaviness weighed him down. All he did was nod.

"Vivian was a good girl. Sweet and kind. Funny, too. Such a good little girl."

The faraway look in Ronnie's eyes revealed a sad innocence, making her vulnerable and lost, searching for something that no longer existed and wishing it back to life.

Ronnie closed her eyes. "Sometimes I can see her right in front of me, and if I try *really* hard, I can feel her. I can smell her skin and her hair. Hear her voice and the way she mispronounced big words."

Finally, Ronnie opened up. The booze made her do it, but she was talking.

*Why didn't you do it eleven years ago, Ronnie?*

Now that she had, Tony was the one who didn't want to revisit the past.

Ronnie opened her eyes, then did something Tony never saw coming but would never forget. She laid her head on his lap and looked up at him with those big brown eyes. Suddenly, love had replaced anger. It had replaced duty. Love had replaced grief.

Tony had been dead inside for so long, existing in a hazy slumber, believing he was over her. Out of sight, out of mind, only takes a person so far.

Now she was here, flesh and bones. The perfect opportunity for him to tell her what she meant to him, what she will always mean to him. Brianna was hot, but she didn't come close to being in the same class as his ex-wife.

Tony petted Ronnie's head. "There's no one like you. You're the only woman who gets to me."

Ronnie sat up. Taking the initiative, she removed Tony's coat and suit jacket. "Prove it."

Tony wasn't that guy—the one who took advantage of drunk women. "I don't think that's such a good idea."

"You don't want me?" Rejection layered her words as she pouted. "I'm still not good enough for you. I'll never be."

She was dead wrong. "That's not true, Ronnie."

Her fingers dug into his thighs, arousing him. He got a whiff of her hair. Smelled like peaches and sunshine. She wasn't a random woman he had taken home from a bar. She was Ronnie, the woman who had been his wife.

*Don't do it,* his brain warned him. *She's still drunk. You'll regret it; she will, too.*

"Show me what I mean to you," Ronnie said, her hands moving up his chest, taking him back to a time when all they needed was each other. "Please, Tony."

There was no need for her to beg. He gladly obliged. Touching her smooth lips, her eyelids fluttered.

A softness Ronnie had only shown for Tony rose to the surface. She was all business at the station. Tonight, she was all woman. He loved that about her. There were so many reasons he had fallen for her. She had taken her greatest passions seriously, being a cop and being his love.

Lost in the sensation of her skin, Tony ached for more of her as he softly kissed her neck.

Ronnie's head collapsed sideways. "Hmm, Antonio." She had only called Tony by his full name during their lovemaking, and in seconds, she filled a decade-long void within him.

Tony sniffed her vanilla-scented skin. She still wore the same brand of lotion. To smell the subtle, sweet fragrance, you had to be close, and Tony was as close to Ronnie as he could get.

His mouth found her parted lips that were waiting for him. He almost refrained from kissing her; the anticipation alone made his head spin with excitement, but who was he kidding? Tasting the sweet aftertaste of alcohol inside her mouth, Tony maneuvered the kiss in slow movements while their tongues got reacquainted.

From Ronnie's throat came a gratifying moan as her fingernails clawed his back. She lunged on top of Tony, and he fell backward into the corner of the couch. Her fingers wove through his black locks as her mouth worked wildly on his.

"Oh Tony," she moaned in ecstasy. "I've missed your hands on me."

He skimmed her shorter hair, familiarity enveloping him. The last time he and Ronnie had sex was two days before Vivian died, when they had decided to extend their brood and began their journey to have another baby, not only for themselves, but for Vivian. For their daughter to have a brother she'd play mommy to or a sister who'd be her best friend.

"This is how we are supposed to be," Tony said, winded.

Then he kissed her—hard, harder than he imagined possible. A deep, hungry kiss, only she could satisfy. Words didn't exist to describe the intensity shooting through him like lightning. He searched for them, but they were nowhere to be found. He concentrated on how their lips perfectly intertwined. Her touch ignited pleasure in him while the battle in his mind refused to retreat as he tried resisting what he knew he shouldn't do.

Tony brought Ronnie with him as he stood, never allowing their mouths to separate. He ignored the warning and told it to shut up as he tore off his tie and threw it on the floor. She feverishly untucked his shirt as he quickly unfastened the row of buttons. Ronnie's hands slid beneath his undershirt and touched his bare skin, making him shudder. In return, Tony nibbled her ear as if it were a tasty dessert before going back to her mouth for seconds, and they staggered to the hallway.

Now was the ideal moment to scoop her into his arms—not to mention terribly romantic—carry her into the bedroom, and make love to her like he never had before.

"Wait," Ronnie muttered against his kisses.

"Don't say it," Tony said with a finger on her lips. "Don't think. Just let it happen."

Ronnie blinked and blinked again, trying to focus. "I... I'm going to..."

Her torso jolted. She pressed a hand to her mouth as her cheeks expanded. She stumbled as she hurried into the bathroom. Tony heard the toilet lid smack against the tank, followed by Ronnie vomiting.

He went inside. She was on the floor, hanging over the toilet.

Tony dropped to his knees beside her. She dry-heaved as if she were about to barf again. Then did.

He held back her hair as she emptied her dinner into the bowl. He flushed the toilet and carefully propped her against the wall. Her eyes had shrunk into slits.

Ronnie prided herself on being in control. If the guys at the station saw her bombed, she'd never live it down.

Tony soaked a washcloth in cold water. He wiped Ronnie's mouth and the vomit on her dress. With a graceful lift, he picked her up off the floor and carried her limp body into the bedroom, then laid her on the bed.

She looked dead, and he checked her pulse.

Tony removed her short black heels and dropped them onto the floor. He opened the second dresser drawer where she had kept her pajamas and still did. Neat freak. Three equal rows of perfectly folded clothes in descending order of color from light to dark. Bottoms, tops, and T-shirts she wore on the weekends while puttering around the house.

Thumbing through the stacks, Tony saw his high school football jersey. Ronnie had kept it after all those years. She used to wear it as a nightgown and looked so hot with white socks and no bottoms, but Tony took a pair of flannel pajama pants and a gray T-shirt instead.

He rolled her onto her side and unzipped the dress, then turned her onto her back and carefully took it off. He sat her up to unhook her bra and removed the garment, sneaking a peek at her chest pressed against him.

*God help me.*

Tony pulled the T-shirt over Ronnie's head and her pliable limbs through the openings, then covered her with the comforter.

He returned from the bathroom with a wastebasket and placed it on the floor next to the bed, just in case. To add humor to the situation, Ronnie started snoring, her button-nose twitching before she drifted off to a deep sleep.

Tony took Ronnie's dress and turned off the light on his way out. In the bathroom, he soaked the stained garment in soapy water.

• • •

Crashing Chet's wedding had been as easy as walking inside the reception hall. The low lights and loud music concealed the stalker's entrance. Half the guests were three-sheets to the wind to have even noticed him standing in the back corner drinking a beer.

It had been worth the drive to see Tony haul Ronnie's drunk butt out of the wedding.

He had followed them to Ronnie's place and sat in the freaking frigid truck outside her apartment building. He watched the row of windows on the third floor, waiting for a light to come on, and minutes later, he saw Tony and Ronnie going at it hot and heavy, before disappearing from the window.

*Nothing like make-up sex. Although it had been a long time for me. Too long.*

Ronnie had even ruined his love life.

# CHAPTER 9

A sickly groan awakened Ronnie as a gurgle vibrated in her throat.

Her throbbing eyelids opened. The relentless pounding in her head made it impossible for her to focus on the blurry object in front of her. Black and white colors smeared together resembling a child's abstract finger painting. A man was in her bedroom, or what she assumed was her room.

Little by little, the fuzzy man became clearer. It was Tony on the edge of her bed, holding a mug. His unbuttoned shirt was wrinkled and his tie was missing, while his normally neatly combed hair was untamed.

"Good morning, sunshine." The slanted grin on his face was reminiscent of the satisfied expression he used to have after sex.

Ronnie tried connecting the pieces from last night as the sketchy events came to her in spurts. The couch. She remembered being on the couch. Tony and buttons. Shirt buttons. A cold, wet thing on her face.

She swallowed; the wretched taste almost made her throw up.

Tony sipped on whatever was inside the mug, but it sounded more like a shrilling slurp. "Congratulations. Your first hangover. How's it feel?"

Ronnie sneered like a pit bull on the attack. "How do you think?"

"It's been a while since I've had one," he said with the mug to his mouth, then took another loud slurp. "I take it your drinking days are over."

Ronnie tried lifting her head that felt like a steel beam. She closed her eyes, begging the darkness to have mercy on her and lessen the excruciating pain. "I think I'm dying. I have a better survival rate of being poisoned. This isn't fun. Why bother?"

"People drink for a lot of reasons."

Ronnie wasn't a dolt; the question was rhetorical. But Tony toyed with her because he could.

"They're happy or sad. Bored." He stopped. She opened one eye, seeing him smile. "Sometimes jealous."

Ronnie held her head. Either the room was spinning from the champagne she had drank like soda or what had happened between her and Tony.

"Did we…" The hangover dwindled her vocabulary. "Do it?"

"Hmm… what do you think?"

He was having way too much fun at her expense. Ronnie's tone sharpened. "If I knew, I wouldn't ask. Now would I?"

Hadn't Tony succeeded in torturing her by bringing that pair of legs to Chet's wedding? *No!* Internal slap to the head. *The wedding!* Ronnie's colleagues had seen her drunk. The miniscule respect she had worked so hard to gain disintegrated after a few glasses of bubbly.

"You passed out before we had a chance to. Technically, you threw up, then passed out."

"But stuff happened, right? We… did things." She made it sound so illicit.

Tony set the mug on the nightstand. "Nothing for you to be embarrassed about."

"Me? Embarrassed?" She scoffed. "You're the one who should be embarrassed. No, ashamed. Taking advantage of me."

"Hold it right there, Ronnie." Offense thickened Tony's tone. "The only thing I *took* last night was good care of you. I got you home safely and put you into bed. And for the record, you're the one who made the first move."

"I did not."

*Wait—did I?*

Trying to remember made Ronnie's head ache even more. It felt as if someone were inside of it, beating the wall of her skull with a sledgehammer.

*Prove it... Show me... Please, Tony,* she heard inside her head. *I did come onto him.*

Mustering the strength to tug on her shirt, Ronnie raised her voice. "Then how did I get this on?" She held her head. "Ow," she whined.

"I put it on you. You puked on your dress. I figured you didn't want to smell it when you woke up."

"You undressed me?"

"Yeah, I did. Nice to know you kept my jersey. You used to sleep in that old thing all the time, but I didn't want you to get sick on it." He pointed to the gray shirt. "So I put you in that."

She raised the comforter to her chin, feeling exposed. "You saw me?"

"Relax, Ronnie. I've seen you naked thousands of times. We were married."

"It's different now."

"Maybe for you." Tony acted very matter-of-fact.

*What man in his right mind would pass up ogling an unconscious, naked woman?*

"Sorry I didn't turn you on," Ronnie mumbled. "Nothing new there."

Tony cupped his ear. "What was that?" Although she knew he had heard her.

"Nothing," Ronnie said, followed by burping champagne-infused gases.

He held the wastebasket in front of her. Waiting, listening to her body through the surging pain, the sensation attenuated.

"I don't need it," she said.

Tony placed the wastebasket on the floor. "Try sitting up." He helped Ronnie as if she were a brittle-boned old woman, then handed her the mug. "Here, drink."

She pushed it away. "I did enough of that last night."

"It's coffee."

Ronnie's shaky hands held the mug, afraid of spilling the brew on the white comforter. Her nose wrinkled after the first sip, and she stuck out her tongue. "It's black. You know I hate black coffee."

"Cream and sugar might make you toss your cookies again." He gestured for her to keep drinking.

Ronnie vacillated between what was worse: the bitter coffee or the hangover. "My tongue feels like nasty shag carpeting that hasn't been cleaned in a decade."

Tony's laugh nearly broke the sound barrier.

She covered her ear, squeezing her eyes shut. "Not so loud."

He patted her leg to get her attention, and she opened her eyes. "I rinsed your dress. It's hanging over the shower rod, but I'd throw it in the washing machine, anyway. Need anything else before I go?"

"You're leaving?" She held the mug in front of her mouth to hide her panic.

"Max is bringing my truck."

Ronnie forced down another revolting sip of coffee, surprised she hadn't upchucked by now.

"Are you sure you're okay?"

"I'll be fine."

Ronnie was embarrassed Tony had seen her hungover and pathetic, but grateful that if anyone had to take care of her, it was him.

She felt small and weak, not the strong woman she had come across as, and often pretended to be. Had it been all an act? Was she that unhinged? Her ex-husband, the one she had divorced, was a free man. She had told him at the lawyer's office to move on with his life, which he did. Tony was going to date; he might even get married again. Before moving back to Hilton, she had assumed he already had. Ronnie couldn't expect him to be single forever. Yet, there he was in a rumpled suit and bedhead hair, taking care of her.

"Tony." *Say it and mean it,* her brain scolded. "Thanks."

His arms straddled her, reminding her of Birchwood Park under the dogwood tree as her thumping heart outweighed her throbbing head.

"Another fact for the record..." Tony leaned forward; the mattress squeaked from his weight. "You still have a killer body."

The words penetrated her flesh.

"Ten years has made you more beautiful." He moved in and softly kissed her, letting his mouth linger on her dry lips. She allowed it, this place of refuge that had once been his home.

"Get some rest," he said and left the bedroom.

## CHAPTER 10

Christmas wreaths and poinsettia plants decorated snow-covered graves at Cold Springs Cemetery. The festive hues may as well have been a dismal gray, as Ronnie knelt in front of Vivian's tombstone. Etched in granite was her daughter's name and minuscule time on Earth.

*Vivian Elizabeth Lombardo*
*December 19, 2005-August 12, 2009.*

Ronnie tried picturing Vivian as a teenager. She imagined her lean and tall, the color of her hair landing somewhere between Ronnie's natural brown and Tony's jet-black hue. Her rounded baby fat thinned out, replaced with mature features.

All Ronnie saw, though, was her baby girl in a casket, clothed in a purple velvet dress and white tights. Tess had bought the outfit; Ronnie had been too distraught to shop for burial clothes for her daughter. Vivian's long hair curled at the ends, splayed over her shoulders. Tucked in the crook of her elbow, her favorite stuffed animal—a bunny she had received in her Easter basket that year.

Ronnie brushed a thin layer of snow off the tombstone's ledge, then wondered what made her do such a frivolous thing. Vivian had been dead for eleven years, but for Ronnie, losing her daughter was as fresh as it had been the day the car hit her. And the day the funeral director had closed the casket. And the moment the graveyard workers had lowered the pink box into the ground. And every day since then.

The memory of that ill-fated summer day haunted her like a ghost.

Gleeful shrieks and laughter formed a cadence of innocence at the neighborhood playground—a new hotspot attracting kids in droves. The smell of fresh-cut grass tickled Ronnie's nose. Clusters of fuchsia and purple New Guinea Impatiens adorned the green space surrounding apparatuses ranging in sizes and difficulty.

Boys and girls sprinted through the obstacle course, requiring minimal supervision from their parents, while three-year-old Vivian insisted on conquering the big-kid slide without Ronnie's body acting as a shield.

Vivian's sudden surge of independence allowed Ronnie time to relax on a nearby bench. Her head balanced on the ledge, absorbing the sun's rays that magnified her drowsy state after a sixteen-hour work shift.

Chores topped Ronnie's list. Laundry, clean the bathrooms, and pay the bills. Going to the playground was at the bottom. She had considered postponing the outing, but she promised Vivian she would take her that day, then out to lunch after. And Ronnie always kept her word.

"Mommy!" Vivian shouted. "Watch me!"

Ronnie lifted her head as her daughter waved wildly at the top of the slide before launching herself through the enclosed tube. She applauded Vivian's accomplishment as the girl ran toward her wearing a yellow shirt and white shorts.

"See, Mommy! I told you I could do it all by myself!"

Ronnie pulled Vivian in for a hug and kissed the child's tender mouth. "I never doubted you for a second, baby girl."

"I'm going to the sandbox now."

Ronnie lovingly tapped her daughter's bottom. "Have fun."

Vivian skipped toward the box, her long brown curls bouncing off her back. She joined the two girls inside, burying her legs in the tan sand. They shoveled silt into red buckets with plastic scoopers and tried making a creation of some sort. Ronnie was too far away to see exactly what.

The sandbox had become Vivian's favorite playground feature after her bare feet touched the beach at Ocean City, Maryland, last month. She had marveled at the "ginormous" ocean—her word—and screeched as the waves crashed over her tanned legs while wading at the shore.

Ronnie slouched on the bench as her stomach growled. The lingering charcoal aroma from the hot dog stand across the street lured parents and kids for lunch. She looked at her watch; it was almost noon. The playground and a pit stop for junk food was a winning pair like peanut butter and jelly.

A blond-haired boy ran after a neon-green ball that cleared the sandbox wall in one smooth bounce. Vivian handed him his ball. His mouth moved, but Ronnie couldn't read his lips. Vivian looked around the sandbox, then at the boy picking his nose, and followed him. They took turns kicking and chasing the ball, and Ronnie assumed, making rules on the fly as they played.

Being an only child brought out the social butterfly in Vivian—much more than it had for Ronnie as a kid.

Ronnie yawned as she watched Vivian run alongside the boy. Her languished eyelids begged her to give in to fatigue. She closed her eyes, letting her consciousness slip away, just for a second, until a horrid shrill of squealing brakes and skidding tires replaced the sweet laughter of childish delight.

Her eyes snapped opened, and she saw the ball rolling down the road. Ronnie screamed until her throat ached and sprinted to where her daughter's lifeless body lay sprawled on the hot pavement.

The sound of crunching leaves brought Ronnie back to the present. She turned around and saw Tony holding a wreath. "I had a feeling you'd be here today," he said.

"It's her birthday." Ronnie's eyes blurred with tears. "Fifteen years old."

Tony placed the wreath in front of the tombstone and sat down next to Ronnie. "I visit her every year. Thirteen was hard. Every year is hard."

Ronnie gazed at the cloudy sky, pleading for a whiff of that new baby smell and to feel Vivian's silky wrinkles. To feel the bond created while breastfeeding her child.

Tony loosely hugged his bent knees. "Remember the week after she came home from the hospital? I don't think we slept all week."

Those were the roughest nights of Ronnie's life, but she wouldn't have traded them for the world.

"I'd nurse her; you'd burp her. She'd sleep for twenty minutes—thirty on a good night—and then we'd do it again." Ronnie paused, musing. "Nurse, burp, sleep, repeat."

Tony had jumped into parenthood with both feet. He had changed diapers and bathed Vivian, fed her breakfast, and rocked her to sleep when she was fussy. He was a hands-on father who cherished every moment, even the unglamorous ones, of raising their daughter.

Ronnie looked out at the cemetery. She envied parents with teenagers, and would gladly endure the phase that makes you want to rip out your hair. Teenagers' mood swings keep parents' guessing, worried, and irritated. One minute, they're embarrassed to be seen with you. The next, they're your best friend. The older they get, the more you begin a sentence with, "Remember when you were little, how you used to…" Their lives are ridiculously superficial with school dances, football games, and parties. You never think they will grow up, then one day they do.

Ronnie imagined Tony being like Tess, overprotective and overbearing, when Vivian started dating. Between being a cop and being Italian, he'd instill the fear of God into every awkward, skinny guy, with one thing on his mind, who wanted to date his daughter. Ronnie and Tony would wait for Vivian to get home, then pretend they were sleeping as she tiptoed down the hallway past their bedroom. They'd lie awake in bed, wishing she didn't have to grow up so fast.

Then the day Ronnie dreaded would come as Vivian announced her plans to go away to college. Outwardly, Ronnie would be the proud mom, bragging to all her friends about her daughter's endeavor, and cry her eyes out the night before she and Tony drove Vivian to the campus to drop her off, then cry the whole way home.

Instead, Ronnie and Tony were at Vivian's grave on her birthday.

Ronnie faced Tony. "You were a good dad. I'm sorry I didn't say it more often."

"I learned by watching you. How you held her. How patient you were. Even when she was screaming her head off. You always knew what to do. You were a great mother, Ronnie. Everyone said so."

She dropped her head. "Good mothers stay awake."

"What does that mean?" Tony asked.

Ronnie was not supposed to say it, but now that she had, things would never be the same between her and Tony.

"I fell asleep. At the playground." She choked on a whisper. "That's why Vivian ran into the street."

Tony backed away, his mind reeling from the secret she'd kept for more than a decade. "What do you mean, you 'fell asleep'? How could you do that? You were supposed to be watching her!"

"I just closed my eyes for a second." Ronnie's voice shook. "I was exhausted from working a double. I'm so sorry."

"It's a little late for that!" Anger shot Tony to his feet. "Why didn't you walk around or leave earlier? If you were that tired, why didn't you just stay home?"

Ronnie burst into tears. "Because I promised to take her to the playground and to lunch!"

"All this time, you lied to me. You made me believe I did something wrong." Tony paced, his hands flapping like Tess's. "I was your husband, Ronnie. What were you so afraid of?"

"This! This moment right now! I couldn't tell you because you'd hate me, just like you do now. But it'll never be as much as I hate myself!"

Tony's countenance dropped, implying he finally understood Ronnie's reasons for acting the way she had. Avoiding him. Not talking. No sex. She had been afraid of losing him, too.

He sat back down. "I could never hate you, Ronnie."

"A car didn't kill her. I did," she said, sniffling. "I killed our daughter because I didn't want her to be mad at me. I only cared about myself."

Tony held Ronnie in his arms, his hand grasping the back of her head. "Shh," he hushed. "Don't do this."

"I didn't deserve to be her mother. I don't deserve to be anyone's mother!"

Tony's firm hand moved in soft strokes over her head. "You loved her. She knew it, so did I. Everyone did. She was so blessed to have you. We both were."

Ronnie couldn't fathom how Tony could be so understanding. She didn't deserve his compassion; it was beyond her comprehension. "It's not supposed to be this way. Vivian wasn't supposed to die. This isn't a place for a child." Ronnie's tears soaked his jacket.

"I miss her, Tony. I miss her so much."

His mouth disappeared into Ronnie's hair. "Me, too, honey."

She screamed, causing her body to tremble. "The pain won't go away; it never goes away! Why did she have to die?"

Tony kissed the side of Ronnie's head, offering small flutters of comfort. "I don't know, baby. I ask the same question all the time. I just don't know."

Ronnie was a cop, and she couldn't protect her own daughter. Every day she helped people, strangers, except for an innocent little girl named Vivian. She'd driven herself crazy with 'what ifs.'

"Do you know how many times I've thought if I had just told her we'll go to the playground another day or to wait until you got home, that she'd still be alive?"

Tony held her tighter. "It was an accident, Ronnie."

"Because of me! I dozed off. Good mothers keep an eye on their children. They don't let them run into the street and get hit by cars, but bad ones do."

"Stop!" Tony grabbed Ronnie's face, making her flinch. "I don't ever want to hear you say that again. You hear me? You weren't a bad mother. Never."

"I was selfish," she whimpered.

"Why? Because you wanted Vivian to have fun? Because you wanted her to play and treat her to junk food? That's not selfish, Ronnie. That's a mother's love."

Her mouth quivered. She couldn't look at him.

"Quit punishing yourself. You've done it long enough. It has to end."

She stayed silent.

"Honey, blaming yourself doesn't change what happened." Tony turned her head toward him. "Miss her, cry because you can't be with her or watch her grow into an incredible woman like her mother, but stop with the guilt. It's no way to live."

Ronnie's head hung. "I tried being mad at the boy for not staying on the other side of the playground, and the driver for not taking a different street. I've even tried blaming the ball. I still can't go near the toy section in Walmart."

She held onto Tony for what seemed like a lifetime. In it, a release had broken. Fear grew deep in her belly, but she owed him the whole truth.

"I knew working the way I did wasn't good for either of us. I needed you and you needed me, but I couldn't bring myself to tell you the truth. Every time I tried, it hurt so bad. The only one I could talk to about it was my dad."

Ronnie had spent hours at Nick's grave, trying to make sense of what had happened. Her last day there, she knew what she had to do. The first step toward healing had to come by grieving the loss of Vivian with Tony. Ronnie was ready to do whatever was necessary. Grief therapy. Marriage counseling. Support groups. All the above. She had lost her daughter, she couldn't lose Tony, too. The night she had returned from Ohio, ready to have a heart-to-heart with her husband, it was Tony's confession about his fling with Kaitlyn that came as a shock.

"I thought you needed Natalie more than me, that she could help you in a way I couldn't," Tony said. "Nothing I did worked. I felt like a failure."

How could Ronnie have let him believe that? It made her sick to think about how she had treated him. She had read every note he left her, then cried in private. When Tony had taken over laundry duty, Ronnie hit a new level of guilt.

"Everything you did for me didn't go unnoticed. You tried harder than most men would've. I knew it then, and I know it now."

Tony's finger traced the trickle of tears down Ronnie's cheeks.

"There's something else you don't know about the double I worked," she said. "It wasn't voluntary overtime. It was punishment."

"I don't follow."

"Sergeant Ortiz had it in for me ever since our self-defense training. He mocked the instructor who paired us together. The big, bad sergeant didn't think little Ronnie was strong enough to flip him onto the mat, but I did. I bruised more than his backside."

"The jerk made you do a double for that?"

"No. He waited for me to mess up, and I did. I forgot to turn on my body cam. He was all too happy to give me my first infraction. I thought about how disappointed Dad was in me. I begged Ortiz for a second chance. He said he'd overlook the incident if I took Pulinski's shift. Apparently, he had tickets to the Pirates game—seats behind home plate."

"Why didn't you tell me?" The tips of Tony's eyebrows pulled to the middle of his forehead. "I would've had a *chat* with Ortiz."

"Because I didn't want my hubby standing up to the department bully. There was no reason for both of us to be on his hit list." Ronnie wiped her eyes. "I should've taken the infraction, but *no*, not me. Having a spotless record was more important. I had to prove I had what it took to be better than the guys while being the perfect wife and super mom at home."

"You're the most driven woman I know. It's who you are."

"What good has it done?" Ronnie let out a heavy breath and recalled their daughter's last moments. "Vivian woke up early that day. I only got a few hours of sleep. She kept bugging me about going to the playground. Remember how she used to hop when she asked a question?"

Tony smiled. "Like she was bouncing on a pogo stick."

"I thought once I was outside and got some fresh air, I'd perk up. The longer I sat on the bench, the more tired I got. It felt as if someone had pulled down my eyelids. The last thing I saw was Vivian running."

Tony's soothing touch gave Ronnie the strength to continue.

"Then I heard it. That awful sound… squealing brakes." The horrific memory made her collapse against Tony, clutching his jacket as she sobbed.

"I'm so sorry you went through that alone." Tony rubbed her back and kissed her forehead. "And Ronnie, I'm so sorry about what I did to you. To us. There's no excuse for it. I'd give anything to undo it, but I can't, and that hurts me more than you'll ever know."

She swallowed a glob of mucus. "You've never said that. That you were sorry."

"I wanted to, so many times. If I had, maybe things would've turned out differently."

Ronnie had heard Tony's apology and felt it as he held her. He moved her between his legs, holding her as they sat on the cold ground. She didn't know for how long.

Forgiving Tony for sleeping with Kaitlyn had seemed impossible, and for a long time Ronnie didn't want to, because if she had, then she'd be the one to blame for her husband's mistake. Being with Tony now, telling him the secret that was the catalyst chain reaction to their divorce, Ronnie knew she owed it to him, herself, and Vivian to reconsider.

She turned and looked at him. "I forgive you, Tony."

A tear fell from the corner of his eye. "I forgive you, too."

Four words from them both began repairing the damage left from years of heartache and guilt. Moments of silence passed, followed by waves of cries from them both, as they finally grieved the loss of their daughter together.

• • •

Careful not to be seen, but close enough to hear, the stalker hid behind a six-foot cross headstone as Ronnie made the confession of the century.

*Isn't that something? Miss Perfect By-the-Book Cop was responsible for her daughter's death.*

His parental heartstrings refused to tug. The stalker felt no sorrow for Ronnie or what she had lost, because she had taken her personal life out on him.

To the right of Vivian's headstone, there was plenty of room for another grave.

# CHAPTER 11

The Lombardo men congregated in the family room while their better halves were hard at work in the kitchen, cooking a Christmas feast. Tony was there physically, but his mind was on Ronnie after seeing her at the cemetery, where he had learned the truth about what led to their daughter's death.

If she had been honest with him from the beginning, they could've worked through their trauma. It wouldn't have been easy, but they'd still be married.

Ronnie had been living in her own private hell. Tony would never fully understand how it felt for her to go through each day knowing one mistake had led to tragedy. He had experienced his share of near parental mishaps in the four years he'd been a father, but nothing close to what Ronnie had gone through.

One night, Ronnie had gone out to dinner with Tess and Cora. Tony had put Vivian to bed and was watching the Penguins hockey game when he heard his daughter yell, "Dadda!" She had climbed out of her crib and was standing on the landing, where he had forgotten to shut the gate. Flying off the couch as fast as he could, Tony caught her just in time before she went tumbling down the steps.

Tess rounded up the guys for dinner. At every Lombardo meal, dinner conversation centered around the typical topics of food, work, and a hefty dose of brotherly razzing to keep the laughter going.

Tony pictured Ronnie next to him at the table. His confidence had been at an all-time high when he invited her to his parents' house for Christmas. To his disappointment, though, and hers, she had declined, having made plans to visit her parents.

The days prior to Ronnie's departure left Tony anxious. At any moment, the Taylors could pull another stunt like the one they did on Thanksgiving. But Natalie and Graham had kept their word, and Ronnie drove to Akron on Christmas Eve.

Tony and his family had assumed Ronnie would be with them for Christmas. Even Rachel missed seeing her again.

Ronnie's absence clung to Tony like a lonely shadow, not likely to leave until after the first of the new year. If she had stayed in Hilton, he had planned on taking her out to dinner at Brookline Restaurant, where they'd had their first date, then to Chet's apartment for his and Mia's first time hosting a party as newlyweds. Or spend the evening at home (now his apartment) like they'd done during their marriage. Steak, shrimp, and twice-baked potatoes for dinner—all cooked by Tony—followed by two movies chosen by Ronnie. One being a chick flick. They'd count down the last seconds, ring in the new year with a kiss, and reveal resolutions they knew they wouldn't keep.

After opening gifts and eating a meal that left the guys rubbing their full bellies, Tony headed home with Tess's traditional bag of holiday leftovers in tote.

John went outside with Tony as the snow fell faster. "Have you heard from Ronnie?"

"I texted her last night. She made it to Akron before the snowstorm."

"Good." A cloudy breath escaped John's mouth as he looked up at the sky. "Looks like it's heading our way. Do you want to spend the night?"

Tony tapped the truck's hood. "I got four-wheel drive. I'll be fine."

"Okay, but do me a favor. Call your mother when you get home. You know how she worries." Before Tony's rebuttal, John rushed to his wife's defense. "I know, you're over forty years old. But you and your brothers are still her babies."

Tony heard the same speech every time he left his parents' house during inclement weather. "I promise I'll call."

He opened the truck door and John said, "Take your time."

"I've driven through worse than this."

"I meant with Ronnie." John warmed his hands inside his pockets. "Your mother and I can die happy knowing she's back in the family."

Tony's parents had years of life left but made their aging seventies sound as if they were on their deathbeds ever since they had bought their burial plots at the cemetery last year.

"What I'm trying to say is, ten years is a long time. Ronnie's changed. You might have to get to know her again." John shrugged. "Meh, but what do I know? I'm just an old man who wants to see his son happy."

John had never admitted it, but Tony had suspected for some time that his father felt responsible for his and Ronnie's breakup. He was the one who had convinced Tony to tell Ronnie about his one-night stand. The whole garden analogy about weeds and deception.

"Ronnie makes me happy, Dad."

"I know she does." John shivered, then hugged Tony before heading toward the house. "Don't forget to call."

"Yes, sir."

While the truck engine ran, Tony swiped a thick layer of fluffy snow off the windshield and windows with a snowbrush. Fat flakes fell from the sky, reminding him of the Christmas snowstorm that had left him and Ronnie stranded at the Lombardos' house.

Tony had offered Ronnie his old bedroom, still in tack with sports trophies and posters, while he bunked on the couch. They had arranged a late-night rendezvous at midnight. As the grandfather clock gonged, Ronnie had appeared at the top of the staircase, the dull yellow hallway light shining on her. Tony had loaned her his famed high school football jersey—the one he had worn during the city championship that would be remembered for more than the two touchdowns he scored.

Seeing Ronnie in the blue and white symbol of his youth, Tony knew he wasn't getting the jersey back, but boy, did he look forward to seeing her in it more often.

Tiptoeing down the staircase, Ronnie then leaped into Tony's arms and kissed him as if it had been two years instead of twenty minutes since they had seen each other as he carried her into the family room that glowed from the Christmas tree's white lights.

Lying on the couch beneath two layers of blankets, temptation, strong and unyielding, had tested Tony's willpower as it did whenever he was alone with Ronnie, but they agreed to consummate their relationship on their wedding night. She'd been old-fashioned like that. The good-girl quality made her even more irresistible.

Four months later, on a sunny Saturday in April, Tony and Ronnie were married at St. Matthew's Catholic Church. That night in their honeymoon suite, she came out of the bathroom wearing a pink silk teddy that matched her blushing cheeks. It was to be expected—her being a virgin.

Tony's own insecurities left him with the burden of meeting her expectations for her first time.

In the truck waiting to get warm, Tony heard the melody and lyrics of "Stand by Me" over the humming motor, the song that had been the anthem of their love. He'd programmed the CD on repeat their first night together, giving them plenty of time to explore each other. He couldn't take his eyes off her. She was beautiful, so innocent and pure.

After they had finished, Ronnie cuddled next to Tony with a sleepy smile, her fingers gliding across his chest. "Was it worth the wait?"

She had no idea.

Tony's superficial, shallow relationships prior to Ronnie had been based on a woman's looks and sex. His selfish player days of making the rounds on the dating circuit, getting what he wanted in bed, then moving on to someone new, ended when he'd met Ronnie.

Sex was no longer just sex. After making love to Ronnie, his wife, for the first time, Tony knew what it meant to be one in body and soul, in the most intimate expression of love between two people.

· · ·

The curry aroma permeated throughout Natalie's kitchen.

Ronnie's mother had prepared a tasty Christmas dinner: ham, au gratin potatoes, glazed carrots, and chocolate cake for dessert. Graham, however, wanted Indian food. The new ethnic restaurant had received rave reviews from his number-crunching colleagues at the accounting firm. Natalie, being the compliant servant she was, had merrily placed a takeout order and paid extra for the last-minute delivery.

She bustled into the kitchen, wearing an apron that gave the illusion she had cooked a holiday meal. Humming "It's the Most Wonderful Time of the Year," she peeked inside the oven and stuck a finger in each container. "Almost done." She licked her finger and closed the door.

Ronnie imagined the food at the Lombardos: Tess's beef tenderloin and Nonna's homemade lasagna. A tureen of pasta e fagioli at one end of the table and mashed potatoes and two kinds of vegetables at the other end next to a basket of warm dinner rolls. For dessert, a selection of homemade Christmas cookies, cheesecake, and cannoli. That was a Christmas dinner, not the meal in her mother's oven.

The Lombardos were a tight-knit bunch, so it went without saying that gifts galore were under the Christmas tree. By the time John and Tess had passed them out, everyone had a stack of presents to unwrap. Within twenty minutes, paper, bags, and ribbon covered the carpet. Then came the Secret Santa gifts. The whole family took part in the tradition. Trinkets and gag gifts topped the exchange.

The spicy smell brought Ronnie back into her mother's kitchen. Compared to the holiday hoopla at the Lombardos, the quietness in Natalie's house choked her.

Ronnie had Graham to thank for that. The Grinch was extra miserable after postponing his New Year's trip to the Cayman Islands until February because of a reservation snafu, forcing him and Natalie to hunker down in snowy Akron. Ronnie had extended her visit, which exacerbated her stepfather's miserable mood.

Ronnie had promised her mother they'd go shopping the day after Christmas and hit the town on New Year's Eve.

Last night, lying awake on a portable cot in her old bedroom that had been converted into a storage room for Graham's junk, all Ronnie thought about was Tony after their text exchange.

*Tony: Just checking to see you made it safe.*

*Ronnie: Got here twenty minutes ago.*

*Tony: How are the roads? A lot of snow?*

*Ronnie: It's getting there.* Snowflake emoji.

*Tony: Not too bad here. Supposed to get a foot tomorrow. It's not Christmas without snow.* Smiley emoji.

*Ronnie: I can do without it.* Sun and palm trees emojis.

*Tony: I'm with you.* Winking emoji. *Merry Christmas, Ronnie.*

Ronnie could've sent Tony drivel texts about the weather and silly emojis for the next hour. She almost called him, then sent one last message before signing off.

*Ronnie: You too, Tony.* Christmas tree emoji.

Natalie hummed a new carol Ronnie didn't recognize as she broached her ex-husband. All holiday cheer vanished from her mother's musical tone. "What do you mean you spent Thanksgiving with him?"

She made it sound as if Ronnie had committed a felony.

"Veronica?" Natalie snapped, questioning her daughter's sanity.

Ronnie inwardly cowered until she noticed her mother's Caribbean tan. Natalie always turned heads. She kept up on her beauty regimen like an athlete training for the Olympics. The right makeup. Her short blonde hair always looked as if she had just come from the salon. The Botox injections around her hazel eyes kept away wrinkles well into her sixties.

"You're the one who canceled, Mom," Ronnie said. "I had nowhere to go."

"He's your ex-husband. Working together is bad enough, but spending a holiday with him and his family? I bet Tess just *loved* that."

*Yes, as a matter-of-fact, Mom, she did. John and Nonna, too. The whole family was over the moon to see me!*

Natalie clashed with Tess the minute she met her impending in-laws during a Sunday dinner at the Lombardos. Graham had stayed behind in Akron, claiming he had a headache. The big baby.

"Can't he take an aspirin?" Tess had asked.

"It's a migraine," Natalie had replied with a gritted smile, "and he's all out of his medication for it."

Tess had been the perfect hostess, was sweet as pie, and outshined Ronnie's mother in hospitality. What irked Natalie more than anything was when she heard her daughter call Tess "Mom."

Tess had packed a dinner for Graham and instructed Natalie to make sure he ate every bite. Food was good for a migraine. It cured any aliment, according to Tess.

Ronnie took the salad bowl and ranch dressing from the refrigerator. "It was dinner. It's not like I slept with Tony."

Natalie folded her arms, implying her daughter was lying through her teeth.

"I didn't!" Ronnie insisted. "We're colleagues."

"Sell it to someone else." Natalie fumbled to untie the apron and slammed it onto the counter. "Veronica, you're falling for him again."

Ronnie let out a laugh even she didn't believe. "That's ridiculous!"

"No, ridiculous is entertaining the idea of getting back together with your cheating ex-husband. I cannot comprehend this... this... infatuation you have with him!"

"Infatuation?" Ronnie echoed.

"Yes, you heard me. Why? Because he's good-looking?"

*You think I'm that superficial, Mom?*

There was more to Tony Lombardo than his appearance and terrific body, but Ronnie's mother hadn't taken the time to get to know him to find out.

"Veronica, you'd do anything for that man, and I don't see why."

*Well, well, well, isn't that the pot calling the kettle black.*

Natalie had been the poster child for doormats for the past twenty-five years.

"He's had a hold on you since the day you two met."

"Then why did I divorce him? Someone with an 'infatuation' would've stayed. He didn't have a 'hold' on me, and if you were—" Ronnie balked at calling out her mother. Natalie didn't know about her marriage to Tony because she wasn't around to see it for herself. "Tony's different."

"How's the cheater different?"

Ronnie felt as though she were a teenager trying to convince her mother the misunderstood bad boy with the wild reputation was really a great guy. "I can't explain it. He just is."

Natalie opened the oven, then slammed the door shut without checking the food. "Men who cheat don't change. They're master deceivers who put on a show, saying and doing all the right things, and the gullible woman falls for it."

"I'm not gullible, Mom, and I resent the accusation."

Natalie took a bottle of Sauvignon Blanc from the built-in wine rack and vehemently popped the cork. "Must I remind you how you fell apart? You were a mess. You hadn't been that upset since..."

"Dad and Vivian died."

Natalie went quiet at the mention of Nick. She poured a glass of wine and drank half of it in a slow sip. "Tony will only wind up hurting you again, Veronica."

"Mom—"

"Hear me out. The minute you turned your back, he slept with another woman in *your* bed. You can't trust him. The next rough patch to come along, he'll take the first teeny-bopper to come his way to forget about his problems."

"It happened once."

"One time too many."

"So make him suffer because of it for the rest of his life? What about forgiveness, Mom?"

"He doesn't deserve it," Natalie said mercilessly, refilling her glass. "He's nothing but a rotten cheater."

*Why won't you believe Tony is different? He has changed.*

Ronnie saw it firsthand the morning after Chet's wedding and had felt it at Vivian's grave as she and Tony finally grieved the loss of their daughter together.

"Veronica," her mother said in a calmer tone. "You're smart, attractive. There are so many men who'd swim an ocean for you. See what's out there."

Natalie tucked Ronnie's hair around her ears as if her daughter were a little girl, proud of her sage motherly advice as Graham entered the kitchen.

"Natty, when are we going to eat? I'm starving."

"A few more minutes, Graham."

Ronnie's stepfather's pouty stance blamed Ronnie for prolonging dinner, and he went into the dining room.

What did a woman like Natalie see in a whiny, balding man like Graham Taylor after being married to Nick? Ronnie's father defined what it meant to be a man. Strong, confident. Smart and funny. He could fix anything. He knew his place as a father and husband and took his role as provider and protector seriously.

"Veronica, it's best to forget this silly notion of you and the cheater. I know what I'm talking about. You might not understand it now, but one day, you'll thank me."

Natalie carried the salad bowl and dressing into the dining room, signaling the end of their mother-daughter talk.

Ronnie's mother had a point—perhaps the biggest one of all. Tony had cheated on her. Forgiveness and change didn't equal trust—and trust was the core of a marriage. Without it, nothing else mattered. Without trust, Ronnie would always suspect he was with another woman as the voice inside her head constantly reminded her of his one-night stand with Kaitlyn.

# CHAPTER 12

*May 2010*

Ronnie hadn't unpacked from her trip to Akron when Tony blindsided her with his sordid admission. Her tone burned with fire. "Who is she?"

Shame prevented her husband from looking at her as he sat on the edge of the bed, staring down at the tan carpet. "It doesn't matter."

Ronnie lurched forward, screaming in Tony's face. "Tell me her name. Now!"

He quietly uttered, "Kaitlyn."

"Kaitlyn! Of course, it's a 'Kaitlyn'!" Ronnie's arms flailed while mocking the name. "Where did you meet *Kaitlyn?* While she was on stage at some whore-infested strip club?"

Ronnie pictured Tony grinning like an idiot, puffing on a stogie while shoving folded bills down the front of the dancer's purple G-string.

The color of his skin tone dropped two shades. "It's not important."

"Yes, it is! Where did you meet her? Tell me!"

He stared aimlessly at the corner by the door and mumbled, "The Grind."

"The Grind?" Ronnie repeated. Had she heard right? "What did you do? See her sitting at a table drinking a latte and ask to sleep with her?"

Tony kneaded his fingertips into his forehead, practically exfoliating a layer of skin. "She works there."

"Kids work at The Grind! Is she even old enough to drive?" Repulsion gutted Ronnie's insides. Her husband had slept with a girl— not even a woman his own age. A child.

Tony stood and moved cautiously toward Ronnie. "I didn't have to tell you. I almost didn't."

"Well! Let me be the first to applaud you for your honesty! What morals you have!" Ronnie smacked her hands together in a slow, sarcastic clap. "I suppose that makes you the hero—no—the victim. The poor, sex-starved man who had no choice but to do a kid who pours coffee. And who does that make me in this story of yours, Tony? The big, evil villain?"

Tony reached for her hand. "I love you too much to lie to you. You deserve better than that."

The instant he touched her, Ronnie pulled it away. "How considerate of you. Too bad you weren't thinking about my feelings when you were rolling around with Kaitlyn."

Tony spoke in a pathetic whisper. "Baby, let's sit down and talk about this."

"Don't call me 'baby,'" she said through clenched teeth. "I'm not your baby, and I'm done talking."

Ronnie threw the suitcase she had brought with her to Akron on the bed and dumped a week's worth of dirty clothes onto the floor. Pointing at the empty case, she ordered him to pack.

After Tony left, Ronnie wept on the floor until her tear ducts desiccated, and she fell asleep. In her hysteria, she had clutched a piece of the broken glass frame, cutting her hand and spilling blood onto the engagement picture of them taken at the dogwood tree in Birchwood Park.

The next day, Ronnie stripped the bed and took the sheets, along with another set from the linen closet, not knowing which one that slut's body had touched, and went into the backyard for an early morning barbecue. She doused the mound of cloth in lighter fluid and struck a match, torching the fabric as the filthy smell of betrayal ascended into the air.

Ronnie waited one day before dropping in on Kaitlyn at The Grind. Her gut twisted into a pretzel when she saw a gorgeous blonde behind the counter.

*That has to be Kaitlyn. Is she even twenty-one?*

Ronnie hoped she wasn't nineteen, not for Tony's sake, but for her own. How embarrassing it'd be if her thirty-one-year-old husband had slept with a teenager.

The girl handed a customer a carryout tray with four to-go cups inside and flicked back her ponytail.

Tony had tried convincing Ronnie to dye her hair. "You'd look extra hot as a blonde," he had said, picturing the new do. Extra hot, his exact words. Ronnie hadn't been hot enough, apparently, and needed chemicals to get the job done. She was a brunette, content with her natural color, not wanting to be someone other than herself.

Ronnie approached the counter as the cheerful barista greeted her. "Welcome to The Grind. What can I get for you?"

"Kaitlyn?" Ronnie said flatly.

The girl's smile drooped. "Yeah."

Ronnie's police uniform sent a frightening message that the barista had done something wrong. And she had. Kaitlyn had been an accessory, a willing participant in a crime against the covenant of marriage.

"I'm Officer Lombardo. I believe you know my husband, Tony."

Kaitlyn let out a terrified squeak. She couldn't look her former lover's wife in the face. "I—I have a customer."

Ronnie turned around, speaking in a daunting cop tone. "Excuse me, ma'am. I'm going to be a few minutes. Would you mind taking a seat, please?"

The heavyset woman murmured but complied.

Kaitlyn cowered behind the coffee urns. Lucky for her, a counter separated her from Ronnie, who was on duty, which was the only thing keeping her from hurdling over it and ripping out Kaitlyn's hair from the roots.

"Why are you here?" Kaitlyn asked.

Ronnie's duty belt squeaked as she moved closer to the counter. "I'm dying to find out why a pretty girl like you can't find a single man her own age. Why you jumped into *my* bed with *my* husband?"

Kaitlyn stuttered, unable to form a coherent sentence.

"You knew he was married. Obviously, you have no respect for that kind of commitment. Then again, you're just a kid who's good at only one thing—and it's not pouring coffee."

Kaitlyn shifted her weight, her limbs jittering. "Can you please leave?"

"No. I won't."

"If you don't, I'll—"

"What? Call the cops?" Ronnie let out a maniacal laugh. "Go ahead."

"What do you want me to do? Do you want me to say sorry? Fine. I'm sorry I slept with your husband. There. I said it. Now can you please go?"

The contrived apology infuriated Ronnie. The slut hadn't taken the last doll from the toy bin during recess; she'd had sex with a married man!

"This isn't a meaningless high school relationship. You destroyed a marriage. Two people who promised to be faithful until death. I want you to live with that knowledge for the rest of your life."

Kaitlyn stared at Ronnie; it hadn't sunk in. The gravity of her actions and how it had affected Ronnie and a myriad of people involved meant nothing to her, because cheap trash like Kaitlyn—the hot, skinny ones—used their body as a bargaining tool for love.

Ronnie walked away as Kaitlyn's immature voice called out, "What about Tony?"

She stopped and turned. The homewrecker stood at a safe distance behind the counter.

"He told me how your daughter died. It's only natural he'd look for someone to turn to since you weren't there for him."

The gall of her. The downright nerve! Her perception was as narrow as her waist. What did she know about burying a child?

"Well, Kaitlyn, Tony's all yours now," Ronnie said. "But before you get too excited, just know there will come a day when you find out he cheated on you. Then you'll know exactly how it feels to have someone you love betray you. But don't come looking for me to cry about it. We have nothing in common, nor will we ever. You're nothing but a skanky piece of trash." Ronnie pulled a quarter from her pocket and dropped it into the tip jar. "That's all you're worth."

# CHAPTER 13

The week between Christmas and New Year's moved slower than a sick turtle as Tony waited for Ronnie to return from Akron. Before briefing, he'd stand outside her office with the hope she had cut her vacation short and he would see her at her desk with her nose to the grindstone.

The station felt empty without Ronnie there. It was the same loneliness that had taunted him after the divorce. The only difference now was he knew she was coming back.

Under an overcast sky, Tony drove on snowy roads to the station that first Monday in January. The forecast called for the gloomy weather to stick around, but not even the grayest of days darkened his hope as the new year signified Tony's second chance with Ronnie.

In the locker room, while changing into his uniform, Tony rehearsed his speech as if he were an actor who had received his big break. He weighed each word with careful consideration.

*Ever since Vivian's birthday, I haven't stopped thinking about you. More than the job brought you back to Hilton. We belong together, and I want nothing more than to go into the new year with you.*

Tony combed his hair, looking in the mirror at each side before splashing on a dab of Ralph Lauren Polo. He took a deep breath and left the locker room.

The tremors in his hands matched the ones in his stomach on the way to Ronnie's office. He hadn't been this nervous about a girl since middle school when he had made out with Lexi Sanders in the back of the library during study hall, but that was how Ronnie made him feel: young, passionate, and scared out of his mind.

Tony knocked on Ronnie's door, assuming she'd be at the station early on her first day back. No answer.

He twisted the knob. Locked.

Tony had time to get a cup of coffee, and as he turned around on his way to the kitchen, he collided with Ronnie. Their heads smacked together; the bone-to-bone contact made a hollow *thump* noise.

His jaw throbbed from the impact as a shooting pain surged through his bottom row of teeth. "Sorry. Are you okay?"

"Yeah. It shouldn't leave a bruise." She looked so darn cute, rubbing her forehead. Her eyes sparked with a flicker of hope. Or maybe it was the aftermath of the collision. "Were you waiting for me?"

Suddenly, Tony was that seventh-grader in the library and searched for an excuse to buy him more time. "You haven't had your coffee yet. I'll come back."

"Wait here." Ronnie unlocked the door and went inside the office, then came out with a police academy mug.

They walked toward the kitchen, engaging in casual conversation. "How was your Christmas?" Tony asked her.

"Quiet. Graham's postponed vacation ticked him off. Other than that, it was fine. How about yours?"

"The usual. A lot of food. Presents. Ma harping on me to quit the force. It wouldn't be a Lombardo dinner without her mentioning it."

As they entered the kitchen, Tony took Ronnie's mug. "Allow me." He poured coffee inside of it, then stirred in three creamers and three packets of sugar—she liked it on the sweet side—and he handed her the mug.

Ronnie sipped the steaming beverage. "Mmm. Perfect," she said with a smile. "What did your Secret Santa get you?"

Tony poured coffee into a Styrofoam cup for himself. "You remember that?"

"It's a Lombardo Christmas tradition, along with Tess's beef tenderloin."

"Which was delicious," he said, patting his belly twice.

"Was it tastier than my Indian cuisine?"

Tony sipped his coffee, confused. "Huh?"

Ronnie leaned her hip against the counter and puckered her mouth as though she had sucked on a lemon. "Graham had a hankering for Indian food. I can still taste the curry."

"Don't let Ma know about that," Tony quipped, knowing how Tess was a stickler for traditional holiday meals as he internally rehearsed his speech one more time.

*Ever since Vivian's birthday, I haven't stopped thinking about you. More than the job brought you back to Hilton. We belong together, and I want nothing more than to go into the new year with you.*

"What did you get?" Ronnie asked, breaking his concentration.

Tony didn't know what she meant, then remembered the Secret Santa gift. He must've been more nervous than he thought if he couldn't remember a question for more than a minute.

"A tie," he answered. "The pattern is a strand of Christmas lights, and yes, it's musical."

"I assume it plays 'Jingle Bells.'"

"And alternates with 'Rudolph the Red-Nosed Reindeer.'"

Ronnie tipped her head back with a laugh. "You'll have to wear it to the Christmas party next year. No, I mean this year. Can you believe it's 2021?"

Tony couldn't have planned a better segue.

"Time flies." He leaned against the counter, taking another sip of coffee. "I was hoping you'd be back before New Year's Eve."

"I was already in Akron. How many chances do I get to spend an entire week with my mom? Did you go out? Like on a... a date?" Quickly, she sipped her coffee.

"Chet and Mia threw a wild party. Well, maybe not that wild," Tony added. "I went there for a few hours, but didn't make it to midnight."

"Old age setting in? Can't stay awake past nine?"

"Too many happy couples. I felt out of place."

"I know what you mean. We went to a Japanese Hibachi restaurant—the ones where the chef cooks in front of you and puts on a show. He made a volcano out of onion rings and lit it on fire. Catapulted shrimp into his pocket and hat. The way he flipped the spatulas and the knives was so cool!"

Tony adored Ronnie's energy as her voice danced with excitement. She glowed; the same way she had before Vivian had died. It was a sign. Ronnie was coming back to him in rivulets, beginning with their lunch at Birchwood Park.

"The food was unbelievable," she said, still reliving the night. "Graham, of course, treated me like a third wheel. But that's typical."

*Graham. What a jerk. Can't he see what an amazing woman Ronnie is? Any man would be proud to have her as a daughter.*

"Seems like New Year's Eve was a bust for both of us," Tony said.

"It's an overrated holiday." Ronnie looked at the clock on the wall, as if she needed to be somewhere.

Procrastinating was over. Time to tell Ronnie what he had been waiting for weeks to say. He wiped his sweaty palm on the side of his pants. "Chief, I need to talk to you. It's important."

"Tony," she said, interrupting him, "when we're alone at the station, call me Ronnie."

This was going better than he had expected.

"Just don't let the guys know. You get bullied more than your share for being my ex-husband."

Tony signaled okay with his thumb and index finger.

"You were about to tell me something?"

"Right. Ronnie, ever since Vivian's birthday, I haven't stopped thinking about you. And…" Tony's mind went blank. Lights out. He hit the panic button and went on an out-of-control-ramble like a moving car with no brakes. "Chet's wedding was good… You know, about what happened, how we talked. Not you getting drunk. That wasn't good. Not that you did anything wrong. It was just, you know, unexpected. For you and me."

*Stupid! Stupid! Stupid!*

Tony exhaled, as though he had been holding his breath in the swimming pool during PE. The speech he had nailed down, the one guaranteed to strike a chord with Ronnie, was a slop of words mushed together.

Ronnie clinked her uneven nails against the mug. With each passing beat, he sensed his second chance waning. "Tony, I'm glad we're friends again, but that's as far as it can go."

Her words knocked the wind out of him. The softness in her tone made it sound as if she had no other choice.

"I thought about us while I was in Akron. A lot. With me being Chief, things could get kind of messy. The last thing I need is the guys accusing me of giving you preferential treatment because we're dating. A platonic relationship is for the best. It's safe that way. Our focus needs to be on the department and our jobs."

*That's a load of crap, Ronnie. What gives you the right to have the final say? What about me and what I think?*

Ronnie resorted to that cockamamie excuse because she knew they had a shot at making another go of a relationship. Using her position as chief as the scapegoat meant only one thing.

"You don't trust me," Tony said. "That's the real reason."

Her eyelids fell. "I want to. I really do."

"You can, Ronnie. Give me a chance to prove it to you."

She looked off to the side. "I'm sorry for my behavior the night of Chet's wedding. Throwing myself at you the way I did."

"Don't be, I'm not. Know why?" Tony caressed her cheek with his knuckles. "Because it meant you still have feelings for me."

Ronnie looked at him the same way she had at her apartment when she laid her head on his lap. That look of wanting him and needing him. That look of love he had seen from her time and time again. "I was drunk. I wasn't thinking clearly and unintentionally led you on. It was wrong for me to send you those kinds of signals."

"What about the cemetery? Was that a miscommunication, too?"

"Absolutely not. I meant everything I said to you. All of it. We both needed that closure. Tony, for the first time since Vivian died, I can live my life again."

*Why are you acting like this is the end? It's not. I can't be just friends with you, Ronnie.*

"Believe me, this wasn't an easy decision," she said. "But if being friends is all we can be, I'll take it."

While counting friendship a small victory, it was the kindest form of rejection.

"How about it?" Ronnie smiled softly. "Friends?"

Tony would have to take what he could get—for now.

"Friends it is."

• • •

Tony unearthed the words as if they'd been floating in the sewer. "Friends. She wants to be friends."

"Don't you?" Max asked.

"Yeah. If we were twelve and going to the mall on a group date." Tony glanced out the window, then back at Max in the driver's seat of the patrol car. "She finally talked about the day Vivian died. She said she forgives me for cheating on her."

John's intuitive advice Christmas night in the driveway echoed in Tony's mind. *Take your time.*

"I'm not giving up, Max. If it means waiting for her to come around, then I'll do it. I don't care how long it takes." He nodded, agreeing with himself.

"You and the Chief belong together," Max said.

"Tell me something I don't know." Tony's voice dipped. "Ronnie's scared. She's talked herself into thinking that I'd be dumb enough to cheat on her again, so she's playing it safe with this whole friends' thing."

"What's your plan?"

Tony tossed his hands in the air. "I don't know. I didn't think I needed one."

"Maybe the best thing to do is take it day by day. Give her time. Be supportive and be a friend. If that doesn't work, beg."

Tony rolled his eyes.

"Joke. I'm joking."

Tony smirked. "Who knows? It might be my last resort."

Static came through the patrol car radio. The dispatcher belted out, "Radio to Sector One. Accident injury on Interstate 45 South. Multiple vehicles in the middle of the highway."

Tony answered dispatch. "Clear, we're responding."

Max hit the lights. The siren blipped, and they sped to the scene.

# CHAPTER 14

Tony paced the conference room. Five minutes with Ronnie was all he wanted before the afternoon drug task force meeting. The sound of footsteps and murmuring grew louder outside the door. He poked his head into the hallway. Max and Chet came inside, followed by the rest of the officers on the team.

Perusing a report, Ronnie entered the conference room and stood at the helm of the table. She dropped the folder. "What's the status of the health classes?"

"The middle and high schools are on board," Max said. "The teachers will have lesson plans ready for February. They'll let me know this week which days to visit the classes."

"Nice work, Officer Brody. The physical ramifications of drug abuse aren't pretty. Maybe grossing the kids out will keep their curiosity at bay."

A bubble of laughter emanated from the officers.

"Chief, the elementary principal is on the fence," Officer Nelson said. "She thinks the kids are too young for a hardcore message about drugs, especially the kindergarteners."

"Her concerns are valid. Telling a five-year-old about drugs isn't easy, but chances are they've already been exposed through television, older siblings, and video games. Sadly, even from their parents."

Tony added his two cents. "Chief, what if we compromise with the principal?"

Ronnie went to where Tony sat and lowered herself onto the edge of the table. "Go on."

"Fourth and fifth graders know about drugs. We can put together a fun assembly for them. Music and games while weaving in the message. If the response is good, then we'll try it out on the younger kids."

"It's worth a shot." Ronnie addressed Officer Nelson. "Present the idea to the principal. If she agrees, we'll work together on a program for the kids."

"I'll call her first thing tomorrow morning."

"Moving on. I've spoken to the director from the New Beginnings Youth Center. She's thrilled to be partnering with the department. I'll be at the center a week from this Friday to meet the staff and kids and brainstorm on ways to get the community involved. Anyone care to join me?"

Tony raised a hand. "I'll go."

"Thank you, Officer Lombardo." Ronnie quickly moved past her appreciation.

"Count me in," Max said.

"Excellent." Ronnie stood and went back to the head of the table. "Eventually, you will all need to stop by and introduce yourselves. It's important for the kids to feel comfortable around us. I'm sure we're the last people they want to hang out with."

Ronnie looked at Tony. "I'm sending out press releases to the news stations and the *Hilton Herald*. I want to get as much media attention on the center as possible. Put the bug in Joey's ear. Maybe he can drum up a few story angles."

"No problem. Now he can quit whining about not getting any leads."

"Good ol' Joey." Ronnie clapped her hands together once. "We're done for now. Thanks, guys."

Tony waited in the conference room for the other officers to leave. "You're doing a great job, Ronnie. Keeping the guys in line and the task force. Kahn made a smart move hiring you."

"Thanks, Tony. That means a lot to me. I appreciate all your hard work. You've shown real leadership. It's always been in you."

Tony's rise in hegemony wasn't why he stayed behind to talk to her, but it broke the ice.

"How about we go out to dinner? Nothing fancy. A burger at the diner." He shot his hands up in defense. "Not a date. Just food. We'll go Dutch."

She smiled, the way a woman does when she was about to turn a guy down. "Sorry, I can't. I'm leaving early."

*For what? A doctor's appointment? An oil change for her SUV? Is she lying?*

"I'm moonlighting." Immediately, she waved a hand frivolously at her joke. "I'm teaching a criminal justice class at Dearborn College."

Ronnie, a teacher? She didn't seem the type.

"Your plate is already full," Tony said. "The station. The task force. And you want to add more to it?"

Defensiveness cut through her tone. "I enjoy staying busy."

Ronnie was doing it again. She was drowning herself in work to keep from avoiding a situation that had her second-guessing her decision. Only this time, Tony played it smart. "Nothing wrong with that, but it doesn't leave time for much else."

"Such as?"

He wanted to say, "us," but it was too soon.

"One class a few hours a week. Piece of cake."

Ronnie didn't need a cheering section, but as her biggest fan, Tony formed one, anyway.

"If anyone can do it, it's you." His sexy smile sweetened the compliment. Sure enough, it made her blush.

"I—I have to change. I can't wear my uniform to class." She headed for the door. "See you tomorrow."

Tony blew a piercing whistle. Ronnie turned around as he handed her the folder off the table. "Have a good class, teach."

• • •

Ronnie lapped the third floor of the college building for the second time, walking past one empty, dark room after another. The echo of her black shoes striking the concrete floor followed her as she searched for her assigned classroom through the frustrating labyrinth. She took a piece of paper from her coat pocket with her chicken scratches on it. *Anderson Hall, room 350*. Rounding the hallway, hoping life existed somewhere on the third floor, Ronnie saw a man leaving an office.

*Finally, a human.*

Her pace sped up to a fast walk. The sound of her clicking heels quickened as she stretched her arm in the air. "Excuse me?"

The man looked in her direction while locking the door.

Ronnie approached him, winded. "Can you tell me where room 350 is?"

The tall man with blond hair stared at her; words had escaped him. He blinked. "Room 350?"

"Yes. I've circled the floor twice, but it's safe to assume I've missed something."

Behind his Gucci-framed glasses were the brightest blue eyes Ronnie had ever seen. "Are you sure you're in the right building?" he asked. "The last room on this floor is 320."

"This *is* Anderson Hall?" Doubt soared in her tone.

He smiled as if he was too timid to answer. "Anderson is on the right of the student union. We're in Tenter Hall."

Ronnie laughed at her goof. "That's what I get for not reading the sign outside the building."

"In your defense, the snow is covering the moniker."

Ronnie reached for her phone at the bottom of her purse and checked the time. "Good, I've got a few minutes. How embarrassing, right? The teacher being late on the first day."

"There are worse things that can happen."

"I suppose." She tucked a loose strand of hair behind her ear. "I better go."

"I'm heading out as well. I'll escort you to Anderson Hall."

"That'd be great." Ronnie tossed the phone inside her purse. "I'm Veronica Callahan. Everyone calls me Ronnie."

The man shook her hand. "Aidan Foster, and you look more like a Veronica to me."

Aidan's smooth voice as he said Ronnie's real name made her feel desirable, yet oddly unattainable.

He led the way down two flights of stairs. "I take it this is your first class as a professor."

Ronnie quickly corrected him. "No, no. Just instructor. Once a week. I'm the Hilton police chief."

His face twisted in astonishment. "How did the police chief get roped into teaching?"

"The wife of one of my officers works in admissions and had mentioned an opening. Something about the instructor having to quit. Family issues, I think. Anyway, the college was scrambling for a replacement for Intro to Criminal Justice. They took the first body that came along. I thought it would be fun."

"Teaching can be. Sometimes."

The cryptic remark sent Ronnie's red flag soaring. "Is there something I need to know?"

Aidan cocked an eyebrow. "I don't want to spoil the surprise."

She bobbed her head slowly. "Guess it's too late to back out now."

Ronnie and Aidan came to the first floor. He held open the door for her as they went outside. "What course do you teach?" she asked.

"Psychology. Primarily upper-level classes for juniors and seniors."

"Ooh. Better watch what I say, or you'll analyze my every word." She laughed. "Sorry, couldn't help myself."

Aidan must've found her humor refreshing because he replied, "Don't worry. I only analyze my students."

*Hmm. Witty, charming. Not bad looking, either.*

He took Ronnie on a mini-tour of the campus as they cut through the quad, surrounded by the library and theater building. They walked to the student union on the pavement portion cleared of snow, where he pointed to Anderson Hall, and they went inside.

While riding the elevator to the third floor, Aidan told Ronnie the backstory behind the building's renovation project. The thought that his articulation and attention to detail would make him an outstanding police officer passed through her mind.

The elevator doors parted, and they walked through the corridor and rounded the corner to the end of the hallway. The last lecture room on the left had a square plaque outside the door with the room number 350 on it.

Aidan glanced at his Rolex. "You've arrived at your destination with a few minutes to spare." Grinning, he added, "I sound like a GPS."

"Where'd we be without it?" Ronnie said as students walked into the classroom. "Thanks for the tour, Aidan. It was nice meeting you."

"You as well." He adjusted the falling strap on his bag over his shoulder. "Hopefully, I'll see you around campus."

*Is this the part where I'm supposed to say, "Let's meet again next week. Or was he asking for my phone number?*

A flirty temerity came over Ronnie as Aidan's stare boosted her self-esteem. "Who knows? Maybe you will."

# CHAPTER 15

Students funneled into the student union dining hall, where the heady smell of processed food sounded the dinner bell. Side-by-side food stations, each with a different cuisine, lined the area like a mall food court.

The pizza booth displayed slices of burned cheese on what resembled a cardboard slab. Next, Mexican. *Burritos and refried beans?* Not before class, Ronnie noted, imagining a gas attack. Moving to the Chinese station, she surveyed the sweet and sour chicken and fried rice through the glass. MSG—an insomnia culprit.

Ronnie settled for a turkey sandwich from the cooler of a mini-mart. At the register, she added a cup of coffee to her skimpy dinner. After paying the young cashier—who was most likely working her way through college—Ronnie turned and plowed into a man, sending a splash of coffee onto his blue shirt as apologies spewed from her mouth.

"Hello, Veronica."

Ronnie looked up. "Aidan?" She handed him a wad of napkins from a dispenser, hoping the dark spot wouldn't leave a stain. "I'm so sorry. I didn't see you standing there."

"No harm done. Just a little coffee." He dabbed the wet spot and looked out at the seating area. "May I join you?"

"Yes, of course."

They walked past a rowdy group of guys reliving last night's "awesome" beer bash and went to a secluded table in the corner. By the time they sat down, the wet, abstract circle on Aidan's shirt had shrunk.

"How was your class last week?" he asked.

Ronnie peeled the cling wrap off the sandwich. "Not what I expected."

Aidan crumpled the moist napkins. "Care to elaborate?"

She mumbled a "hmm," trying to summarize a three-hour class in one sentence. "Do students always look like they're unconscious?"

"Or that they'd rather be collecting garbage along the highway?"

"Sounds like you've seen a few of those before."

He leaned across the table and confessed, "More than I can count."

Ronnie was relieved she wasn't the only teacher boring the students. "One guy nodded off the entire class. I was afraid his head was going to snap off his neck. Another student doodled more than she took notes. Then there was the cellphone issue. I had assumed they knew about no texting in class."

"The average attention span is forty-five minutes, which presents a challenge for a three-hour evening class."

"Got any suggestions? I'll try anything. I'm not too proud to admit I'm desperate." Ronnie bit into her sandwich, eager for a few hidden gems of wisdom.

"Good teachers are creative. You need to pique students' interests." Aidan stroked his clean-shaven chin. "You're the police chief. You must have plenty of stories. The good, the bad, and the ugly. Tell a few if they relate to the material you're teaching. Students like stories. It breaks the monotony of lecturing and shows them you're a normal person."

*Stories, of course!*

With two decades of police work under her belt, Ronnie had seen more of the unusual and the peculiar than she thought existed.

"How about a field trip?" Aidan suggested. "Bring them to the station. Maybe to a lab where there's DNA testing or the evidence room."

"CSI Hilton style?" Ronnie's clever side made a rare appearance around Aidan.

"Yes. Something like that." He grinned, the same sophisticated smile Ronnie had noticed last week. "Or a project. Split them into groups of three or four and use class time to have them work on their presentations."

"Those are great ideas, Aidan. You've got me more interested in the class, and I'm the one teaching it!" She sipped her coffee. "You came through for me again."

"My pleasure, Veronica."

"Aren't college students here to learn and plan for their future?" Ronnie asked before biting into her sandwich.

"Don't be too hard on yourself. It's a common misconception among first-time teachers. I believed the same notion three years ago."

Ronnie and Aidan continued talking about teaching and their courses while she observed features of the attentive psychology professor she hadn't noticed until now, such as the tiny mole below his left eye and an immovable wave of hair above his tall forehead.

She finished eating her sandwich and drank the last ounce of lukewarm coffee, then rummaged through her purse for her phone. Ten minutes left until class. She gathered her purse and black bag—a replica of Aidan's she had bought after noticing his. "I'm glad I ran into you. Literally."

"Likewise." As Ronnie stood, so did Aidan. "Veronica, I'd like to see you again. Off campus. Will you have dinner with me tomorrow evening?"

"You mean a date?"

He adjusted his glasses, watching his feet shift. "Yes, a date. Six o'clock."

Ronnie hadn't been on a date in two years since her relationship with Mark. The divorced father had his sons every weekend, which made for some strange dates as the four of them went everywhere together, making Ronnie the stepmom stand-in to the introverted boys obsessed with video games.

Her prerequisite before dating a new guy was to know more than his name and his vocation. Although Ronnie had only two brief encounters with the attractive college professor, her womanly instincts green-lighted her to have some fun. "I'd love to have dinner with you, Aidan."

They texted each other their phone numbers, she gave him her address, and then he walked her to her classroom. Aidan didn't tell Ronnie which restaurant they were going to, but she'd bet a week's paycheck it wasn't the diner near the station.

Between lecturing and visualizing the clothes in her closet, the butterflies in Ronnie's stomach took flight early while she explained to her students a suspect's rights after being arrested.

The last thing on her mind was her lesson.

She had a date for tomorrow night.

• • •

Beneath the soft glow of the dining room and the flickering candle on their table, Aidan Foster read the menu like a man who had dined at a French restaurant a time or two. His silver suit, black dress shirt, and charcoal-tinted tie coordinated with his sophisticated personality.

Ronnie had resorted to her elf-green dress, the same homely garment she had worn to Chet's wedding. Once again, she deemed her choice bland compared to her swanky surroundings. As soon as she got home, she would dispose of the outfit that made her feel inadequate.

Had Ronnie known Aidan would make reservations at one of Hilton's most expensive restaurants, she would've bought a new dress. Her mundane wardrobe ranked her clothes far below spectacular on the fancy meter for the classy French restaurant, Le Cep, where the maître d' had placed a linen napkin over her lap.

Their waiter approached the table with a bottle of Chardonnay Aidan had ordered and poured the wine into Ronnie's glass, causing her stomach to rumble with remembrance from the last time she had drunk like a sailor. She politely stopped him at the halfway mark. The only way to make it through dinner was by taking sips between bites of food.

Ronnie browsed the menu, trying to interpret French dishes written in a cursive font. "I've never eaten French food, except for French fries and French toast." She cringed. "Bad joke, sorry."

Aidan laughed, finding her either comical, or he did it to be polite. "Being a novice, allow me to make the recommendations for you." His eyes fell down on the menu. "For the first course, a bowl of the lobster bisque, followed by the coq au vin for your entrée."

"I have a pretty good idea what the soup is, but coq au vin? Never heard of it."

"It's the French's version of chicken and vegetables in a Burgundy sauce."

*Great. Just what I need. More wine.*

Ronnie closed the menu. "Sounds delicious. Coq au vin it is."

"Excellent choice, mademoiselle," Aidan said with a French accent. "For dessert, which do you prefer? Chocolate mousse or raspberry and crème crepes."

Ronnie drummed her fingers on the table. "Chocolate is a girl's best friend. Although, the crepes sound good, too."

"You get the mousse, I'll take the crepes, and we'll split them. Problem solved."

She raised a flirty eyebrow. "Sharing food so soon?"

"Why wait?" Aidan closed his menu. "I know what I want when I see it."

His ardent gaze caused a rush of warmth to spread over Ronnie's neck. Aidan differed from the other men she had dated. The urbane intellect's physical attractiveness came through in a studious sort of way. His refined personality enhanced his manliness. Clearly, Ronnie and Aidan were opposites, but as the saying went, opposites attract.

The waiter returned and took their orders. While waiting for their meals, Ronnie probed her date.

"Did you always want to be a professor?" she asked and took the smallest possible sip of wine, as you would during communion at church.

"It was the back-up plan I assumed I'd never need. After medical school, I received my license, became a board-certified psychiatrist, and opened a practice."

"Ah. So it's *Doctor* Foster."

"Only on paper," he said, lamenting.

"Why? What happened?"

"I'd been treating a patient with several disorders. OCD, anxiety, and trauma from her childhood. At the end of one of our sessions, she said she was in love with me. I told her our relationship was strictly professional—doctor to patient—but she wouldn't hear of it. I terminated her as a patient and recommended she see a female colleague of mine. Instead, she made my life miserable and filed a lawsuit against me, citing I had made inappropriate advances toward her. None of it was true, of course."

"I was investigated. My license was nearly revoked. Three-quarters of my patients left. It was the worst time of my life. As much as I didn't want to, I closed the practice, which made me appear even more guilty."

*Talk about life kicking you when you're down.*

"What happened with the lawsuit?" Ronnie asked.

"She eventually dropped it when her lawyers realized they had nothing on me. I knew I didn't say or do anything to mislead her, but I second-guessed myself as a doctor. If I hadn't done anything wrong, why couldn't I help her? What if I couldn't help any of my patients?" Aidan fixated on his drink and held the stem of his glass, swishing the wine. "Apparently, the adage is true. Those who can, do; those who can't, teach."

A piece of Ronnie's heart broke for him. "Teaching is a noble profession, Aidan. You're making a difference, even if it doesn't always feel like it."

"Very profound. Maybe I should go to you for sessions." He lifted his glass as if he were toasting her and sipped the wine. "Enough about my defunct venture. I want to know more about Veronica Callahan. What made you decide to become a police officer?"

Nick instantly came to Ronnie's mind. "My dad was a cop. He talked about the force with so much passion, so much pride. Wearing that uniform meant the world to him. Being a cop means putting others before yourself. It's not about power or what you can get away with." She fiddled with the silverware next to her plate. "I always knew I'd have a career in law enforcement. Nothing else competed for my attention."

"Earning the position of police chief is very impressive. He must be so proud of you."

"I hope so." Ronnie raised her glass to her mouth. Suddenly, she needed that wine. "He died when I was twelve."

Aidan's smile dropped, either from shock or embarrassment. "Veronica, I'm so sorry. Do you want to talk about it?" He closed his eyes with regret. "Forgive me. It's the psychiatrist in me."

"There's nothing to apologize about. You didn't know."

"How did it happen?" Aidan asked, as if he knew Nick's line of work had resulted in his death.

Ronnie sipped her wine. Not even alcohol had the strength to numb her as she recalled her father's final moments. "He was an officer until the last year of his life when he became a detective in the narcotics unit. He'd been working undercover as a buyer. One night, he went to make an arrest, but the dealers got spooked. I'm not sure what gave him away. They caught wind he was a cop, and the sting went south. One dealer had a gun and fired two bullets into my father."

Three weeks after Nick's murder, Ronnie went to the dingy alley where her father had lain on the cold ground, bleeding to death. She had to see for herself where he had taken his final breath.

"I can only imagine how traumatic that was for you, Veronica," Aidan said. "Being so young. Losing him that way."

For months, Ronnie had had nightmares about Nick's murder. In every dream, wearing her Janet Jackson nightgown, she'd been with her father, warning him, but he couldn't hear her as she stood by and watched him get shot.

"I try not to dwell on it," Ronnie said. "I remember the good things about my father instead."

"Such as?" Aidan took both of her hands in his with confidence, his full attention on her.

Ronnie's smile stretched from ear-to-ear. "He was the biggest baseball fan I had ever known. We went to a lot of Cleveland Indians games. I'm from Akron, Ohio," she said, clarifying the geographical distance. "Dad was always coaching me and reminding me to choke up on the bat and to step into my throws."

"You played baseball?"

"My first year in Little League, I played second base. It was my favorite position. The next year, the coach stuck me in the outfield. I wanted to quit, but Dad wouldn't let me. He told me to give it my all and be the best center outfielder I could be."

"That's excellent parenting advice."

"He didn't mean just baseball. I figured that out when I got older. Sticking it out, honoring commitments. Dad was big on loyalty and keeping promises."

Ronnie blinked back tears. A first date wasn't the time to cry.

"It didn't take much to make him happy," she said. "He found joy in little things. Going for a walk in the woods. A good steak. Working around the house. Most men bellyache about cleaning the gutters, but not my dad. He'd be on the ladder, whistling while scraping out wet, rotted leaves."

Aidan's thumbs massaged Ronnie's hands. "Those are wonderful memories, Veronica, and the best thing about a memory is that no one can take it away from you."

Talking about Nick was easier for Ronnie than talking about Vivian. Her father died trying to make the world a better place; his heroic actions were proof. Vivian died because of Ronnie's negligence, making it harder for those sweet memories of her daughter to flow.

Their food arrived, dissipating the heavy conversation, and then came dessert. The dining room had thinned out by their second cup of coffee, and Aidan drove Ronnie home.

Inside her apartment, he helped her out of her coat. "Funny how things work out. I didn't expect to see you again. The campus is big. Odds of running into you were slim."

Aidan rubbed the middle of his forehead with his finger. "I have a confession."

"No good comes from that," she jested.

He hesitated. "I was milling around outside of Anderson Hall when I saw you. I followed you into the student union."

Ronnie hung her coat in the closet. "Our bumping into each other wasn't accidental?"

"Completely premeditated. I hope you're not upset."

"Flattered is more like it. Since we're exposing our secrets, I *may* have been scoping out the quad for you, too."

Silence descended over the room, and with it, an intensity settled in Aidan's blue eyes that Ronnie felt cut through her. He pulled her against him. "I haven't told you how beautiful you look tonight."

"Actually, you did." The compliment swelled her confidence, even in that God-awful green dress.

"It's worth repeating," he said.

Ronnie rose onto the balls of her feet to meet him halfway as he bent down and gently kissed her. She scored him an eight for technique. No one gets a ten on the first try. Aidan's mouth hovered close to hers as he spoke. "I want to know everything about you, Veronica. Everything."

He pressed Ronnie's flaccid body close to his and deepened the kiss, causing certain body parts to tingle, and she bumped the rating to a ten.

# CHAPTER 16

With her fingers on the keyboard, Ronnie replayed her date with Aidan for the hundredth time that day. They had listened to classical music in his Lexus during the ride to Le Cep. His impeccable, chivalrous manners showed as he opened all the doors and helped her with her coat. He had laughed at all her jokes. They had shared dessert—her half of chocolate mousse and crepes larger than his.

It was their goodnight kiss, however, that had left her dizzy with wonder as she contemplated the evening being more than one date.

The blinking cursor on Ronnie's computer screen reminded her of a yellow signal light, warning drivers to proceed with caution.

She took a notepad from her desk drawer and drew a vertical line down the center of the page. At the top, she scribbled *pros* in one column and *cons* in the other. The antiquated method had steered her in the right direction over the years when decisions left her teetering the fence.

Ronnie listed Aidan Foster's positive attributes under the pros' column:

*Smart*
*Attractive*
*Kind*

*Conversationalist*
*Stable*

She reviewed the list and reviewed it again. Her answers lacked depth, to a degree. Aidan's good qualities were visible, yet shallow, as if they were floating on the surface.

Onto the con column.

He had flaws, everyone does, but it was too early to identify them after one date and two conversations on campus. Aidan had aced their date. He had said and done everything right from the moment he had arrived at Ronnie's apartment to dinner at Le Cep to their unforgettable kiss.

Aidan had made his feelings for Ronnie known. They'd been on her lips and in her body as the psychiatrist said goodnight without words. She'd be foolish to pass up a promising relationship with a man as captivating as Aidan who found her worthy of his time.

Tapping the pen against the desk, she hunted for a few cons to fill the empty column. There had to be something about Aidan Foster that turned Ronnie off. She was desperate to find it and make him imperfect. The beat of the writing utensil annoyed her as much as digging for an unknown that wasn't hidden. Then she found it buried in the truth as she wrote *Tony* in the con column.

Aidan's biggest downfall—the only one until now—he wasn't Tony. No man would ever be Tony Lombardo.

*That's what I need. Someone the opposite of Tony.*

Ronnie's friends' policy between her and Tony ensured that, over time, she would no longer see him as her ex-husband—the man she almost reunited with—had it not been for Natalie's rant on Christmas Day. "*You can't trust him. The next rough patch to come along, he'll take the first teeny-bopper to come his way to forget about his problems.*"

Although Ronnie had forgiven Tony for cheating on her, his infidelity was like a faded scar. She wouldn't risk going through that kind of pain ever again. Who would?

The romance between her and Tony was dead. Done. Over. Finished. No more passionate, carried away moments in her apartment. Holiday dinners at the Lombardos? Never again. No flirting. Nothing. Ronnie and Tony were friends. Colleagues. Dedicated cops. Their new relationship was nice and neat in one little box.

A knock on the door scattered Ronnie's thoughts like marbles dropped on a glass floor. She crumpled the paper and threw it into the wastebasket. "It's open."

Wanda, the receptionist, came in with a bouquet of vibrant pastel-colored flowers as big as her fist, with a giant purple bow tied around the neck of a white vase. She placed the arrangement on the desk. "Someone must really like you."

Ronnie plucked the sealed envelope from the plastic stick and took out the card. The nosey receptionist stood next to her on her tippytoes looking over her boss's shoulder for a glimpse at the mysterious sender's signature, and Ronnie pressed the stationary flat against her chest. "I can take it from here, Wanda."

The receptionist wrinkled her nose, then left the office.

Ronnie read the card. *To many more memorable evenings. Love, Aidan.*

The short, sweet, to-the-point note caused the yellow signal light to flash faster.

Ronnie went to text Aidan to thank him for the flowers, but decided a phone call was more considerate. He answered on the first ring. "Right on time."

"Excuse me?"

"I have a break between classes. I had the delivery set for exactly one o'clock. That way, I'd know you had received them."

The floral fragrance smelled like spring as Ronnie touched the velvety soft petals. "I've never seen a more beautiful bouquet, let alone gotten one. The flowers are gorgeous, Aidan."

"As gorgeous as you, I hope." His sultry voice caused her flesh to break out into goosebumps. "This means I can ask you out on another date for tomorrow afternoon."

Ronnie slouched in her chair as though she were a teenager talking to her boyfriend in her bedroom before bedtime. "I should play hard-to-get, but life's too short."

"I'll pick you up at three, and before you ask where I'm taking you, it's a surprise."

She swiveled delicately. "One hint. Please?"

He hummed tenderly. "I can't resist that sweet plea."

"I am pretty irresistible. So, the hint?"

Aidan paused. "Dress warmly."

She vetted for more details. "Something outdoors?"

"You'll find out tomorrow. Goodbye, Veronica."

"Bye, Aidan."

Ronnie ended the call. She reached into the wastebasket for the balled sheet of paper and smoothed it with her palm.

Under the pro column she wrote *Romantic*.

• • •

Tony finished his afternoon patrol and returned to the station for the meeting at the New Beginnings Youth Center. He asked Max to take a separate patrol car so he and Ronnie could ride together. Any time alone with her was one step past friends.

"You didn't send them?" Max had an expression that said he had let the cat out of the bag when he assumed Tony had sent the flowers.

The news sucker-punched Tony.

"Maybe they're from her mom," Max said. "Is it the Chief's birthday?"

"Natalie wouldn't send flowers to Ronnie's wake. And her birthday is in March."

Curiosity and dread tangled at the thought of another man vying for Ronnie's affection.

*Who is this guy? Where did she meet him?* He had too many questions that needed answers.

Tony slapped Max on his back. "I'll meet you at the center."

He almost believed Max's ridiculous notion that Natalie had sent the flowers until he went inside Ronnie's office. The invisible sign only Tony saw above the bouquet flashed garish neon lettering that read, Guy, Guy,

Guy, and he acknowledged the massive arrangement on steroids. "Nice flowers."

Ronnie sniffed a budded pink rose cupped in her palm. "Yes, they are."

He tried reading the card held in place on the plastic stick, but she subtly turned the vase around so that he couldn't see the sender's name.

Pretending to check emails on her phone, Ronnie said, "We should head over to the center."

"Max already left. You can ride with me."

Winning Ronnie back wouldn't happen overnight. Of all the obstacles standing in Tony's way, he hadn't foreseen another man being one of them.

In the patrol car on the way to the center, Ronnie stared out the passenger window. The quietness as Tony drove made him feel as if he and Ronnie had regressed. One step forward, two steps back.

Tony knew exactly how Ronnie felt at Chet's wedding when she saw him with Brianna. He felt the same way visualizing his ex-wife with another man, but he needed to get a read on his competition, every detail, to know what he was up against.

"Who sent the flowers?" he asked nonchalantly.

"A friend," Ronnie answered.

*She's on to me.* "Maggie Richmond?" Tony guessed, baiting her.

"No." Ronnie hesitated, debating whether to disclose his name. "Aidan Foster."

Tony hummed as if he were thinking. "Who's he?"

"A professor at the college."

*Making the rounds with the faculty already?* He took a small breath. *Take it easy, Tony.*

"He's got good taste. The flowers, I mean."

Ronnie's grimace showed her agitation. "We had dinner last night."

A date. She went on one date, and the guy had sent her flowers—and not the wimpy, wilted ones from the grocery store. Judging by the bouquet, this Aidan had paid a small fortune.

Tony loosely handled the steering wheel. "Where'd you go?"

Ronnie sighed softly, implying she was tired of playing twenty questions. "Le Cep."

"The French place?" Anyone who could afford Le Cep had more than a few bucks in the bank. "Pretty pricy for a first date." He assumed as much.

"I suppose. I didn't look at the prices."

*That's what Ronnie is into these days—guys with fat wallets.*

The meadow of flowers on her desk implied Aidan had it bad for Ronnie. Question was, did she feel the same about him?

Grand gestures like dinners at expensive French restaurants and breathtaking flowers were a way to a woman's heart. But Ronnie was different. That stuff didn't impress her. She'd choose takeout over fine dining any day. Tony and Ronnie went back decades; he had known everything there was to know about her. Aidan had been on one date with her. There was no comparison.

"I didn't know professors made that kind of money," Tony said.

Ronnie loosened her rigid posture. "All right, Tony. Point heard and received."

"What do you mean?" He played dumb, but she saw through his facade.

"From what I've observed, Aidan is quite comfortable financially. He's a nice guy, and we had a nice time last night. End of story."

Tony stared through the windshield and mumbled, "A nice time."

"You and I agreed to be friends," Ronnie said, reminding him.

Again with the infamous F-Word. It sounded worse every time she said it. "Yeah, I remember. And as your friend, can't you tell me about the guy you're dating?" Sarcasm stung his tongue.

"Not when you act like that."

Ronnie had that look in her eye, the one that said she was warming up for a fight. Her snippy tone could reach firecracker status in seconds. Fast. Loud. Fierce. Her sharp words could saw a person in half.

Tony cooled the flames while faking his way through the lie. "Ronnie, I'm fine with it. You're free to date whoever you want."

Her expression said she believed otherwise. "Let's not talk about Aidan. We're almost at the center."

Tony stopped at a red light. "Your call, but like I said, I'm fine with it."

*They're right. It does get easier with each lie.*

• • •

Tony and Ronnie joined Max inside the center as the woman behind the glass window phoned the director's office. The door opened a minute later, and a short, stocky woman came into the lobby.

"Paula Crowe. Great to finally meet you." The director shook Ronnie's hand with both of hers as if the chief were a savior. "Your partnership is a godsend."

Ronnie introduced Paula to Tony and Max, and the three of them followed the director as she delivered the bad news.

"The state's been chopping our funding with a butcher knife for years. We've cut here and there to survive, but this time," Paula said with a shake of her head, "they've gone too far. Seventy-five percent of our funding—gone."

"Did they give a reason?" Tony asked.

"Just the same vague excuse. 'There's not enough money in the budget,' which is code for, 'get someone else to bail you out.'"

Tony grunted. "Then where are my tax dollars going?"

"Good question. I can tell you this, they're not helping nonprofits like the center. Think of us as the third-class passengers on the Titanic. And we all know how that story ended."

"But these kids need help," Max said.

Paula led the trio through the swinging double-doors and into the facility's epicenter. "As long as state workers and politicians get their pay raises and hold on to their seats, they don't care about teen drug addicts. We're on our own if we want to stay open. I'm kicking myself for not contacting private donors a long time ago."

Ronnie, Tony, and Max toured the center as Paula outlined the program's principal objectives: counseling, mentoring, and college and career advisement.

"The staff believes in these kids. It made me so angry they had to take a pay cut, I could spit nails, but not one person complained," Paula said. "They encourage the kids to not let their past dictate their futures, letting them know we all make mistakes, but there are second chances."

Tony and Ronnie looked at each other as if Paula were talking about marriage.

"What demographic of kids end up here?" Ronnie asked.

Paula tucked a curly strand of copper-colored hair behind her ear. "Contrary to popular belief, the majority are from middle-class, two-parent homes in the 'burbs. Why they use varies. Everything from typical peer pressure to neglectful parents. Others are curious and get hooked."

Tony hadn't thrown his full support behind the cause Ronnie was so passionate about. Selfish motives had him volunteer for the drug task force, and he felt like a fraud as Ronnie listened intently to Paula.

The director gathered the teens from the homework and counseling rooms and had them sit in an open area with rows of chairs. Using two fingers, she blew a shrill whistle at the three boys shooting hoops. They jogged down the basketball court and joined their peers.

Paula cupped her hands around her mouth. "All right, settle down," she shouted over the chatter. "This is Police Chief Veronica Callahan and Officers Tony Lombardo and Max Brody."

They each flicked a slight wave.

"The Hilton Police Department is partnering with us to raise awareness about the center. I want you to give them your full attention." Paula stepped aside as the teens applauded.

"Hi, I'm Veronica, but my friends call me Ronnie." Her smile permitted them to do the same. "We're excited to be here and are looking forward to getting to know you all."

Pride ballooned within Tony. Ronnie had a way with kids. She treated them like human beings, meeting them at their level. She was in uniform, but you'd never know it by the way she interacted with them.

"You should be proud of yourselves. It takes a lot of guts to get help. No matter what anyone says about you, you can turn your life around and go after your dreams."

Tony knew Ronnie and Vivian would've had a close mother-daughter bond. No matter what Ronnie believed, she'd been the best mother to their little girl.

Ronnie hopped back onto the table, her legs dangling. "We all know someone who has struggled with drug addiction, whether personally or indirectly."

A skinny boy with glasses blurted, "What about you?"

Paula dipped her head at the teen with shaggy blonde hair and black roots. "Kevin. Your manners."

"Sorry." He raised a hand, and his arm was marred with reddish skin bruised from needle marks. Ronnie called on him, and he asked again, "Who do you know that's an addict?"

"I have a friend from high school whose brother overdosed. He spent his whole adult life as an addict. He'd be clean for a while, then go back to drugs, until it killed him. One morning, an employee from a UPS store found his body behind the building."

Kevin raised his hand. "Why did he start using?"

"My friend, his sister. She gave him a joint one day after school, thinking it would be funny to see him high. To this day, she blames herself."

A girl who belonged in a cheerleading uniform raised her hand.

Ronnie pointed to her. "What's your name?"

"Maddie," she said.

It was hard to imagine a pretty kid like her doing drugs.

"Hi, Maddie. What's your question?"

"Did anyone close to you die from drugs?"

Ronnie hesitated, lightly swinging her legs. "Yes, but he didn't use."

The girl's long brown ponytail on the top of her head swung like a pendulum. "I don't get it. How could he be an addict if he didn't use?"

"My dad was a detective. A drug dealer shot and killed him."

A redheaded teen with a buzz cut raised his hand. "Did they ever catch the guy who did it?"

"He committed suicide after killing my father. He was only nineteen. Nineteen years old and his life ended because of drugs. Because one day he wanted to see what it was like to get high. Because of drugs, a woman is without her son. I don't have a father. And my mother buried her husband."

*Keep going, baby. You got this.*

Tony's inner encouragement was all he could do to help Ronnie get through the painful memory of losing Nick.

"Have you ever thrown a stone into a lake or river?" she asked the group.

A few kids nodded.

"The stone is small. It doesn't seem like it can do much damage. But after it hits the water, what happens?"

Kevin went to shout out the answer, then raised his hand. "It makes a ripple."

"Exactly. The ripple multiplies, becoming wider and wider. That joint or painkiller or cocaine line won't ripple unless you take it. Doing drugs is like a ripple. It affects everyone around you."

Ronnie spoke to the group for another ten minutes before she and Max mingled with the kids, while Tony felt more like a security guard. The teens had baggage. Lots of it. How could he relate to them? What was he supposed to say to a fourteen-year-old who had snorted coke every day? Or popped OxyContin as if it were candy.

"Here I am, five feet from a cop without an urge to bolt."

Tony turned around and saw a boy dribbling a basketball. It was now or never. "Hey. I'm Tony."

"Jesse."

"How long have you been at the center?" Good question. Simple and nonintrusive. Better than, "What did you get hooked on?"

Jesse stopped dribbling the ball and rested it on his hip. "A year."

The teen talked to Tony about his mom, Doreen, and his sister, Lola. He mentioned wanting to play Major League Baseball, but knew the narrow path of that dream. He planned on one day counseling teens who had believed the lie that drugs solve problems.

Tony listened more than he talked, seeing past the teen's drug addiction as Ronnie and Paula joined him.

"Dude, if it weren't for this place, I'd be like your friend's brother," Jesse said to Ronnie, "lying in some parking lot dead. It's because of Paula I'm clean. She rides me pretty hard, but it's only because she cares."

The director slung her arm around the teen. "You've grown on me, Jesse. I'm proud of all the kids, but this one right here," she said, jiggling his shoulder, "he's come a long way. A far cry from his first month."

Jesse covered an eye, grinning with embarrassment.

"He tried making life miserable for me. It didn't take him long to find out about my tenacity. Then one day he broke down and cried like a baby. We both knew that was the first day of his new life."

If Vivian were alive, she'd be a few years younger than Jesse, dealing with the same peer pressure he had. Tony hoped his daughter would've made the right choices. He couldn't bear to see her live with the consequences, like the kids around him.

Driving back to the station, Tony couldn't stop thinking about the center. It was a lifeline for people like Jesse. If it closed, kids right now struggling with drug addictions may not live to see their eighteenth birthday.

"Thinking about the center?" Ronnie said to Tony.

He looked at her with a sidelong glance. "You know me so well."

Tony and Ronnie had a kooky ESP connection between them. They finished each other's sentences and used the same words to describe something. It was freaky.

Tony hit the steering wheel with his palm. "There's gotta be a way to keep the center open. What about what Paula said about private donors?"

"We don't have time to fill a financial hole that wide. The center's fiscal year ends May thirty-first. If the state doesn't reconsider by then, we're screwed."

Tony wagged his finger. "Not if we do a blitz."

Ronnie rolled her eyes. "Forget about football, Lombardo. Now's not the time."

"You have been following the game. Impressive, but no. I didn't mean football. What about a fundraiser? A glamourous event for rich people with lots of money to blow on a good cause."

Tony waited for Ronnie to commend his idea as brilliant or call him a dope. She clapped her hands once, shouting, "Like a gala!"

"Exactly. Black-tie. Expensive dinner."

She added, "With an auction and lots of media coverage."

Tony and Ronnie looked at each other simultaneously and spoke in unison. "Joey."

They high-fived each other. Tony entwined his fingers between hers, holding their joined hands in his lap.

"Tony, don't," she said, loosening her hand.

He didn't know what was sadder: the dulcet tone in her voice or how cold it felt when she pulled her hand away from him. "Sorry," he said, gripping the steering wheel. "Got a little excited, is all."

Ronnie went quiet and stared out the passenger window the rest of the way back to the station.

# CHAPTER 17

Ronnie's suggestion for a fundraiser left Paula Crowe ecstatic. Time being their adversary, Ronnie called on their biggest weapon to spread the word. The media.

Tony, Max, Chet, and the rest of the drug task force officers waited with the reporters in the conference room for the presser to begin as Ronnie and Paula came inside.

"Thank you for coming," Ronnie said from behind the lectern, with Paula at her side. Photographers hiding behind their cameras took a barrage of pictures from different angles. "I'm pleased to announce the Hilton Police Department has partnered with the New Beginnings Youth Center. For those of you who are unfamiliar with the nonprofit organization, the center offers counseling, mentoring, and career advisement to recovering teen substance abusers. The timing of this partnership is impeccable. We've learned the center is in jeopardy of closing because of cuts in state funding. We're asking the Hilton community to help us to keep that from happening. Joining us today is the center's director, Paula Crowe."

Ronnie and Paula switched spots. Scanning the audience, her eyes locked with Tony's. She quickly turned her attention back to Paula, pretending she hadn't seen him wink at her.

"I've been the center's director for fifteen years," Paula said. "Our program has saved so many young lives. Kids who believed they wouldn't amount to anything are now in college. Many have careers and families of their own. But what about the kids who won't get that chance if the center closes?" She waved a pointed finger at Ronnie. "Because of this woman and her officers, the center has an excellent shot at staying open."

Paula watched her hands grip the sides of the lectern.

"As a former drug addict, I know what these kids are going through. It took me a long time to get clean, longer than I had wanted. If there had been a place like the center when I needed help, maybe I would've made better choices. I believe every kid has potential. Each one deserves the same opportunities as the sober kid. Look, I'm the captain of the ship. If it goes down, I go down with it. Here's hoping it doesn't come to that."

Joey raised a hand with a pen between his fingers. "Joe Lombardo, *Hilton Herald*. Ms. Crowe, there's talk about a fundraiser. Can you give us the details?"

"Because of the drastic cut in funding, we need private donors. The fundraiser is a black-tie dinner and auction. We're asking the community for support, individuals—large and small businesses—anyone willing to help. All proceeds go directly to the center and future education and outreach programs."

Joey butted in, cutting off the reporter behind him. "When's the fundraiser?"

"Ah," Paula hesitated, "this kind of event takes a year to plan. We don't have that much time. We're aiming for early May."

"That's three months away," Joey said.

Paula bobbed her head. "Yep. The donors are out there, but we need your help."

A woman from Eyewitness News 5 spoke quickly, preventing Joey from dominating the interview. "What about ticket prices? And where's the fundraiser going to be held?"

"We're working on all the specifics. We'll have more information soon."

Paula answered two additional questions, then turned the presser over to Ronnie, who thanked the reporters as they left the conference room.

Tony slapped Joey on the back as he walked by. "Thanks, little brother."

Joey reciprocated the goodbye with a punch to his big brother's arm. "You owe me."

Tony approached Ronnie and Paula at the lectern. "Nice job up there, Paula."

"Thanks, Officer Lombardo. This fundraiser will save the center, I just know it! With all this publicity, I can see a deluge of donors! Chief Callahan, I can't thank you enough."

Ronnie stared at her ex-husband with admiration. "Thank Tony. He came up with the idea."

"It was a team effort," Tony said, then tapped his finger against his belt.

"I know that look, Lombardo," Ronnie said and pointed to her head. "What's going on in there?"

"We want big donors, right?"

"The bigger the better," Paula said.

"Exactly. People with a grand in their wallet as if it were pocket change want to see where their money is going. It's about more than a building staying open. It needs to be personal."

Ronnie trundled a hand. "As in?"

"A real-life example. Say, for instance, one of the teens as a guest speaker."

Ronnie dragged out her words. "You. Are. Good."

Tony playfully punched her arm. "Don't sound so surprised."

Ronnie tapped her chin, smiling, as she glanced up in thought. "I see event planning in your future, Officer Lombardo."

"Thanks for the vote of confidence, but I'll stick to being a cop." He grinned. "How about Jesse? He'd be perfect."

"Yes!" Paula's copper curls bounced as she shot her arms up like a football referee, signaling a touchdown. "He'll do it. I know he will. If he doesn't, I'll force him!" She let out a hearty chuckle. "I have a ton of work to do and not much time to do it. I'll call Jesse. That'll be one thing to cross off the list." She whacked Tony on the back. "You're a keeper."

Tony and Ronnie headed to her office, brainstorming logistics. Venues, caterers, and businesses to hit up for donations.

"We can count on Dad," Tony said. "He's always willing to help community projects."

"Do you think he'll donate to the auction, too?"

"I don't see why not. Custom cabinets are a big-ticket item. The kind we need to hit our goal."

Tony leaned against Ronnie's doorway. "Since we're on a roll, I hate to see it end. Let's head over to my apartment; I'll spring for a pizza. You pick the toppings. Even if it's pineapple and ham."

"On the *whole* pizza?" she said with a smirk.

His mouth curled into a playful cringe. When it came to pizza, Tony turned into a carnivore who liked his pie loaded with every variety of meat.

"You can't say you don't like it if you've never tried it."

When they were married, every time they ordered a pizza, Ronnie had hounded him about tasting the Hawaiian-inspired dish. She'd hold a slice to his mouth and beg him to take a bite, but he refused. He wished he had appeased her back then. "Okay. I'll do it for you, but only for you." Tony stepped backward into the hallway. "I'll order the pizza. Meet me at my place at six."

"Tony, wait." She fidgeted with her fingers. "I'm sorry, but I can't."

"Ronnie, it's work. I'm not trying anything here. I'm cool with the whole 'friends' thing." *Liar, liar,* his brain taunted.

"It's not that. I can't come over because I have plans with Aidan."

"Oh." *Another date. How many was that? Two now?* "Where's the professor taking you this time?"

"The Carnegie Museum of Art. There's a new exhibit featuring work from the neo-impressionist era he wants me to see."

Tony's face contorted with confusion. "You don't like art."

"It's not on my top ten list, but one evening won't kill me. Who knows?" she said with a bouncy shrug. "It might grow on me. I can take up painting as a hobby."

Tony feared Ronnie was turning into this guy's puppet. French restaurants. Art shows. What about her interests? "You're certainly becoming one for the finer things in life. A pizza from Johnny Brock's is hardly in the same league as art from the neo-impressionist era."

"That's your opinion." Ronnie's eyes harden. "If you want, I can give you a full report of my evening in the morning."

Her sarcastic offer scraped his heart. Tony didn't care about art or want a play-by-play of her date with Aidan. All he wanted was Ronnie at his apartment, sharing a pizza with him.

The writing on the wall said Aidan wasn't going away any time soon. As Tony had done and probably would do again, he hid his jealousy, poking through his spurious smile.

"Can't wait to hear all about it. Chief."

• • •

Ronnie left the station and drove to her apartment as her thoughts about her relationship with Aidan took over.

His surprise on Saturday of a horse-drawn carriage ride was one for the books. They had snuggled in the red velvet seat with a blanket over their laps, eating gourmet cheeses and chocolate-covered strawberries and drinking wine. The ride took them through the north end of town lined with Victorian homes and century-year-old buildings safe and sound under preservation.

Ronnie wondered if a man like Aidan, clothed in culture, could adapt to an afternoon at PNC Park for a Pirates game or eat takeout in sweatpants while watching a cheesy 80's movie.

Instead, she had to rush home and dress her best to view artwork she didn't understand. Tony's offer of pizza and gala planning sounded much more fun.

In the two dates Ronnie had with Aidan, the subject of marriage and children hadn't been broached. For all Aidan knew, Ronnie was a single, career-focused woman who wasn't ready to settle down with a family. Her reluctance to disclose her marriage to Tony and Vivian's death became easier. Eventually, Ronnie would tell Aidan about her past but convinced herself now was not the time. It was only their third date.

She came to a stop sign. Truck headlights blazed through the back window, blinding her. She flipped the rearview mirror up and continued driving.

The truck followed her—too closely. If Ronnie slammed on the brakes, the front end would be in her back seat. She refused to speed because some idiot was tailing her bumper.

The driver flicked the headlights, trying to communicate with her.

She double-checked her lights. On. Her blinker. Check. She listened for a flat tire. Nothing but smooth pavement. No warning on the dashboard that a door was partially open.

"What?" She lifted her palm, questioning him as if he could hear her.

The truck swerved from side-to-side. Ronnie pulled over to get his license plate number, but he made a sharp left turn onto Davidson Road.

# CHAPTER 18

Once the media ran with the news about the imminent gala, ticket sales soared and generous proprietors offered services to offset the costs. The owner of a vintage warehouse had waived the thousand-dollar rental fee to hold the gala there. A rental company had committed to supplying chairs, tables, lighting, and decorations. Also at no charge. Thanks to John Lombardo's connections, Pittsburgh's most renowned catering company had agreed to feed five hundred guests in exchange for free advertising on every piece of promotional material from now until the big night.

Joey owned the story on the center's quest to remain open, becoming one of the *Hilton Herald*'s rising journalists as his articles on the facility's history and Paula Crowe's years of drug addiction graced the front page.

As Paula updated Ronnie on a weekly basis regarding gala business, it wasn't long before their joint effort to save the center grew into a friendship. She had called Ronnie at the station one afternoon with new donations to add to the auction block while weaving Tony's name into the conversation.

"Uh, what's the story with you and Officer Lombardo?" Paula asked, her tone eager for the dirt.

"There isn't one," Ronnie answered, as if her seven-year marriage to Tony had never existed. "I'm his boss."

Paula laughed. "Not so fast. I got eyes; I see how he looks at you."

"Really, Dr. Phil. How does Tony look at me?"

"Like he wants to rip off your uniform and throw you onto the desk."

What was funnier about Paula's speculation was that it was most likely true. Ronnie knew all she had to do was give her ex-husband the okay and they'd be back together faster than a sprinting jackrabbit.

"Come on, girlfriend. Any secret office fling you want to divulge? I won't say a word to anyone. I promise."

The director was bound to find out Ronnie and Tony were once Mr. and Mrs. Lombardo. It was better for Ronnie to spill the beans than for Paula to hear it from Tony.

"Brace yourself, Paula."

"Sounds juicy. Are we talking like a trashy romance novel?"

"Sorry to disappoint you." Ronnie paused. "Tony's my ex-husband."

Silence stretched on Paula's end, making Ronnie think she had dropped the phone. "You're pulling my leg."

"Nope. Married seven years. Divorced for eleven."

"You'd never know it. You two act as if you like each other."

"We do. We're friends. We agreed to put the past behind us."

"If I had to work with my ex, I'd kill him." Paula laughed so hard she snorted. "Crap. I just made a death threat to a cop."

"I'll let it slide this time."

"Ronnie, why on earth did you let Tony go? He's delicious. I'd have no problem waking up next to that every morning."

Neither had Ronnie. She remembered him wearing a Steelers T-shirt and striped boxers to bed and how his ice-cold feet tucked against her legs. The man had refused to wear socks, but she didn't care. It was an excuse to get as close to her as possible.

She broke away from the memory. "Paula, there's more to marriage than looks and sex."

"I know, but it helps." She let out a raunchy laugh.

Ronnie had dreamed of having a man like Tony for a husband. He was fun and made her laugh. They had shared similar interests and opinions, from sports to politics. Their dedication to the force was the driving connector between them. Tony had been the only person she could confide in about the job's grueling moments. But aside from law enforcement, commonalities, and the physical stuff, there was more to Tony Lombardo only Ronnie had seen and experienced that she could never express in words, and that was how he made her feel safe without even trying.

Ronnie checked her phone for the time. "I have to go, Paula. Aidan's picking me up at the station."

"Who's Aidan?"

"Just a guy I'm seeing."

*Just a guy?* The flippant remark was a slap in the face to the man she'd been dating for five weeks. Aidan had wined and dined her with exquisite outings to the symphony and art museum, spent a boatload of money on extravagant flowers, and lavished her with adoring compliments.

"Bet Hottie's not happy about that," Paula said.

"Tony's fine with it."

*He'll never be fine with it, and you know it,* Ronnie's brain chided.

Paula's tone flattened. "Sure he is. And I believe in unicorns, too."

Ronnie didn't have time to tell Paula about the Tony and Ronnie anthology. Her divorce was a conversation for another day. "Tony and I are friends. That's all there is to it."

"Which is a subtle way of saying you two still have the hots for each other."

"Goodbye, Paula." Ronnie drew out her friend's name in a sweet farewell.

"Keep me posted." Paula snickered. "About the gala, too."

Ronnie changed out of her uniform and into a pair of jeans and a sweater, reapplied her makeup, brushed her hair, and then went into the lobby where she waited for Aidan.

He arrived promptly at five o'clock wearing brown pants, a tan cashmere sweater, and a black overcoat with leather gloves, which posed the question: Did the man own a single pair of jeans, a shabby sweatshirt, and grubby sneakers?

Aidan kissed her hello and did an obligatory scan of the station. "This is where you work."

The unimpressed tone was to be expected from a dignified man like Dr. Aidan Foster. Blue-collar and crime clashed with his world of wine and art.

Ronnie looked around the lobby with pride for the law. "Yep. This is where it all happens."

Most significant others would have requested a tour. Aidan hadn't, and Ronnie didn't offer.

She and Aidan said good night to Wanda at the front desk. Ronnie was halfway out the door when a man's voice bellowed, "Got a minute, Chief?"

The moment she had dreaded snuck up on her like a killer in a horror movie. Her ex-husband postured himself like an imposing father inspecting the new guy taking out his daughter.

Wanda's rattling throat noise implied she'd seen this coming. Give her a bucket of popcorn, and she was all set for the show.

Ronnie switched to Chief Mode. She was the department's top brass. There was no room for intimidation from her subordinates, especially Tony. "Yes, Officer Lombardo. What is it?"

"I need to update you on the health classes at the schools."

"Thank you. I appreciate your efficiency, but we'll discuss it on Monday." Tony waited for Ronnie to introduce him to the guy she'd been hiding from him for over a month. "Officer Tony Lombardo, this is Dr. Aidan Foster."

Aidan extended his arm, clueless. "It's a pleasure to meet you."

Tony peered down at Aidan's gloved hand, then reluctantly shook it while staring at Ronnie but speaking to Aidan. "Where you two off to?"

"Vinoski Winery in Rostraver," Aidan said. "Have you ever been there?"

"A winery?" Tony cackled, pointing rudely at Ronnie. "Keep an eye on this one, Dr. Foster."

Aidan's forehead wrinkled as his smile drooped. "Pardon?"

Ronnie hooked Tony's bicep and pulled him aside. She had gotten drunk once, and he made her out to be a lush. Her voice ran deep in a seething whisper. "That was uncalled for."

"Lighten up. It was a joke."

"You may think you're the next Jerry Seinfeld, but I don't find you funny. Keep your inappropriate comments to yourself, Lombardo. That's an order."

Tony folded his arms. "Too afraid to let the *uptight* professor know you got hammered? Does he find that kind of behavior *vulgar?*" he asked with a snooty accent.

Aidan pulled back his coat sleeve, revealing his Rolex. "Veronica, we should get going. It's an hour's drive to Rostraver."

"I'm coming." Ronnie glared at Tony as if she were burning a hole in his head. "I'm warning you, Lombardo. Watch your mouth."

She returned to Aidan's side and held his hand. Her affection rendered a smile from her boyfriend and a snarl from her ex-husband.

"If I were you, Aidan, I'd take the wheel on the way back," Tony said.

Aidan's eyes narrowed. He stepped forward and came nose-to-nose with Tony. "If you have something to say, I suggest you be a man and say it."

Ronnie moved between the men. They looked as if they were squaring off for an after-school fight with a pregame of trash talking. "Aidan, Tony's just bantering. We all poke fun at each other. It comes with being a cop." She turned to Tony and spoke through gritted teeth. "Isn't that right, Officer Lombardo?"

*Please, Tony, don't. Don't let Aidan know we were married. If you care about me at all, you'll keep that big Italian trap of yours shut!*

Tony stared Aidan down as if the psychiatrist were a deplorable thief. To some degree he was. He had taken his woman from him. "Whatever you say, Chief."

Aidan grinned, artificial as plastic flowers. "I suppose I'll have to adapt to police vernacular. Won't I, Officer Lombardo?"

Tony's eyes begged Ronnie not to leave with her yuppie date, and she looked away, knowing the power they had on her. She slipped her hand inside of Aidan's. "Come on, let's go."

They passed by Wanda, the first link in the gossip chain with a front-row seat to what was sure to be the rumor of the day.

Ronnie wondered what made her let Aidan pick her up at the station. Then she remembered. He had insisted.

• • •

Ronnie read the brochure aloud as she and Aidan walked through the Castle at the Vinoski Winery. "It says there are thirty-four rooms, including fourteen bathrooms, eight bedrooms, and three living rooms." She folded the pamphlet. "Phew. I'd hate to be the cleaning lady."

Aidan ignored her bad joke, and she continued reading.

"No two rooms have the same ceiling or crown molding."

Aidan hadn't spoken since he and Ronnie had left the station, making for a long car ride. Tony's rude behavior poorly reflected law enforcement and her leadership as chief. She continued paraphrasing the brochure.

"Jay Lustig was the original owner of the Castle before becoming an owner of the Pirates. Turns out he was a big baseball fan." Ronnie displayed a goofy grin. "I like him already."

She was practically talking to herself and pointed to the event listing. "Look at this. They're having a Murder Mystery Dinner next month. That sounds like fun."

Aidan didn't answer.

"Let's do it. Of course, I am a cop," she bragged facetiously. "You know, all those clues. I have an advantage."

"Yes, you do." Aidan's tone was colder than the temperature outside.

At the wine tasting station, he swished a goblet of Cabernet in a circular motion to release air. Before performing step two—the sniffing process—

he placed the glass on the rustic ledge. "What did Tony mean about keeping an eye on you?"

Ronnie wished she had smooth things over on the way to the winery. "I told you, Aidan, it was harmless bantering."

"Veronica, I'm a psychiatrist. I can read body language better than anyone. Tony has a problem with you."

Life would be less complicated if that were true. Dealing with a hostile officer such as Ortiz was easier than dealing with one who was in love with her.

Ronnie picked up her goblet. "It's an inside joke that stopped being funny. Nothing more."

"Care to share it?"

Ronnie scrambled for an explanation that didn't include her and Tony almost sleeping together had it not been for her hugging the porcelain throne. "I'm not a big drinker, and since we were going to a winery… well, it was ironic. Kind of humorous when you think about it."

Aidan forced the goblet down as she went to take a sip of wine. "Why didn't you tell me?"

"You're a wine connoisseur. I didn't want to embarrass you."

"Veronica, we've been dating for five weeks, and you're keeping secrets from me. That's unacceptable."

"It wasn't malicious, honest."

Honesty. Ronnie hadn't been honest with Aidan since they had met. Did that make her a liar? Her secrets were like cancer, eating away at her.

"If you kept something as insignificant as not drinking wine from me, then what else are you hiding?"

Hiding. It sounded so sneaky. Dirty, too. Her distaste for alcohol hadn't compared to the truth about her and Tony.

"Veronica, it's clear there's more than a friendship between us. But if you don't feel the same way about me as I do about you, we can't continue this relationship."

Ronnie placed her hands on his chest and looked up at him with adoring eyes. "Oh, Aidan. Do you really think I'd still be seeing you if I didn't have feelings for you?"

But her declaration came up short in quashing Aidan's suspicions. "What's the story between you and Tony? I don't doubt there's one. Not with the amount of hostility you two exhibited."

Ronnie's stomach plummeted, the same feeling akin to falling in a dream. Telling Aidan she and Tony had been married was one revelation Ronnie wanted done on her terms when she was ready, and she was far from ready.

For five weeks, she had hidden a substantial piece of her life from Aidan. Now she risked losing him because of it.

"Aidan... the truth is... Tony and I...." Ronnie's parched throat wouldn't allow her to say the words, "were married."

Aidan slouched, staring at Ronnie. It was the first time she had seen him in poor posture. "You and Tony, what? Dated?"

Ronnie swallowed to lubricate her throat. "We were married."

Aidan stepped back from her, as if she had a severe case of body odor.

"It was a long time ago," Ronnie said in her defense. "We've been divorced for eleven years."

It could've been a hundred years and it wouldn't have made up for her lying to Aidan. "Now you work together. How sweet."

"It's a professional relationship. Amicable. We're friends."

"Officer Lombardo didn't seem too friendly to me," Aidan bit back.

Ronnie laughed nervously to disguise what Aidan knew all along. "Tony's like a big brother. He's Italian. You know how they are. That whole protect the family thing they do."

"I'm not a fool, Veronica. He may act all Mafia protective with his actual family, but you're his ex-wife. That little show back at the station wasn't typical police bantering. He doesn't approve of you dating and wants you back."

Of course, Tony wanted her back. Otherwise, he wouldn't have acted like the jealous ex-husband that he was. Then there was Vivian, Ronnie's darling angel. The best parts of her and Tony that made up a perfect little girl, whose life had ended before it had had a chance to begin.

Suddenly, Ronnie's secret marriage didn't compare to the torture of losing a child. Her moist eyes stung as a tear ran down her cheek. "We had a daughter. Vivian. She was three and a half when she died."

Aidan closed his eyes as if admonishing himself for being too hard on Ronnie. "Sweetheart, I'm so sorry. Come, let's sit down." Aidan led Ronnie to a table. "Was she sick?"

Ronnie shook her head. "No. A car hit her."

Aidan groaned, as if he felt the torment that had been living in her for more than a decade. "How did it happen?"

Ronnie relived that fateful day in August, from the double shift Ortiz had blackmailed her into working to the moment she had dozed off and Vivian ran into the street. Aidan cringed, as if he had witnessed the deadly hit.

"I let my guilt about what I had done consume me. I couldn't be around Tony. All I did was work. We went from a happy family to two strangers." Ronnie glanced at her shaky hands. "He wound up cheating on me, and I divorced him."

Ronnie had exposed all her skeletons in the closet. Her father's murder. Tony's affair. Vivian's fatal accident. It wasn't until that night at the winery that she realized the burdensome toll of those secrets until she'd been honest with Aidan, and he held her while she cried in the tasting room. Every tear felt like a cleanse, ridding her body of toxins. She mourned Vivian every day. There were times when her loss hit her hard, like tonight. Once she had stopped crying and rested in Aidan's embrace, he stood her to her feet and drove her home.

At her apartment, Ronnie kissed Aidan with an overwhelming urgency. It wasn't their normal goodnight kiss. Removing his coat, then hers, her body cried out for his.

"It's been an emotional night for you, Veronica," Aidan said, holding her tight, as if he were afraid to let go. "We don't have to if you're not ready."

"I don't want to wait. I can't." Ronnie kissed Aidan, winding her leg around his, and stroked his calf with her foot. She needed someone to show love to. Someone alive who could reciprocate that love.

They went into the bedroom. Their clothes on the floor made a path to the bed, where he answered her need. More than once.

While Ronnie hadn't planned on making love to Aidan that night, sometimes the best moments in life were the unplanned ones.

# CHAPTER 19

The sun hung on the horizon like a giant, bright orange spot as Ronnie ran down Grimsby Avenue. The mild temperature for late March was a sign of warmer days ahead.

She hadn't been on a three-mile run since returning to Hilton, and it showed in her lackluster performance as her pace slowed halfway through. Sweat dripped down her face. The crisp air burned her lungs while thoughts of work and her personal life clogged her mind.

Five weeks until the gala. Her students had returned from spring break tanner. She and Aidan had added physical intimacy to their relationship since their date at Vinoski Winery.

Back at her apartment, Ronnie gasped for air as she clocked the run at thirty-two minutes, six minutes slower than her personal best. The embarrassing time needed work.

After taking a shower, she cooked scrambled eggs and toast, which, by a miracle, she didn't burn, and brewed a cup of coffee. While eating breakfast, she read Joey's latest gala article in the *Hilton Herald*.

Ronnie deserved a day off from the station—especially on her milestone birthday.

Forty.

Natalie had sent Ronnie the same gift she had ever year since her daughter was eighteen. A greeting card with a check inside for one hundred dollars. Underneath Hallmark's birthday wishes was a mediocre, sentimental message from her mother.

*Happy Birthday, Veronica. It's hard to believe you're 40. Have a wonderful day. You deserve all the happiness in the world. Take care and hope to see you soon. Mom.*

Natalie had signed her name, not Graham's. She never did.

After breakfast, Ronnie went to the grocery store to stock up on the essential food items of bread, coffee, microwaveable meals, and potato chips. She then cleaned the apartment from top to bottom, scrubbed the kitchen and bathroom floors, and did two loads of laundry, all by one o'clock. Her birthday dinner with Aidan at Marco's Italian Ristorante wasn't until six.

Ronnie propped her feet on the coffee table and turned on the television. There was nothing on but frivolous soap operas and goofy game shows where contestants made fools out of themselves for money. She turned off the TV and went into her bedroom to retrieve her gun from the safe inside her closet. Practicing her shooting skills at the firing range was a productive way to spend the afternoon.

Her phone buzzed with a cryptic text from Captain Rosario. *Need u @ the station. Urgent.*

She frantically typed, *What's going on?*

The phone buzzed. *Tell u when u get here.*

She typed, *On my way,* and left for the station.

Birthday or not, when duty called, Ronnie answered. Driving to the station, she listened to each local radio station for breaking news reports. Lieutenant Mills could handle an administrative emergency, which meant something severe had happened that required her presence. Was one of her officers in an accident? Or shot? She floored the gas pedal, driving twenty miles over the speed limit.

Ronnie power-walked past Wanda at the front desk as the receptionist leaned over the edge and shouted, "Captain's waiting for you in the conference room!"

Ronnie threw a hand in the air, signaling she had heard Wanda. Rounding the corner, she burst through the door and into the conference room as a manly shout of "Surprise!" made her jump.

Officers and detectives applauded her, whistling. On the table was a cake with white frosting and her picture on it with *Happy Birthday, Chief!* Wanda came in with a lighter and set forty candles ablaze that took Ronnie two tries to blow out.

After cake and small talk, the guys returned to work while Tony stayed behind to clean up. Ronnie rested a curled fist under her chin. "This has your name written all over it."

"There was no way I'd let you sneak under the radar," he said, collecting the paper plates. "Not on your fortieth."

Tony and Ronnie had patched things up after their confrontation the day Aidan met her at the station. Little did he know he had unwittingly drawn Ronnie and Aidan closer because of his boorish behavior.

In her office the following Monday, Tony made amends. "I'm sorry about the way I treated you the other day," he said. The Tony from the past would've never made the first move, let alone be the first one to apologize.

"Apology accepted," she said.

He folded his arms and stared at the ground. "It's weird seeing you with another man. It'll take some getting used to."

*Now you know how I felt when I saw you with Brianna.*

"Aidan's a great guy, Tony. He's smart and funny, very kind. Give him a chance. You might like him."

"Right," Tony laughed, muttering under his breath, "when hell freezes over."

Ronnie licked the last blob of frosting off her plastic fork. "I'm glad there were no 'over the hill' jokes."

"I warned the guys to go easy on you." Tony wore a smile that said he had her back. "Do you feel any different?"

"No. Should I?"

He took her plate. "I'm not sure. I didn't."

"How could you? You don't exactly look over forty."

"Thanks for noticing." Tony strode to the trash can with a cocky swagger and dumped the garbage inside. "You don't look so bad yourself. For an old lady."

Ronnie's mouth dropped in laughter. "Tony!"

"I'm kidding," he said, busting her chops as if she were Max or Chet. "You're like a fine wine, Ronnie. You get better with age."

She smiled, feeling all warm inside. Aidan always complimented her, but when her ex-husband did, it was different, and she couldn't understand why. "Thanks for the party, Tony."

He stored the half-eaten cake in the bakery box and slid it aside. "It's not over yet. A birthday party isn't a party without gifts."

Ronnie turned and glanced around the conference room. There was not a present in sight. When she looked back at Tony, he was holding a small package wrapped in pink paper with a white ribbon the size of a box of jewelry. "Happy birthday, Ronnie."

"You didn't have to get me a present."

Tony held out the box closer for her to take. "I know I didn't have to. I wanted to."

"The cake was plenty," she insisted.

He turned her hand up and slapped the box into her palm. "Stop being a pain in the butt."

Ronnie threw her hands on her hips. "Is that anyway to talk to the birthday girl?"

"Yeah, if you keep standing there arguing with me." Tony's voice softened. "Open it. Please."

She untied the ribbon and tore off the paper. Removing the lid, Ronnie tipped the box upside down and caught a blue velvet case. The hinges squeaked as she opened it, and she let out a silent gasp at the teardrop-shaped locket encrusted in sparkles that looked like the real thing. "Are those diamonds?"

"The jeweler seemed to think so," Tony said with a chuckle.

The extravagant gift blew her away. "This must've cost a fortune!" Ronnie hid her eyes with a hand, embarrassed by her bluntness. But Tony's smile only grew as he watched her fumble with the box. She shut the lid. "I can't accept this. It's too much."

"Nothing's too good or too much for you." Tony opened the lid. "Look inside the locket."

Ronnie freed the dainty roped chain from the slits and set the case on the table. Prying the seam apart, she drew in a sharp breath. Staring back at her was a picture of Vivian on her lap. Their faces pressed side-by-side as Vivian's tiny hand was curled under Ronnie's chin.

"It's my favorite picture of you two," Tony said with a beat of sadness.

Ronnie touched the photo. "Mine, too."

"I thought it'd be nice to have a picture of her. You had left the photo albums at the house after the divorce. I have them at my apartment. If you want a few back, let me know. No pressure. Whenever you're ready."

Ronnie didn't know when that would be, but she hoped soon. For now, the locket was a start.

"May I?" Tony asked, taking the necklace.

He fastened the locket around her neck, his hands gently caressing her skin as she held back her hair. Twisting the teardrop right side up to see the photo, Ronnie blinked back tears. She closed the locket and pressed it to her skin, feeling as if Vivian's heartbeat had come back to life. In a way, it had. Ronnie's, too.

She held the locket between her fingers as if it were a rare gold coin. "I don't have the words to express what this means to me other than thank you."

Simultaneously, they embraced one another. Ronnie rested one side of her face against Tony's chest as he stroked the back of her head with his firm hand. Time had stopped, taking her to a safe place only he could provide, where she lowered her guard and floated in a pool of vulnerability.

Tony lifted Ronnie's chin. She closed her eyes to keep from looking into his. Those all-powerful dark brown eyes she couldn't resist. Perfect contentment urged her to stay with Tony, but Ronnie had to be strong. "I have to go," she said quietly and started to leave. Tony grabbed her hand, stretching her arm like taffy.

Someone had to be brave and let go. Ronnie knew it had to be her.

. . .

Dinner at Marco's Italian Ristorante called for a new dress. Ronnie had splurged and had gone to LeAnn's Boutique, where she and Rachel gabbed like best friends as Joey's girlfriend went from rack to rack on the hunt for the perfect dress. If she didn't like one, she'd wrinkle her perky nose as if she had smelled expired milk. Rachel honored her word, adding her forty percent employee discount.

Ronnie applied an extra layer of eye shadow and smacked her lips together to even out the shiny red lipstick. She fussed with her hair more than usual, but left it down. An updo was beyond her skill level.

Standing in front of a floor-length mirror, Ronnie examined the sexy black sleeveless number that blew that awful green dress out of the water.

She put on a new pair of high heels, then chose her silver hoop earrings from her minuscule jewelry collection. One accessory remained. She freed the locket from the blue velvet case and stared at Vivian's picture before clasping the medallion around her neck.

"Don't cry, Ronnie," she told her reflection in the mirror. "It's your birthday. Time to celebrate."

Aidan arrived at six o'clock dressed in a sharp black suit with a dozen red roses. He offered Ronnie his elbow, escorting her outside to the white limo parked next to the curb. Her boyfriend knew how to celebrate in style.

The driver tipped his hat and opened the door. "Happy birthday, Miss Callahan."

Inside Marco's Italian Ristorante, Aidan handed their coats to the coat-check girl and whispered into the maître d's ear. The man in the tuxedo bowed slightly. "My pleasure, sir." He held two menus in the crook of his arm and led them to their table.

Aidan and Ronnie followed the maître d' through the hallway adorned with sculptures and paintings, and into the main dining room. Giant chandeliers shimmered against wine-colored walls as a strolling violinist serenaded the diners at each table.

The maître d' gestured to a jutted ledge with a private table for two and wingback chairs next to a gas fireplace. "Is this satisfactory, sir?"

Aidan looked at Ronnie for approval. "Veronica?"

She could not have asked for a more glamourous setting. "It's perfect."

Aidan pulled out Ronnie's chair, and the maître d' handed them their menus. "Stefan is your waiter this evening. He'll be here shortly to take your order." The gentleman smiled at Ronnie, showing no teeth. "Happy birthday."

After ordering two appetizers and their entrées, Aidan reached inside his suit pocket for a box wrapped in gold paper and placed the package on the table. "Happy birthday, Veronica."

The spoiled princess Ronnie had dreamed of wanting to be became a reality. She unwrapped the box, savoring the anticipation, and removed the lid. Inside was a sleek watch with a shimmering jeweled band and a square face.

Aidan took the liberty of attaching it around her wrist. "It syncs to your phone. You can call, text, go online, all without having to rummage through your purse for your cell."

Fancy yet functional. Classy yet practical. The perfect birthday gift from her boyfriend.

"Thank you, Aidan. I love it." Ronnie modeled the high-tech gadget. "How does it look?"

"Amazing." He brought her hand to his mouth and pressed his lips to her skin. "Like you."

Ronnie showed Aidan her appreciation for the watch and what had become a string of compliments with a seductive kiss.

Turning forty agreed with Ronnie, giving her everything she needed. A fulfilling career that carried on her father's legacy, and a fairy tale relationship—until Prince Charming pointed to the locket around her neck. "Is that new?"

Ronnie twiddled the teardrop metal, wishing her boyfriend was like most men who were oblivious to things like women's jewelry. "Um... yes, it is. It's a birthday gift."

"From whom?" Aidan asked, pulling away from her with a noticeable change in his voice.

Ronnie fiddled with the linen napkin on her lap and cleared the frog in her throat. "Tony."

Aidan's eyes shrank to a villainous stare. "He bought you a necklace?"

The chastising tone made her feel as if she had broken the unspoken rules for ex-spouses.

The waiter arrived with their appetizers of calamari and tomato bruschetta. Aidan coldly thanked the server and waited for him to leave. "An intimate gift, wouldn't you agree, Veronica?"

An intimate gift, yes, but not one Aidan could understand because he hadn't been a parent who lost a child. Ronnie opened the locket. "It's of Vivian and me."

She assumed once Aidan saw the photo of her dead daughter, he'd pity her. He didn't. "She looked like you," he said in a toneless manner.

Ronnie snapped the locket shut. She bit into a piece of bruschetta bread and handed him the platter. He waved, passing on the appetizer.

"What's it like working with Tony?" Aidan asked, not in an inquisitive sort of way.

He hadn't mentioned Tony Lombardo's name since the night at the winery. It was a good run while it lasted.

Ronnie chewed the crunchy bread more than she needed to, turning it into a garlicky tomato goop. "It was awkward at first, more for him than me, but we're professionals. He's an officer. I'm the police chief." *Drop it!* her brain barked at Aidan as she took another bite of the bruschetta.

Aidan took a hard sip of wine. "I'm not comfortable with the arrangement."

Ronnie dabbed the corners of her mouth with the napkin. "I don't see why."

Aidan's icy stare could extinguish the fireplace. "You're my girlfriend, Veronica. I shouldn't be forced to share you with him."

"Tony and I are divorced. There's no sharing to be had. Besides, I'm the one who ended the marriage."

"Because he committed adultery."

The jab aimed at Tony hit Ronnie instead. "You don't have to remind me of what he did. I lived it. I was there when it happened."

"If he hadn't, you'd still be married to him."

"Yes, but we're not. Tony and I are friends. We've moved past the past. As a psychiatrist, don't you classify that as a breakthrough?"

"If you were my patient and not a woman I care deeply about."

Ronnie sipped water from her glass. "Sounds hypocritical to me."

Then, silence. And plenty of it until the waiter returned with their meals. He set Ronnie's plate in front of her announcing, "Veal Milanese with fettuccine Alfredo for the lady. Tortellini and truffles for the gentleman." He placed Aidan's meal down and bowed. "Enjoy."

Once the server was out of earshot, Aidan unfolded his napkin with a hard snap and placed it over his lap. "Do I have a reason to worry?"

Ronnie held her fork and knife to cut her meat. "Beats me. Are you looking for one?"

"I don't have to look too far, now do I?"

"What are you saying?"

Just then, the roaming violinist approached their table with a romantic melody that agitated Aidan. "Do you mind?" he said to the musician. "We're trying to have a private conversation." The man's bow hit a sour note as he stopped and went to another table on the other side of the restaurant. Aidan turned to Ronnie. "If our relationship is going to continue, Veronica, I need to be certain there's nothing between you and your ex-husband."

She cut into the meat. "Tony and I are no longer 'Tony and Ronnie.' We've been apart longer than we were a couple. Yes, we have a history. But that's all it is."

"History has a tendency to repeat itself," Aidan said.

Ronnie dropped her utensils, and they clinked against the plate. "Is this how the evening is going to be, Aidan? Filled with snarky cliches? Okay, my turn then—"

He raised a hand, cutting her off. "There's no need for childish behavior."

"Childish! You're calling me childish when you're the one bent out of shape over a little gift!"

"Little gift?" he repeated, as if she were out of touch with reality. "How much did the 'little gift' cost, Veronica?"

"I have no idea. I didn't ask," she snapped. "I'm not that rude."

"Judging by its appearance, I'd venture to say Mr. Lombardo spent a few thousand dollars. If not more."

"And so what if he did? What do you suggest I do? Fire Tony for buying me a gift. Will that end your insecurity?"

Aidan growled. "I'm not insecure."

"Could've fooled me," she bit back. "I'm not as smart as you when it comes to the human psyche. I'm just a cop. But I don't need a doctorate to see my boyfriend has a big problem with my ex-husband."

"There wouldn't be one if you'd keep your distance from him!" Aidan raised his voice so loud, the couple at the next table stopped and stared.

"How do you suggest I do that, *Doctor* Foster? He's one of my officers."

Aidan glared at her with a snide smile. "Perhaps not accepting jewelry is a good place to start."

"Still can't let go of the necklace?" Ronnie bobbed her head, amused. "You have no business telling me what I can and cannot accept as a gift. This isn't Tony's way of trying to win me back." She deepened her voice and puffed out her chest, imitating a cocky man. "Buy the ex an expensive gift. She'll forget all about what happened and come running back. Maybe that works on some women, but not me."

Ronnie extended the necklace, and Aidan looked away as if it burned his eyes. "This is about Vivian. I haven't seen a picture of my daughter in years, and when I look at the locket, when I *wear* this locket—because Aidan, I'm going to wear it—I'm thinking of her, not Tony."

Her argument didn't sway him. "I'm sorry, Veronica. You failed to convince me."

Ronnie pushed away her plate. "I'm not hungry."

"Maybe it's best to call it a night," he added.

"Fine by me." Ronnie whipped her napkin hard onto the table as Aidan flagged their waiter.

On the ride to her apartment, Ronnie and Aidan sat at opposite ends of the limo. Staring out the window at the community she had sworn to protect and serve, she imagined how the evening should've gone. A delicious dinner, followed by a walk along the river, then back to her apartment. So much for that scanty purple negligee she had bought specifically for tonight.

Too late to think about what could have been. Instead, Ronnie relived the better moments of her fortieth birthday. The surprise party at the station, and Tony's gift. Those were memories worth taking with her.

The limo stopped outside her apartment building. "Don't bother coming inside," she said to Aidan while gathering her purse and the container of leftovers. There was no point in letting a meal that sublime go to waste.

Aidan grabbed her hand and pressed a button to raise the privacy glass. "We can't end the evening this way."

Ronnie ripped her arm loose. "There's something you need to know about me, Aidan. When I'm this angry, I advise the best thing for you to do is to leave me alone."

She exited the limo and slammed the door.

In her bedroom, Ronnie looked at her reflection in the mirror, not knowing the next time she'd get to wear the black dress. "It was fun while it lasted."

She changed into her pajamas and went into the kitchen, taking the container with her to the couch, where she ate a cold dinner alone on her birthday.

Aidan's accusation held partial truth. Ronnie and Tony had a child together; they had shared a life. Years and memories don't disappear into an abyss, as much as her boyfriend wanted them to.

Ronnie touched the locket, picturing Tony at the jewelry store hunched over the display case and driving the salesperson nuts until he found what he was looking for. Her fingertips ran over the rough diamond surface.

She took her phone off the coffee table to text Tony. A quick, *Hi*, or another, *Thank you* for the necklace.

Typing T and O, his name appeared. Her finger dangled over the message box, then she closed out of the screen.

Ronnie turned on the TV and channel surfed through the stations. The opening credits for *Pretty in Pink* scrolled across the screen. She camped out on the couch, watching the movie she had seen a hundred times, but tonight, related to the teenage love triangle as if it were her own.

Ronnie had a lot in common with Molly Ringwald's character, Andie, not because she too had a boy's name. Both had two different men fighting for their affection. Ronnie sympathized with Duckie, who tried wooing Andie—the girl he had loved forever. Andie and Duckie were cut from the same cloth, bringing comfort and familiarity to their relationship. Then out of nowhere, dreamy, sophisticated, BMW-driving Blane rolled into Andie's life, and she fell for the rich kid from the wealthy section of town. In the end, Andie chose Blane and Duckie stepped aside.

Tony wasn't likely to capitulate so easily, and she questioned if her heart could ever fully belong to Aidan.

After the movie, Ronnie brushed her teeth and went into her bedroom. She unclasped the locket and stared at the photo of her sweet Vivian. "Good night, baby girl. Mommy loves you."

She kissed the picture and secured the locket into the blue velvet case.

# CHAPTER 20

Ronnie read the instruction manual for her new watch while reliving last night.

A dozen red roses. The limo ride. A romantic table for two at Marco's, where Aidan watched with anticipation as she opened his gift. Funny how fast the evening had turned disastrous because of two words: Tony Lombardo.

Ronnie's impeccable birthday celebration took a nosedive because of a locket.

Back to the watch. The GPS emergency contact feature.

Who from Ronnie's small circle was worthy of the dubious honor? Natalie made the most sense, being her mother, but distance disqualified her. What could she do from Akron except wait and worry?

Up next, Tony. Perish the thought.

Ronnie's ex-husband... an emergency contact? That only made Aidan's case against her airtight, which left one person. Aidan, her boyfriend, or was he?

They hadn't spoken to each other since the limo driver brought her home. Ronnie had cooled off and was ready to talk, expecting to have received a call or text from Aidan by now.

While typing Aidan's name and phone number into the feature, Wanda came inside Ronnie's office and handed her a manila envelope. "This just came for you, Chief."

"It wasn't with the rest of the mail?"

"No. The genius who sent it wanted to save sixty-three cents on postage." Wanda huffed. "It was stuck between the crack of the front doors. Cheap and lazy."

Ronnie inspected the mysterious envelope with no return address or postage. Just *Police Chief Veronica Callahan* typed across the center. Her cop instincts soared to high alert. "Thanks, Wanda."

After the receptionist left, Ronnie squeezed the package from top to bottom. She sniffed along the seal, then used a letter opener to slice open the top. Inside was a single sheet of paper. She pulled it out and read nine words typed in a bold font across the middle.

**HOPE YOU ENJOYED YOUR BIRTHDAY.
IT WAS YOUR LAST.**

Ronnie dialed Detective Kurt Ashe's extension. "Come to my office. Now."

He appeared in the doorway within seconds and closed the door. She handed him the note. His bushy salt and pepper eyebrows leaped above his glasses. "Someone sent you this?"

Ronnie straightened her posture, exuding a brave front. "Yes. It was stuck between the doors of the front entrance."

Detective Ashe read the ordinary white sheet of printer paper again, searching for clues invisible to the naked eye. "Any idea who?"

"No. Check the surveillance video outside the station and send the envelope and the paper to forensics, but keep it quiet. I don't want this getting out. Not yet anyway. It could be a dumb prank."

Detective Ashe waggled the sheet of paper. "This is a death threat, Chief."

Ronnie's skin prickled at the words death and threat.

"Try to trace where it came from," she said. "Tell forensics to bump it to the top of the list. I want answers before I leave today. No one is to know about this—especially Lombardo."

His eyebrows collapsed in confusion as to why Ronnie singled out Tony before lifting them back up. "Oh, yeah. The whole ex-spouse thing."

Ronnie had forgotten she was talking to a gruff detective instead of Paula. He made her relationship with Tony sound juvenile.

"It's too early to make any conclusions. Why have Tony worry when there may not be anything to worry about?" She smiled a little to lift the heaviness. "And he's got a bigger mouth than Wanda."

Detective Ashe stood to his feet. "Whatever you say, boss."

• • •

Steam rose from Ronnie's skin as she soaked in hot water. Scraping her butt across the bottom of the bathtub, she tilted her head back into the water before going under. She popped through the surface and slicked back the plastered strands from her eyes.

The bath failed to relax Ronnie. A bottle of tranquilizers couldn't knock her out.

Nearly twenty years as a cop without a death threat until today. Criminals she had arrested had cursed her, using every four-letter word combination and then some, but never threatened her life.

Surveillance video outside the station had captured a man wearing a black hooded sweatshirt that covered his head. Sunglasses, gloves, and a bandana from his nose down to his chin concealed his face.

The crime lab came up empty on evidence. No trace of DNA on the paper or envelope. Criminals had a tendency of being clumsy, leaving behind their identity with something as small as a strand of hair or half of a fingerprint. Whoever had sent the threat knew to wear gloves. He had known not to write Ronnie's name on the envelope, excluding the need for handwriting experts.

Someone knew Ronnie, knew about her. If he had known it was her birthday, he knew a lot more.

*Aidan?*

He was mad last night, but mad enough to threaten her?

The probability of Ronnie being watched, followed, concerned her as she remembered the erratic driver from a few months ago. He wasn't drunk or reckless. He was sending her a message.

*The truck! It couldn't have been Aidan!*

If her boyfriend won't wear jeans, Ronnie doubted Aidan would drive a rattletrap truck like the one that had been tailing her.

The sound of the ringing doorbell pulled her back into the present and her body flinched, sending a slosh of water over the rim of the tub.

Ronnie put on her bathrobe, letting the terrycloth fabric act as a bath towel to soak up the excess water. She looked through the peephole. No one was there.

The bell rang a second time, causing her heart to bang against the wall of her chest. Again, she looked through the peephole, and again, no one was there.

Ronnie dashed into the bedroom and took her gun from the safe. She released the safety and cocked it once. Bullet in the chamber. She unlocked the door and flung it open in one swift motion while aiming the weapon straight ahead.

"Holy crap!" Aidan shouted, followed by a crunching noise. He had never uttered a crude word in front of Ronnie, and sounded like a frazzled man for once.

With his hands up, his head motioned at the gun. "Veronica?"

It was as if Ronnie had been outside her body, then returned when she noticed the weapon aimed at Aidan and slowly lowered it.

"Is that how you greet all your visitors?" Sarcasm rolled off Aidan's tongue.

Ronnie wiped the water droplets on her face with her sleeve. "I didn't see you through the peephole. After you rang the bell again, you still weren't there. I freaked out for a second."

"I bent down to tie my shoe. Then a second time to retrieve the flowers."

They both looked at the bouquet pinned under Aidan's foot. He sighed as he picked up the battered arrangement and collected the scattered petals.

"I'll put my gun away," she said, as he walked past her into the apartment.

Ronnie locked the weapon in the safe and went back into the living room, where Aidan tried bringing the marred bouquet back to life. "You left them in the limo," he said.

*Right. Our first fight.*

Ronnie touched a limp petal. "Even the crushed ones are still gorgeous."

The patronizing compliment went unnoticed as Aidan handed her the bouquet. "Veronica, I am so sorry."

She arched a squashed rose to even it out with the bunch. "I should be the one apologizing. I pointed a loaded gun at you."

He shook his head. "No, not the flowers. Well, yes, the flowers, but mostly, I'm sorry about last night. I ruined your birthday."

"No. You didn't," she mumbled, sitting down on the couch.

"That's kind of you to say, but false nonetheless. There's no excuse for my behavior. No textbook explanation other than plain jealousy."

Aidan sat down next to Ronnie. If clothing reflected moods, then Aidan's said devastated as he sat hunched over with his tie loosened and top shirt button unfastened.

"There's no easy way to tell you this, so I'll just say it." Hurting Aidan was the last thing Ronnie wanted to do, but she needed to be honest. "Tony wants to get back together with me."

Aidan's head hung in defeat, as if he had already lost her. "I would, too, if I were him."

"I can't stop his feelings for me. It's one of those things. We were married. We had a child, but even though she's gone, Vivian is still a link between us."

Aidan stared at the floor. "I understand. It is what it is."

"I'm sorry having the locket upsets you."

He shrugged. What else was he supposed to do?

Ronnie imagined herself in Aidan's shoes. Would she be furious if he had received an expensive, personal birthday gift from an ex-wife? Depends. If she wanted him back, you bet.

"Here's the thing, Aidan." Ronnie reached across his lap and held his hand. "I chose not to get back together with Tony. I chose *you*."

Her words were like CPR, reviving his wounded heart. Aidan looked at Ronnie the way he had so many times since meeting her on the third floor in Tenter Hall, and she knew he believed her.

"Last night, there was something important I had to tell you," he said.

Two months had been a reasonable timeframe for Aidan to say the L-word. A phony fortune teller would've predicted correctly, and Ronnie played along. "I'm listening."

"I had a speech prepared."

"Of course, you did," she said, interrupting. "Sorry. Go ahead."

"After dinner, I wanted to take you to the Mt. Washington Observation Deck to see Pittsburgh glowing from three hundred and sixty-seven feet. It's where my grandfather told my grandmother he loved her for the first time. I wanted to do the same with you."

Aidan stared at his hands as if he didn't know what to do with them. He had put so much care into the evening, and it didn't go as planned. No wonder his blue eyes looked so sad. "I've loved you since our first date at Le Cep, Veronica. I wanted the first time I told you to be special."

Ronnie touched Aidan's cheek. "I don't need flashy. You could've told me while walking me to my apartment or during dessert. Or now. Just like you did."

"You're not disappointed?"

"No. Because I love you, too."

Aidan wrapped his arms around her, and she heard him sniffle, but felt his smile imprinted on her neck. "I can't tell you what it means to me to hear you say that."

Ronnie grinned. "Should I say it again?"

"Yes." Aidan drew back and kissed her. "As much as you want."

"I love you, Aidan."

Ronnie did. He was good to her and for her. How could she have suspected him as the sender of the threat?

"There is something else I need to tell you." He took her hands, as if he were about to propose. "My mentor, Dr. Jacobson, is retiring from Englewood Counseling at Guidepost Complex. He's asked me to take over his patients. Veronica, I'm going back into private practice. My first session is next week."

"What about your classes?"

"The semester is almost done; I'll do both until then. It's going to be hectic—sixty, seventy hours a week. We may not see much of each other, but it'll only be for a few months."

Sacrifices were a part of life. Ronnie had made her share in order to advance in her career. If Aidan had to work long hours to get where he wanted to be, she'd support him the entire way. "I'm happy for you, Aidan. I'm behind you a thousand percent."

"You're the one I have to thank."

Ronnie didn't see that coming. "Me? What did I do?"

Aidan stroked her damp head. "You've been through hell and back, Veronica. Losing your father and your daughter. A divorce. Most people would've let all that tragedy keep them hostage, but not you. You went after your dream with fearless tenacity. Just knowing you gave me the courage I needed to try again." No one had ever praised her with so much passion. She felt unworthy and happy at the same time. Aidan muttered, "You've changed my life," as his tender lips on Ronnie's thanked her.

"This calls for a celebration," she said.

"Our new relationship or my job offer?"

"Both."

"There's no one else I'd rather celebrate with than the woman I love." Aidan stood. "I'll go home and change and be back in an hour."

"Let's stay in tonight." Ronnie pulled him down onto the couch. "We'll order a pizza and hang out here and watch an old movie on TV. By old, I mean from the eighties."

Rows of lines formed on his forehead. "Like teenagers?"

"Yeah." Ronnie unknotted his tie. "We can make out like teenagers, too."

"Will you let me get to second base with you?" he asked with a dirty smirk.

*Hot dog! Aidan used a baseball analogy!*

Ronnie unbuttoned his shirt. "I was hoping for a home run."

He let out a sexy moan while untying her robe. "Put me in the game, coach."

Food could wait. They peeled off their clothing and acted on Ronnie's suggestion right there on the couch. When they had finished, Ronnie ordered a large pizza with pineapple and ham.

"I've never had it," Aidan said, "but I'll try anything once."

Ronnie changed into a pair of blue athletic pants and a long-sleeve T-shirt, dried her still-damp hair, and tied it into a short ponytail. No makeup.

The pizza came thirty minutes later, hot and tasty. Ronnie had three slices; Aidan had four. From the hallway closet, she took a blanket and spread it across their laps, and snuggled next to him as she flicked through the stations and came to *Back to the Future.*

Ronnie watched Marty McFly travel back in time and change history, wishing she had the same sci-fi powers. Picturing herself behind the wheel of the DeLorean time machine, she punched in the date, August 12, 2009.

How different her life would've been if she had stayed awake that day at the playground. On the bench, she would've watched Vivian play in the sandbox as the neon-green ball bounced inside. As her daughter and the blond-haired boy kicked the ball, the second Vivian went toward the road, Ronnie would've shouted, "Vivian! Stop!" and run to her daughter.

The girl would've cried as Ronnie scolded her for telling her never to run toward the street again. The blond-haired boy would have scampered away with his ball while the black Toyota drove down the road.

Ronnie would've walked the toddler to the hot dog stand for lunch, then driven home, where they both would've taken an afternoon nap.

Tony would've come home from work to find Ronnie waving her hand through the burned smell coming from the oven.

Tiny footsteps would've charged into the kitchen. "Daddy, Daddy, you're home! I missed you!" Vivian would've said in a squeaky voice, then leaped into his outstretched arms and kissed him.

She would've rubbed her tiny hands on his five o'clock shadow and told him he felt scratchy, before jumping down and disappearing into the family room to watch a cartoon.

Tony would've saved dinner, somehow, and later, after tucking Vivian into bed and reading her two stories, one about farm animals the other about princesses, Tony and Ronnie would've gone to their bedroom and made another Vivian.

# CHAPTER 21

Ronnie pulled into a parking lot filled with Mercedes, Jaguars, and Bentleys. A Ferrari, too.

*Cha-Ching!*

Three intense months of preparations all came down to tonight's gala. Planning the fundraiser had helped take Ronnie's mind off the death threat at times, and although the note left her on edge, she hid it well. No one was the wiser. The isolated incident wasn't to be taken lightly, and the cop in her remained extra vigilant.

Ronnie tipped the valet and went inside the warehouse that radiated with vintage charm. Classic and modern styles meshed in harmonious congruency, creating an elegant venue for the high-class fundraiser. The cold warehouse had been converted into a warm, inviting space for five hundred wealthy guests.

Original wooden beams ran across the thirty-foot ceiling. Strands of white lights looped outward from the center and down the faded brick walls like drizzling water on a shower door. Tables draped in purple linens, for the color representing addiction recovery, surrounded a parquet dance floor.

Walking through the crowd, Ronnie smiled and waved at donors as if she were on a first name basis with Hilton's elite as they socialized during cocktail hour. A drink in one hand and a plate of scrumptious hors d'oeuvres in the other. The stuffed mushrooms and bacon-wrapped shrimp had Ronnie on the lookout for a roaming server. She spotted Paula instead, who waved at her as though she were signaling a plane on a taxi runway.

The women exchanged hellos and hugs, carrying smiles saying, *We did it!*

Paula wore a black dress with a short jacket outlined in onyx beading, while her tamed kinky copper curls were in a simple updo. "Where's Aidan?" she asked Ronnie at their reserved table near the stage.

"He had a full patient load. He'll be here by the time dinner's served."

Between classes on campus and evening counseling sessions, Aidan worked around the clock, as he had predicted. Juggling two full-time jobs had put a dent in their dating life, reducing their time together to once a week. Ronnie handled the temporary arrangement like a champ, being the supportive, patient girlfriend. Tonight, however, she wanted her boyfriend with her to see there was more to being a cop than issuing traffic tickets and arresting criminals.

Paula stepped back for a better look at Ronnie. "The belle of the ball."

Ronnie bathed in the compliment as she blended in with the rich women in sparkly evening gowns and men in designer suits and tuxedoes. The bodice of her blue dress fit like a Band-Aid. The remaining see-through material flowed to her ankles. Strappy, color-matching heels completed the ensemble. No ordinary dress would do for an occasion like the gala.

"What's this?" Paula lifted the locket around Ronnie's neck, letting it lie on three fingers. She studied it as if it were a priceless ancient artifact.

"It's just a necklace I wear on special occasions." Ronnie would never hear the end of it if Paula knew Tony was the generous benefactor of the locket with Vivian's picture inside.

Servers clad in black and white uniforms with hors d'oeuvre trays weaved around the guests. Then, in a graceful choreographic move, which appeared rehearsed, a mingling group parted ways. There stood Tony, as if out of thin air.

Ronnie's breath hitched, caught in her throat. He strode toward her and Paula in a black tuxedo and bowtie that was similar to the one he had worn on their wedding day.

Paula let out a high-pitched whistle. "Hot stuff, coming through! We should throw you in the auction lineup. You'd bring in some big bucks!"

Tony smiled modestly. "Maybe next year."

"Do it for the center, Tony! We're counting on you!" Paula joked with a boisterous laugh.

Ronnie could see it now: Tony on stage strutting his stuff as drooling women shot paddles in the air faster than the auctioneer calling out the bids.

"Where's your date?" Tony asked her. She abandoned the daydream. He made Aidan out to be an escort Ronnie had hired from a service for desperate women too ugly to get a date on their own.

"*Aidan,*" Ronnie emphasized, "will be here soon." Assuming Tony had brought a date, she scoped the room for a young, gorgeous woman. "Who's tonight's lucky lady?"

"Going stag." He seemed proud to be alone. So unlike him.

"Tony Lombardo doesn't have a date for Hilton's biggest event of the year? Talk about front-page news. Where's Joey when you need him?"

Tony posed like a model with a hand in his pocket, his stare cutting through her. "The woman I wanted to bring had other plans."

"Ha!" Paula belted out.

Ronnie played along with Tony's game, for his sake. "Canceled at the last minute, did she?"

A forlorn look crept into his beautiful, dark eyes. "Yeah. You can say that."

Ronnie saw Jesse moving through the crowd toward the reserved table. Either his suit was a hand-me-down or off the rack from a discount store. Bless his heart, he wanted to make a good impression.

The teen introduced his mom, Doreen, to Ronnie and Tony. She looked as nervous as her son.

"Do you have your speech?" Paula asked Jesse.

"Uh-huh. In my pocket." His lips turned a grayish-white, and he looked as if he were about to puke. "A lot of people are here. What if I screw up or sound stupid? They don't care about what I have to say."

Tony slung his arm around Jesse. Since meeting the recovering addict, he had visited the teen at the center once a week and on the weekends. He had taken him to the batting cages and out for burgers. So much of who Tony had become mirrored the kind of person Nick was. "Is what you have to say the truth?"

Jesse lowered his head. "Yeah. I guess."

"Then nothing you say is wrong. It's your story. No one knows it like you."

"Tony's right," Paula said. "Jesse, you don't have to be perfect. Just be you."

Tony hugged Jesse, Italian style with a slap-pat. "You can do it. We all believe in you."

Pressure swelled behind Ronnie's eyes, tears forming at the thought of Tony giving fatherly advice to a teenaged Vivian and the other children they had planned on having.

*Get a hold of yourself, Ronnie. Tonight's about the center.*

"What's wrong?" Tony asked Ronnie as he caught her staring at him. He wiped his skin. "Do I have something on my face?"

"No. It's fine."

*More than fine.*

He checked his shirt for an unfastened button.

*Don't get me started on your chest.*

Joey came by to say a quick hello before joining the other reporters interviewing affluent doctors, lawyers, and business owners.

A staffer from the catering company informed Paula dinner was ready to be served as Max and Audrey and Chet and Mia arrived.

Jesse and Doreen sat down at the reserved table. Tony pulled out Ronnie's chair for her and sat next to her. To her right was an empty seat. Of all nights for Aidan to be late, he had to pick the most important evening of her career.

*Where are you, Aidan?*

Paula went on stage and stood behind the podium. "Good evening, everyone. Welcome to the first New Beginnings Youth Center Gala. I'm Paula Crowe, director of the center."

A thunderous applause erupted.

"This fundraiser is possible because of our partnership with the Hilton Police Department. I'd like to take a moment to recognize two members of the force who made it happen: Police Chief Veronica Callahan and Officer Tony Lombardo." Paula looked down at the table where they sat and bounced her hand. "Stand up, you two. Let everyone get a good look at ya!"

Tony and Ronnie smiled and waved, receiving their recognition.

"To all our new donors. Through your generous support, you're changing and saving young lives. You're providing hope for their futures, and from the bottom of my heart, I thank you."

Another round of applause.

"Enjoy your dinner and get ready for an incredible auction!"

A five-piece band played instrumental music during the meal, and after dessert, Paula returned to the stage.

"Is everyone having a good time?" She spoke loudly into the microphone, stirring up the energy in the room. "Before we begin the auction, you're about to meet one of the reasons why you're here tonight."

Ronnie thought she saw Aidan at the entrance, but it was only a server. She pressed the sides of her tech-savvy watch and the face lit up, revealing the time. 7:25. Her annoyed sigh caught Tony's attention, causing him to smirk as he knew the reason for her irritation.

"I can tell you about this young man, but we've asked him to share his story. Before he does, I have something to say." Paula looked at Jesse at the table. "I'm so proud of how far he's come. It's an honor to call him my friend. Ladies and gentlemen, Jesse Hughes."

The spotlight followed Jesse on stage to the podium. He took a folded piece of paper from his pocket and smoothed the creased paper. "I've played baseball since I was a kid," he said quietly. Paula whispered in his ear. He raised his head and moved his mouth closer to the microphone.

"One day, my dad said, 'Jesse, do you want to be a baseball player someday?' I told him, 'I already am,' but he meant professionally. We dreamed about me playing in the majors, but when I was twelve, I lost more than a dream. My life fell apart the day my dad died in a car accident on the way to one of my games. I started hanging out with the wrong crowd. I was thirteen the first time I smoked pot. It was fun getting high because I didn't feel sad about losing my dad. But soon, it wasn't strong enough. I tried acid. That wasn't enough, either. Then I tried coke. At fifteen, I was hooked on crack. You're probably wondering how a kid my age gets money for drugs."

Jesse drummed his fingers nervously on the glass. "I stole. I stole money from my mom and my friends' parents. I even locked my little sister in the bathroom and took her piggy bank money. She'd been saving it to buy me a new mitt, so I'd go back to baseball and quit using."

Ronnie's heart sank, along with everyone else's.

"I overdosed a few weeks later. I woke up in the hospital, wishing I was dead. Wishing the last puff of the crack pipe had done me in. I went through a month of rehab." Jesse glanced up. "I don't want to talk about that. It was that bad. Then my mom heard about the center." He looked at Paula next to him. "I hated it, and I hated Paula. But she didn't quit on me. My life was worth saving. It wasn't too late for me. I've worked hard this past year to get my grades up and stay clean. I'd be lying if I said it was easy. It's not. But because of the center, I have a place to go to for counseling and encouragement, away from bad influences. I'll be graduating next year. For the first time since my dad died, I'm excited about my future. I want to go to college and help young people like me who believed life wasn't worth living."

Jesse folded the paper. "Thank you for your donations."

His speech moved guests to tears as women dabbed their eyes with their napkins. The men, too. He received a standing ovation as he went to his seat.

Paula thanked Jesse, then noted the paddles on the tables and introduced the auctioneer.

The band returned to the stage after the auction with a slow jazzy tune. Again, Ronnie looked at her watch. 8:40. Still no Aidan. She almost called him when Tony stretched out his arm as if he were a gallant gentleman from the nineteenth century. "How about a dance, Chief?"

Tony's request elicited a memory of Vivian's last Christmas Eve. "Santa won't come unless you're sleeping," Ronnie had said, as she covered the toddler with the bedspread.

Vivian yawned. "How does Santa know I'm sleeping?" she asked, rubbing her tired eyes.

"He has special powers. That's what makes him Santa. It's just like the song says, 'he knows when you're sleeping, he knows when you're awake.'"

The little girl had believed the innocent fib and went to sleep while Tony and Ronnie wrapped presents and assembled toys late into the night. The family room had resembled Santa's workshop, and they were his elves.

After Tony had tucked the last present under the tree, Ronnie crawled on her hands and knees collecting debris when she heard music coming from the stereo. Tony lifted her up, and they danced as the paper beneath their feet crinkled.

Ronnie placed her hand in Tony's as the wailing saxophone at the gala directed them onto the crowded parquet square. She hadn't danced with him since that Christmas Eve night and feared falling out of step with his rhythm. For a man with an athletic build, Tony was a smooth dancer.

Their hands joined. She wasn't nimble by any means, but didn't have to concentrate on the steps because with Tony, he led and she followed.

His stare rode her body up and down. "The dress looks incredible on you, Ronnie."

She had hoped he would notice. "I can't take all the credit. Rachel picked it out. She said it complimented my hair color and skin tone."

"She's right." Tony motioned at Ronnie's throat with a tilt of his chin. "The locket's a nice touch."

"It fits perfectly." Ronnie held the necklace for a moment, then tugged Tony's lapel. "You always looked nice in a suit."

"Nice?" He sounded borderline offended. "That's all?"

Ronnie rolled her eyes at his sad attempt to get her to fawn over him. "My mistake. You've always looked hot in a tux. Is that better?"

He grinned. "You think I'm hot?"

She refused to answer.

"I take that as a yes."

Tony pulled Ronnie forward to close the chasm big enough to fit a horse between them. Her feet skidded against the floor, causing her to bump into him. Before reclaiming her space, he locked his arm around her waist. He looked up as if he were outside, gazing at the stars. "You did all this, Ronnie."

"I had a lot of help." She resisted the temptation to touch his clean-shaven chin.

His eyes met hers. "You're so compassionate. The way you care about people. I see it in whatever you set out to do and accomplish."

She felt herself blush at the compliment.

"It felt good, you and me, working together again. A team," Tony said while his stare lured Ronnie to a dangerous place that had once been her safe-haven. "We were always good like that, and not just on the force."

He'd been her partner on the job and her partner in life.

"The last time we danced—"

"Christmas Eve, 2008," Ronnie answered, reading his mind. "What made you think of that?"

"How can I not?" While holding Ronnie's hand, Tony's index finger broke free and touched her chin, then glided down to the base of her neck in a slow, sexy motion. "Remember what happened after we danced?"

He hadn't forgotten. Neither did Ronnie, as she remembered how they had shed their clothes and made love on the floor next to the presents under the tree.

"You do," Tony said, pleased the memory made her too shy to answer.

Ronnie's feet felt glued to the floor, yet her body rotated, and she saw Paula and Max watching from the table. God only knew what they were thinking. From their smiles, Ronnie had a good idea. "We have an audience."

Tony's fingers rode the bumps of her spine as he pressed his cheek to hers. "In that case, let's give them something to talk about."

The cologne emanating from his skin could not contain Ronnie from moaning as she inhaled the intoxicating fragrance. "Ralph Lauren."

In a husky tone, he whispered in her ear, "I wore it for you."

Ronnie's body shivered with excitement as her hand went from Tony's bicep to the back of his neck, where her fingers feathered through his hair.

She could have danced with Tony forever, but it wouldn't have made up for the years they'd been apart. His pace slowed down. "We need to talk somewhere where we can be alone."

Ronnie watched Tony's dark eyes work their magic on her, knowing the last thing they'd do was talk, until she spotted Aidan scanning the crowd. She saw the confusion wash over Tony's face as she abruptly pulled away from him. "Thanks for the dance," she said and walked away.

Tony followed her as she approached Aidan. She convivially pointed at her watch.

"I know. I'm unbelievably late." Aidan kissed Ronnie with a generic peck on the lips. "My last patient was double-booked erroneously. It was an important appointment. I couldn't turn him away."

*But it's okay you're two hours late to something that's important to me.*

Ronnie accepted her boyfriend's apology with a disappointed grin. "Better late than never."

When Aidan saw Tony, he pulled Ronnie next to him and tactfully groped her hip. A simple message that said she was his. "Good evening, Tony."

"Aidan."

Tension ran thicker than the day the two men had met at the station.

Aidan stiffened. "Thank you for keeping Veronica company in my absence," he said with sincerity as phony as a three-dollar bill.

"The pleasure was all mine," Tony replied coolly.

Aidan turned to Ronnie. "I'm so sorry I wasn't here sooner, sweetheart. Allow me to make it up to you."

Ronnie stared at him, curious. "How?"

"You'll see." Aidan looked at Tony with a smug smile. He led Ronnie to the dance floor, where he twirled and dipped her. She burst out laughing as Tony watched the exhibition from the sidelines.

"What did I miss?" Aidan asked Ronnie.

She looped her arms around his neck. "Everything."

"Give me the highlights."

"Dinner was delicious. It made Le Cep seem ordinary."

Aidan looked at her suspiciously. "I highly doubt that."

He had the right to his prerogative. "The auction was a hit. I lost track after two hundred thousand dollars, but the best part was—"

"That wasn't the best part? What can outshine bringing in that kind of money?"

"Jesse." Ronnie tilted her head back in delight. "I wish you'd been here to see him give his speech. He's a great kid. I know he's going to make something of his life."

Aidan nodded while his incredulous countenance said otherwise.

"He wants to become a counselor for recovering teens. You can be his mentor and introduce him to the other therapists at the practice."

Aidan smiled apologetically. "Now's not an ideal time, Veronica."

"I didn't mean tomorrow morning. In a few weeks. I know you're busy, but it'd mean a lot to Jesse."

Aidan looked past her and into the crowd. "We'll see."

"We'll see?" she repeated. "What you're really saying is no."

"I'd be more than happy to help Jesse *once* my schedule frees up. Right now, it's full. I warned you it'd be this way."

"School is almost over."

"There's another..." Aidan paused, weeding through his vocabulary, "prospect that I will need to give attention to. At least, I hope so."

"You're already working two jobs. What are you planning to do next? Write a book?"

"This one is special and well worth it."

Ronnie brusquely stopped dancing and folded her arms. "Okay, Aidan. What's going on?"

Before Ronnie could blink, he dropped to one knee.

"Until I met you, I hadn't experienced unconditional happiness. My life has purpose and meaning because of you. When I think about my future, you're in it. Veronica Callahan, I want you to be my wife." Aidan pulled a black box from his pocket and opened it. "Will you marry me?"

The room blurred. Ronnie felt dizzy, staring at the diamond ring secured in the slit. Couples formed a circle around Ronnie and Aidan, waiting for her answer. The shock from an unexpected proposal rendered her momentarily mute.

"Veronica?" Aidan said only her name, but in it asked her a second time to marry him.

Ronnie's voice constricted as she uttered a weak "yes." She affirmed her answer, louder. "Yes. I'll marry you."

Aidan slid the ring onto her trembling left finger, and this time, planted a searing kiss on her while the crowd applauded.

Reporters caught wind of the engagement and circled Ronnie and Aidan like predators on prey, with bright lights from cameras shining on their faces. Photographers snapped pictures. Aidan spelled his name for the reporters and answered a barrage of questions that was noise to Ronnie.

Tuning out the ballyhoo, she saw Tony look at her the way he did the night he had told her about Kaitlyn. Only this time, Ronnie was the one who had thrown the javelin through his heart.

He looked as if he were having a panic attack, searching for somewhere to hide and lick his wounds, then disappeared into the crowd.

In the middle of the media frenzy, Joey's vicious glare at Ronnie labeled her a traitor.

. . .

After Aidan's marriage proposal knocked Tony out of the running, the devastated cop hightailed it out of the gala and past the stalker at the entrance.

Watching those three was like watching a cheesy soap opera. Tony actually thought he had a shot with Ronnie on the dance floor, her looking all feminine for once. The stalker hadn't seen a more gullible doofus than Lombardo. He didn't know whether to laugh or feel sorry for the schmuck.

Even he hadn't seen Aidan's proposal coming. If only Ronnie could've seen Lombardo's face when the shrink pulled out the ring. He was better off being kicked in the jewels—it would've hurt less.

The stalker grunted, watching those asinine reporters flock to the lovebirds as if they were royalty.

*Look at that pompous snob, acting as if Ronnie were some sort of grand prize. The guy has no idea what he's getting himself into, marrying that kid killer. Lucky for him, he won't find out.*

## CHAPTER 22

Every time Tony closed his eyes, he saw Aidan on bended knee, sliding a ring onto Ronnie's finger, which made for a sleepless night.

The next morning in the kitchen, he poured Corn Flakes into a bowl and drowned them in milk. He ate a spoonful of cereal, and a droplet of milk dribbled down his chin. Wiping it away reminded him of touching Ronnie's chin when they had danced. What a knockout she was in that blue dress.

Tony's second chance with Ronnie had slipped through his fingers faster than falling sand in an hourglass. The signs were all there. How she had looked at him. The way she had held the back of his neck while her face pressed against his. Ronnie had wanted Tony as much as he had wanted her. Words expressing a reconciliation were unnecessary, because sometimes saying nothing said it all. If Aidan hadn't shown up when he did, Tony knew the night would've turned out differently.

He took the bowl of cereal to the couch and turned on the television. The morning news anchor on Channel 5 introduced a report on the gala. Video of the donors and Jesse at the podium, then the real story.

"The money raised isn't the only news from last night." The upbeat woman sounded as if she were announcing the winner of a beauty pageant.

"Hilton Police Chief Veronica Callahan is engaged after her now-fiancé, Dr. Aidan Foster, proposed to her on the dance floor."

After the media had swarmed the happy couple, Tony bolted. Watching Ronnie say yes tore him up inside. Hanging around for the celebration hurt worse.

He ate another spoonful of mushy flakes. The soggy cereal went down hard as he watched Ronnie and Aidan being interviewed.

"Where did you two meet, and how long have you been together?" a reporter asked, sticking a microphone in Aidan's face.

"I met Veronica on the Dearborn College campus this past January. I was leaving my office and there she was." He looked at Ronnie adoringly. "We've been together ever since."

The camera stayed on them as another reporter asked, "Were you planning to pop the question tonight, Dr. Foster?"

Tony sneered, sarcastically mimicking Aidan's title.

"I've had the ring in my pocket for a week, waiting for the right moment. As soon as I saw her, I knew tonight was the night."

Back to the first reporter. "Chief Callahan, did you see Dr. Foster's proposal coming?"

Ronnie processed the question before answering. It was obvious only to Tony that by the look on her face, she didn't have an inkling that she'd be engaged by nine o'clock. "All I have to say is Aidan's full of surprises."

The longer the interview went, the more shy Ronnie became. She was used to being in front of the camera, conducting press conferences at the station. But this was her private life on display for all of Pittsburgh to see. It was a different ball game. While Aidan appeared comfortable being the center of attention, Ronnie seemed as if she wanted to slink away from the crowd.

Aidan unabashedly kissed Ronnie while the cameras continued rolling.

Tony couldn't eat another bite. He went into the kitchen and dumped the remaining cereal down the garbage disposal.

• • •

Ronnie stirred her coffee, but it was her mind that was swirling as her unexpected marriage proposal stole the spotlight from the center.

*What was Aidan thinking? The gala, of all places!*

That euphoric sensation a woman feels the first twenty-four hours of her engagement hadn't bubbled inside of Ronnie for no other reason than Aidan had picked the wrong place to ask her to marry him.

For a man as methodical as Aidan, he had proposed on a whim. Or did he? A roomful of five hundred people made it hard for Ronnie to say no.

Every morning newscast had the story. The local radio stations dropped a blurb about it, too. Ronnie hadn't seen the morning edition of the *Hilton Herald* but assumed the article landed on the front page.

Joey.

The Lombardo who'd been like a little brother to Ronnie made her feel like Benedict Arnold. Would the witty journalist report objectively as his writer bylaws commanded, or would he spin the article against her?

Ronnie had learned quickly Italian families have a superglue-like bond, loyal to one another until the end. When you hurt one of them, you hurt them all.

She sipped her coffee, but not even the roasted beans lifted her sunken spirits.

Ronnie left the station kitchen and was inside her office when Tony tromped by. In her haste to set the mug down, coffee spilled over the rim and formed a puddle on her desk. She dashed out the door. "Tony, wait!" She sped to a jog. At his side, she kept pace with his fast strides. "Please, let's talk."

He ignored her and continued walking.

Ronnie grabbed Tony's shoulder, twisting his taut torso toward her. "Stop and listen to me!"

The soles of his shoes skidded against the cement floor, echoing in the hallway. "Ortiz will have my head if I'm late," Tony said with a face like stone.

"I'll handle Ortiz."

Tony looked down at the diamond the size of a boulder on Ronnie's ring finger and lifted her hand. "Careful. You can hurt someone with that thing."

Ronnie's engagement ring from Tony wasn't nearly as big as the two carat, custom-designed monstrosity Aidan had boasted about, but she had adored it as if it were the Hope Diamond. It never left her finger. Ever. Not in the shower or at bedtime. While running or washing dishes. The ring had been with her until the day their divorce was final.

Ronnie pulled rank and her hand from Tony's grip. "In my office. Now."

His heavy footsteps followed her, and he slammed the door. "What are you thinking, marrying a guy you've only known for a few months?"

"I was unaware of the time requisite between dating and marriage," she answered.

Tony bypassed her snarky remark. "Are you sleeping with him?"

"You're way out of bounds, Lombardo! My private life isn't to be discussed at the station with anyone, namely you!"

Tony's eyes hardened. "Answer me. Are you sleeping with Aidan?"

"Not that it's any of your business, but yes, I am. That's what two people in a relationship do." Ronnie took a tissue from a Kleenex box on her desk and wiped away the coffee ring around the mug. She muttered, "I highly doubt you've been abstinent for eleven years."

Tony had no comeback and ended the inquisition into her sex life. "How much do you know about Aidan?"

She balled the dirty tissue and threw it into the wastebasket. "Enough."

Tony's hands flailed. "Wow! That says it all!"

"You want specifics? Okay. His birthday is September eighth. He has one sister, Lucy. He graduated from Duke University. He's allergic to cats—"

"Don't get smart with me, Ronnie. I'm not in the mood. I meant important stuff. How does he feel about you being a cop?"

The question stunned her. "He's very supportive."

"Is he? Because we both know the stress and demands of the job. If your spouse can't support you, it makes it that much harder."

Tony was right. Understanding a cop's life without being one was impossible.

Ronnie and Aidan rarely talked about her position as chief. Their conversations had revolved around his practice—keeping patient information confidential, of course. They were both in the business of helping people, each career important in different ways.

Tony continued to grill Ronnie. "Does he want kids?"

Ronnie shuddered at the idea of having a baby. Failure haunted her every time she saw a woman and child together, at the grocery store or walking inside the elementary school in the morning on her way to the station. Constant reminders of what she had lost swarmed her thoughts. Fear made her believe it could happen again.

"Where are you going to live?"

Would Aidan's home in the ritzy Wellington Heights neighborhood be her home, too, or would she just be moving in?

"Stop!" Tony's bombardment made Ronnie's head throb. "Please, just stop."

"This is all going too fast." Tenderness carried Tony's tone. "You're rushing into something you're not ready for."

Too fast? No. Ronnie was forty and not getting any younger. She'd been alone for more than a decade, punishing herself for Vivian's death and driving her husband into the arms of another woman. Pain had formed a barrier around her heart, protecting her from getting hurt again. Now, to be with Aidan, who was head over heels for her, why wouldn't she want to spend her life as Mrs. Foster?

Ronnie rolled back her shoulders. "There are couples who knew each other for a week and got married and lived to celebrate their sixtieth wedding anniversary."

Tony grunted. "You were always a sap for that crap."

"What on earth are you babbling about?"

"You act tough, Ronnie, but you're a sucker for romance in the most unconventional way. You never could make it through a movie without crying. Problem is, you confuse those storylines with real life. The Hollywood fairytale of boy meets girl, they fall in love, and live happily ever after." Tony snapped his fingers rapidly. "One, two, three, there you have it."

Ronnie felt emotionally naked. She flashed a cocky grin. "I suppose I have you to thank for that. Look at us. We had dated only six months when you proposed."

"You can't compare the two. You know it was different with us."

Within a year and a half, Tony and Ronnie had dated, got engaged, and were married. Not technically a big screen romance, but it was her romance.

"Do yourself a favor, make it a long engagement. Over time, you'll come to your senses."

Ronnie's throat dried up. "We've already set the date. July third."

Tony's jaw dropped. "Two months!"

"Aidan's not a procrastinator. It's one of the many qualities I like about him." She bit back with regret as the word "like" flew out, and Tony jumped on her slip of the tongue.

"Like?" he echoed. "Shouldn't someone getting married love their fiancé?"

"I wouldn't be marrying him if I didn't," she snapped.

"People do it all the time."

"Not me."

Tony crossed his arms. "Then say you love him."

He stared, waiting. Ronnie huffed. She would do anything at this point to shut Tony up. "I love Aidan. Happy?"

"My happiness isn't important. It's yours I'm worried about." Tony went behind the desk to where Ronnie stood. "Do you want to marry Aidan? Not out of obligation or because he gave you a rock the size of Mount Rushmore. Do you want to live your life with him?"

Ronnie didn't owe Tony an explanation, nor did she have to defend her decision. For the first time since the divorce, she was happy. Tony wouldn't take that away from her. "Look, Lombardo. You can either be a friend and support me or keep your opinions to yourself. You choose."

Tony's lips formed a thin, angry line. "You're making a mistake."

"Then it's my mistake to make."

"What about *us*, Ronnie?" He cupped her face in his hands. "Last night, we were so close."

Had she led Tony on? Was it Chet's wedding all over again? The way Ronnie had danced with Tony, letting him hold her so closely. The innuendos of their sex life. How she had touched him. Women with that kind of boldness who didn't follow through had a name. They're called teases.

"Don't touch me like that," Ronnie said, backing away. "We're friends. That's it."

"Keep telling yourself that. Let me know when you believe it." Tony slammed the door on his way out.

Ronnie plopped into her chair as the sparkling rock atop her finger reminded her of the Fourth of July, 2002.

She and Tony had gone on a bike ride along the Three Rivers Heritage Trail, followed by a picnic in Point State Park in Pittsburgh. At sunset, he had them move to a less crowded spot. Lying on a blanket, they snuggled while waiting for the fireworks over the confluence of the Allegheny and Monongahela Rivers forming the Ohio River.

The sky had filled with colors. Booming explosions and crackling had made it the typical fireworks celebration until Tony lifted Ronnie to her feet.

"We're not leaving, are we?" She looked up at the sky. "There's still the grand finale."

All was quiet as spectators waited with anticipation for the big ending. Tony dropped to one knee. He opened a black box and said two simple words. "Marry me."

Ronnie jumped on Tony, and they toppled onto the ground as she rolled on top of him.

"I hope that means yes," he said, tucking her dangling hair behind her ears.

Ronnie kissed him in between a series of yeses. "A thousand times, yes!"

There Tony was, flat on his back as he plucked the ring from the box. "Can I put this on you?"

Ronnie was so excited she had forgotten that part, but it'd be a memorable moment to tell their kids.

Tony slid the square-cut diamond onto her finger. The fireworks went off in sync with the joy exploding inside of her as they kissed during the grand finale under a fiery sky above.

## CHAPTER 23

"My phone is ringing off the hook!"

Paula bit into a chicken sandwich, drunk with giddiness as if she had won the Pennsylvania Lottery. Donations for the center continued pouring in days after the gala. To celebrate, Ronnie met the director for lunch.

"Jesse's speech won everyone over," Ronnie said. "There wasn't a dry eye in the house."

"Or maybe it was your marriage proposal!" Paula shrieked. "How are we going to top that for next year?"

Ronnie sipped her Sprite. She would endure Chinese water torture before admitting to Tony her engagement left her with doubts. "Do you think Aidan did it on purpose?"

Paula's forehead furrowed. "Uh, yeah. That's how marriage proposals usually work."

Ronnie bit into her cheeseburger, then wiped her mouth with a napkin. "What if Aidan proposed the way he did to stick it to Tony?"

"You're reading too much into this."

"Think about it, Paula. Of all the places to propose, Aidan chooses the gala? Not that it wasn't kind of sweet—it was, if you like that kind of attention, which I don't. The gala was about saving the center, not asking me to marry him in front of hundreds of people. One of whom is my ex-husband."

Paula slurped her coffee. "What did Tony say?"

"What I expected. It's too soon. I don't know Aidan well enough. I'm making a mistake. And he loves me."

Paula's eyes widened. "Tony said he loves you?"

"Not those exact words, but the implication was there. It has been for months."

"You'd have to be in a coma not to see that man loves you. But do you love him?"

The simple question had two possible answers. Yes or no. Only one created a dilemma. "What if I did?" Ronnie said. "How can I love two men at the same time?"

Paula bit into her sandwich. "Easy. One you love. The other, you're *in* love with." She chomped her food. "Big difference, Ronnie."

She tapped an overcooked French fry against her plate. "Tony and I have a complicated past."

"I had a feeling there was more to your breakup than irreconcilable differences, but I didn't want to pry."

There was a time when Ronnie had lumped Tony in with the rest of the scumbag cheating husbands. But she had changed. Tony had changed, and he didn't deserve to have his image tarnished because of one remorseful mistake. "He slept with another woman," Ronnie said, followed by a quick redemption. "But it was only once."

Paula's mouth stretched into a line, as if a blast of wind had pulled back her skin. "Ouch."

"That's not the worst of it."

Ronnie finally told Paula about Vivian's accident. How she could still hear her hysterical screams as she rocked back and forth, cradling her daughter's lifeless body in her arms on the side of the road while strangers mourned with her. And through her guilt, she pushed Tony away, which led him to finding solace in another woman.

"You poor thing," Paula said, reaching for Ronnie's hand. "It all makes sense. No wonder you won't give Hottie the time of day. I thought it was your tacky way of flirting with him."

Ronnie chewed a French fry. "I'm not that good at flirting, Paula."

"Hey, I get it. Infidelity ended my marriage, too. Keeping your distance guarantees you won't get hurt."

"Could you ever love Ricky again after what he did?"

"I don't want to love Ricky again," Paula answered bluntly. "Anyway, it's different."

"How? They both cheated."

"Ricky didn't slip like Tony. My snake of an ex-husband slithered into one bed after another right after our vows. If it had been once, meh, maybe we could've worked it out."

Paula's optimism made Ronnie feel like a heel. Tony had made a mistake, but one was all it took for her to end their marriage. "Tony wanted to go to counseling. He would've jumped off the Smithfield Street Bridge if I told him to. He was willing to do whatever it took to save our marriage, but I walked out on him."

"You're not a quitter, Ronnie."

Slightly offended, Ronnie said, "I didn't say I was."

"No, but you feel like one." Paula looked at her with a sad smile. "Look, you did what you had to do. Your daughter died. Your husband strayed. I know it wasn't easy leaving Tony."

*You're right, it wasn't, because I loved him. I still do. You already know that though, don't you, Paula?*

"Can you ever forgive Ricky?" Ronnie asked.

Paula's eyebrows arched as if the answer were obvious.

"Guess not."

"The only good that came from my screwed-up marriage was the center. After me and Runaround Ricky split, I had to get a job for luxuries like food and shelter."

Ronnie dipped a French fry into a blob of ketchup and swirled it back and forth. "I've forgiven Tony, but I don't trust him. If I forgive him, isn't trust part of that?"

Paula ate the last piece of her sandwich. "Not necessarily, but in your case, I hope so."

Whether or not Paula was right, Ronnie was engaged to be married to another man. Her focus should be on that, not her ex-husband. "Do you like Aidan?" she asked.

Paula shrugged. "He's a nice guy and makes you happy, but what I think is irrelevant. I'm on Team Tony and not ashamed to admit it."

Ronnie laughed softly. "At least you're honest."

"It's one of my better characteristics," Paula said and finished her coffee.

Thank God for Paula. Ronnie didn't know what she'd do without a friend like her. Just as they'd finished their meals, John Lombardo came into the diner. Ronnie waved at him, and unlike Joey's visible disapproval the night of the gala, the man who was once her father-in-law smiled sweetly back at her.

Paula turned around. "Who's that?"

"Tony's dad." Ronnie's somber tone sounded as if John had died.

Paula whistled. "I see where Hottie gets his looks. Nice picture into the future, huh?"

"Is that all you think about?"

Paula squinted pensively. "Yup. Pretty much."

The hostess handed John a takeout container. He walked over to Ronnie's booth. She smelled the sweet scent of varnish and sawdust on him as they hugged and introduced him to Paula.

"From the center, right?" John said.

"Yes. It's nice to meet you, Mr. Lombardo."

"Mr. Lombardo was my dad. He's been gone for years. Call me John." For a split-second, Ronnie saw Tony in the way her ex-father-in-law smiled. "I hear the gala was a big success."

"We had an incredible turnout. Better than we dreamed," Ronnie said. "Thank you for your donation and the auction item. It was more than generous."

"I do my part whenever I can." His eyes shifted to Ronnie's engagement ring.

She nervously twisted the band. "It was unexpected."

"For a few people." John's kind smile made her feel like a backstabber. He lifted his to-go box. "I gotta head back to the factory. It was nice meeting you, Paula."

"You, too, John."

He pressed two fingers to his mouth and blew Ronnie a friendly kiss while heading for the door.

"Now he's a father-in-law worth having," Paula said.

Ronnie flopped down into the booth.

*Don't I know it.*

• • •

Ronnie checked her watch for the fifth time. Aidan had texted her to meet him in the student union dining hall to discuss plans for the wedding. She had ten minutes before her class and texted him just as he hurried toward her table.

"Two more minutes and I was going to leave," she said, deleting the message.

He kissed her and sat down. "Sorry, sweetheart. I was on the phone with the club. Good news. I booked the banquet hall for the reception."

"The country club? The one you belong to?"

His serene blue eyes danced. "It'll be your club, too, come July third."

Country clubs were all the same. The men lived on the golf course, and the women belonging to frou-frou organizations had lunches on the patio.

"The ceremony will be on the greens at three, cocktail hour at four during pictures, and dinner at five," Aidan said, sounding like a wedding coordinator.

Ronnie and Tony's marriage ceremony had taken place at the church the Lombardos had attended since he was an infant, followed by the reception at The Italian Gardens in Pittsburgh.

She couldn't envision her second wedding at a country club. "Aidan, there are a lot of venues. Can't we see what else is available?"

"The event manager needed an answer today. There was a last-minute cancelation. Do you believe it? Great timing," he said with a grin implying the venue was meant for them.

Suddenly, the reality of marrying Aidan hit Ronnie hard. The engagement. The wedding. Living with Aidan for the rest of her life. It was all real. It was all really happening.

Her reluctance about the club made Aidan realize he had overstepped his groom duties. "You're displeased I went ahead and booked it, aren't you?"

The excitement on his face fled, but Ronnie let him have his moment. "Aidan, it's fine. I would've done the same thing. You made the right decision."

He sensed her feigned approval. "Veronica, what's wrong?"

"Nothing."

*Add lying to the list.*

"Didn't I tell you there are to be no secrets between us?" Aidan said, scolding her. "Tell me what's upsetting you."

That was a good question. Ronnie should've been thrilled about getting married, but they had been engaged less than a week, putting her in the race of a lifetime to meet an urgent deadline. "Maybe we're moving too fast."

Aidan's face tightened. "Does this have anything to do with Tony?"

Ronnie rolled her eyes. "Not that again."

"You do want to marry me?" Doubt came through his tone, stripping his confidence.

She held up the back of her hand in his direction. "No, I always walk around wearing engagement rings from men I don't intend to marry."

"Then what's the problem?"

*Tread lightly, Ronnie.*

"I feel as if we're sprinting through this."

Somehow, her answer had struck a chord. "Sweetheart, we only have two months. Less, actually. We can't drag our feet."

"Then maybe it's best to wait until the fall or spring. Part of the fun of a wedding is the planning."

Tony's voice clanged in Ronnie's head like a church bell. *"Do yourself a favor, make it a long engagement. Over time, you'll come to your senses."*

"Veronica, I've waited for you my entire adult life," Aidan said. "Even July seems like an eternity. Once we solidify the bigger plans, it won't seem so rushed. I promise."

*One tally mark for Aidan; zero for Ronnie.*

"You're right."

"Two words I won't hear as a married man," he joked. His phone dinged with an email notification. "That was quick."

Ronnie leaned over to see the screen. "What is it?"

Aidan scrolled through the message. "A sample itinerary of our honeymoon."

Ronnie threw herself back into the chair. "Don't tell me you booked that, too."

"No, I didn't." He jiggled his head as if she were overreacting.

Ronnie and Tony had chosen their honeymoon together. They had both wanted a warm location by the water and had narrowed down their choices to Cancun. Tony had joked that they would be sure to get "killer Mexican food" compared to the restaurants in Hilton, which couldn't cook a decent burrito to save their lives.

When they hadn't been tanning on the beach or swimming in the Caribbean Sea, Tony and Ronnie were getting their money's worth in their hotel room with three to four lovemaking sessions each day.

"The club is one thing, but the honeymoon?" Aidan said, interrupting Ronnie's wandering mind. "There are so many details to discuss. I want your input on our two-week European excursion."

Her eyes just about fell out of her head. "Europe?"

"Yes." Aidan stared at her as if they had already agreed to travel overseas.

Ronnie and Tony had talked about going to Italy for their twentieth anniversary. Driving along the Tuscany countryside loaded with vineyards. Walking hand in hand as they visited the Colosseum and the Vatican. And the food! The authentic cuisine would be something to tell Tess about.

"Two weeks is too long to be away from the station," Ronnie said. "I can't take that much time off."

Aidan tilted his head condescendingly. "Yes, you can. You're the police chief."

"I realize that, Aidan. But my job is incredibly demanding. I'm in charge of the entire department."

"Surely there are other officers who can fill in for you."

"Well, yes. Captain Rosario is second-in-command. But jaunting around Europe for two weeks seems irresponsible."

Aidan stowed his phone inside his suit pocket. "Veronica, it's our honeymoon. What better way to spend it than in Europe? It'll be fantastic! Spain, France, Italy, Greece. Touring the most romantic cities with my wife."

The tempting trip prodded Ronnie. Aidan wanted to give her the world. What kind of woman would she be if she did not let him? "I'll think about it."

He sighed. Her compromise perturbed him. "Fair enough. After the honeymoon, there are other things to consider."

Trepidation came through in her tone. "Such as?"

"Once I get into a routine with my patients, we can have a baby."

Ronnie's stomach clenched, as if someone had pulled on it from the inside. "You want children?"

He chuckled. "Why wouldn't I?"

"You never mentioned having kids." Ronnie assumed Aidan, being reserved and proper, would find whiney kids with runny noses undignified. Kids were messy and noisy. Demanding and sometimes unruly, among other unattractive traits.

He held her chin in his hand. "Sweetheart, how can I not want to make a child with you?"

*How can I not*? Tony had quoted the same phrase while reminiscing about their Christmas Eve dance. Ronnie hadn't seen him since the morning in her office after the gala. He'd been avoiding her, but it was best to put some space between them until he came to accept her impending nuptials, which, according to her calendar, should be right about never.

"Veronica, a baby is another extension of our lives. A child as beautiful as his or her mother."

Being a psychiatrist meant being in-tune with emotions. Ronnie naturally assumed Aidan detected all her insecurities that went into motherhood. Apparently, he didn't.

"Aidan, I'm forty. My biological clock is winding down."

Leaning in, he kissed her with a sultry grin. "Then we have our work cut out for us. Thankfully for you, I'm up for the challenge. As many times as it takes."

Aidan was a good lover. Gentle. Romantic. Passionate. After making love, he'd hold Ronnie in his arms and dote over her, telling her how beautiful she was and complimenting her lovemaking. He was a talker, but she liked that. He was a psychiatrist. Talking was what they did.

Lately, however, Ronnie's mind wandered to Tony. Thoughts of an ex-husband while having sex with a future husband may seem normal for some women, even laughable, but not to Ronnie. She had mentally cheated on Aidan more than once.

"After the baby's born, you can retire," he said.

*Retire?*

"What did you say?"

Aidan laughed. "You don't expect to continue working as the police chief." Aidan made the notion out to be a no-brainer, that she should know better than to believe a career in law enforcement and raising a child didn't mix.

Ronnie went on the defense. "I'm too young to quit working, and I love my job."

"You misunderstood, sweetheart. I don't have an archaic mindset. The man provides while the wife stays home with the kids. I'm in favor of women working and you still can. Just not as the police chief. There's your course at the college. Add another class or two, if you want. And there's a day care on campus."

In an instant, Ronnie's life had stopped being her own. "You have everything planned out."

"Most of it. The rest will fall into place." He kissed her goodbye. "I have to go. I have a six-thirty session."

Ronnie hid her discomfiture and any sign of uneasiness, avoiding another lecture on keeping secrets. Thankfully, she didn't have to try too hard. Aidan's mind was on his patient as she watched his long strides take him out of the dining hall.

Ronnie made the short trek to Anderson Hall.

*He wants a baby. He wants me to quit the force.*

Being a cop meant the world to Ronnie. Her position as police chief was more than a job. It was what she was born to do. If Aidan took that away from her, he'd be taking away her identity.

Had Tony been right? Was she moving too fast?

No, couldn't be. Ronnie chalked it up to nerves. Fear of failing as a wife and a mother tried dwarfing what mattered most, which was that Aidan loved her. He wanted what was best for her.

Ronnie dismissed the premature talk about retirement. She'd deal with it if the time came. No baby; no reason to retire.

*There's no guarantee I'll get pregnant. I could stay on the pill without him knowing.*

More secrets.

Ronnie went inside Anderson Hall to teach her last class of the semester.

## CHAPTER 24

The stalker sat on the couch with two pronounced stains on the cushions and fabric tears on the armrests. Dilapidated furniture coordinated with the chipped paint and scuff marks adorning the dingy white walls. A matted brown carpet—with who knows what embedded into the crunchy fibers—was harder to ignore.

He didn't have time to stew over the shoddy décor. More pressing matters had him on a mission as he clicked Play on the DVD remote.

She appeared on the television screen, as beautiful as the day they had met, wearing a yellow ankle-length sundress. The gentle breeze sent her long blonde curls airborne as she repeatedly tucked the tendrils behind her ear while pushing the little boy on a swing. He wore jeans, a T-shirt, and a red baseball cap. He was five then.

A scream from the apartment above interrupted the stalker's trip into the past, bringing him back to the present.

"Boy, I said, 'shut up!'" a raspy voice shouted, followed by the crack of a slap and another shrill scream.

The stalker turned up the volume to drown out the noise.

The hole-in-the-wall, one-bedroom apartment was all he could afford. He hated living in that apartment and the despair it represented. He hated what he heard and what he saw.

Arguments from neighbors seeped through the paper-thin walls as they fought over money, and more often, who was cheating on whom. Doors slammed all day long, alerting him when people left and came home. Begs of mercy cried out from children beaten for not doing something as simple as putting their dirty plates into the dishwasher.

The stalker finished his beer in one gulp and crushed the can. Three remained in the six-pack next to him. He had become accustomed to drinking his dinner but had yet to get used to the musty, mildewy stink of his crappy apartment. He detached another can from the plastic ring, snapped back the tin tab, and guzzled the warm beer.

Alcohol didn't dull his memory of what he had lost as he watched the video.

The woman chased the boy in a fenced-in backyard. She grabbed him from behind and shouted, "Gotcha!" twirling him overhead. His laughter came through the loudest. He had a lot of energy that day. One of the few days that year.

The stalker scowled before taking a hard swig of beer and pausing the video. He left the couch and went into the bedroom, where a twin mattress without a box spring lay on the floor.

He put on black leather gloves and took a pair of scissors and a copy of the *Hilton Herald* out of a plastic bag. A small cage with three white mice inside sat on the edge of the bed. The stalker knocked on the plastic dwelling, sending the rodents running in frenzy circles. He took the cage, newspaper, and scissors back to the couch and resumed the video.

After it ended, he watched it again from the beginning. He unfolded the *Hilton Herald*. At the bottom of the front page, he read the article headline aloud. "Police Chief Says Yes to Marriage Proposal at Gala." He cut out the article and photo of Ronnie and Aidan and placed it on the floor by his feet.

The stalker watched the mice scurry in their enclosed, temporary home.

*What kind of life is that for a mouse? Being trapped.*

He could relate, being trapped in unfair confinement for years. Unable to have contact with people other than those branded like him. Nights were lonely, giving him time to plan his revenge while lying on a thin cot masqueraded as a bed.

He took a knife from his pocket, opened it, and fingered the blade. "Time to put the rodents out of their misery."

# CHAPTER 25

The *Hilton Herald* article about Ronnie's engagement meant nothing to her. The words smeared across her photo in what appeared to be blood did.

**YOU WON'T LIVE TO SEE YOUR WEDDING.**

As with the first threat, another envelope with Ronnie's name was stuck between the crack of the front door entrance of the station. She had concluded the first message was a disturbing prank but couldn't brush off the second one as easily.

Ronnie phoned Detective Ashe to her office. He had that *I told you so* expression but knew the drill and left with the bloodstained newspaper clipping while calling forensics.

The surveillance video outside the station showed the same man's face concealed, as it had been the first time. Waiting for word from the forensics team drove Ronnie mad, so she went home to worry in private. Approaching her apartment, she broke out in a cold sweat when she saw door debris on the ground.

Knowing he might still be inside, Ronnie drew her gun from her holster and carefully pushed the lopsided door hanging on one set of hinges. Inside, she inspected the living room for movement, listening for the slightest sound. In the bedroom, she looked inside the closet, under the bed, and behind the door. She went into the bathroom and pulled back the shower curtain. Nothing. The hallway closet was empty, too.

Ronnie lowered the gun as she entered the kitchen. Taped on the refrigerator was a copy of the engagement article with another blood-smeared message.

**YOU TOOK MY LIFE. NOW I'M GOING TO TAKE YOURS.**

Her shaky hand stored the gun in the holster. She called Tony from her watch, waiting five long rings before he answered. "What do you want?" he snapped.

Ronnie raised her arm and spoke into the watch, stopping in between, as if she were having an asthma attack. "Tony. I need you. Come, now."

Tony's anger vanished. "Ronnie, what is it? What's wrong?"

She took a deep breath, calming herself, but her voice still shook. "Someone broke into my apartment."

"Are you okay? Are you hurt?"

"I'm fine." Ronnie's cop instincts nudged her to take another look through the apartment while Tony was on the line. She went back into each room. "He's gone, but he left a note."

"What kind of burglar leaves a note?"

*The kind who wants me dead.*

"I'll explain when you get here. I'm calling Detective Ashe now."

"I'm on my way."

Detective Ashe and Tony arrived at Ronnie's apartment within minutes of each other. The detective took notes and dusted for fingerprints in each room while Ronnie filled Tony in on the death threats.

As she told him about the truck that had followed her from the station, Ronnie sensed an inevitable tongue-lashing from her ex-husband. Tony's nostrils flared like a bull when he heard about the note the day after her birthday, and once Ronnie got to the two gory newspaper clippings, his jaw was pulsating.

"You waited until now to tell me?" he said, admonishing her.

"I didn't want you to worry," she said. "I thought it was a prank."

Tony flipped his hands in the air, flabbergasted at how the police chief, of all people, could be so naïve. "This is serious, Ronnie! It's nothing to screw around with!"

She coiled her arms around her waist in a hapless attempt to make her feel safe in her home. It didn't work. Nothing did.

Tony ran a hand over the back of his head. "Blame isn't the issue. What we need to do is find this guy and lock him up."

Some creep had been in Ronnie's home, but for how long and what else had he done besides leave another threat? The thought of him in her bedroom rifling through her drawers, touching her undergarments, made her want to get rid of every article of clothing she owned as she pictured his sunken footsteps on the carpet.

The break-in surpassed an invasion of privacy and a thief's desperation to take property that didn't belong to him. Someone wanted Ronnie dead and wouldn't stop until her body was on a table in the morgue.

"Do you have any suspects in mind?" Tony asked as Ronnie gnawed on her unmanicured nails. He grabbed her shoulders hard with a shake. "Think, Ronnie! Is there *anyone* you've come in contact recently who wants to hurt you?"

"No! If you hadn't noticed, I lead a boring life. I go to work. I come home. I see Aidan. The end."

Tony went quiet at the mention of her fiancé. He tapped his finger on his hip in an eerie beat. "Coincidence how this all happened after you met him."

Ronnie rose to her fiancé's defense. "Aidan is incapable of doing such a heinous act."

"He's a psychiatrist." Tony pointed a finger at his head. "Maybe the doctor has got a few screws loose. Tomorrow morning, I'm running a check on him."

"You know you can't do a random check on someone without a reason. It's against the law."

"Ronnie, you got three death threats," Tony said, holding up as many fingers.

"There's no evidence indicating Aidan sent them. Therefore, we cannot run a check."

"Considering the police chief's life is in danger, I vote yes to bending the rules."

"You won't find anything," Ronnie said with a snarky tone.

"What makes you so sure?"

Ronnie never intended on anyone finding out what she'd done, but Tony was relentless. The only way she could get him to drop the preposterous theory that her fiancé was out to kill her was to tell Tony the truth. Short of blurting out proof of Aidan's innocence as Detective Ashe went from the bathroom to the bedroom, Ronnie leaned in close toward Tony and whispered, "I already ran a check on him."

"And?" Tony asked, acting a little too eager for her findings.

"Not even a parking ticket."

Tony wasn't sold. "We can't rule him out, Ronnie. He doesn't need prior convictions to be considered a suspect."

She folded her arms across her chest. "How convenient for you."

Tony's eyebrows knitted together. "What does that mean?"

"If Aidan is behind this, it would be one way to get him out of my life."

Tony's eyes grew with exaggeration. "You got me, Ronnie! You cracked the case!" He rubbed his hands together like an evil genius. "My master plan was for you to get involved with a guy who's trying to kill you, so that you'd come running back to me. Aidan would be history, and I'd be the big hero!"

He flicked his wrists with irritation and paced back and forth from the couch to the television.

Ronnie went up behind Tony, appalled at her attitude. "I'm sorry. This whole thing has got me a little crazy." She placed a gentle hand on his back. "I pushed you away once. I won't do it again."

Tony turned only his head to look at her, then as he circled around, brought her in close for a hug. "Even if you've known Aidan for years, it doesn't mean one day he can't snap. The world is nuts, and it's only getting worse."

He didn't say anything she didn't know or had already thought of herself, but she still believed her fiancé had nothing to do with the threats and break-in.

Detective Ashe's presence in the hallway caused Ronnie to break away from Tony. The detective went into the kitchen and took the newspaper clipping off the refrigerator, secured it inside a plastic bag, then dusted the surface for fingerprints. He answered his phone on the first ring. "Ashe." He listened with a stoic expression too hard for Ronnie to interpret and ended the call.

"That was the crime lab. It's animal blood, most likely from a rodent." Detective Ashe held up the baggie. "I'm guessing it'll be the same for this one, but it still needs to be sent in."

"The guy has a file," Ronnie said. "He doesn't want to be traced."

"But still freak you out," Tony added.

"He's doing a bang-up job." Ronnie hoped the sicko had left behind DNA, but even she knew the likelihood of that was slim. "Any prints?"

Detective Ashe put his hands on his wide hips. "Nothing. Not on the doorknobs or the fridge. Anyone clever enough to use rodent blood isn't going to leave prints." He pointed to the door. "What are you going to do about that?"

"I'll take care of it. He delivered his message. He's not coming back tonight." A busted doorframe was the least of Ronnie's worries as she walked Detective Ashe into the hallway.

"Call me if you need me. Doesn't matter what time. Okay?"

"Thanks, Kurt." Ronnie went back inside and gently shut the fragile door.

Tony drew his gun from his back holster and placed the weapon on the coffee table. "I'll take the couch. You shouldn't be alone tonight. Not with the door the way it is."

For once, Ronnie didn't argue. Tony spending the night took the edge off her, doubling her protection with both of them trained in firearms.

If the guy was stupid enough to come back, they'd be ready.

• • •

From the hallway, Ronnie watched Tony sleeping on the couch, and it reminded her of their movie dates at home. Halfway through the DVD, they would lie sideways on the couch, with Tony molded to Ronnie from behind as his breath warmed her skin.

The remembrance made her touch the back of her neck as her rational voice told her foolish feelings, *Go back to bed*.

She took a blanket from the hallway closet. Careful not to wake Tony, Ronnie laid the heavy gray velvet covering over the thinner blanket he had insisted was warm enough.

It was the second time Tony had spent the night at Ronnie's apartment—both of his own accord as his way of protecting her. He had propped a kitchen chair underneath the doorknob. It wasn't the most durable form of security, but the best he could do under the circumstances.

Ronnie had done her due diligence, making sure her overnight guest was warm. Although it was time for her to go back to bed, she sat down on the floor next to the couch, observing the steady rise and fall of Tony's torso as he breathed. The moonlight flowed through the window, illuminating his face, and she had forgotten how long his lashes were until his eyelids started twitching.

*Are you dreaming about me, Tony? I still dream about you.*

Ronnie scolded her inner thoughts. As she stood, Tony's arm ejected from underneath the blanket, and he grabbed her thigh, causing her to jump and shriek.

With his eyes still closed and a lazy smile, he said, "Can't sleep?"

Ronnie pushed his hand off her leg. "I was thirsty. I came to get a glass of water."

He opened his eyes and lifted his head, looking down at the extra blanket.

"The apartment is cold at night," Ronnie said before he could ask. "It's an old building with a faulty heating system."

Tony pulled her down onto the couch. "Still wearing my jersey to bed."

Ronnie forgot she had it on. Tony stared at her bare legs, and she tried hiding them by stretching the blue shirt over her knees. Looking down at the shirt that had become her nightgown, she rubbed the silky fabric between two fingers. "It's comfy."

He touched her face. "Thanks for checking on me."

Her head sprang up. "Stop doing that!"

"Why?" His thumb circled her cheekbone. "Don't you like it?"

"Not particularly." Yet she continued to let him caress her skin.

"Liar," he said with that sexy smile. "You'd make a terrible poker player."

"I'm not one for playing games."

Tony continued caressing her skin. "Your eyes used to flutter whenever I touched your face. You thoroughly enjoyed it, from what I remember."

Ronnie wouldn't allow their past to cloud her judgment and numbed herself to his touch. "It was a long time ago. It's inappropriate now that I'm engaged."

But being promised to another man didn't faze Tony as he wiggled back against the couch and lifted the blankets. "Lie next to me."

The invitation to share the narrow space made her freak out. "I didn't come out here to snuggle with you!"

"Then why did you?" He looked over his shoulder at the kitchen. "It wasn't to get water. I didn't hear the faucet running."

"I drink bottled water."

He sat up on his elbow. "It's okay to be scared. I know you don't want to be alone."

"I'm a big girl, Tony. I stopped being afraid of the dark when I was eight."

"Come on," he said, patting the cushion. "We'll keep each other warm. Like the time at my parents' house during that snowstorm."

Ronnie sprang to her feet. "Stop with the memories!"

"No." He pulled her down onto the couch. "The best times of my life were the ones with you. Remembering is all I have left of us. Don't take that away from me, too."

Ronnie would stay up until dawn with Tony retelling stories of their past if it meant it could eradicate the psycho roaming the streets who wanted her dead. She ran her hands over her face, exhausted but unable to sleep. With her head bowed, she spoke quietly. "I'm scared Tony. I'm really scared."

He took her hands in his. She should've pulled away, but his touch made her feel safe. It always had, and she wished to God she'd stop having those feelings for him.

"Look at me, Ronnie." She did as he asked. "I'll do whatever I can to protect you because in my heart, you'll always be my wife."

*Why does he say things like that?*

Ronnie stood and pulled the blankets to his chin. If she didn't, she would've crawled under the covers with him. "I'm going back to bed."

She was in the hallway when Tony called her name, and she turned. Sitting up, he looked at the couch, then back at her. "There's room here for two if you change your mind."

## CHAPTER 26

Ronnie drank her coffee in the kitchen while the building's maintenance crew repaired the busted door. She barely heard Aidan call her name over the noise from the grinding drill. Outside the doorway, utterly confused, he stepped over the toolbox on the ground and past the two men.

"What happened to the door?" he asked.

Telling her fiancé a crazed man had threatened to kill her wasn't a conversation Ronnie wanted to have over the phone. She had kept another secret from Aidan, and with her poor track record of disclosure, this was a moment she had dreaded since seeing pieces of her door outside her apartment.

Ronnie pulled out a kitchen chair. "Have a seat."

Disconcertment crossed Aidan's face as he lowered himself into the chair.

"Can I get you a cup of coffee?" she asked him, sounding like a waitress.

"No," he snapped. "You call me at the crack of dawn and tell me to come over—that it's important. I arrive to see your door off the hinges. Then you ask me if I want coffee?"

"Thanks for the recap." Sarcasm coated Ronnie's words as she sat down.

"Veronica, please," Aidan said, tired of the runaround. "What's going on?"

Ronnie took a long sip of her coffee. "Someone broke into my apartment last night."

"What?" Aidan's eyes stretched while stuttering, "W-when? W-who?"

She touched his forearm for him to calm down. "I wasn't here when it happened."

Aidan exhaled. "Thank God. Did he take anything?"

"It wasn't that kind of burglary," she said, glancing at the mug.

The same confused look he'd had when he arrived showed up a second time. "I'm not well-versed in law enforcement, but to my limited knowledge, there isn't any other kind."

"He left a death threat," Ronnie said, followed by a sip of coffee. "Someone's after me, Aidan. It's not the first message he's sent."

Aidan listened as Ronnie told him about the mysterious driver and all three threats. She prepared for a tongue-lashing because she had kept more secrets from him. Instead, he asked, "Who knows about this?"

"Detective Ashe." Her voice trailed off. "And Tony."

"Why did I even bother asking?" Aidan's face screwed in disdain. "Surely you told your ex-husband but left me in the dark. Tony's known about this since day one!"

Ronnie felt her insides boiling. Her fiancé acted like a selfish brat, more concerned about being one up on her ex-husband instead of her safety.

"Let's get a few things straight, Aidan," Ronnie said. "One, it's not a competition. Two, Tony didn't know anything until last night. The only person I told was Detective Ashe, because I needed him to send the evidence to forensics."

"How could you stay here alone, Veronica? Why didn't you come to my house?"

Ronnie glowered at Aidan. "Right. Leave my apartment with a busted door."

He pointed vehemently at the living room. "Then I would've stayed here!"

She sipped her coffee. It went down hard.

Aidan's eyebrows rose high above his glasses. "Oh, I see," he said with an eerie calmness. "Why would you need me here when Tony spent the night?"

"On the couch," she blurted, as if that lessened the situation.

"I'm sure he did," Aidan mumbled.

"Tony's a trained officer. It made sense for him to stay here."

Aidan looked away, shaking his head in disbelief.

"Do you honestly think I had sex with my ex-husband on the brain after some nutcase breaks into my apartment and threatens to kill me?"

Aidan adjusted his glasses; his face flushed with embarrassment. "I didn't mean to imply—"

"No, you flat out accused me of sleeping with Tony!" Ronnie's voice carried to the doorway, where the men stopped what they were doing and stared. She left the table and dumped the remaining coffee down the drain, slamming the mug down in the sink.

*How dare he even think such a thing!*

Aidan's chair scraped against the floor. Standing behind Ronnie, his long arms wrapped around her, and he kissed the back of her head. "I'm sorry, sweetheart. I didn't mean it. I know you're not that kind of person. It does make me feel better knowing you weren't alone."

Ronnie's tension from the break-in and threats melted at Aidan's touch and sincere apology. She turned around, and they embraced. "I'm sorry for not telling you sooner, Aidan."

"It's okay. I understand," he said and kissed the top of her head. "I think it's prudent for you to take a temporary leave from work."

"And do what? Stay in my apartment all day. Not go outside. Stop living life." Ronnie looked up at Aidan. "I can't do that. That only gives this guy more time."

"What if something happens to you? I can't even think about—"

"I have my gun on me all the time. I'll tell my officers the situation. They can patrol the neighborhood and be on the lookout for anything suspicious."

"That's it?" Hopelessness pinged Aidan's words.

"There's no DNA to trace him. Until he makes a mistake, there's nothing I can do. I can't bring in every male in Hilton and the surrounding Pittsburgh area for questioning."

Aidan pinched Ronnie's chin with authority. "Until this is over, you are to stay in constant communication with me. Understood?"

"Yes," she replied meekly.

"I want to know where you are at all times, and how long you'll be gone. You are to check in with me each time you leave the apartment, the station, and the college. No arguments. I mean it, Veronica."

"I'll do whatever you want, Aidan. I promise."

"Good." He released her chin. "What's on your agenda for today?"

It wasn't even eight o'clock yet, and Ronnie felt as if she were a gas tank on empty. All her energy had been sucked out of her. "Just the station, then home."

"Fine. Get your bag. I'll follow you to work."

"Aidan, you don't have to do that."

"Veronica, I insist. I have plenty of time before my ten o'clock class. My last session is at five-thirty. As soon as I'm done, I'll come over and spend the night. You are not to be alone."

The maintenance crew gathered their tools. One of the men called out from the doorway, "You're all set, ma'am."

Ronnie thanked the crew as Aidan looked at his watch. "We better get going." He hugged her tighter than Tess Lombardo and kissed the top of her head. "I love you, Veronica."

"I love you too, Aidan."

# CHAPTER 27

Ronnie left the station from the back entrance, looking for the final exams she vaguely remembered stowing inside her bag. She'd been reporting her daily agenda to Aidan as he had ordered and as she had promised, while he locked the new deadbolt on her door. He had practically moved into her apartment after the break-in. Seeing his toothbrush on the bathroom sink and clothes hanging in her closet made her feel as if they were already married.

She found the exams in the center pouch. The pages moved like an animation as she thumbed the stack, counting the copies.

"Taking off?" a voice from behind her said. She jumped and dropped the papers.

Ronnie chased after the exams, blowing across the parking lot. "What are you still doing here?" she asked Tony as she crouched on the pavement.

He squatted, collecting the papers near him, and handed her the stack. "Working a double. Max is, too. Three officers called in sick."

She shoved the exams inside her bag and headed for her SUV. Tony nipped at her heels as he followed her across the lot. She glanced over her shoulder. "I don't remember hiring you as my bodyguard, Lombardo."

Her joke fell flat; Tony didn't find it funny. "I'll follow you to the college."

Ronnie unlocked the door with the key fob; the headlights blinked. "I don't need a police escort."

"There's no harm in having extra protection."

"Then what? Call in the Secret Service? Perhaps a bulletproof motorcade? I'm not the President of the United States."

"He's still out there, Ronnie. You need to be vigilant. You're a cop. You know that."

She opened the driver's door, tossing her purse and bag onto the passenger seat. "Tony, I appreciate your concern—"

"Concern?" he echoed in astonishment. "Global warming is concerning. This is your life. The guy isn't an amateur."

"Which means he won't try anything in broad daylight. The college is safe. Students and faculty are still moving about, and campus security is patrolling the grounds."

Tony scoffed at the mention of campus security as if they were second-rate officers. "How long is the exam?"

"Students have three hours, but they'll probably finish in two."

He folded his arms over his chest and nodded. "All right. I'll be there to make sure you get home safely."

"The campus is lit more brightly than Times Square. There are surveillance cameras everywhere." Ronnie grinned with a hint of teasing in her voice. "Besides, it's outside our jurisdiction. You don't want to get reprimanded again, do you?"

"You're worth the infraction." Tony glanced up, as if he were pondering the universe. "There's an old saying: 'It's better to ask for forgiveness than permission.'"

Ronnie balanced her fist on her hip. "Who says I'll forgive you?"

Tony rammed an invisible dagger between his pecs with a *thud*. He winced in feigned drama, staggering as if she had stabbed him. "Ouch! No! Bl-blood."

"Your dying scene needs work. I wouldn't count on the Oscar just yet."

While Ronnie wanted to stay and continue her flirty bantering exchange with Tony, she had a roomful of students waiting to take their final exam and call it a semester. She got inside the SUV; her left leg hanging out. Nicely, but firmly, she said, "Lombardo, as Chief, I'm ordering you to do your job. Patrol your sector, not Dearborn College."

Ronnie shut the door and pressed the ignition button. Tony knocked on the glass, and she rolled down the window. He leaned through the opening, adamant on protecting her. "Call or text me when the exam is over."

"Ever since the break-in, Aidan's forced me to check in with him like clockwork. I can't pee without telling him first."

Tony sighed, shaking his head. "Geez, you're stubborn."

"I'll be fine."

"Promise?"

"When have you ever known me to break a promise?" she said and laughed.

But Tony didn't. His face was serious, one that said he meant business. "Be careful." Reaching through the opened window, he touched her face just enough to make her eyes surrender at contact before getting carried away.

She put the SUV in reverse and backed out of her reserved spot. At the exit, she saw Tony in the rearview mirror watching her from a distance and turned onto the road.

• • •

The first student handed in his test after an hour, while the last one finished hers forty-five minutes later, making Ronnie wonder if she'd made the questions final-exam worthy as she walked through the college parking lot.

She longed for home and could almost feel the softness of her gray sweatpants against her skin and taste the takeout dinner from Athens Deli while she and Aidan graded papers.

Inside her SUV, Ronnie went to call her fiancé to tell him she was on her way home when she heard a click, followed by a knife blade snapping open below her chin. "Hello, Ronnie," came a man's voice from the back seat.

Fear paralyzed her vocal cords, preventing her from screaming, as she choked on her own breath.

"Give me your gun," he ordered.

She didn't move.

"I know you have it on you," he said, pressing the knife into her skin. "I hate repeating myself."

One quick move, and he'd slit her neck open. "It—it's in my back h-holster," she stammered.

"Get it."

The man released some of the knife pressure and hovered the blade in front of Ronnie's neck as she leaned forward to remove the gun.

"Nice and slow." He commended her obedience. "That's it. Good girl."

Holding the loaded gun, she risked missing her target from the way she was positioned.

The man traded the knife for the gun and held the barrel under her chin, followed by a clicking noise from the switchblade. "Start the car."

His familiar voice sent her eyes to the rearview mirror for a glimpse of the madman in the back seat.

"Look straight ahead." He sank the barrel deeper into her skin. "The curiosity must be killing you, but you'll find out soon enough."

Ronnie's trembling hand accidentally put the gear shifter into NEUTRAL. She popped it into DRIVE, and the vehicle juddered.

"Don't try anything cute or Aidan will be a widower before he's a groom," the man warned her, then ordered her onto the highway.

Her hands strangled the steering wheel, turning her knuckles white as a pool of sweat formed in her palms. The speed limit sign prompted an idea as she drove through a thirty-mile-an-hour residential zone. Cops set traps along the mile-stretch, parked with radar guns aimed out the window. How ironic? Breaking the law might save her life. She floored the gas pedal, and the speedometer soared to fifty.

"Slow down!" the man barked, and she slammed on the brakes. "We don't want to get pulled over, now do we?"

Ronnie felt a vibration on her wrist as her phone rang. The man in the back seat reached inside her purse with a gloved hand and held the device in front of her. Aidan's pictured filled the rectangular screen. "If it isn't the impending groom."

The missed call went to voicemail. Seconds later, she felt another vibration. This time, she had received a text. Two minutes had passed before Aidan called and texted again.

The crazy man snickered. "Dr. Foster is persistent."

Ronnie followed the man's directions, every stop and turn, taking them farther from the Dearborn College community and miles outside of Hilton.

She finally asked, "Where are you taking me?" then wished she hadn't as his sinister cackle prickled her skin.

"Somewhere no one will ever find you."

. . .

Tony entered the main entrance of Dearborn College. More than a dozen buildings were on campus, and it occurred to him he didn't know which one Ronnie's class was in.

He drove down each aisle of the parking lot at a crawl, combing the rows for a white Toyota 4Runner. Ronnie was crazy to think he would let her walk across campus at dusk by herself while a psycho had threatened to kill her. Tony didn't care the college was out of his jurisdiction. He'd take the slap on the wrist for another infraction because Ronnie's safety surpassed his ego.

He patrolled three parking lots a second time with no luck. It was eight o'clock, and Tony remembered Ronnie had said the three-hour exam wouldn't take that long. She must've just left, but he wouldn't know for sure until he heard it from her, and he dialed her number.

Her phone rang once. Twice. Three times. "Come on, answer," he mumbled impatiently before hearing her voicemail greeting. *"Hi, this is Ronnie. Leave a message,"* followed by a beep.

"It's me. I'm at the college. I know. I deliberately disobeyed an order. You can chew me out tomorrow." Driving toward the exit, still looking, he said, "I don't see your SUV. You must be home or on your way. Call or text me to let me know you're okay. I sound like Ma." He paused. "See ya later."

As soon as Tony pulled onto the highway from the campus, he had a troublesome feeling something wasn't right.

Things weren't as they'd appeared.

• • •

Ronnie drove to an undisclosed location with the gun's barrel pressed deep below her chin. Her only weapon—her gun—had the power to take her life.

The madman in the back seat had yet to reveal his identity or motive for wanting her dead. "Turn here," he ordered.

Ronnie drove down a desolate dirt road with pockets of thick brush on each side and no houses. She passed a road sign: DEAD END AHEAD. It was a killer's ideal dumping ground to stash a body, which made her believe this was no impromptu abduction. The man had thoroughly detailed his plan, and she imagined, felt great satisfaction in choosing this spot.

The sun had set. Through the evening darkness, Ronnie saw a dilapidated farmhouse and ramshackle barn when she remembered the emergency GPS on her watch.

In the middle of nowhere, she doubted there was a nearby cell phone tower to pick up a signal, but the technology on her wrist was her only hope. Ronnie discreetly moved her hands to the six o'clock position on the steering wheel. After a few swipes, she hit the emergency icon, and the man ordered her to turn onto the gravel driveway.

• • •

Tony made a pit stop at the station after leaving Dearborn College. First to the restroom, then to the kitchen for coffee. That bothersome feeling gnawed at him like a persistent stomachache and intensified when Max came in the kitchen with a worrisome look on his face.

"Aidan's here," he said. "He said he needs to see you."

Only one reason Tony could think of would make Aidan come to the station without Ronnie. Tony dropped the Styrofoam cup in the sink, letting coffee splash onto the wall, and sprinted to the lobby, with Max behind him.

Both times Tony had seen Aidan, the professor's demeanor had brimmed with sophistication— unlike now as he paced back and forth like a junkie.

"Where's Veronica?" Aidan shouted at Tony. "Where is she?"

Tony's heart pounded with trepidation. He hadn't heard from Ronnie, either, and assumed she was being her stubborn self by not calling him as he had asked.

"I've been waiting at her apartment. She should be home by now. I've called and texted," Aidan said, on the verge of hyperventilating. "She hasn't responded. Something's wrong, Tony. I feel it."

Trained officers stay calm in every situation, but inside, Tony was freaking out. "Aidan, are you positive she didn't stop anywhere on her way home? The grocery store or to get a bite to eat?"

"No," Aidan answered sharply. "She explicitly told me this morning she was going straight home after the exam. Even if she hadn't, why wouldn't she answer when I called or call me back?"

His phone dinged, sending him scurrying into his pocket for the device.

Tony could feel himself breathe as air reached his lungs. The text had to be from Ronnie. She was safe.

But the bewildered expression held on Aidan's face didn't confirm Tony's relief. "What is it?"

"An address. 1723 Townline Extension in Bowman."

"Bowman's so small, it doesn't even have a zip code," Max said. "There's nothing but woods and vacant land."

Aidan's eyes widened. "It's Veronica! She's in danger! There's an emergency GPS signal on her watch. It sends a text when activated!"

*Why didn't you get to the college sooner?* Tony thought.

He'd have time to beat himself up later for his rookie mistake after he found Ronnie.

All Tony had to do was look at Max and his partner knew what to do.

"Right behind you," his best friend said, and he and Tony raced to the door as Aidan followed them.

"I'm going with you."

"No!" Tony said. "Stay here!"

"She's not your wife!" Aidan shouted.

Tony balled his fists. If he hadn't been a police officer, he would've knocked Aidan out in one punch and the guy would be on the floor, seeing stars. "She's not yours, either, Aidan." Tony pointed at the ground. "Stay put. Leave the station and I'll have you arrested."

In the patrol car, Tony called Ronnie again, praying for her to answer, hoping she had accidentally triggered the emergency text or there was a glitch in the GPS. Fear bounded him with thoughts that he had seen her alive for the last time earlier that day. Fury scolded him for not insisting on standing guard outside her classroom.

One agonizing ring after another, until her voicemail greeting. *"Hi, this is Ronnie. Leave a message."*

Tony hung up. "No answer."

Max flicked on the siren and lights and sped toward the tiny town of Bowman.

## CHAPTER 28

The madman wedged the gun between Ronnie's shoulder blades and marched her past the vacant farmhouse with scuffed gray clapboard siding. Overgrown grass and dead shrubs bordered the dwelling. She suspected the two smashed windows on the second floor were the handiwork of bored kids with nothing better to do than to vandalize an abandoned property on a lazy Saturday afternoon.

The barn was just as bad. The derelict structure's slanted door balanced on a set of hinges, while gaps between tattered, chipped planks the color of faded red paint made up the side facing Ronnie.

Once inside the darkness, except for slivers of evening dusk streaming through missing planks and two small windows, the man used the gun to nudge Ronnie forward. She lost her balance and stumbled. This was her chance. She wouldn't die without a fight.

Ronnie spun around to hit him, but he blocked her desperate move and punched her in the eye. She fell to the ground, whimpering. He straddled her, pinning her down, and backhanded her across the face.

Dragging her across the dirty, cold floor, he bellowed, "Get up!" pulling Ronnie to her feet. "I dare you to try that again, Chief."

He slammed her against a post and wrenched her arm behind her back. Ronnie's throbbing eye felt as if it were about to explode; her vision blurred. Metal clanked, and a handcuff pinched her skin.

"Ah," the crazed man said, snapping the second cuff. "It's been a long time since I've done that."

Then it clicked, so to speak. Cops use handcuffs. The man's voice. His precision on not leaving DNA. The mysterious stalker who wanted Ronnie dead had stood with her on the same side of the law. In a drawn-out whisper she said, "Luke Tillerson."

The man came around from behind the post. He flicked a cigarette lighter, cutting a flame through the darkness. "You remember. I'm touched."

Luke lit a tarnished lantern next to his feet. The yellow glow revealed hay piles and rusty tools.

With a sneer that made the hairs on Ronnie's arms stand, he dangled the handcuff key and put it into his pocket. "At my sentencing, I warned you that you'd pay for what you did. I wasn't bluffing." He made a *tsk, tsk* noise with his tongue.

Luke shoved the gun down the front of his pants; the trigger exposed for quick access. His baggy jeans and stained white hoodie made him look two pegs shy of a homeless man. His onetime meticulously trimmed reddish-brown beard was straggly, while his crew cut had grown as long as Ronnie's hair.

"I did my time behind bars. All eight years, thanks to you." He took a spool of rope off the ground and cut two pieces with the knife. "I was the best detective Scottsdale had until you came along."

"*Good* cops don't steal drugs from the evidence room and sell them to *kids* on the streets," she said.

Luke threw the knife and spool of rope on the ground. "I had a good reason!"

Ronnie's phone rang. Luke removed it from the hoodie's front pouch. "Guess who? I'll give you a clue. It's not your fiancé."

*Why didn't I listen to you, Tony?*

"I'm impressed, Ronnie," Luke said, stuffing the phone into the pouch. "Tell me, just between us cops. Do you get a rise from bossing Lombardo around? Is it your way of getting even with him for cheating on you with that smokin' hot chick from The Grind? Although, from what I've seen, you've both have gotten past all that. Water under the bridge, as they say. Yep, you and Lombardo are pretty cozy."

Luke went behind the post and tied one rope around her ankles. "Someone loved me once. I had a family. A wife and a son. But you took them from me."

"You did it all on your own," Ronnie said.

He nearly strangled her with the second piece of rope and spoke with rage into her ear. "When your kid's got cancer and the chemo and radiation bills are a hundred grand, you need to get creative. You didn't see it that way, though. No, not Miss Perfect By-the-Book Cop. You're nothing but a squealer. Cops have a bond, Ronnie. Blue brotherhood."

Gasping for air, she replied, "Stealing... drugs was wrong. Made the wrong... choice."

Luke loosened his hold. "Hmm. Choice. It's interesting you use that word. I haven't decided what I'm going to do with you. Don't get me wrong, I'm still going to kill you. The question is *how*?"

He tied the knot around her neck, then stood in front of her. "Tell you what, I'll let you pick. Here are your choices. Option A." He whipped out the gun and pressed it to her forehead, making her shriek. "Do it now—quick. One bullet between your eyeballs and be done with it."

He withdrew the gun.

"But what's the fun in that?" Stepping closer, he said, "Option B."

As Ronnie turned her head, he grabbed her face with one hand, pinching her cheeks hard. "Look at me when I'm talking to you!"

She trembled and nearly lost control of her bladder.

"As I was saying. Option B. Make you suffer, like I suffered for eight years in that hellhole prison waiting for my family to visit. Wishing they'd answer the phone. Hoping for a letter from my wife—her handwriting has a whimsical flair. A drawing from my son or a note telling me about school or what sports he plays. I didn't even get a lousy picture! Not one. I don't even know what my son looks like now! You know why I didn't get any of those things, Ronnie? Hmm?" Luke scratched his greasy hair. "Because three months into my sentence, my wife sent me divorce papers. She left me because I did the only thing I knew to do for my family. That's gratitude for ya."

He returned the gun to the makeshift holder. Taking the phone from the pouch, he turned it off and stuffed it into Ronnie's pants pocket, staring at her with a sadistic grin that gave her the chills.

"It's a shame to let you go to waste." Luke pressed his body against hers. The smell of stale beer and the stench of menthol cigarettes lingered on his breath. "Eight years is a long time to go without doing a woman."

He touched Ronnie's cheek with the tip of his nose. She squeezed her eyes shut, her chest heaving. He sniffed her, then slowly licked her neck. "You taste like vanilla—my favorite."

Being raped was every woman's worst nightmare. On the Scottsdale force, Ronnie had taken several statements from sexually abused victims. She never forgot the terror in their eyes as they spoke of the attacks and imagined she had that same look right now. Restrained to the post without a way to fight back, all Ronnie could do was beg for mercy. "Don't... please, don't," her voice quivered.

Evil permeated Luke's eyes as he burst into cunning laughter. "Nah. You're not my type. I have a thing for blondes."

Squatting, he rubbed a wad of hay between his fingers. "Nice and dry." He stood, wagging his finger. He had an idea. "Here's what I'm going to do for you, Chief. I'm going to speed up the process."

Luke picked up a gasoline can off the ground, and Ronnie frantically tried breaking free, hoping the rotted post would snap in half.

"Don't tire yourself out," he said, pouring the fluid onto the hay. "You're not going anywhere."

Ronnie was trapped with no way out. Luke was going to torch the barn. She could almost hear the hay crackle and smell the smoke, feeling it fill her lungs, cutting off her air supply. She was better off being shot than being consumed by flames.

Ronnie was going to die. She closed her eyes and saw a vision of Nick and Vivian. Soon, she'd see them for real.

. . .

The patrol car came to a rolling stop. Tony pointed to the 4Runner in the driveway. "There's Ronnie's SUV!"

Max requested backup into the radio's microphone on his shoulder.

Exiting the patrol car, Tony searched for signs that Ronnie was alive, but the night's stillness had him fear he was too late. "Check the house, Max. I'll take the barn."

"Got it." Max cuffed Tony's shoulder. "Be careful."

Tony reciprocated the warning with a slap on his buddy's back. "You, too."

He drew his gun and blended into the dark, ominous night, walking like a stealthy thief across the grass when suddenly, he felt Ronnie's presence getting stronger with each step he took. She had to be alive. Tony peeked around the barn door. A light bounced off the ground. His quiet footsteps took him inside, where he saw Ronnie bound to a wooden post.

Tony's heart raced, beating viciously against the wall of his chest, thankful she was alive, but mad as hell at the man who had kidnapped her.

*I swear I'll kill him if he hurt her.*

Ronnie lifted her drooping head. Tony raised a finger to his mouth with a silent "shh." The man came into view, dousing a pile of hay in liquid.

Tony sniffed. Gasoline.

"All done." The man dropped the empty can and stood next to Ronnie. "One spark and this place will be a blazing inferno in no time."

Tony came out from hiding with his gun aimed at the guy as if he were a paper target at the shooting range. "Don't move!"

But the man was quick and pressed the gun's barrel under Ronnie's chin as her tiny whimper traveled across the barn to Tony. "Your team is smarter than I gave them credit for, Chief," he said in a calm tone, implying he was in charge. "Hand over the gun, Lombardo."

"Don't do it, Tony!" Ronnie shouted.

The man grabbed a clump of Ronnie's hair and yanked it back, making her yelp. "Still barking out orders, aren't ya?"

Tony was one of the department's best marksmen, but without a clean shot, he risked hitting Ronnie. The hay under his feet snapped as he took a step, his eyes fixated on the stranger. "Drop your weapon! Now!"

The man slid the gun to Ronnie's temple. "One more step and the last thing you'll see will be bits of her brain splattered all over."

"Take it easy," Tony said. "Step away from her. Put the gun slowly on the ground and your hands where I can see them."

"Don't talk to me like I'm a lunatic!" the man screamed. "I used to *be* you, a respected cop. I helped people." He pulled Ronnie's hair again; she shrieked in pain. "Then *she* ruined my life!"

"I don't know what this is all about," Tony said.

"You wanna know what happened, Officer Lombardo? Okay, I'll tell you. You see, your ex-wife here turned me in. She couldn't mind her own business. She ratted on me like a ten-year-old tattletale. I spent eight years in prison. Thanks to her, I lost everything! My wife, my son, my job. All because she couldn't keep that BIG, FAT yap of hers shut!"

Tony's training had prepared him for situations like this. He knew exactly what to do, but this wasn't a random stranger. His wife—that's right—his wife's life hung in the balance. Tony kept the guy talking. "Killing her won't change anything."

"Yes, it will," the stranger said in a pleasant tone. "It's called revenge, and it's *so* deliciously sweet."

Tony would've pummeled the guy unrecognizable if he hadn't had a gun to Ronnie's head.

The man moved the barrel down Ronnie's jaw to her chin and used it to turn her head toward him. "Everything comes full circle, Chief. You took my wife from me. Now it's your turn to lose someone you love. I can't think of a better way than for you to watch your precious Tony die." In a seething whisper he said, "Say goodbye to hubby, Mrs. Lombardo."

The man aimed the loaded gun at Tony, followed by rounds of popping gunfire. Tony fired three shots, but not before the man got two into him and his body plunked on the ground.

"Tony!" Ronnie screamed.

The man collapsed, and on his descent, he knocked over the lantern. It rolled into a pile of gasoline-soaked hay, igniting the straw. Flames raced through the hay and up the walls.

Tony groaned and made it onto his knees. Holding his left shoulder while the blood drained from his body, he moved toward Ronnie in a slow crawl, dragging his legs behind him.

She banged her handcuffed hands on the post. "The key's in his pocket!"

Tony used his free hand to pull it out of the dead man's front pocket. He couldn't think about the pain, he had to save Ronnie. Standing had never been so painful and exhausting as he unlocked the cuffs, but fumbled with the knots.

Ronnie pointed to the knife on the ground. "Over there, Tony!"

Staggering toward the knife, struggling to breathe, he picked it up and ripped through each rope in one swipe, freeing Ronnie. He dropped to his knees, pushing her. "Get outta here!"

"No! I'm not leaving you!" She hoisted him onto his feet, but his legs buckled and he fell again.

"Max! Help!" Ronnie shouted as he sprinted inside the barn and skidded to the ground like a baseball player sliding into home plate. Without hesitating, he threw Tony over his shoulder.

"OW!" Tony screamed.

Cracking wood, followed by a sharp snap.

"Go! Go!" Ronnie shouted, pushing Max from behind as they ran out the door just as a fiery beam tumbled and the brittle roof caved.

Max lowered himself to the ground and rolled Tony onto the grass. He radioed for help in the microphone. "Officer down! I repeat OFFICER IS DOWN! I need an ambulance and fire truck at 1723 Townline Extension, Bowman. Hurry!"

Ronnie tore off the blouse over her tank top and moved Tony's head onto her lap. She pressed the pink shirt against his shoulder, staunching the spewing blood. "It's going to be okay, Tony. The ambulance will be here any minute."

Blood soaked through the shirt. Ronnie bunched it again and put a clean section of material over the wound. She unfastened the top two buttons of Tony's uniform shirt and clutched the St. Christopher medallion.

Tony squeezed Ronnie's arm with what little strength he had, letting her know he was fighting, as the fire's orange glow reflected off her. She became a blurry sketch; he was losing consciousness.

"Hang on, Tony. Hang on." Ronnie kissed his head while rocking back and forth. "Please don't leave me," she pleaded, sounding a thousand miles away.

His blood-drenched hand stretched up and touched her cheek.

If this was how he was going to die, he couldn't have asked for a better way than in Ronnie's arms.

## CHAPTER 29

Ronnie held her cold blouse, soaked in blood. Tony's blood.

She had followed the ambulance to Allegheny General Hospital in Pittsburgh, the closest level one trauma center. The paramedics had passed the gurney to a team of doctors and nurses on standby, who rushed Tony into an ER room, then did a CT scan. An hour later, he was in an operating room.

After a nurse asked Ronnie a lot of questions, the woman offered to contact the Lombardos. Ronnie should've been the one to make the call, but she chickened out. How could she tell John and Tess over the phone that their son had taken a bullet saving her life?

Ronnie called Aidan and told him to meet her at the hospital. In the ER waiting room, she scrolled through the missed calls and texts from her fiancé, but it was Tony's voicemail minutes after Luke had taken her off the campus that she listened to, hoping a recording wouldn't be the last time she would hear his voice.

*"It's me. I'm at the college. I know. I deliberately disobeyed an order. You can chew me out tomorrow. I don't see your SUV. You must be home or on your way. Call or text me to let me know you're okay. I sound like Ma."* He paused. *"See ya later."*

If Ronnie had let Tony follow her home from the college, none of this would've happened. He would've seen Luke hiding in the back seat of her SUV, arrested him on the spot, and would now be filling out a report at the station. Luke would be behind bars, Ronnie could walk freely without fear of another threat, and Tony wouldn't be in a hospital fighting for his life.

Ronnie listened to Tony's voicemail a second time as Aidan ran through the emergency room doors. He nearly smothered her as his shaky hands glided roughly through her hair. He held her so tightly; she coughed as he pecked her with rapid kisses, but stopped when he saw the blood blotches on her face. "Veronica, you're hurt!"

She touched her cheek. "It's not mine."

"Let me see you." Aidan studied her. For what, Ronnie didn't know, and apparently neither did Aidan. His eyes, however, shook with fury at the rope burn across her neck.

"I'm fine." Ronnie intercepted his hand that reached for the raw line of scraped skin. He opened her hand, staring at the dried blood embedded in her palm. "I'm okay."

Through the window, Ronnie saw the Lombardos dash across the lit parking lot and into the emergency room entrance.

"Where's Tony? Where's my baby?" From the look of Tess's puffy, bloodshot eyes, she had cried the entire way to the hospital.

"He's in surgery," Ronnie said.

Tess whimpered. "How did this happen?"

"What was he doing in a barn?" Joey asked, like a concerned brother and not a reporter.

"Who was the guy who shot him?" Vince wanted to know.

"Why was he working nights?" Tess asked. "He's on the day shift!"

The barrage of questions had them talking over one another in a cacophony of noise. John blew a hard whistle. "Everyone, shut up!"

The family obeyed his command.

"Start at the beginning, Ronnie," John said to her. "Don't leave anything out."

The Lombardos listened as Ronnie told them about the death threats and the break-in. Cora and Nonna both gasped. Ronnie painted a watered-down version of the horrific details from the moment Luke held her at knifepoint from the back seat to how her watch's emergency GPS led Tony to the barn in Bowman.

Tess noticed Ronnie's bloody blouse, knowing it was her son's blood. She punched down against the air with her fists. "I knew one day something like this would happen. I just knew it!"

John held his crying wife as her wailing traveled to the floor above them. "Tony's a fighter, Tess. He's not gonna let a bullet get the best of him."

Nonna, Vince, Cora, and Joey girded Tess from behind. Ronnie moved with caution toward the Lombardo clan. "Tess?"

The woman stiff-armed Ronnie, keeping her at bay. She looked into her former mother-in-law's perennial loving eyes that now blamed her for Tony's critical condition.

"Let's leave them alone." Behind Ronnie, Aidan placed his hands on her shoulders and gently guided her away from the family circle that alienated her.

"I need to do something," Ronnie said. "Will you come with me?"

"Of course, sweetheart."

They went to the information counter, where a receptionist had ended a phone call. "Excuse me?" Ronnie said. "Where's the chapel?"

The woman pointed to the ceiling. "Third floor, honey." She patted Ronnie's hand. "I'm praying for him, too."

Ronnie and Aidan rode the elevator and followed the signs to the chapel. The brightly lit mini-church contrasted with the movies' portrayals of a dark room with rows of flickering candles and a woman in despair kneeling at the altar with her hands folded in prayer.

Sitting on the hard wooden pew closest to the door, Ronnie stared at the metal cross on the wall in front of her. The symbol of one man's sacrifice who had died for the sins of the world.

When she and Tony were married, they had attended Mass at St. Matthew's, although not as faithfully as other church members. Vivian had been baptized as an infant with Vince and Cora as her godparents. Ronnie and Tony had planned on their daughter's milestones as a Catholic. First Confession, First Communion, and Confirmation.

Ronnie had followed the rules, but it didn't immunize her from losing the ones she loved the most.

"Do you believe in God, Aidan?" she asked.

He squirmed in his seat, but Ronnie was too disorientated to question what made him uncomfortable about God. "I think a force exists. Whether it's God, I can't be certain. There are those rarities that have no explanation. Miracles and supernatural experiences, but I'm not totally convinced."

"Then, you're an atheist?"

He thought before answering. "Technically, an agnostic."

Add religion to the subject list they hadn't discussed. Ronnie's soon-to-be husband was on the fence about God.

The chapel offered hope to those clinging to an invisible belief that something much greater had the power to save. Yet, how many prayers went unanswered?

"I believe in God," she said. "But I don't know why he doesn't answer every prayer."

Aidan hunched over, the tips of his fingers forming a triangle. "I'm sorry, Veronica. I don't have an explanation."

A man of Aidan's intellectual curiosity must've had theological discussions with some of his patients. If he questioned God's existence, he was more suited and prepared with clinical reasoning and science inside the four-walls of his office versus a hospital chapel, where he was a fish out of water.

"It doesn't hurt to pray, right?" Ronnie said. "Some prayers do get answered."

Aidan gathered her into his arms. "If it makes you feel better, sweetheart, you say all the prayers you want."

Ronnie did just that, only not out loud.

*The last thing I deserve is a favor. But please, God, let Tony live. He has a family that loves him and friends who care about him more than he knows. I've already lost Dad and Vivian. I can't lose another person I love.*

Life without Tony would expand the void left by Nick and Vivian, causing an urge to justify why she had gone to the chapel when she could've easily prayed in the waiting room.

"Aidan, I know you don't have warm and fuzzy feelings for Tony, and I'm not asking you to. But he's one of my officers. I feel responsible. I can't go home until I know he's all right."

Her fiancé kissed the side of her head. "Veronica, we're not leaving the hospital until he's out of surgery."

Ronnie didn't expect her fiancé and her ex-husband to become best friends. To have a beer at The Tavern after work and swap Ronnie stories. Yet, the worst of times have a tendency to bring out the best in people. If that were true, then it seemed Aidan had turned a corner.

"Let's go downstairs," he said. "I'll buy you a really bad cup of coffee. We'll get some for the Lombardos, too."

As they stood, John came into the chapel.

"Is Tony out of surgery?" Ronnie asked him faster than he could say hello.

He sadly shook his head. "Not yet, hon."

"Mr. Lombardo, we're putting out positive thoughts for Tony," Aidan said.

John's smile held him back from crying. "Thank you. We'll take all we can get."

As Aidan went into the hallway, Ronnie said to him, "I'll be down in a minute."

He knew she wanted to be alone with John. Again, he didn't argue. "I'll get that coffee."

John lifted his heels in a rocking motion, the same way Tony did when he didn't know what to say. "That's your fiancé? Nice fella."

"Aidan's a wonderful man." Perhaps more now than twelve hours ago, although she had sounded as if she needed to talk herself into it. "Shouldn't you be with Tess?"

"The boys are with her. I came here to check on you."

Ronnie sat down in a pew, guilt overwhelming her. "Tony's the one you need to worry about, not me."

Tony was fighting for his life because he had saved hers, and his father wanted to make sure *she* was okay. Who does that? Who? The Lombardos.

The kindest, most loving family Ronnie had ever had the honor of knowing, and one time, had been a member of.

"Why can't I worry about both of you?" John asked.

She stared at her lap to keep her from seeing the look on his face when she said, "Because I'm not family."

John nudged Ronnie's leg and said, "Scoot over." He sat down next to her. His manly voice softened, reminding her of Nick. "Ronnie, you'll always be my daughter."

Before she could blink back tears, Ronnie buried her face in John's chest, bawling. The Lombardo men had a knack for knowing what to say to turn her into an emotional mess.

John let Ronnie cry. When she had finished, he took a handkerchief from his pocket and covered her nose with the cloth as if she were a child. "Blow." She blew out two whoppers of mucus, and John bunched the snotty rag back into his pocket.

"Tess hates me," Ronnie said.

John's bewildered expression said she was nuts. "Who says?"

"I saw the way she looked at me, John. You did, too. Everyone did. She blames me for Tony getting shot. She should. It's my fault."

"Tess is in shock." John consoled Ronnie with an arm around her. "You know how long I've been married? Forty-seven years. That's a long time to know a person. As God as my witness," he said, as if he were taking an oath, "I can say without a shadow of a doubt, she doesn't hate you."

Ronnie snuggled closer to John. "What if Tony dies?"

"My son's a mule. Stubborn. He's been that way since the day he was born, and even then, he refused to come out. Tess was in labor for twenty-eight hours."

"I know. She mentions it every year on his birthday. It's her reminder of what she had to go through to get him here."

"Food and guilt are her biggest weapons." John chuckled. "Did you know Tony was accident-prone as a kid?"

"Tony? I don't believe it."

"It's true," John said with raised eyebrows. "He had so many bruises, cuts, and broken bones, I thought child welfare services was going to take him away. One time, he and Vince were wrestling in the treehouse I'd built for them. Tony fell out. Fifteen feet. Broke his ankle. He sliced open his hand on a circular saw in my wood shop. What a gusher that was. He had enough stitches to make a quilt. All the spills he took off his dirt bike put us on a first-name basis with the hospital nurses. Tess was ready to bubble wrap him."

If the stories hadn't come from John, Ronnie wouldn't have believed them. Tony had agility, control, and skills. And while his klutzy childhood should've made Ronnie laugh, a bullet wound didn't compare to his past accidents. "This isn't a bruise or a fall. Tony was shot," Ronnie reminded John.

He patted her shoulder. "I know, hon. I know."

"I'm cursed. Every person I care about ends up dying. My father. Vivian. Tony could be next."

"Ronnie, your father was murdered. You had nothing to do with that."

"He had the day off. He wasn't supposed to go to work. If I had begged him to stay, he'd still be alive. But I let him go. The *big* detective I was so proud of!"

"You could've pleaded until you were blue in the face, and he would've still walked out that door because he had a job to do."

*Like father, like daughter.*

"Did Tony tell you?" she asked John. "About how I fell asleep when Vivian got hit."

"He did," John said, glancing upward. "Hon, it was an accident. We all know that."

"It wasn't supposed to happen! I was supposed to be the smart, responsible cop. I was supposed to be observant and sharp."

"You made a mistake."

"I've made a lot of them, John." She looked up at him. "I practically threw Tony at Kaitlyn."

John pointed a waving finger. "Tony's a big boy. No one forced him to do anything. He takes responsibility for what he did."

"If I had given him a second chance, he wouldn't be lying on a table in the operating room. What happened tonight *is* my fault." Ronnie looked at the cross. "Maybe this is God's way of punishing me for the divorce. You're not supposed to get divorced. It's in the Bible."

"Ronnie, God doesn't work like that."

"Believing in God and going to church doesn't give you a pass, John. Bad things happen to good people. Anyone who's ever meant anything to me dies." She looked at him. "I'd run far away if I were you."

"Stop being overdramatic. You sound like a typical Italian woman." John squeezed Ronnie. "Tony has the best doctors working on him. He's going to be fine."

If only John's positivity and optimism would rub off on Ronnie. "You don't know that. Anything can go wrong in the OR."

John sighed, trying to get through to her. "Ronnie, we're all here for a reason. We're all called to something. Vince and I make cabinets because people need them in their homes. Joey informs the public with his articles. Tess's passion for food means her family will never be malnourished."

*What a jokester. Just like Tony.*

"Hilton needs good cops. The town has the best with you and Tony in uniform. He's not done with his calling; neither are you. That's how I know he's gonna make it."

Aidan's patients pay two hundred bucks a session. John gave her one for free. She looked at him, and for a second, she saw Nick.

"If you say so. Dad."

• • •

In a room off of the surgery wing, Ronnie, Aidan, and the Lombardos sat on thin-cushioned chairs as uncomfortable as the couch that felt like a piece of plywood. Waiting.

Laced heavy with worry, the sterile, cold room reeked of stale coffee from the pot that had been heating on the burner. The coffee Aidan had bought for Ronnie and the Lombardos wasn't much better. They didn't need caffeine to keep them awake. Their adrenaline did that for them. An obese man lying on the couch squirmed for hours in between his naps. When he moved, the couch springs squeaked like a sick cat.

One a.m. marked Tony's third hour of surgery. Ronnie whispered to Aidan, "It shouldn't take this long to remove a bullet."

"It doesn't mean something went wrong," Aidan whispered back, but everyone heard him. "Internal injuries are a process. Surgeons complete one task before moving onto the next. I'm not an expert, but I assume they need to stop the bleeding first before they do any repairs. The bullet hit his shoulder. Not any organs, which is good news."

Ronnie shivered, rubbing her bare arms, not wanting to wear her bloody blouse that looked like a gruesome Halloween costume.

The door opened. A petite woman wearing green hospital scrubs came inside. A mesh-looking cap tied around her head and face mask below her chin, thin elastic straps still looped around her ears. "Lombardo Family?"

Everyone immediately stood. Ronnie and Aidan stayed at a distance.

"Follow me." The woman led them to a separate room resembling an office where you hear the best and worst of news.

"I'm Dr. Blumrick." She assumed correctly John and Tess were Tony's parents. The surgeon's youthful appearance made her look younger than Ronnie.

"Tony's out of surgery and in the ICU." She removed her mask. Her blonde hair tumbled as she took off the cap. "Both bullets went through his clavicle."

"The collarbone," Aidan clarified to Ronnie.

"He was shot twice!" Tess shouted, crying as John intervened.

"Honey, let Dr. Blumrick talk." He looked at the surgeon. "Go ahead, Doctor."

"One bullet hit his subclavian artery. We repaired it, but there was massive hemorrhaging. He'll need blood transfusions for several days."

Tess made the sign of the cross, practically strangling her rosary beads.

"The second bullet just missed the brachial artery by an inch. There was no exit wound, which meant both bullets were lodged inside, but we got them out."

"What about his shoulder?" John asked. "Is there any permanent damage?"

"Luckily, the bullets didn't hit any nerves, so there's no loss of feeling in his hand or arm. Sometimes there are bullet fragments, but not in Tony's case. His arm will be extremely sore and bruised. With PT I expect him to regain full mobility of his shoulder in about six weeks."

"How long will he be in the hospital?" Vince asked.

"Two to three days in ICU, then we can move him to a regular room for another three days or so. Once his body can make its own blood, he can go home. He's going to be weak and fatigued for a while because of the hemorrhaging."

The doctor worked in a trauma center; she treated patients with life-threatening injuries every day. But for Ronnie, and she presumed the Lombardos, it made her head spin.

"We'll watch for infection, but I don't foresee that being an issue," Dr. Blumrick added. "Being in a barn with dirt, debris, and feces, there's a greater risk of infection. We cleansed the wound, or what I call it, power washed it. We had him on antibiotics during the surgery, and just to be on the safe side, will give him a few more doses the next couple of days."

"Can we see him?" Joey asked.

"Yes, but only for a few minutes. He's in a medically induced coma."

"A coma! Oh, John!" Tess threw herself into her husband.

"It's standard procedure for this kind of injury, Mrs. Lombardo. He'll be on the ventilator until tomorrow. Just to warn you, it's not like what you see in the movies. He's hooked up to a lot of machines, a lot of IVs. It's difficult to see someone you love like that, but as bad as it looks, he's sleeping. We want to keep him comfortable."

Tess sniffed, composing herself. "I can handle it. I'm his mother. Let's go."

Everyone headed for the door as the doctor stopped Ronnie. "I'm sorry, ma'am. Just immediate family."

John took Ronnie's hand, pulling her along. "She is family."

The doctor conceded with a sighing, "All right."

Ronnie looked at Aidan apologetically.

"Go ahead, Veronica," he said. "I'll be in the ER waiting room."

She left with the Lombardos, and they followed Dr. Blumrick to Tony's room on the ICU floor.

"Two at a time," the doctor said firmly. "Five minutes each."

After John and Tess came out of Tony's room, Tess was crying. Vince and Cora went in next, followed by Joey and Nonna.

"Was it as bad as the doctor said it would be?" Ronnie asked Joey.

The youngest Lombardo brother held a mischievous grin. "The guy gets shot and still looks like a stud. The nurses will be fighting over who gets to feed him Jell-O." He lightly punched Ronnie in the arm. "You're up."

Ronnie braced herself for what she was about to see and went inside Tony's room. She had seen tragedy spilled onto the street, where car accident victims covered in blood with missing limbs were pulled from the wreckage. Homicide scenes, where murder victims lay in their own pool of blood, while detectives gather evidence and the medical examiner determined the time of death. She had coped with it because it was part of the job. Dr. Blumrick was right. It's harder when it's someone you love.

The flat beeping sound of the monitor alternated between the humming machines, sounding like air compressors.

Circular patches connected to wires hooked to machines covered Tony's bare chest. Ronnie counted five IV bags, one with crimson red liquid that must have been for the transfusion. She cringed at the sight of the thick arterial line in his neck filling his body with blood.

Ronnie stood on Tony's right side, far away from where the bullets had plunged into his shoulder, now covered in huge bandages, while staring at the tube down his throat and a thinner one up his nose that transported meds. He didn't look at all like Tony.

*Joey's such a liar.*

"Hey, Tony. It's Ronnie. I don't know if you can hear me, but if this is your way of trying to get my attention, you need to rethink your strategy." She held his hand, careful not to disrupt the cannulas. "Sorry. Stupid joke."

Gently, she stroked his fingers. "You gave us quite a scare, but the doctor said you're going to be as good as new in no time. I knew you would be. You're strong. You're a fighter." A tear ran down her cheek. "There are a lot of people who need you, Tony. They're depending on you. Me included."

Dr. Blumrick came inside. "Time's up."

Ronnie wiped her face and waited for the doctor to leave. "I'll be back tomorrow." She kissed Tony's forehead, then whispered in his ear, "I love you."

• • •

Ronnie and Aidan went to the hospital the next day to visit Tony. He was off the ventilator by noon, and an oxygen mask replaced the breathing tube.

His quivering eyelids opened. His hoarse voice sounded like Darth Vader. "Ronnie."

Tony pulled the oxygen mask halfway down before Ronnie put it back over his nose. "You need to keep this on," she said.

He closed his eyes as a nurse came in to change two of his IV bags.

"I feel so helpless," Ronnie said to Aidan. "I can't do anything."

"You can give blood," the woman said.

"That's a brilliant idea," Aidan agreed. "My blood type is O. Sweetheart, what's yours?"

Ronnie couldn't remember the color of the bra she was wearing, if she had remembered to even put one on at all. "I'm not sure. A positive, I think."

"We can use all types. The blood bank is on the first floor." The nurse attached both IV bags. "He'll be like this for another day. I'll let him know you stopped by when he's awake."

Tony opened his eyes again, using all his strength. "Ronnie," he said, followed by a slow breath that fogged up the mask. "Stay."

Then he fell back asleep.

# CHAPTER 30

Aidan hadn't left Ronnie's side since last night. After their succinct visit with a sleep-induced Tony, Aidan drove Ronnie to her apartment. He called the practice to reschedule his sessions for the week while he stayed with her. The mild sedative he had prescribed made her sleep most of the afternoon while he lay next to her in bed. Food had been the furthest thing from her mind, but Aidan insisted she eat to keep up her strength, and he made her a bowl of chicken noodle soup and a cup of tea.

The shooting made national news before Ronnie could call her mother. Natalie showed up at her apartment with a suitcase, sobbing.

Aidan ordered gyros and Greek salads from Athens Deli for dinner. Ronnie noticed his skittish behavior as he left to pick up the takeout, afraid to leave her alone, even though Natalie was there. He kissed Ronnie goodbye. "I'll be right back. Call me if you need me."

She smiled softly. "We'll be fine."

As soon as Aidan closed the door, Natalie cooed over her daughter's fiancé. "You've hit the jackpot. Aidan's smart and handsome. Successful. Did you see how he didn't want to leave you? What an angel!"

Ronnie sipped her lukewarm tea. "He's almost too good to be true."

Although Natalie had met Aidan under dire circumstances, Ronnie's fiancé and mother had connected instantly. She knew they would. While his interests in wine and art made him seem somewhat pretentious, Aidan could win over a biker gang.

"He's the real deal, Veronica. A mother knows when her daughter has found the one."

*Unlike Tony. Right, Mom?*

Natalie had acknowledged her ex-son-in-law's bravery and gunshot wounds with a phony sympathetic look. "I hope he's okay," was all she had said. The man had two bullets removed, not his tonsils.

Natalie stood, smoothing her beige linen pants, and paced the area between the living room and kitchen, trying to find something to do. Ronnie was finally alone with her mother and didn't know if she'd get another chance like it again. "Were you disappointed in me?" she asked.

Natalie froze, followed by a guffaw. "What in the world are you talking about?"

"Growing up, you and I weren't exactly close. I wasn't into girly stuff."

"And that means I'm disappointed in you?" Natalie went to the kitchen and opened the dishwasher. "You were busy playing catch with your father and going to baseball games."

"That's not an answer. Were you disappointed I didn't turn out like you?"

Natalie held two clean mugs by her pinkie. "Where do these go?"

"Mom, leave those alone. I'll put them away later."

Natalie closed the dishwasher door. The lull surrounding them intensified their conversation. Ronnie had always known the truth. Now she was about to hear it from her mother as Natalie sat down on the couch next to her. "I was jealous of the bond between you and your father. That bond was supposed to be me and you."

"Dad and I had a lot in common. I liked what he liked."

"I know I took it too personally, but it felt like," Natalie paused, fidgeting with her fingers, "that you didn't like me."

Her mother's childlike honesty was pitiful. "Mom, it was just... easier with Dad."

"Yes, I suppose it was." Natalie wore a brave smile. "He was fun, not too serious. You idolized him, which didn't help." Ronnie ignored the backhanded compliment. "The way you looked up to him gave him more reasons to keep working those hours, keep taking those risks. He wanted so much for you to be proud of him."

"I was. He was a great cop, a great dad and husband." Ronnie always wanted to be like her father and had spent her life after he died striving for his respect.

From the faraway look in Natalie's eyes, Ronnie saw Nick in her mother's thoughts. "The signs were there. I knew you wanted to follow in his footsteps before you did—and that scared me."

Ronnie didn't ask why, because she already knew.

Natalie looked at the ceiling as if she were talking to Heaven. "I used to pray it was just a phase, and you'd change your mind. That one day you'd come home from school and say, 'Hey, Mom, guess what? I don't want to be a cop. Let's go shopping.'" She elbowed Ronnie with a grin. "But that didn't happen. So there I was, sick with worry, waiting for a call from someone I didn't know, saying, 'I'm sorry, ma'am, your daughter was killed in the line of duty.'"

Natalie's face scrunched, her eyes releasing tears not only for her daughter's brush with death but also for her late husband's murder. "Nick had a head like a rock. He put being a cop before being my husband. If he had to choose, I'd always lose. Then I lost in the worst way. Every day, I still see it. Opening the door, those two officers on the porch removing their hats."

The night of Nick's murder had been a real-life nightmare. Ronnie had woken to her mother screaming. She ran downstairs to the entranceway, where Natalie sat on the floor, wailing in the arms of a cop. Ronnie knew her father was dead.

"The day your father died, we had a fight. Another one of our fights about the force. I was so mad that I threatened to leave him if he didn't quit. He laughed at me, as if I were a dimwit. I told him to stay at the station and not to bother coming home. Then I stormed out of the house."

Natalie sniffled. "Not a day goes by I don't regret those words. I can't take them back, and I can't bring Nick back, either."

Hearing her mother bare her soul touched Ronnie in a way she didn't expect. She had selfishly mourned her father, unaware Natalie had suffered in silence, and they cried tears they should've shed together long ago. "If you had to do it all over again, would you still marry Dad, knowing he was a cop?"

Natalie wiped her eyes, smearing her mascara. "In a millisecond."

"But how if you hated his job?"

"Because love that strong is a terrible thing, Veronica. It comes into your life without permission. It messes with your head. One minute it makes you happy, the next it makes you miserable. It won't leave, no matter how many times you tell it to." She mused, smiling. "And thank God it doesn't."

"Do you love Graham the way you loved Dad?"

Natalie dabbed her eyes with a Kleenex from her purse. "He was a good distraction. I didn't use him," she clarified, "but it's not the same as it was with your father."

Ronnie and Natalie had been oil and water for forty years, but that night, they'd never been more alike. Nick had been the love of Natalie's life; Graham was a safe replacement—although not because he was an accountant. Her mother's story mirrored her own. Tony had been the love of Ronnie's life, yet she found safety in marrying Aidan.

"Veronica," Natalie said, "what kind of love do you have for Aidan?"

For the first time, Ronnie's mother treated her like a woman instead of the baseball tomboy who had refused to go shopping with her. Dabbing Ronnie's teary eyes with the used tissue, she surmised, "Something tells me Aidan is your Graham."

Their unprecedented talk had broken down the invisible wall between them, and without Ronnie having to confirm her mother's suspicions, Natalie's expression said she already knew as her ringing phone interrupted them. She huffed when seeing the Caller ID and blew her nose. "Hello, Graham." She listened, then huffed again. "I'm sorry you're bored. It's a beautiful night. Why don't you go for a walk?"

Ronnie heard her grouchy stepfather's murmuring complaints through the phone.

"Graham, I've only been gone a few hours. Isn't there anything on TV?"

Natalie looked at Ronnie with yielding eyes, the ones her mother had every time Graham pouted until he got his way.

*Here it comes. Any second, she's going to fold and will be back in Akron in time for a late dinner with stepdaddy.*

Then a miracle happened. Natalie's nostrils flared as she pursed her collagen lips. "You listen here, Graham. My daughter has just been through a horrific, harrowing ordeal. I'm staying as long as she needs me!"

Ronnie couldn't believe her ears; her jaw went slack.

"Good night, darling." Natalie stretched the words with sweet sarcasm. She ended the call and laughed harder than Ronnie had ever heard.

She was so proud of her mother, but asked, "Why'd you do that?"

Natalie hugged Ronnie. "Because I know how it feels to come in second."

• • •

Tony had spent two days in the ICU before being transferred to a private room on the second floor, where he stayed for three more days confined to his bed with nothing to do but sleep and watch television.

The news stations ran continuous updates on the shooting with interviews from Captain Rosario, who said a lot without saying anything. Neighbors Tony hadn't talked to, but they acted as if they were best friends, and well wishes for a speedy recovery from community leaders and residents.

Max and Chet had stopped by to visit, joking that Tony would do anything to get out of patrolling Sector One. Paula and Jesse also stopped by, and, of course, Tony received two daily visits from his parents and brothers.

Footsteps entered his room. He assumed it was his nurse, Anita, coming to check his vitals.

From behind the curtain, Ronnie appeared with a cellophane-covered basket and a giant green bow. He was glad it wasn't Anita.

"Hey!" Tony said, smiling bigger than he had in weeks. He almost didn't care Aidan was there, too. "It's about time you showed up. I was beginning to think you were avoiding me."

"We wanted to wait until you felt better," Ronnie said.

Aidan's phone rang. He answered, "Yes, Felicia." Listening, he sighed. "I told you to forward all my calls to Dr. Wagner." He nodded. "All right, hold one moment." He turned to Ronnie. "I need to take this. It's a patient. I'll be right back."

*Take all the time you need, Doc.*

Aidan brought the phone to his ear. "All right, Felicia. Put her on," he said as he left the room.

Tony studied Ronnie's pale appearance. She hadn't been sleeping well—he could tell by her cloudy eyes. She had on a Pirates baseball hat, her hair in a ponytail. A Nike sweatshirt and jeans. She looked beautiful.

Except for the bruised skin beneath her eye. Tony clenched his teeth. "Did Tillerson give you that shiner?"

"It looks worse than it feels." Ronnie gingerly poked the puffy skin. "It's a scratch compared to being shot."

"If the bullets hadn't killed him, my bare hands would've."

Ronnie stared at Tony's side where the bullets from her gun had plowed into his left shoulder. "How do you feel?"

"Like someone sliced me open." He pressed the button on the bed rail. The mattress rose in a slow, mechanical climb.

"You look a lot better than you did a few days ago with all those wires and tubes sticking out of you. It was awful seeing you like that."

Tony had been groggy for two days and remembered little, other than when the oxygen mask finally came off, and he was down to two IVs. He jutted his chin. "Is that for me?"

"Yep." She listed each snack in the basket: "Chocolate-covered pretzels, honey-roasted peanuts, caramel corn, and trail mix."

Tony circled a spoon through the fruit cocktail cup with more syrup than fruit, then pushed away the lunch tray. "Sounds better than the slop here."

"I'll put this on the dresser. Unless you want something now?"

"Maybe later."

Ronnie placed the basket next to the arrangements of flowers, some with balloons that said, "Get Well Soon."

She poked the rubbery chicken on the plate as if it were roadkill. "Seems a tad overdone." The mashed potatoes shaped into a mountain had the same density. "How are the potatoes?"

"They taste like wallpaper paste."

"There's not much hope for those canned peas, is there?" she joked.

"No." He pointed to the chair at the end of the bed. "Have a seat."

She eyed the door as if she were hatching an escape plan. You would've thought Tony had offered her a seat in the electric chair. "I should go. You need to rest."

"Talk to me, Ronnie." He sounded as if he had the onset of laryngitis. "Please."

She sat down on the hard plastic chair as a voice came over the hospital intercom paging Dr. Kellenberg to fourth floor pediatrics. Tony flexed his fingers as if he were directing a moving car into a tight parking spot. "Come closer."

She lifted her butt, scraping the chair legs against the floor. "I hear they're kicking you out tomorrow."

"Can't come soon enough. My bags are all packed. I'll be staying with Ma and Dad for a few weeks." He resisted closing his heavy eyelids. "The media are having a field day."

"That's an understatement," Ronnie said with a lift of her shoulders. "The big guns are here, too. CNN, MSNBC, and Fox News had camped out at my apartment building for two days. Max and Chet had to escort me and Aidan to his car."

"It's like the paparazzi," Tony joked.

She put on black sunglasses from her pocket and pinched the bill of her hat. "Thus, my disguise. You might want to consider one, too. There's a crowd of hungry reporters outside waiting to interview the heroic cop."

"I promised Joey the first interview. He'll finish me off if I renege."

Ronnie took off the sunglasses. "I'm not ready to go on camera and answer questions like, 'Chief Callahan. How did it feel to have a madman tether you to a post and set the place on fire?'"

Tony couldn't erase that image from his mind. He never would.

"I'm talking to a counselor. I had my first session yesterday. Aidan recommended a colleague at the practice who deals with traumatic experiences. He said he can make you an appointment, too, when you're up to it."

Tony still wasn't jazzed about Aidan, but the guy was trying. "I'll think about it."

A Black woman around Tess's age came into the room. "How's my favorite patient?"

"Anxious to get outta here," Tony said, shifting his numb butt.

She looked at his lunch tray and propped a hand on her curvy hip. "Now, I know the food here isn't Momma's cooking, but you gotta eat something. You'll whittle down to nothing. You're too handsome to be a scrawny little man."

"You try eating it."

The woman replaced the remaining IV bag. "Shoot, honey. Not on your life."

"Ronnie, this is my nurse, Anita," Tony said.

"Hey, I know you," the woman said to Ronnie, while holding a thermometer at Tony's temple. "You've been on the news." Anita wrapped a band around Tony's good arm and he stuck a finger into the opened clip to get his oxygen level. "You're the police chief from Hilton." Anita looked at Tony with a big grin. "You saved her life!"

The machine beeped, and the nurse removed the band and clip. "Mm-hmm. Handsome and heroic. If only I wasn't married." She smiled at Ronnie. "I'm glad you made it out of there alive."

"Me, too, Anita," she said.

The nurse pointed at Tony. "Don't go anywhere, Mr. Hero. I'll be back later to take your vitals again and get your autograph!"

"Yes, ma'am."

After Anita left, Ronnie said to Tony, "I bet the nurses started a 'Tony Lombardo Fan Club.'"

"I am a celebrity of sorts," he said with a laugh. "So. What else is new with you?"

She hummed in thought. "Internal affairs is investigating the shooting."

He cleared his dry throat. "It was self-defense."

"Right. Ashe got a search warrant for Tillerson's apartment. He found three dead mice, newspapers with the gala article ripped out, and gloves. Between evidence and video from your body cam, the district attorney would be a moron to bring charges against you."

The room felt heavy talking about Luke Tillerson, the shooting, and murder charges.

"Have your parents been by yet?" Ronnie asked.

"I saw them this morning. Dad had to drag Ma out of here by her hair. They'll be back later." Tony held back a wince as he adjusted the position of his injured arm. "Dad told me about your talk with him in the chapel. It got me thinking."

"About what?" Ronnie shifted in her seat, cracking her knuckles.

Tony swallowed, eyeing the pitcher on the overbed table. Before he could ask, Ronnie poured water into a plastic cup and handed it to him. He sipped it, and suddenly, the love he had for her ached more than the hole in his shoulder from the bullets.

"You were saying?" she said.

Tony had hoped he wouldn't have to mention his infidelity. He hated talking about it. "If I hadn't cheated on you, we'd still be married. None of this would've happened." Taunting images rolled through his mind. "What Tillerson did… What he almost did to you—"

"He didn't, so don't think about it as if he had."

"I'm sorry, Ronnie. I'm sorry about what happened with Kaitlyn. I'm sorry about being so weak that I threw away the best thing that ever happened to me."

"Tony, stop. You wouldn't be in a hospital bed if it weren't for me." He wanted to believe her, but couldn't. "You were right. I gave up on us, on our marriage. If I would've stayed and worked out our problems, I would've never joined the Scottsdale force. Never turned Tillerson in. If there's anyone to blame, it's me, Tony. Not you."

Ronnie was still as stubborn as ever. "We can go back and forth all day. You say it's your fault, I say it's mine. That cancels each other out, and no one is to blame."

"But it's—"

"Ronnie, enough. Let's not talk about it. Okay? It's over."

"Agreed. You need to concentrate on your recovery so you can get back to the station, where you can irritate me under more acceptable circumstances."

At the sound of footsteps, Aidan rounded the curtain. "Sorry about that," he said, putting his phone into his pocket. Aidan held Ronnie as he extended an arm to Tony. "I can't thank you enough for saving Veronica's life. You brought her back to me. I'll be forever grateful."

Tony shook Aidan's hand in an unspoken truce as he lay trapped in the bed, forced to watch another man with the woman he loved. "Her watch is the real hero. Without the GPS, we wouldn't have found her." Had it not been for Ronnie's quick thinking to send an emergency text from her fiancé's gift, she would've died.

"Tony, if there's anything you need, please let us know." Aidan took Ronnie's hand. "It's time to go, sweetheart."

"You don't have to leave," Tony said, more to Ronnie than Aidan. "I'll ask Anita if I can go for a walk, if you don't mind pushing me in a wheelchair."

Tony went to hit the call button. Ronnie looked at Aidan as he decided for them both. "You need to rest," he said to Tony with a half-hearted smile. "Losing the amount of blood you did will leave you fatigued for a while."

Tony was exhausted, but seeing Ronnie gave him a burst of energy.

"Aidan's right," Ronnie said. "Rest is the best medicine."

At the door, she turned and waved, mouthing the word, "bye."

## CHAPTER 31

Ronnie arrived at John and Tess's house Saturday morning armed with two grocery bags of ingredients for sauce and meatballs, eager to learn from one of the greatest chefs on the planet.

She had waited until Tony moved back into his apartment after recovering at his parents' house for three weeks before calling Nonna to ask for a cooking lesson on how to make sauce.

In the basement kitchen, Ronnie seasoned a pound of spareribs with salt and pepper and cooked them inside the kettle.

"Enough to brown the sides," Nonna said, as Ronnie flipped the meat with a pair of tongs. "They say pork is bad for you, but look at me. Ninety-two, I'm still here. You need pork in the sauce. It flavors it beautifully."

Nonna's commentary proved both entertaining and sagacious.

After Ronnie poured cans of diced tomatoes and added fresh herbs into the kettle, Nonna handed her the sugar bowl.

"Don't you mean salt?" Ronnie said, hoping not to embarrass the old woman. It was a simple mistake. They both looked similar. Given her age, it wouldn't come as a surprise if she had confused the two ingredients.

"No. Sugar," Nonna said, shaking a correcting finger. "It cuts the acidity of the tomatoes."

Ronnie felt foolish for doubting the woman who had learned to cook before she could walk. She gathered a clump of sugar between her fingers and released it in a swirling motion over the sauce.

The first time Ronnie had tasted Nonna's sauce, it was Heaven on Earth. She hadn't known something so delicious existed. The Lombardos must've thought she had come from a deserted island where there was no such thing as tomatoes the way she had fawned.

Nonna hummed a tune while stirring the sauce with a wooden spoon, then put the lid on the kettle and turned on the burner. "Slow and low," she said to Ronnie. From the cupboard, she took out a bowl and announced, "For the meatballs."

Ronnie followed Nonna's step-by-step instructions. She cracked an egg over the ground pork and the ground beef in the bowl, dumped in one cup of bread crumbs, tossed in more herbs, and added grated parmesan cheese. "Do you have a spoon to stir this?"

"No spoon, honey." Nonna forced Ronnie's hands into the meat. "Mix. *Squeeze* the meat."

Ronnie grimaced as the slimy substance squirted between her fingers.

Nonna encouraged her protégé as she worked the mixture. "That's it, honey. Now flip it over. Make sure it's well combined."

Ronnie rolled all the meat into balls and put them into a cast-iron skillet with oil. She turned the burner on high.

"Low," Nonna reminded her.

Ronnie lowered the gas, shrinking the blue flame.

After cooking the meatballs for a few minutes, Ronnie removed them from the pan and used a paper towel to soak up the excess grease before adding them into the kettle of sauce. She turned up the flame.

Nonna gently admonished her. "Slow and low."

Ronnie reduced the flame. "But it's not cooking." It was more of a question than a rebuttal.

"It's cooking," Nonna assured her, bobbing her head. "Slow and low. Like making love."

The old woman's sensual analogy caught Ronnie off guard. "Nonna!"

Talking to your parents about sex was awkward, but talking about the deed with a woman as old as Nonna rose to another level of embarrassment.

"What?" Nonna shrugged. Modesty apparently was not one of her weaknesses, if she had any at all. "Cooking *is* like making love. You take your time. Get to know what works. Experiment. In the end, you have something delicious. Like what you and Tony had."

*We sure did.* Ronnie quickly shook off the memory before staying in the past one minute too long.

Bringing Tony dinner was the least Ronnie could do. It just so happened that Aidan was out of town for the weekend.

Nonna dipped two pieces of homemade Italian bread into the sauce and handed one to Ronnie. "What's it need?" she asked and ate the bread.

Ronnie waited on her palate, chewing the moist bread. "I'm not sure."

"Yes, you know." Nonna patted her belly. "Your gut. What's it say?"

Ronnie took a stab in the dark. "Um... more oregano?"

"You trust yourself. The other secret to cooking is to trust what you taste and listen to your gut." Ronnie added three dashes of the herb into the kettle and stirred the sauce, then put on the lid. "Now, we wait."

If Ronnie's batch turned out half as good as Nonna's, she'd be happy. She couldn't wait to see Tony's reaction when he found out she had made the sauce.

Nonna brewed a pot of coffee, then shuffled to the pantry. "While we wait, we eat and talk." She returned with a Tupperware container of homemade Italian cookies and unsnapped the lid, releasing an aroma of sugar, butter, and a whole lot of love. Nonna offered her student first pickings. Ronnie politely took a biscotti and a cuccidati. The old woman lifted the container. "More, honey, take more." Ronnie took two pizzelles, knowing she'd go back into the bucket for another cookie before leaving.

Nonna dunked her biscotti into her coffee and bit into the log-shaped cookie. "This fiancé of yours... Do you love him?"

Aidan was the opposition and the last person Ronnie wanted to talk about to a Lombardo. "Yes, Nonna. I do."

She heard the old woman thinking, *"You loved my grandson once, too."*

Nonna took a cuccidati from the container and bluntly asked, "What about Tony?"

The old woman had never been one to mince words. Ronnie knew Nonna would mention Tony sooner or later and snapped a pizzelle in half, then bit into the severed wafer-thin cookie. "I care about him a lot. He's a good friend and will always be special to me—not just because he saved my life—but because he gave me Vivian."

Nonna smiled, satisfied, for Ronnie's sake. "Honey, Italians know two things. We know food, and we know love." She held Ronnie's face in her cold, bony hands. "*Mio nipote* loves you, and *you* love him."

Denying Ronnie's feelings to someone as intuitive as Nonna was futile. "Sometimes love's not enough and you're better off as friends."

"*Si, si.*" Nonna sipped her coffee. "But the heart is stronger than the mind."

*My heart decided to make a special meal for my ex-husband, even though my mind kept trying to remind me I have a fiancé.*

• • •

Tony's shoulder and arm had ached for weeks. The painful swelling took its sweet old time going down. A ghastly shade of purple around the shoulder seeped down to his chest, making him look as if someone had bludgeoned him. He wore a special sling with a Velcro strap around his waist to keep him from moving his arm. The one highlight of his day was going to physical therapy because it was the only time he could take the sling off, while his therapist, a former Marine named Seth, worked the wounded arm.

Tess had fed Tony like a king and had spoiled him like a prince, but her relentless nagging about him retiring drove him crazy.

"See what happened? What if you're not so lucky next time?" Tess had said. Every day. "This is a sign, Tony. It's time to turn in your badge."

By the end of the third week of his recovery, Tony had regained his strength and didn't need an afternoon nap like an old man. Tess had badgered him to stay longer, but he preferred to take care of himself and went back to his apartment.

As the days dragged on, Tony grew more restless. The days blended with no distinction between a weekday and the weekend. He had gone on a daily walk around the neighborhood, read a legal-thriller novel, and binge-watched two Netflix reality shows as the mindless entertainment provided a few laughs.

Tess had sent Tony home with enough prepared meals for a month. Surveying the rows of containers in the refrigerator, his tastebuds told him they wanted meatloaf, and he nuked a chunk of it in the microwave. While waiting for dinner to warm up, Tony turned on the television and went to ESPN to watch Sports Center before the Pirates game. A knock rattled the door.

*Gotta be Ma.*

Tess wouldn't stay away if a firing squad surrounded the building. She had made many unannounced visits to Tony's apartment. At this rate, staying at his mother's house would've saved her a full tank of gas.

Tony squinted through the peephole, grinning. A silver lining shone through his boring day, and he opened the door.

"Hi, Tony." Ronnie entered without an invitation—not that she had needed one. She was always welcome. It was her first time in his apartment, and she did an unimpressed scan of his bachelor pad.

"What are you doing here?" Tony asked, shutting the door.

"Checking on Hilton's most famous patient." She gasped, gawking at the ugly bruise on his left side with a gauze bandage taped over the incision. "Tony! Your shoulder!"

His shirt was off. It was easier that way. He glanced at the area in question. "It's sore, as if I did a hundred bench presses. But it feels better every day."

"Oh. Okay." Ronnie took him at his word, but there was still a glimmer of doubt in her eyes. She lifted a green canvas bag. "Hope you're hungry. I have plenty for two."

The microwave dinged as the smell of reheated meat filled the room.

She extended the bag toward him. "If you already have dinner, I'll just leave this for you."

"No!" he said. "Stay. We'll add the meatloaf to whatever you brought."

Tony turned off the television and followed Ronnie into the kitchen, where she set the bag on the counter. She looked comfortable in her weekend clothes. Black athletic pants and a white Under Armour T-shirt. Her hair pulled back in a ponytail.

"I'll go put on a shirt," he said.

"You don't have to change on my account. If you're more comfortable like that, I'm fine with it." She smiled. "I've seen you a time or two without a shirt."

Tony had made a similar comment the morning after Chet's wedding, when she found out he had seen her naked. He didn't want to risk her leaving and decided it was best for both of them if he covered up. "I'll be right back."

He went into the bedroom. Lifting his wounded shoulder to put on a T-shirt hurt too much—not that he'd dare tell Ronnie. Bypassing the pile of clothes on the floor, he took a blue button-down shirt from the closet and went back to the kitchen, fumbling with the sling.

Ronnie tossed the shirt over her shoulder. "Let me help."

If dressing him was the only way she'd touch him, Tony would take it and relish every second.

She unfastened the Velcro around his waist. He ducked as she moved the diagonal strap over his head and removed the sling. Standing next to his injured shoulder, she held open the shirt. "Can you straighten your arm?"

"No problem." He tried and winced.

"Sorry," she said, as if she had inflicted the pain.

"I'm okay."

From the bottom, she gently raised the sleeve over his arm, then came around to his right side and he inserted his good arm into the hole. Tony watched Ronnie's hands move down the row of buttons, fastening each one, before she put on the sling and attached the Velcro band.

"Is that comfortable?" she asked.

"Very." Curiosity nearly got the best of Tony as he refrained from mentioning Aidan. Did the psychologist know his fiancée was in her ex-husband's apartment?

At the counter, Tony stood behind Ronnie and tugged the rim of the canvas bag to peek inside. "What do you have in there?"

She removed two Tupperware containers. "I made sauce and meatballs."

He tried not to laugh. "You made sauce?"

"Yes, *I* made sauce," she said with an adorable snarky imitation. "The real thing. Not the stuff from a jar. Homemade, all the way down to fresh herbs."

Ronnie had all the ingredients for an Italian meal spread out on the counter: a box of spaghetti, vegetables for a salad, and a loaf of bakery bread.

"And for dessert, your favorite." She waited, creating an air of anticipation before the big revelation.

Tony grinned. "Tiramisu?"

She took out a white box from the bag. "From Costello's Desserts. Baking is a whole other beast."

"I'm getting the royal treatment. I should get shot more often."

Ronnie's face hardened like steel. "Don't say that! Don't you ever say that again!"

"Whoa, take it easy." Tony raised his healthy arm in defense. "It was a joke."

"It's not funny. Nothing about that night is."

*You idiot! What a dumb thing to say! You're not the only one who almost died.*

"You took a bullet for me, Tony. No, you took *two* bullets, and I saunter in here with dinner, as if I can repay you with spaghetti." She leaned back against the counter and lowered her head. "I didn't even thank you for saving my life."

The shooting was as fresh for Ronnie as it was for Tony. The nightmares had tapered off, but every day he saw Tillerson, evil as the devil himself, reminding him of not only his brush with death, but how he nearly lost something more important. Ronnie.

"I did what I was trained to do. Any cop would've done the same," Tony said, choosing his words carefully. "As far as repaying me, you being alive is thanks enough."

"Because of me, you almost died," she said.

"Didn't we agree not to talk about it? No more blame."

But it wasn't the end for Ronnie.

"What if Tillerson had shot you in the chest, like my father?" She bit down on her shaky lower lip. Again, her head drooped. "All I see is you on the ground, bleeding. I can't stop thinking about it."

Cops risk their lives every day they are in uniform. They know there's a chance they might not make it home. No call was out of the realm of danger—from a routine traffic stop to an undercover sting. Knowing that didn't stop the hurricane of emotions when someone you cared about got hurt in the line of duty.

When Tony saw a gun pointed at Ronnie's head, nothing mattered to him except getting her out of the barn alive, even if he had to give his life to do it.

"Hey?" he said.

She looked at him.

"I'd take ten bullets to keep you safe."

Sorrow swam in her warm brown eyes. "Same here." She glanced at the food on the counter. "I need to use the bathroom, then I'll start dinner."

He cocked his head toward the hallway. "Second door on the left."

Ronnie returned a few minutes later. "Do you need me to do a load of laundry?"

"That's not necessary."

"Judging by the pile of clothes on your bedroom floor, I say it is."

He stared at her. "Snooping around my place, are you?"

"I walked past your bedroom. The door was open, and there they were. You weren't that messy when we were married."

He pointed to the sling. "Try doing laundry with this thing on."

"Claimed the one-armed man," she quipped.

"You hate doing laundry," he reminded her.

"Not today. Where's a basket and the soap?"

"Are you sure?" He gave her a leery stare. "You don't have to try so hard."

Ronnie balled her fists on her hips. "Lombardo, I suggest you shut it and take what you can get. This is a onetime offer, and the expiration date is rapidly approaching."

He lifted his right arm in surrender. "Okay, if you insist."

Ronnie followed Tony to the hallway closet that had a mishmash of stuff inside. She put the detergent inside the laundry basket and went into his bedroom, then came out with a mountain of clothes in the basket.

"I'll throw these in the washer," she said on her way to the door. "Where's the laundry room?"

"Second floor at the end of the hall. Follow the noise from the washing machines."

"Got it. Be back in a few."

Ronnie was gone seven minutes—Tony kept track.

Back in the kitchen, she sifted through the cupboards for two pots—one for the spaghetti, another for the sauce and meatballs. She filled the pasta pot with water and turned the burner on for it to boil.

Tony went up behind her, tempted to wrap his good arm around her and nuzzle her smooth neck. "Need any help?

"I know I wasn't the greatest cook when we were together."

He cocked an obvious eyebrow.

"Okay, I was awful! If it weren't for you, we would've starved or gotten fat from takeout, but I can boil spaghetti." She shooed him away. "Go. Sit and relax."

"I've been relaxing for weeks." He sounded bored. "I've had my fill."

"Fine, you can stay. But don't help me. I want to do this myself."

He stepped out of her way. "I won't lift a finger. I'll just sit back and watch the show."

Ronnie moved through the kitchen like a woman who knew what she was doing. She chopped the vegetables for the salad and cut the loaf of bread into thick slices. The real test came when it was time to heat the sauce and meatballs. She turned the burner on high, and Tony's tastebuds shivered at the imminent charred sauce. If Ronnie ruined dinner, it would devastate her.

*That's too high, Ronnie. It needs to be low.*

As if she heard his inner thoughts, she lowered the flame to a simmer and stirred the sauce occasionally. When the water reached a boil, she took out the spaghetti from the box. About to snap it in half—a big no-no among Italians—she instead dropped it into the pot whole.

"I'll check the laundry." She issued a playful warning. "Don't. Touch. Anything."

Tony popped a cherry tomato from the salad into his mouth. "Affirmative, Chief."

Ronnie returned a few minutes later. "The laundry is in the dryer."

She stirred the spaghetti; it still looked al dente. While the pasta finished cooking, she set the table and poured two glasses of Arizona Iced Tea. She grated a block of parmesan cheese into a bowl and put the salad, dressing, bread, and a stick of butter on the table.

Back to the spaghetti. With a fork, Ronnie fished two strands from the boiling water for her and Tony to taste-test. He approved. After straining the spaghetti, she coated it in sauce and meatballs in a serving bowl.

She pulled out his chair. "Dinner is served."

Ronnie filled Tony's dish with spaghetti and four meatballs. She buttered a slice of bread and added it to his plate. She prepared her plate, and they split the chunk of meatloaf.

Tony sniffed the sauce. It smelled better than he expected. He twirled a chunk of spaghetti around the fork and ate it, making "mmm" noises as he chewed. "You said you made the sauce."

She bit into a slice of bread. "I did."

He pointed the fork at the food. "This is Nonna's sauce. I'd know it anywhere."

Ronnie seemed happy he had noticed. She had done a better job than she thought. "I went to your parents' house for a cooking lesson."

"The meatballs, too?"

"Meatballs, too," she echoed proudly.

Tony broke one in half with his fork and took a bite. "They're better than Nonna's. But if you tell her I said it, I'll deny it."

Ronnie grinned. "It'll be our little secret."

After they had eaten a second helping of spaghetti, Tony and Ronnie sat at the table and talked. The same feeling he had at Thanksgiving returned.

The one that felt as if they were still married, except for when he looked at her engagement ring that told him they weren't.

"How's work at the station?" Tony asked her. "Is everyone behaving?"

"Like Communist soldiers, but I doubt it has to do with my leadership. I think they feel sorry for me about the shooting. They're going out of their way to be extra nice to me. Even Ortiz. My first day back, he bought me a jelly doughnut."

Tony raised his eyebrows. "Wow. If I were you, I'd milk it for all it's worth."

"I intend to." She took a cucumber slice from the salad bowl and ate it, crunching.

"I can't wait to get back to work," Tony said, relaxing against the chair. He lifted his wounded arm. "First, I gotta get rid of this sling."

Ronnie drank the last drop of Iced Tea. "Two more weeks before it comes off, right?"

"Yep. Sleeping is uncomfortable, but the hardest part is taking a shower."

Ronnie looked down at her plate with a flirty grin. "Sorry. Can't help you there."

Tony turned his body for her to get a good look at the sling. "I did take a couple of bullets for you."

"And bathing you is my penance?"

"Perhaps," he answered and winked.

Her cheeks turned a rosy shade as she stood. "I'm not a nurse who makes those kind of house calls, Lombardo."

*Whoops. Took that one too far.*

"Ronnie, you're not gonna leave because of that, are you?"

She stood next to him, her hand on the back of the chair as she bent down, close enough to smell the sauce on his breath. "No."

The dreamy look in Ronnie's eyes made Tony's pulse race. A few inches separated their mouths from touching. All he had to do was move in, just a little, but she backed away as if she had caught herself getting too close.

"The laundry is done," she said. "I'll go get it."

Tony cleared the table and put the leftovers in the refrigerator. Ronnie returned from the laundry room and dropped the basket of clean clothes next to the couch. She washed the pots and stowed them in the dish holder to air dry.

"Wanna watch the Pirates game while I fold?" she asked, turning on the television.

He sat down on the couch. "Ladies and gentlemen, she cooks, does laundry, *and* is a baseball fan. What more does a guy need?"

"Ha-ha. You're so funny."

Ronnie tipped the basket of clothes upside down and sorted them into categories: socks, T-shirts, pants, and underwear. Tony watched her more than the game. She folded one pile before moving to the next as if she'd been doing his laundry for the last eleven years. Her attention on the game while folding was impressive. For the underwear pile, she didn't flinch, which meant she was numb or comfortable folding his boxers.

Ronnie made neat piles ranging in color brightness from light to dark, like the clothes in her drawer. She stacked them into the basket and went into the bedroom, where Tony heard drawers opening and closing. She called out, "Ready for dessert?"

Watching the game, he replied, "You bet!"

She stowed the basket inside the hallway closet, then went into the kitchen and cut two large squares of tiramisu. "How about a cup of coffee?"

"Sounds great."

Ronnie plucked two K-cups from the spinning stand and brewed one cup at a time in the Keurig machine. His was black; hers was with milk and sugar. She placed Tony's dessert plate and mug on the end table and returned with hers as she sat down next to him. Taking a bite, she moaned. "This is so good."

"I expect a homemade dessert next time," he joked, taking a bite.

She bumped his good arm with hers. "Right! That'll happen!"

They watched the rest of the game, shouting at the players as if they could hear them through the television, and ridiculing the ump's calls. In between cheering for the Pirates when they scored and high-fiving each other on a good play, Ronnie and Tony added their commentary.

The game ended with a Pirates win, and it was time for Ronnie to go home. With each step she took toward the door, Tony's simplistic evening of having dinner and watching baseball with Ronnie slipped away into what would be a wonderful memory.

He tried devising another reason—or excuse—for her to stay. "Thanks again for dinner and for doing the laundry. I had a great time."

"Me, too. It was fun."

Tony looked at his arm in the sling. "I'll have to keep this thing on longer if it means you taking care of me."

"Don't push it, Lombardo." Ronnie poked him in jest. "I need you back at the station."

"Ah, she can't survive without me," he said with gentle mockery. "Now, does that make me the best officer on the force, Chief Callahan?"

Confusion fell across her face.

"Thanksgiving," he said. "You ragging on me during dinner?"

Ronnie's jovial countenance turned serious. "That was just a show for your family."

Tony read between the lines and knew she had meant more than him being a cop.

She turned the knob and opened the door a crack, her indecision to leave coming through in her hesitation.

Tony pushed the door shut with his foot, the click echoing through the silence. From behind, he wrapped his good arm across her chest and spoke softly in her ear. "Stay."

Ronnie curled her hands around Tony's arm, her breathing accelerating. "That's tempting."

To make his offer more enticing, Tony created a path of kisses along the curve of her face. Her head sank sideways while she softly hummed along with the rest of her body before she turned around and faced him.

"I came to cook you dinner, not end up in bed with you."

"That wouldn't be so bad. Would it?" He kissed her lips. "Ronnie, I want you to be the last thing I see before I fall asleep and the first thing I see when I wake up. I need to feel you next to me. Baby, I've missed you so much."

Ronnie tried throwing him off track with her humor. "I'm a wreck in the morning."

"Not from what I remember." Tony sensed her fear, not of him, but of herself.

"Trust me, it's not a pretty sight."

His hand glided over her head. "Impossible. You always look amazing."

Sadness came through Ronnie's tone as if she were apologizing. "Have you forgotten that I'm engaged?"

Nothing could sever what Tony and Ronnie had, not even another man. "Our connection still exists, Ronnie. It's too strong to break. You feel it, too. I know you do."

His mouth pulled at her irresistible lips, her mouth dissolving into his. He placed her hand flat on his chest, not knowing what vibrated more, her shaky hand or his rapid heartbeat.

"Stay. Just one night," Tony murmured. Because one night alone with Ronnie was all he needed to convince her they belonged together.

"What about your shoulder? The sling." She was considering it; she was going to stay.

Tony glanced at the blue cloth. "I'll power through the pain. It hurts a lot less than being without you."

Ronnie moved away from him. "I'm sorry. I can't do this."

But she wanted to. He saw it in her eyes and felt it as he kissed her again.

In her rush to leave, she fumbled with the doorknob. "Good night, Tony."

# CHAPTER 32

Ronnie watched the foot traffic on the street below through her apartment window. The activity reminded her of an opening scene from a Hallmark Channel movie. An elderly man walked his furry white dog past a group of gabbing teens, and a young couple with two kids sat on the patio of Fred's Tasty Treat eating ice cream cones.

She had grown fond of the neighborhood over the last ten months. New renters were slated to live in her apartment after she moved into Aidan's house in Wellington Heights. Residents of the posh development on Hilton's lucrative east side with grandeur homes in a newer cul-de-sac adhered to rules enforced by the Homeowner's Association. Backyard campfires—including portable firepits from Home Depot—were banned. Laundry hanging outside—forbidden. Outdoor gatherings ended by eleven o'clock. Homeowners received fines if they slacked off on maintaining their landscape.

Ronnie couldn't picture Aidan mowing the lawn and trimming the shrubs. She didn't have to; he had hired a lawn service to do it for him.

She was one week away from becoming Mrs. Aidan Foster. Ronnie Foster. Veronica Foster.

Despite her initial irritation toward her fiancé's decision-making without her, Ronnie had allowed Aidan to do most of the legwork. She'd been through wedding preparations before, Aidan hadn't. Truth be told, she was relieved he took the reins of his own volition. She had made it easy on herself by agreeing with his choices, except for their honeymoon.

Europe was off the table. They had compromised on a ten-day Caribbean cruise instead. Ronnie had a stock of Dramamine in case she got seasick her first time on a ship. Green gills weren't attractive.

Each box had been check-marked. The final headcount for the reception. The flowers, the cake, the limo, the band, and all those extras Ronnie deemed insignificant. The only thing left was to say, "I do."

Her phone rang; it was Tony. She waited two rings, then answered with a cheery, "Hi!"

"Got any plans today?" he asked.

Aidan had been scarce lately, making a name for himself at the practice. He had pampered and babied Ronnie for weeks following the shooting, then dove back into work, trading one hectic schedule for another, filling his appointment book with additional evening and Saturday sessions. Conferences had him out of town. Last weekend it was Chicago. This weekend, Boston.

Ronnie fluffed a couch pillow. "I'm swamped. Why?"

"Guess who nabbed two tickets to the sold-out Pirates game?"

She played along. "I'll take a wild guess and say you."

"Ding, ding, ding! Correct! Ronnie, you're our grand prize winner! What do we have for the lady, Bob?" Tony pretended to be a game show host, then deepened his voice like an announcer. "One FREE ticket to the game!"

She laughed, tossing the pillow onto the couch. "How did you manage such a coup?"

"I cannot reveal the details of the mission. It's top secret."

Ronnie went to the kitchen and took a soda from the refrigerator. Twisting off the cap, she said, "Why not ask John or Vince to go with you?"

"Can't. They're working."

"On a Saturday?" Suspicion blanketed her words. "The factory isn't open."

"Uh… there's an emergency order. It can't wait until Monday. Vince probably screwed up something."

Ronnie sipped her drink. "Max or Chet?"

Tony boomeranged with "Dance recital and house hunting, respectively."

She sealed the cap and put the bottle back into the refrigerator. "That leaves me. Your last hope. What an honor." Ronnie pictured Tony's sly smirk, the one teetering between cocky and confident.

"Ah, but wait. Perhaps I saved the best for last."

*How corny. Typical Tony.*

"What do you say? You and me at PNC Park. Hopefully, another win for the Pirates."

The difference between spending the night at Tony's place and going to a baseball game with him was huge. Ronnie deemed the outing as innocent as Thanksgiving at the Lombardos' house.

"Depends on the seats," she said. "I won't consider anything less than behind home plate or third base."

"Upper deck outfield won't cut it?"

She hummed facetiously. "I'll make an exception this once."

"I can still wear you down."

If that were true, she would've slept with him the night she had cooked him dinner.

"Pick you up at noon," he said.

Ronnie heard the smile in his voice. It was the same one in hers. "I'll be ready."

Changing into a pair of jeans, Ronnie reminisced about her goodbye at Tony's apartment. She daydreamed of waking up in his bed, nestled in his brawny embrace, while his unshaven jaw softly grated on her skin.

Quickly, she ended the fleeting fantasy—that's all it was, a fantasy. Nothing had happened at his apartment, and she was confident nothing would happen today, either.

Ronnie put on a Pirates T-shirt while engaging in the laborious act of justifying an afternoon with her ex-husband.

*For crying out loud, it's a ball game!*

Thousands of fans were her unofficial chaperones. PNC Park was hardly the place for Tony to make a move on her.

Ronnie freed the locket from the blue case and opened it. She smiled at Vivian's sweet face and clasped the medallion around her neck.

What would Aidan say if he knew she was going to a baseball game with Tony? she thought, fastening her watch around her wrist. Or that she had cooked him dinner the night Aidan was in New York City. The next day, when Ronnie's fiancé had come home, he was too busy talking about the Big Apple to ask her about her weekend.

She put on her Pirates hat and reached for her mitt on the shelf in her closet. Punching the glove, she loosened the stiff leather.

Aidan's tune toward Tony had changed after Tony had saved Ronnie's life. He no longer scowled at the mention of his former nemesis.

*That settles it. Going to a ball game with Tony was fine. Two baseball fans. It was innocent.*

Ronnie punched the glove again.

So why was her stomach tied tighter than a sailor's knot?

• • •

Tony arrived at Ronnie's apartment in a Pirates T-shirt and hat. She was glad to see him without the sling. "How's the shoulder?" she asked.

He slowly rotated it, as if he were stretching before a workout. "It's getting there. Still a little stiff." He swatted the bill of her hat. "Let's go."

They drove to PNC Park and made it to their seats in time for the first pitch. Sitting under blue sunny skies as a light breeze passed over them, it was a perfect day to be at the ballpark.

Watching the players in the dugout, Ronnie remembered going to games with Nick. They'd eat junk food and chew stringy Big League Chew gum. He bought her souvenirs—the number-one foam finger and pennants for her bedroom walls. During the seventh-inning stretch, they'd split a box of M&Ms.

A food vendor strolling up the aisle shouted, "Popcorn! Peanuts! Get your popcorn and peanuts. Five dollars each. I got popcorn. Peanuts!"

Tony flicked Ronnie's arm. "How about a hot dog? Ketchup, mustard, and relish?"

"It's not a ball game without one." She reached for her wallet.

He stopped her. "It's on me."

Tony returned a few minutes later, carrying two cardboard boxes filled with food.

"The hot dog was plenty!" Ronnie said.

"We might as well do this right." Tony handed her one box. Next to the hot dog was a container of nacho chips smothered in beef, cheese, and salsa, and a bottle of Sprite. He had an identical meal.

Ronnie placed the box on her lap and bit into the savory hot dog. "Mmm. Yummy."

"Ball games have the best dogs."

"Why do you think that is?" She took another bite. The meaty flavored tasted better the second time.

Tony bit into his hot dog, and a dollop of relish landed on his nachos. He chewed while thinking. "Maybe it's being outside. Or that it's something simple. Good things don't have to be fancy."

"True. It's the little things." Ronnie lifted her hot dog. "Junk food." She gestured toward the field. "Baseball." She looked at Tony with a little smile. "Good friends."

"Or best friends." A beat of sadness came through in his tone. Tony tapped the corner of his mouth, referring to hers. "You got a little mustard right there."

Ronnie went to wipe it away, but Tony did it for her. "I got it." The yellow glob was long gone, but he continued slowly wiping her face with a napkin.

"Thanks." Ronnie ate a nacho chip, followed by a refreshing sugary gulp of soda.

During the sixth inning, a foul ball sailed toward them. Ronnie scrambled for her mitt as Tony shouted, "It's yours, Ronnie!"

She jumped and caught it. Touting victory, she raised the ball in the air as fans in her section cheered. Tony elbowed her, pointing to the jumbo screen where she had made her debut.

After the game, Tony and Ronnie celebrated the Pirates win with roast beef sandwiches and French fries at a fast-food restaurant with an indoor ice cream parlor.

"You still haven't told me how you got the tickets," Ronnie said.

Tony looked at her with a sneaky grin. "I have my ways."

"I'm sure you do." She ate a French fry. "They were John's tickets."

Tony slurped lemonade through a straw. "You can't prove that."

"Yes, I can. The parking lot at the factory was empty."

"Yeah, so?"

"There was no *emergency* order, which makes me believe Max and Chet didn't have plans, either."

"No, that part was true." Tony bit into his sandwich. "A customer gave Dad the tickets as a thank you."

"Lying to your boss." Ronnie wagged her finger. "Shame on you, Lombardo."

"It's not lying when you have a good reason," he said, chewing. "It was the only way I could think of to get you to spend the afternoon with me. Baseball is your weakness. You can't resist a game. It was the perfect set-up." He wiped a napkin across his mouth. "Besides, we always had fun at Pirates games."

*Too bad today was our last one.*

After they had finished eating, Tony took Ronnie's tray to the counter. He returned with a bowl of her favorite ice cream—chocolate chip cookie dough—and slid it in front of her. "Dig in."

"Are you trying to make me fat?"

He sat down with his bowl of mint chocolate chip. "A few extra pounds won't hurt you. Ma thinks you're too skinny as it is."

While eating ice cream, Ronnie watched a little girl in the kiddie play yard run from the obstacle course to the stationary horse on a spring. The wind blew her long brown hair as she rocked back and forth, giggling.

Ronnie twisted the locket around her neck as Tony looked through the window. "She's cute. Remind you of anyone?" he asked.

Ronnie scraped the spoon aimlessly along the inside of the bowl. "Every little girl reminds me of Vivian."

"Do you want to talk about it?"

Ronnie pulled away from her trance. "Talk about what?"

"Whatever's on your mind," Tony said and ate a bite of the green ice cream. She stared at her bowl. He reached across the table and took her hand. "You can tell me anything."

Ronnie stared out the window, knowing what Tony was about to hear sounded morbid. "Have you ever wondered what your last moment before you die would be like?"

The way he lifted his eyebrows implied he hadn't expected that. "Not really."

"The night of the shooting, all I thought about was how I was going to die alone in a filthy barn. I didn't know what the last thing I was going to see before everything went black. Some hay or a beam. One of the broken windows. Luke. Then I saw her."

"Her? You mean Vivian?"

Ronnie nodded. "Dad was holding and kissing her. They were smiling and laughing. Then they looked at me, and I heard Vivian. She said, 'Come on, Mommy,' and they were both waving for me to join them, and I wanted to. I wanted to die." Ronnie faced Tony. "Then I saw you, and I knew it wasn't time to go."

Tony rounded the booth and sat next to Ronnie. They said nothing and finished eating their ice cream. Talking about death the way Ronnie had had a way of killing a conversation.

The ride back to her apartment was a quiet one as Ronnie reflected on her afternoon with Tony at the ballpark and their talk. She assumed Tony was in his own world of reflection, as he hadn't spoken, either.

He pulled up to the curb of Ronnie's building, and without asking, walked her to her apartment and followed her inside. After removing her sneakers, she doubled over in pain.

"What's wrong?" he asked, assisting her to the couch.

She lowered herself onto the cushions and placed her hat, mitt, and fly ball onto the coffee table. "I think I ate too much."

"I've seen you eat more at a Lombardo birthday party."

Ronnie lay on her side, curled up with a hand on her belly. "My stomach isn't what it used to be."

Tony smirked. "You act like you're geriatric."

Ronnie winced as another painful wave rolled through her gut. "I'm not twenty-five anymore."

Tony glanced around the apartment. "Where's the antacid?"

She pointed at the hallway behind her. "Bathroom. Medicine cabinet, top shelf."

Tony returned with an Alka-Seltzer pack. He dropped two tablets into a glass and filled it with water from the kitchen sink, activating the fizzy remedy.

Ronnie rose slowly from her side as he handed her the glass, and she drank half of the medicinal liquid. "Yuck."

"Maybe it wasn't the food." Tony sat down next to her and felt her forehead. "You don't have a fever. That rules out appendicitis."

"It could be the flu. It's going around." She burped and finished the rest of the grayish drink in one gulp. Bubbles shot up her nose. "I hope it's not food poisoning."

"Doubt it. We ate the same thing, except for the ice cream. I'm fine. Besides, you'd be puking. A lot more than you did after Chet's wedding."

Ronnie closed her eyes briefly. "Don't remind me."

Tony sat with his elbows perched on his thighs. "Speaking of weddings, are you still going through with yours?"

She glared at him. "Of course. Why wouldn't I?"

"A lot of brides get cold feet."

Ronnie lifted her legs and wiggled her toes. "Mine are nice and toasty." She winced; another gurgle shot through her lower abdomen.

Tony tucked a pillow against the couch arm. "Lie back down." He swung her legs onto the couch and took the glass, placing it on the coffee table. Sitting close to her, his firm hand rubbed her belly in circles with the gentleness of a dove.

The sensation made her tingle with familiarity. She fantasized about him lifting her shirt, his head descending to her exposed midsection, where his mouth and her softness would meet while her fingers laced through his hair. Slowly, he'd move toward her, one kiss at a time, up her body, then gently lie on top of her.

"Feeling any better?" he asked.

She exited the daydream and admitted, "A little."

As much as Ronnie wanted to credit the antacid, it was Tony's attentive bedside manner that had settled her stomachache.

When she was pregnant with Vivian and had a wicked case of morning sickness during the first trimester, Tony had made sure there was always a box of saltine crackers on the nightstand. He had bought a mini-fridge for their bedroom, stocked with ginger ale. He would lie next to her in bed and rub her stomach, telling her what a wonderful mother she'd be, and that he was the luckiest man because she was carrying his child. Her midnight cravings had peaked at seven months, and he had made multiple trips to the kitchen when she had requested odd combinations—cottage cheese and Doritos or applesauce with raisins and whipped cream. One time, Tony had cooked Ronnie a pork chop and fried eggs at two in the morning.

"You're always taking care of me," she said.

"It's easy to do."

The heat of his stare drew her in as she studied every part of him that had once belonged to her while he fingered the locket cradled in the hollow dip below her neck. Ronnie longed to hear the words Tony had said all the time. Words she now knew that dangled on the tip of his tongue.

He leaned toward her, tilting his head to kiss her. Their mouths nearly touched when her phone rang, startling them both. Aidan's name and number appeared on her watch, and the pit in her stomach contracted. "It's Aidan."

Tony fell back against the couch. "Impeccable timing, as usual."

Ronnie answered the call with a gleeful, "Hi!"

"Hello, sweetheart," Aidan said. "How are you?"

"Great." Ronnie stood and went into the kitchen, although Tony could hear her. "How's the conference?"

"Fantastic. I forgot how interesting these meetings can be."

Three days with a hundred psychiatrists discussing mental health issues wasn't Ronnie's idea of interesting.

"The only downfall is not being with you," Aidan lamented, "but I'll be home before you know it."

"I'm counting the hours," she said.

"The next conference is in September in Atlanta. You should come with me. We can make a mini-vacation out of it."

"Sounds like fun. I've never been to Atlanta."

*Maybe I can catch a Braves game while Aidan rubs elbows with his colleagues.*

"What do you have planned for the rest of the evening?"

*Besides almost cheating on you?*

Ronnie went back into the living room. Tony looked at her as if telling her to hang up. "Oh, not much. Just hanging out at home. I'll probably watch a movie."

"Just think, Veronica, one week from today, we'll be married. I can hardly wait!"

"Me, too," she said.

With that, all hope Tony held onto like a life preserver floated farther out to sea.

"Sweetheart, I hate to say goodbye," Aidan said, "but a few counselors and I have dinner reservations before our evening seminar."

Good. Ronnie didn't know how much longer she could go on letting Aidan believe she was alone while Tony sat on her couch. "Have fun. I'll see you at the airport tomorrow."

"Can't wait. I love you, Veronica."

Ronnie stared at Tony while saying, "Love you, too," to her fiancé.

She ended the call, wishing Tony would disappear from her apartment. He complicated her life. She didn't have time to deal with her feelings appropriately, not when she was days away from marrying another man. "I'm a little tired," she said and pointed near the vicinity of her bedroom. "I'm going to lie down."

He stood. "Yeah, I gotta get going."

Tony's heavy, burdened feet thumped across the floor as Ronnie followed him to the door. "Don't bother making a seating card for me. I won't be at the wedding." He grunted. "I'm surprised I was even invited."

Aidan was the one who had written Tony's name on the guest list, which made her think he had done it to rub Tony's nose in watching his ex-wife get remarried.

"You saved my life," she said. "I think that deserves an invitation."

Ronnie fought Tony's emotional hold on her. The pain of wanting him and the life they once had lay buried in the catacombs of her heart.

"I'll see you when I get back from my honeymoon," she said.

He opened the door without looking at her and muttered, "Congratulations" and left.

Ronnie hugged her abdomen. The ache had returned to her stomach and to her heart.

# CHAPTER 33

The morning of Ronnie's wedding, Natalie arrived at her daughter's apartment bright and early with her mother-of-the-bride dress, beauty caddy, and breakfast—croissants and fresh fruit—while Graham sulked at the hotel.

At the kitchen table, she glided the last brush stroke onto her daughter's pinky. "There. All done." She twisted the nail polish cap shut and blew on the wet nails. "Now wave your hands like this."

Ronnie copied her mother's demonstration. Her nails had to be perfect.

Natalie's home manicure had saved Ronnie an appointment to one of those overpriced salons, where the girls chatted more than a gossip columnist. Prior to the paint, she had rubbed oil onto Ronnie's nails and clipped the layers of dead skin, which she informed Ronnie was her cuticle. With a file that felt like sandpaper at one end and silk at the other, she had rounded each nail evenly.

Tired from all that waving, Ronnie switched to blowing. Natalie packed her manicure kit with tools Ronnie didn't know the names of, then moved onto the next beauty item on the list.

"Where's your cosmetic bag?" she asked.

Ronnie blew on her nails. "Do I need one?"

Her mother's countenance said every woman must own a cosmetic bag. "Where do you keep your makeup?"

Ronnie motioned to the bathroom. "Top drawer of the sink."

She heard her mother shuffling through the contents in the drawer. "Is this all you have?" Natalie shouted from the bathroom.

"Yep." Ronnie touched a shiny nail. The blush-colored paint was still tacky.

Natalie returned to the living room with the cosmetics and opened her purse. "You can borrow mine. I always carry extra." She took Ronnie's gown from the hallway closet, thoroughly inspecting the shimmering garment from every angle. "Gorgeous. So different from the first one."

The dress Ronnie had worn when she married Tony was her style: straight, strapless with a small train. The gown Natalie scrutinized weighed twenty pounds and had that princess look, complete with a big poof, lacey veil, and an encrusted rhinestone tiara.

"It's nice," Ronnie said. "Aidan will like it."

Natalie noticed her daughter's perfunctory tone. "You're the one wearing it. If you don't like it, then why did you buy it?"

Ronnie blew on her nails. "I can suck it up for one day. It's just fabric."

Natalie laid the dress over the chair. "Where are your shoes?"

"Bedroom closet."

Natalie retrieved the modest white pumps and held them against the dress. Noises accompanied her pout.

Ronnie knew that sound. "What's wrong?"

"Nothing." Natalie moved the shoes over the dress like a metal detector. "The shade is a smidge off."

Ronnie couldn't see it. "No one will notice my feet."

"I suppose." Natalie shook her head in a disappointed way and sat down next to Ronnie. "Let's see how your nails are doing." She delicately touched a nail and looked at her finger—no smudge. She tested the remaining nine. "Done, but be careful. They're still fragile."

Natalie's mother-daughter moment had finally arrived. The one she had dreamed about since the day Ronnie was born: beauty tips, clothes, and giggling about boys. Well, the boy part was minimal.

"I bought a curling iron. We can put your hair in an updo and curl the ends." Natalie drew Ronnie's hair together with contemplation, followed by that pout and more noises. "Your hair doesn't seem long enough. Why didn't you make an appointment with a hairstylist? Those girls can do anything."

"I want to wear it down."

Natalie released the hair, displaying the same fake smile Ronnie had seen her whole life whenever her mother disagreed with her choices.

After Ronnie's nails had dried, her makeup was on, and her hair was to her liking, Natalie helped her daughter into the gown she had never intended to buy.

The saleswoman had the dress marked sold the minute she saw Ronnie surveying the racks. She held out the dress. "When the designer sketched this, she had you in mind."

Ronnie touched the conglomerate of pearls and rhinestones with enough shine to make a disco ball. "Thanks, but it's not me."

"Don't be hasty! At least try it on."

Ronnie appreciated the woman's enthusiasm, but knew what she wanted. "I'm looking for something less flashy. Simple, yet elegant."

"Oh, honey, no! Think big! All eyes will be on you. Every woman wants to look like a princess on her wedding day."

Royalty wasn't what Ronnie was after and continued bypassing more of the same dresses.

"Trust me. As soon as I saw you, I knew *this* was the dress for you." The woman thrust the gown at Ronnie. She flipped over the price tag and realized why.

Short of leaving Hilton's only bridal shop, she had appeased the pushy saleswoman and tried on the dress designed for Cinderella. Did that make the woman her fairy godmother?

Glittery dollar signs floated in the saleswoman's eyes. "We've found our dress."

*Our? Since when did this become your wedding, too?*

Natalie finished buttoning the gown from behind and attached the veil. Five thousand dollars later and Ronnie's wedding dress had looked better on the rack than it did on her.

The bell rang, and Natalie opened the door. A man in a black suit tipped his cap. "Hello, ma'am. I'm your limo driver, Edward."

Ronnie glanced at the packed boxes in the living room. The next time she stepped foot into the apartment, she'd be a married woman.

Ronnie and Natalie went inside the limo with the rest of the bridal party: Paula—her maid of honor, Maggie Richmond, Aidan's sister, Lucy, and Ronnie's impending niece, Nina, as the flower girl.

The limo driver pulled away from the curb and headed to the Rolling Hills Country Club.

It felt like Aidan's wedding and not Ronnie's, but it was too late for her to do anything about it.

• • •

Tony sprinted around the water fountain and onto the golf greens, past a trio of violinists engrossed in the performance of a lifetime. The country club was an ideal wedding venue—for anyone other than Ronnie.

Rows of white chairs with elaborate pew bows constructed of silk, ferns, and roses lined both sides of the aisle. Tony scanned the crowd of guests and spotted Audrey and Max.

"Casual is in these days, but isn't that a bit overboard?" his best friend said.

Tony looked down at his T-shirt and shorts. It hadn't occurred to him to change his clothes. One minute he was lying on his bed feeling sorry for himself, looking through photo albums of him, Ronnie, and Vivian. The next, he was in his truck, speeding down Nichols Drive toward the club.

"I'm stopping the wedding," Tony said.

Max quit laughing when he realized Tony wasn't joking. "You're serious?"

Chet and Mia arrived and sat next to the Brodys. "Run out of clean suits, Lombardo?" Chet said.

"Don't need one, Dalton. Ronnie's not marrying Aidan."

Max's expression claimed Tony was delusional. "Buddy, it's over. You tried, but the Chief has moved on. Maybe you should do the same."

"That's hardly optimistic advice coming from a relationship expert like you."

"Reality trumps optimism."

"No!" Tony said. "Until Ronnie walks down that aisle, I still have a chance."

Max leaned in with a warning. "She'll rip you limb from limb if you make a scene."

"I won't do anything to embarrass Ronnie." Tony looked back at the clubhouse. "I need to find her. She won't go through this charade once she hears what I have to say."

"It's about time you got here. What took you so long?" Paula approached Tony wearing a turquoise bridesmaid dress. "Nice outfit, by the way."

"Thanks. It's the talk of the town. Where's Ronnie?"

"The bridal suite. Follow me."

Tony and Paula went inside the banquet room from the patio entrance. The tables were set for the reception and a favor on each plate had a tag that read: Aidan & Veronica, July 3, 2021. The bartender lined up champagne flutes. Turquoise cloths draped two tables by the entrance. One with a five-tier cake. The other for the gifts.

The bridesmaids and groomsmen in gray tuxedos went outside. Tony didn't see Aidan and assumed he was in his own room for the groom.

"You're cutting it close, Tony," Paula said. "Ten minutes until the ceremony. Is that enough time?"

"It'll have to be. I'm not leaving here without Ronnie."

"Don't bet on it."

Tony instantly recognized the woman's voice that had enough disdain to fill a nuclear reactor. He turned around, but the summer heat wasn't hot enough to thaw his ex-mother-in-law's icy daggers.

"Hello, Natalie. You look lovely."

She walked around Tony and stood in front of him. "Sucking up won't score you any points."

It was worth a shot, although true, contrary to what Natalie believed. She looked stunning in the silky floor-length dress and matching jacket, the same color as the bridesmaids' dresses. Diamond droplet earrings shimmered against her short blond hair. Thanks to her injections and enhancements, she hadn't aged in eleven years.

"I'd say it's good seeing you, but I'd be lying." Natalie clasped her hands in front of her rigid body with an unapproved glare that rode up and down Tony. "You could've *at least* worn a suit."

He ignored the criticism because now wasn't the time for a war of words with the woman. "If you'll excuse me, I need to talk to Ronnie."

Natalie's arm shot out straight, blocking him. "You can give your congratulations to Veronica and Aidan at the reception."

"It'll be too late by then."

Natalie's hate for Tony burned hotter than volcanic lava. She fearlessly got in his face and snarled. "This is Veronica's wedding day. You had your chance, and you blew it. Big time."

Paula stood behind Natalie, pointing at her watch. Time was running out. Tony had to get to the bridal suite before Ronnie made the biggest mistake of her life.

"Natty, what are you doing in here?" Graham said in that geeky, high-pitch whine Tony remembered so well.

"I just had to check on something, darling."

"Well, hurry up!" he said. "I'm all alone out there. I don't know any of these people."

Natalie exploded. "I'll be out in a minute!" Her husband flinched, and he left through the patio entrance. "Tony, I'm grateful you saved Veronica's life—I am. But if it weren't for *you*, that maniac wouldn't have tried to kill her in the first place. You put her in danger," she said. "You started this whole thing when you cheated on her!"

For someone like Natalie, who wasn't as forgiving as Ronnie, consequences were lifetime reminders of mistakes. "You think I don't know that? That I haven't thought about it every day since it happened. I can't change the past, Natalie. But I'll live the rest of my life doing whatever I can to give Ronnie the future she deserves."

Natalie scowled. "My, my, still the narcissist. You think you can just come in here, tell Veronica you want her back, and she'll drop her bouquet and leave Aidan at the altar?"

"This is Ronnie's life. It's her choice, and she needs to make it without any interference from you."

A man dressed like a manager came out from the kitchen. Natalie snapped her fingers. "Excuse me, Jonathan?" She gestured politely at Tony. "Please remove this man from the premises. He's not on the guest list."

Jonathan stared at Tony as if he were a toad. "Is that true, sir?"

"Not exactly."

"Club policy prohibits nonmembers on the property. Only invited guests from members are allowed. You'll have to come with me."

The man gripped Tony by the elbow the way he'd handle a criminal. He yanked his arm free. "Get your hands off me. I'm a cop!"

Tony's vocation didn't intimidate the club employee. "Well, *officer*, you're trespassing."

Natalie waved and smugly mouthed "Bye-bye" to Tony as Jonathan led him past the cake table.

*That viper.*

"Paula!" Tony shouted, "tell Ronnie I was here!"

Natalie pushed the maid of honor from behind toward the exit. "Come along, Paula. You're needed outside."

Tony passed a room with a sign on the door that read Bridal Suite. He halted. "Please, I need to talk to the bride. It's important. Just one minute, then I'll leave. I promise."

The club's henchman must've been in the wrong line when they were handing out emotions. His eyes never left Tony as he pressed a button on the cordless headset around his head and spoke into the microphone. "Security, please report to the bridal suite."

"Come on, man! Don't do that!"

In seconds, two men appeared, one on each side of Tony, and they escorted him down the hall as he yelled, "Ronnie!"

The men dragged Tony outside and shut the double doors in his face. Scenarios on how to get back inside all ended with him in the back seat of a patrol car.

There was only one thing left for him to do.

• • •

Ronnie opened the door and peeked into the hallway. She could've sworn she had heard her name and closed the door.

The crinoline beneath her gown rustled as she paced while rehearsing her vows in the bridal suite. Two notecards acted as her cheat sheets. She tried memorizing the first one, but halfway through, her mind went blank, and she read the line aloud.

"I'm the happiest woman in the world to have found you." Ronnie erased the sentence. "Cheesy."

She rewrote the line. "I can't wait to spend the rest of my life with you." Grumbling, she scratched a pencil mark through the cliché.

Traditional vows were easier. The ones where the minister said, "Repeat after me." Aidan had insisted on reciting their own vows, calling the exchange a romantic dedication.

*Dedication?* Not Pulitzer Prize writing, but wasn't imitation the highest form of flattery? Ronnie scribbled her thoughts onto the notecard.

"Today, I dedicate my life to you."

Ronnie imagined Aidan's vows drew inspiration from a famous poet. The best she had was, "Today, I dedicate my life to you." How lame.

She could improvise on the spot. Just say whatever came to mind, but if Ronnie froze, she'd embarrass herself and Aidan in front of two hundred people.

Ronnie felt the pressure closing in as she grappled with how to express her feelings for her soon-to-be husband. Saying you loved your better half had become insurmountable, and the truth had never been clearer.

Emotion like that doesn't need to be crossed out and rewritten if you are truly in love. It's already there.

Ronnie read the second notecard, erasing another artificial sentiment. "Five minutes from getting married and I can't nail down these vows."

*It's a sign, Ronnie. Open your eyes and read it!*

Her phone rang, and she hurried to answer it. Her heart leaped; it was Tony. She went to the window, hoping he had changed his mind about coming as she looked for him through the throng of guests. "Hi. Where are you?"

"In the club parking lot. Your mother had me thrown out."

Of all the times for Natalie to stick her nose where it didn't belong.

"Ronnie, I need to talk to you."

"Go around the building to your right. There's a side door. I'll meet you there."

She snuck out of the bridal suite and down the hallway without being seen. She opened the emergency exit door and saw Tony walking toward her taking confident, powerful strides.

"You came," she said as her voice cracked in quiet disbelief.

What got him there didn't matter. He was there, and all Ronnie wanted him to do was hold her.

"You look as beautiful as you did on *our* wedding day," he said.

*No, don't think about that. Don't think about one of the best days of your life.*

"I only have a few minutes, Tony. What did you want to tell me?"

He blurted, "September seventeenth, two-thousand one."

A date Ronnie would never forget. "The day I joined the force as a rookie." She didn't see the correlation between her first day as a cop and Tony's urgency to see her.

"Before we met, I was happy being a cop and a bachelor. Marriage and kids weren't part of the plan for a long time. Maybe never. Then everything changed when you showed up that day—scared, but you hid it well. Determined—some might say too ambitious. And way too good for a jerk like me." Tony held Ronnie's hands as if they were saying vows to each other. "I knew I had met my wife and mother of my children. I was sure of it. I still am. Only now, I have this ache whenever I'm not with you. I can't have you partially in my life."

Ronnie's lips quivered. "Please don't do this to me. Not now."

Tony curled his hands around the back of her neck as she touched the locket with Vivian's picture. "I love you, Ronnie. I've always loved you, and I always will."

Softly, he kissed Ronnie and her legs went numb the instant their lips joined. She slithered her arms around him. He felt so, so good.

"I'm hanging on by a thread." Tony pressed his forehead against hers. "Don't marry Aidan. Marry me, Ronnie."

She looked into his eyes—those eyes with persuasive power—but they couldn't sway her. Not this time. "I have to go. The ceremony's starting."

His face collapsed. He looked as if he were going to be sick. "No, Ronnie. Please."

She touched his hands that hadn't left her neck. With her eyes closed, she rested one side of her face into his palm, rubbing her cheek against it to feel his warmth one last time. "I'm sorry, Tony."

He let go of her, and she waited for his next move. Would he toss her over his shoulder and take her anyway? Would he set off the emergency fire alarm as a distraction? Would he stand there and argue with her? No. Tony did none of those things. He said nothing as he opened the side door entrance and left. It was over between her and Tony. Again. And it ripped through Ronnie like a knife, hacking at her heart.

"Miss Callahan! There you are!" The club's wedding coordinator jogged toward Ronnie and handed her her bouquet. "It's time to get married."

• • •

Guests stood at the first beat of the wedding march, watching Ronnie make that memorable walk to the altar—alone. She had better odds of getting struck by lightning than having Graham give her away. When she had married Tony, John Lombardo had had the distinct honor of escorting her to the altar and welcoming her into the family.

Ronnie's pace slowed to a near standstill as she scanned the bride's side for Tony. She knew it was a longshot before Max's pitiful stare made it official.

Natalie's countenance shone brighter than the sequins on her jacket, while Graham's puss screamed his discontentment. The photographer lowered the camera, perplexed by the sad bride.

Ronnie and Aidan stood under the arbor covered in roses, lilies, and carnations from arch-to-arch.

The minister looked up from his book. "Dearly beloved, we are gathered here today to witness the marriage of Veronica Elizabeth Callahan and Aidan Paul Foster. Marriage is an institution formed by God."

Ronnie broke out into a cold sweat. "Stop!" she shouted at the minister.

"Excuse me?" he said. "Are you okay?"

Ronnie stammered, "I—I—"

Aidan whispered in a low, angry voice, "Veronica, you're embarrassing me."

Ronnie grabbed a hunk of her gown and dashed toward the clubhouse as the guests let out an astounded gasp. The minister shrugged as if he didn't know what was going on.

"Ladies and gentlemen, I apologize," Aidan said. "Thank you for your patience. We'll be back in a moment."

Aidan chased after Ronnie. He caught up to her and spun her around. "Veronica, what's going on?"

Her voice crackled. "I'm sorry, Aidan. I am so sorry, but I... I can't marry you."

He turned around at the guests, watching from a distance. Grabbing her elbow, he pulled her inside the clubhouse through the patio entrance, where two servers were flirting with the bartender.

"Go find something to do," Aidan ordered them, as if he had authority. The trio quickly scattered.

"What do you mean, you can't marry me, Veronica?"

Ronnie couldn't pretend to deny her feelings. "I'm in love with Tony."

Aidan's eyes ached with betrayal. "You've been seeing him behind my back, haven't you?"

*Ouch, that hurt.*

"I didn't sleep with him."

Aidan grunted, appalled by Ronnie's honesty. "Is that supposed to make me feel better? Because it doesn't!"

"Aidan, I didn't mean for this to happen." Ronnie reached for him, but he backed away. "I'm—"

"Don't. Don't say you're sorry and that you care for me. It's patronizing, and it's cruel." He paced in a small circle, quiet, before shouting, "I trusted you!"

"No, you didn't. Not from the moment you found out about Tony. That's why you wanted to get married so quickly. Once I became your wife, you knew I'd be faithful. That I wouldn't do to you what Tony had done to me."

Ronnie had turned the tables on the psychiatrist—and Aidan knew it.

"That's complete nonsense," he snapped. "I wanted a brief engagement because I didn't want to wait a year to get married. There's nothing wrong with that."

"I don't believe that, Aidan. Neither do you."

His calm tone mixed with bitterness. "I see how you look at him. I had hoped one day you'd look at me the same way."

Ronnie had hoped for the same thing. She had tried. She had tried so hard, but Nonna was right when she had said, "*The heart is stronger than the mind.*"

Aidan took a deep breath. "I would've given you everything you wanted, Veronica. But with Tony around, it would never have been enough."

He tugged on the bottom of his jacket. His face tightened as a stoic expression was the only way he could get through the next few minutes.

"There are two hundred guests we owe an explanation to," he said. "The least you could do is to be there with me when I tell them."

"Of course." Nothing Ronnie could do or say would absolve her for jilting her fiancé at the altar, but at least she wouldn't be a coward.

Aidan and Ronnie went outside and walked down the aisle. The saleswoman from the bridal shop was right. All eyes were on Ronnie. How could they not be after she'd run off the way she had?

They faced their guests. Aidan cleared his throat. "Thank you all for coming. Unfortunately, there isn't going to be a wedding."

Murmuring and furrowed foreheads rippled through the crowd. Natalie held her head as if she were battling a migraine. Graham rolled his eyes so far back in his head, they nearly got stuck there.

"Veronica and I care deeply for each other but have decided marriage isn't part of our future." Aidan's articulate, poised demeanor covered how he was breaking apart inside. "It's best we part ways amicably. We're sorry for the inconvenience."

He left and went inside the club, his groomsmen and his parents following him. Ronnie hadn't expected a goodbye hug or a sweet sendoff—that would've been selfish of her.

Whether or not Aidan realized it, he had come into Ronnie's life for a reason—if only for her to become the person she had always denied herself. For that, she'd always love him.

Dumfounded guests stood, wondering whether to go or stay. Natalie flew out of her chair and charged toward Ronnie. "Have you lost your mind? Go after him!"

"It won't change how I feel."

"Yes, it will! Being married will make you forget about Tony." Natalie grabbed Ronnie by the shoulders. "You and Aidan are a good match. Don't you want to be happy?"

*We're not tennis partners.*

If anyone understood Ronnie's predicament, it was Natalie. "Mom, I don't want a 'Graham.' I *need* a 'Nick.'"

At the mention of her father's name, Natalie's watery eyes sailed over to her curmudgeon husband. Her hands went up in surrender. "Go."

Ronnie had broken two hearts in one day, but now she could repair one of them.

"Are you okay?" Paula asked as she and Max approached Ronnie.

"Never better. I have to find Tony."

"What are you doing standing around here for? Go after your man!"

Ronnie tossed the bouquet to her best friend, then panicked. "I don't have my car! Paula, can I borrow yours?"

"I rode over in the limo."

Max reached into his pocket and threw her his keys. "Here, Chief. Take mine."

"Thanks, Max!"

Ronnie ran across the greens and into the parking lot. She pressed the alarm on the key fob and followed the annoying honking noise to Max's Chevy Malibu. She sped out of the country club and yanked off the veil. The wind caught hold of it and sucked it out of the window. She never liked it anyway.

Like a movie montage, she reminisced about scenes from her life with Tony. Their first ride in the patrol car—he had insisted on driving. Their red, runny noses while sipping hot cocoa during their ice-skating date. The Sunday dinner when she had met the Lombardos.

Ronnie pulled alongside the curb of Tony's apartment building. Between running and hauling the gown up three flights of stairs, she had put in a workout equivalent to going to the gym. Her fists banged on his door with a thunderous pounding. "Tony! Tony, please open up! It's Ronnie!" She rang the doorbell, hitting it like a machine gun. "Tony!"

He wasn't home.

In the car, she looked for her phone. "Crap! I left it at the club." There wasn't time to go back and get it, and she drove toward John and Tess's house.

Ronnie heard a blip and saw flashing lights in the rearview mirror. She smacked her hands against the wheel and pulled over. "You've gotta be kidding!"

Officer Chambers appeared at the window. "Are you all right, Chief?"

"Of course I am. Why?"

He stared at her, drowning in white fabric. "Um...license and registration."

"I don't have it on me."

The rookie officer fumbled through his lecture. "I... uh.... clocked you going fifty-five in a thirty. Driving without a license is another citation. No seat belt." He hemmed and hawed around before adding a fourth violation. "Um, you took that stop sign like a yield sign."

Ronnie's officer had done his job. She'd be sure to acknowledge him on Monday. "Chambers, I can explain later. Then you can decide whether you want to write me up that ticket."

"Yeah. Sure. No problem."

She threw the car in DRIVE.

"Chief?"

Ronnie huffed. "What, Chambers?"

He stretched the harness across her lap. "Buckle up."

She clicked the buckle over the mountainous material. "Good work," she said and pulled back onto the road.

The images resumed. Tony's marriage proposal on the Fourth of July. Him holding her hand in the delivery room as Vivian entered the world. The three of them trudging through a foot of snow, making a snowman, followed by a fun snowball fight. Girls versus guy. Family picnics in the park.

Birchwood Park. The only place that meant as much to Tony as it did to Ronnie.

She slammed on the brakes and cranked the wheel. The tire-screeching U-turn in the middle of the road just missed an oncoming car, whose driver signaled his anger by laying on the horn and cursing. Ronnie floored the gas pedal and raced down Washington Street to Stovemeyer Road.

She forgot the speed bump into the park entrance and drove over it so fast, the car landed with a hard *thump*.

Driving on the paved path, she went past groups of grillers, tanning women, and cornhole matches until she spotted Tony's truck and parked in the empty spot next to him.

Ronnie lifted the dress and ran toward the dogwood tree. Tony's words at the lawyer's office echoed in her mind. *"Love's there. It hasn't left. I love you, Ronnie, and I know deep down you still love me."*

Her love for him hadn't left. Not after Vivian had died and not after his affair. Not after she had ended their marriage and moved to Scottsdale.

Ronnie ran past four boys in their swim trunks licking popsicles, staring at the strange lady running through the park in a wedding gown.

Oh, what she must have looked like.

Tony sat on the ground under the dogwood tree, staring lifelessly ahead as if he had blocked out the world around him.

"Brings back memories, huh?" Ronnie said.

He spun around.

She wheezed, hunched over with her hands on her knees. "Woo! If you ever want a good workout, run through the park wearing a wedding dress."

She lifted the bottom of her poofy gown and plopped down next to him.

"Does your husband know you're here?" Tony asked.

"Funny thing happened after you left. There I was, standing next to Aidan under this beautiful archway of flowers. The minister started the ceremony with the whole, "Dearly beloved," speech. And…I couldn't go through with it."

"There had to be a reason. What was it?"

Ronnie knew Tony was going to drag this out. "You know the answer."

"I want to hear you say it." His dark eyes pulled her in, and she gladly let them.

"There's someone else."

Tony grinned, playing along. "Anyone I know?"

"Perhaps. When I was twenty-one, I got paired up with this cop at work. He was attractive and overly confident. Thought he was something special."

Tony wanted to hear more of the story. "What happened? Between you and this guy."

"He desperately tried getting my attention," Ronnie said in character. "He was *relentless*."

Tony held up a finger. "Persistence is a virtue."

"I suppose. Well, I threw him a bone. I figured one date would satisfy his ego, and he'd move onto the next challenge."

"Did your plan work?"

"Not exactly. It turns out his cocky exterior was an act." Ronnie's voice softened. "I misjudged him. I assumed things that weren't true to keep from getting hurt."

"You're human. You're allowed to make a mistake," Tony said. "How's the story end?"

"We got married and had a beautiful daughter. Unfortunately, we split and went our separate ways. As angry as I was, I still missed him so much. I called him once, but he'd changed his number. Before I knew it, I was in Hilton at his parents' house."

Tony interrupted the story. "When?"

"Two years later. On our anniversary." Ronnie paused. "I sat in the car for twenty minutes. The longer I waited, the more afraid I got. What if he was seeing someone or engaged? Or married."

"He wasn't—to all three."

"If I had known that," she said, bowing her head, "well, there's no point in thinking about what could've been."

Tony lifted her chin with one finger. "This guy sounds pretty incredible to have you run out on your wedding."

"He is, but he's not perfect. Neither am I." She took his hand and kissed it. "It's you, Tony. It's always been you."

Their mouths met and moved like a graceful dance, swaying side-to-side, keeping in perfect harmony with their love.

Ronnie's eyes blurred with tears. "I'm so in love with you, Tony."

He flashed her one of those sexy smiles. "It took you long enough to admit it."

She chortled. "You know how stubborn I am."

"You?" He blew a mouthful of air. "Never."

Tony dove towards her with a kiss so deep it reached her soul. Ronnie felt complete and whole. She found the missing part of her life in him and promised herself never to let go of it again.

"You'll always be *my* Ronnie." His voice was raw with passion, yet sweet in delivery.

She traced the outline of his chin. "Antonio."

"It'll be different this time, better than before, because I know how it feels to live without you. It hurts more than any pain I could ever experience." Tony cupped her face in his hands. "I won't let you down again."

"I know," Ronnie said as happy tears fell. "Because I trust you."

He tilted his head up, watching the branches dangle over them. "The first time we were at this tree, I told you two things. Do you remember what they were?"

"Yes. I'll never forget them."

"Don't, no matter what." Tony kissed her eyelids and lifted her to her feet. "Dance with me."

Ronnie looked around. "Here?"

"There's no better place."

The tree limbs wobbled as a gust of wind passed through. Pink petals fell onto Ronnie's dress as she and Tony danced under the dogwood tree while he crooned the words to "Stand by Me."

# EPILOGUE

The pain from seventeen years ago sparked Ronnie's memory. She had declined an epidural and was regretting her decision for natural childbirth.

The steady string of beeps from the monitor was a good sign as she lay on the bed in a hospital birthing room with her knees bent and her legs spread. Her brief rest was over. It was time for another push.

Dignity aside, she grunted, while every muscle in her body screamed obscenities at her during the grueling delivery.

Tony held her hand, cheering her on. "That's it, baby. You're doing great."

Having another child hadn't replaced Vivian. Instead, it added to their family.

Ronnie had told Tony she wanted to have his child again, and it moved him to tears. She had embraced another chance at motherhood, welcomed it wholeheartedly for the first time in more than a decade, because she knew with Tony by her side, she could do anything.

Being older, she had warned him conceiving may take longer or not happen at all, but assured him they'd have lots of fun trying.

It turned out age wasn't a hinderance as Ronnie got pregnant in two months. She had surprised Tony with the news during a romantic spaghetti and meatball dinner, complete with candles and music.

Time had a way of mending the hardest of broken hearts, giving Ronnie lessons she would take with her on her journey. Age had given her wisdom, making her stronger and more confident. And Tony, well, Tony had given her the best gift of all—a brand-new life, making her a mother again at forty-one.

"The head is crowning." The doctor looked up from the end of the bed. "Got a couple more pushes left in you?"

Ronnie grimaced. "Do I have a choice?"

"Sorry to be the bearer of bad news."

The baby felt crammed in her birth canal forever. Pain and exhaustion made her irrational, but one look at Tony made it all worthwhile.

He had read *What to Expect When You're Expecting* cover-to-cover. He had gone with her to all her doctor's appointments and multiple sonograms—her age put her at a high-risk status. They had taken a four-week Lamaze course at the hospital. Tony had been the most engaged father-to-be in the group, asking questions and tending to Ronnie like a mother hen. He had spent a Saturday afternoon at Oh Baby! buying everything from furniture to travel gear to feeding, thoroughly researching each product's safety rating.

Despite Ronnie's swollen feet and achy lower back, Tony had made her feel desirable with a new wardrobe of fashionable maternity clothes, including a sexy red dress she had worn to Brookline Restaurant for their last dinner out alone before the baby.

The doctor raised his head. "Okay, Ronnie. Let's get this push out of the way."

He tried making light of her pain, as if he knew what she was going through! Men.

She pushed. The hardest one yet.

"Great job!" he said, praising her. "You're almost there."

Tony dabbed Ronnie's flushed cheeks with a damp cloth. Twelve hours earlier, he'd been with her when she had her first contraction in bed. He had stayed with her all night, being a supportive coach, breathing with her as a contraction came. He fed her ice chips to moisten her dry mouth and walked her around the room.

"Did I ever tell you how lucky I am that you're having my child?" he asked.

"Only a few thousand times, but it can't hurt to say it again."

"I'm the luckiest man. Thank you for having my child." He brushed a sweaty clump of hair away from her eye. "You're the strongest woman I know."

Ronnie managed a smile through the pain. "I love you, Tony."

"Right back at you."

The doctor lifted his head. "All right, Ronnie. One more good push should do it."

Tony adjusted his grip. "This is it. Here we go."

Balancing on her elbows, bearing down as hard as she could, Ronnie let out a scream, then heard a piercing cry.

The doctor beamed as if it were his first delivery. "Congratulations! We got a boy!"

"A son? We have a son, Ronnie!" Tony laid a hard kiss on her.

The doctor held out a pair of scissors. "Dad, would you care to do the honors?"

Tony went to the end of the bed and snipped the umbilical cord.

Ronnie moved side-to-side for a glimpse of her son. "Is he okay? How does he look?"

"Slimy," Tony joked, "but beautiful. Takes after his mother already." He returned to Ronnie's side. "I am so *proud* of you."

"Thanks," she said and collapsed against him.

The doctor measured the screaming newborn on the table as nurses cleaned him up. "Seven pounds, three ounces. Twenty inches long."

While another nurse tended to Ronnie, Tony recorded their son's first video on his phone. Once mother and son were ready, a nurse carried the baby swaddled in a hospital cloth and hat and placed him in Ronnie's arms.

His mouth stretched open like a fledgling as he yawned. She brought him close for a whiff of that new baby smell. It was the best scent next to Tony's cologne.

Ronnie turned to her husband with tears in her eyes. "We're a family again."

"Like we were always meant to be." The boy's tiny hand curled around his daddy's finger.

Ronnie looked at the infant as his eyes opened. "Hello there, Nicholas John Lombardo. We've been waiting for you."

One year earlier, Ronnie and Tony had returned to Ocean City, Maryland, for an intimate beach wedding, where they'd had their last family vacation with Vivian.

All the Lombardos were there—John, Tess, Nonna, Vince and Cora, the twins, Joey, and Rachel—the newest soon-to-be Lombardo with a wedding planned around Valentine's Day.

Natalie and Graham were there, too. Ronnie wouldn't allow her stepfather's cranky mood to spoil the day. He needed a miracle to change, but Natalie had—slowly—and eventually accepted Tony as her son-in-law again.

Max and Audrey, Chet and Mia, and Paula were part of the celebration. Tony and Ronnie wouldn't think of saying "I do" without their truest friends there.

John had walked Ronnie down the sandy aisle but made her promise it would be the last time. It was a promise she gladly made and one she would easily keep.

Rachel had gifted Ronnie with a wedding dress resembling her first one. Natalie had hounded her daughter to make an appointment with a hairdresser, but she wouldn't. She wanted her mother to do her hair and told Natalie to bring her curling iron.

And Tony. Once again, the man had looked fabulous. He matched the beach theme in a white dress shirt and a tan vest and pants.

The vows had come easily, the way Ronnie knew they would.

Facing each other, holding hands, Tony made his promise. "This past year has taught me about second chances, what it means to love, and to never give up. Ronnie, you are my heartbeat. Without you, I'm not alive. I promise to live the rest of my days with you by my side. To laugh with you, cry with you, and grow old with you. Ronnie, you are the only woman I've ever loved and will ever love."

Then it was Ronnie's turn. "If someone told me a year ago that I'd be here about to become your wife, I would've laughed in their face. The best decision I ever made was coming back to Hilton because Tony, you are my home. No matter what curveball comes our way, we'll get through it together. Everything I am, all I have, I give to you because I will love you until I take my last breath."

When it was time for the ring exchange, Ronnie was ready to see the bands Tony had chosen. He wanted it to be a surprise, and it was.

Max handed Tony the rings. Two symbols of their past lay in his palm. His original wedding band and hers—the one she had left at the divorce signing.

"I used to stare at it, hoping, praying one day it'd be back where it belonged. Now it is." Tony slid the conjoined rings on her finger. "Ronnie, I give this ring to you as a symbol of my promise to be faithful to you alone, to be the man and husband you deserve all the days of our life."

The minister nodded at Ronnie to do the same.

She held up the ring. "This is never coming off ever again," she said and put the band on his finger. "Tony, I give this ring to you as a symbol of my promise to be faithful to you alone, to be the woman and wife you deserve all the days of our life."

After the minister pronounced Tony and Ronnie husband and wife, they walked barefoot on the shore toward the rushing waves.

Ronnie brought her bouquet to her nose. She inhaled the magnificent scent of white roses and tossed them into the ocean. "We love you, Vivian. See you one day soon, baby girl."

Their little girl's giggle soared above the mighty current, the sweet sound of innocence still alive in their memories and in their hearts.

Dear Reader,

First off, thank you for your interest in *Under the Dogwood Tree*. I understand the subject matters of infidelity and the death of a child can be highly emotional and often difficult to read about, although the story hadn't started that way.

One morning, about twelve years ago, I was in the bathroom (of all places) getting ready for church when a thought popped into my head out of nowhere that began with "What if?" Writers love that phrase because it's the beginning of a project that they pour their hearts and souls into. I filled in the blank of my "What if?" with "What if a man's new boss was his ex-wife?" I had originally envisioned the concept as a television series, but I quickly put the idea on the shelf. I wasn't a Hollywood producer, just a wife and a mother who liked to write.

Fast-forward nine years. I had written my first women's fiction novel and wanted to crossover into the romance genre. I had kicked around a few ideas when I remembered my "What if?" Characters, scenes, conflict, and resolve had started to take shape, and the story went from ex-spouses working together to infidelity and grief.

So many married couples find themselves in turmoil. Marriage isn't easy. It's hard. It can be messy. It's challenging, and then there is regret. A harsh word or an action that hurts the one you love the most, although that had never been your intention. Marriage can also be the place where you find safety and security. A place of familiarity and comfort. A place you never want to leave.

For Tony and Ronnie, they'd experienced it all. But even in the darkest moments of their relationship, the only thing that got them through it was love.

*Under the Dogwood Tree* isn't just a romance novel about a hunky man and pretty woman in a few steamy scenes. It's about how love is bigger than any mistake a person can make. My hope is that *Under the Dogwood Tree* provided food for thought, as well as entertainment, causing you to look within yourself and gauge your love and forgiveness for your significant other. And to know that anything worth having is worth fighting for.

–Kari Wirth

# ABOUT THE AUTHOR

Photo Courtesy of Kristy Tasca Photography

Kari Wirth entered college studying fashion merchandising, but after completing an English Composition course, she graduated with a master's degree in journalism from Ball State University. She has written for newspapers, broadcast news, radio, and blogs Along the way, she had decided to write a book. Her debut novel, *Return to Garrison*, was released in October 2020. *Under the Dogwood Tree* is Kari's first contemporary romance novel. She's always working on a new project but still finds time to read novels that inspire her, get in grueling daily workouts at the gym, and is an avid runner. She lives in New York with her husband and their son.

# NOTE FROM KARI WIRTH

Word-of-mouth is crucial for any author to succeed. If you enjoyed *Under the Dogwood Tree,* please leave a review online—anywhere you are able. Even if it's just a sentence or two. It would make all the difference and would be very much appreciated. Like me on Facebook. Follow me on Instagram and Twitter. And check out my website, www.kariwirth.com.

Thanks!
Kari Wirth

We hope you enjoyed reading this title from:

www.blackrosewriting.com

Subscribe to our mailing list – *The Rosevine* – and receive **FREE** books, daily deals, and stay current with news about upcoming releases and our hottest authors.
Scan the QR code below to sign up.

Already a subscriber? Please accept a sincere thank you for being a fan of Black Rose Writing authors.

View other Black Rose Writing titles at www.blackrosewriting.com/books and use promo code **PRINT** to receive a **20% discount** when purchasing.

Made in United States
Orlando, FL
15 November 2023